THE DINOSAUR HUNTER

ALSO BY HOMER HICKAM

Torpedo Junction
Rocket Boys
Back to the Moon
The Coalwood Way
Sky of Stone
We Are Not Afraid
The Keeper's Son
The Ambassador's Son
The Far Reaches
Red Helmet
My Dream of Stars (with Anousheh Ansari)

THE
DINOSAUR
HUNTER

A NOVEL

HOMER HICKAM

THOMAS DUNNE BOOKS

ST. MARTIN'S GRIFFIN

NEW YORK

This is a work of fiction. All of the characters, organizations, and events portrayed in this novel are either products of the author's imagination or are used fictitiously.

THOMAS DUNNE BOOKS.
An imprint of St. Martin's Press.

THE DINOSAUR HUNTER. Copyright © 2010 by Homer Hickam. All rights reserved. Printed in the United States of America. For information, address St. Martin's Press, 175 Fifth Avenue, New York, N.Y. 10010.

www.thomasdunnebooks.com
www.stmartins.com

The Library of Congress has cataloged the hardcover edition as follows:

Hickam, Homer.
    The dinosaur hunter/Homer Hickam.—1st ed.
      p. cm.
    ISBN 978-0-312-38378-7
  1. Ranchers—Fiction. 2. Paleontologists—Fiction. 3. Murderers—Fiction.
  4. Fossils—Fiction. 5. Dinosaurs—Fiction. 6. Montana—Fiction. I. Title.

PS3558.I224D56 2010
813'.54—dc22

                                         2010035890

ISBN 978-1-250-00196-2 (trade paperback)

First St. Martin's Griffin Edition: February 2012

10 9 8 7 6 5 4 3 2 1

To Frank Stewart, fellow dino boy

1

OLD BILL COULTER USED to say a quiet day in Fillmore County is a temptation to God and sure enough, come sundown after a day of blue skies and fair winds, distant pulses of lightning began to play along the horizon, heralding a big storm on its way. Our barn cats, Rage and Fury, came scratching and begging for entrance, and when I answered the door, they flew past me and disappeared inside. Those old cats weren't scared of much but when a real thunder thumper was bearing down on us, they seemed to prefer the doubtful safety of my dented old trailer to their sturdy barn. Since I was suspicious of mice under my refrigerator, they were welcome. "Just hold it down, boys," I admonished them. "This old cowboy needs his sleep." Which, because of the time of the year, was the unvarnished truth.

Since the heifers had started dropping their calves in March, sleep was a precious thing on the Square C and I sure didn't plan on losing any shut-eye over bad weather, especially since there wasn't a thing I could do about it. I shooed the cats off my bunk and climbed under the covers, intent on proving that old saw that cowboys could sleep through anything but a stampede.

The storm hit us around midnight with a flash of lightning and a mighty rumble of thunder. Then came the rain with a steady rattle on the skin of my metallic domicile while more heavenly electricity flew through the air. The next boom of thunder shook the trailer so hard, the door on my little microwave oven flew open. Rage and Fury jumped up on my bed and hissed at me like it was my fault Montana was trying to kill us. I yelled at the cats and they slunk off while I pulled the covers over my head, doing my best to ignore the storm, which kept banging away. I might have succeeded except the vision of a small, black angus heifer formed in my mind. Some bull had nailed her late when we weren't looking and she was about to drop her calf. My boss lady had advised me to keep a sharp lookout for trouble. "Every two hours on this one, Mike," Jeanette Coulter had commanded. "She's got a small pelvis and that looks to be a big calf."

Lying there beneath the covers, all nice and cozy, I realized I had failed to check on that little heifer even once, mainly because I'd spent the day focused on Jeanette's pride and joy, a John Deere tractor, which had thrown a cog. I took an entire minute trying to talk myself out of getting up, but I finally gave in. That almost-mama might be out there in awful pain. I had to check on her, storm or no storm.

The cats watched me from atop the refrigerator while I pulled on my rubber boots and slung on my yellow slicker. "Hold down the fort, boys," I said, then pushed out into the howling rain and wind. My trailer was slanted down a dirt road about a quarter mile from the main house so by the time I got to what we call the turnaround, I was muddy to my knees, soaked to the bone, and generally miserable. Another way of putting that, I was a cowboy ready to go to work.

I headed over to the holding pen with my fingers crossed that all was well. But it wasn't. In fact, it was a pretty desperate situation. I allowed myself the pleasure of a string of fine curses, then headed to the house, pounding on the door and yelling for Jeanette to get up. Her bedroom window scraped open and I stepped back off the porch. "What the devil do you, want, Mike?" she called.

I only had a moment, in a flash of lightning, to see that she was naked as a jay. Her breasts were a wondrous sight, even as I stood in the mud of the yard, rain flowing off the curl of my hat like water out of a pitcher. The lightning flash died and before the thunder reached us, I collected myself and yelled, "That little heifer in the pen, her calf's stuck!"

A bolt from above lit everything up again, and I saw her mixed expression of anger and disappointment. I knew what she was thinking. I should have caught this earlier and she was right. "Chains do?" she demanded.

She was referring to the chain-and-pulley system in our barn that we used to pull a stuck calf out. I waited for another rumble of thunder to finish, then yelled up the bad news, "Gotta cut her, I think."

Jeanette stared at me for a long second, then said, "All right, Mike. Get her in the surgery," and then slammed shut the window, cutting off the finest view I'd had of her in the ten years I'd worked on the Square C.

I headed for the holding pen. By then, the heifer was down in the mud, breathing hard. My heart went out to her, poor thing. She had always been an outsider to the herd, standing alone most of the time, feeding on the hay left over after the other cows had their fill. Now she was in trouble, big trouble, her calf jammed in her birth canal, a situation, which would kill them both if we didn't do something about it damn quick.

I heard Ray Coulter calling my name. Ray's a good kid. Seventeen years old, tall like his daddy with fine features like his mother, smart as paint and a hard worker, too. There aren't too many places left where they make them like our local boys and girls. By the time they're eight years old, they can ride a horse and drive a tractor, crack open the block of a truck engine, and shoot a rifle or a handgun and hit what they're aiming at. They respect their elders, too, even when we don't deserve it.

"Over here, Ray," I called back.

Before he could get to me, Ray slipped in the cold wet swamp of the holding pen and went down hard in the mud and manure. If that had happened to me, I'd have turned the air blue with some elaborate cussing, but not Ray. He just picked himself up and made his way on over. Like I said, a good kid. A ranch kid.

By then, it was a wild scene in the corral, the rain roaring and the thunder hammering and the lightning strobing us in stuttering blue-white flashes. "Help me get her up!" I yelled, trying not to sound too hysterical. Together, we grappled with the heifer, both of us going down a couple of times before we finally got her on her feet. She stood there trembling, her mouth foamy with drool, her eyes rolling, and her nose flared. All bad signs. Then she started to moan. "She's trying to push her calf out," Ray said.

"Well, she can't," I replied. "And I don't think chains are gonna work, either."

"A C-section, Mike?" I saw his eyes light up. "I've never seen one of those!"

"Well, Ray, I think tonight's your lucky night. Your mom's probably already waiting for us."

Ray and I pushed and pulled the heifer through the double doors that led to the surgery, then clamped her neck in a steel rail catch. This, of course, didn't make her happy, and she rattled the walls with panicky squalls. I kept talking soothing cow talk to her but she wasn't much consoled. Cows are smart. She was in trouble, she knew it, and she doubted a couple of idiots like me and Ray were going to get her out of it. Truth was we couldn't. Only Jeanette could and the operation she was about to perform in that cold, concrete room didn't allow much error. I didn't know another rancher in Fillmore County who would attempt what she was about to do. But then, they're not Jeanette Coulter.

Jeanette was in her green scrubs. She finished washing at the sink and gave me and Ray the once-over. "Well? I can't do a thing, you two covered in gumbo and cow shit! Get yourself over to the sink and wash up!"

Ray and I slunk past her, stripped off our rain gear and shirts, scrubbed our hands, faces, and upper torsos, then pulled on clean white T-shirts that were kept in a cabinet beside the sink for just that purpose. Jeanette watched us, then said, "Not that I don't trust you, Mike, but we're gonna check this little mama before I cut her. Ray, you do it."

I confess I was grateful that she'd picked Ray over me. Pushing my hand up inside an expectant mama cow isn't exactly my favorite thing to do. But Ray smiled like his mom had done him a favor, got out the K-Y, and ran his arm up to his shoulder.

When Ray did his duty, I made certain I was a good piece away from that heifer's head. I saw a cowboy lean in close to a cow's head one time, just to scratch her ears while the vet was inserting his hand in the other end, and he got his clock cleaned for his trouble. Three cowboy teeth went flying and everybody, including the vet, laughed out loud. Even the cowboy grinned, showing the big, bloody gap in his teeth. "You gonna buy me thum new teeth, bossth?" he asked before spitting blood. The boss rancher provided a long stare at his employee before replying "Nope," and he didn't, either.

"Calf's backward, Mom," Ray reported. "Its legs are all tangled up, too."

Jeanette pressed two fingers to her forehead, closed her eyes, then shot me a look like it was all my fault, which I guess it was, me and that damned bull. "All right, looks like we got to do this thing. Mike, you set me up. Ray, you shave. I'll do the epidural."

Ray got to work with the electric razor, and I set out the hemostats, scalpels, needles, and sutures our surgeon would need. When Ray was finished, I applied antiseptic over the shaved area. By then, Jeanette was done with the epidural and the little mama's legs were quivering. I released the catch and Ray and I did our best to let the cow down easy. "You hold her, Ray," Jeanette ordered. "Mike, you get over here and help me."

I took up station beside Jeanette. When she glanced at me, I gave her a reassuring smile, which earned me a full-bore, Jeanette Coulter frown. She turned back to the heifer and cut decisively. "Lidocaine," she ordered and I squirted it in, numbing the separated tissue. She cut deeper, a spray of blood erupting from the wound. I patted the droplets off her face with a damp cloth while she applied a hemostat to the bleeder. When she took up the scalpel again, she cut delicately into the muslin-thin wall of the uterus with her reward being a pair of black hooves that pushed through the opening. "Get it, boys," she ordered and Ray and I immediately complied, lifting out the slippery calf and swinging it clear. It had to weigh at least a hundred pounds, a lot of calf for such a small cow.

"Looks to be a heifer," Ray reported.

"Wipe the mucous off its face before it suffocates," Jeanette ordered. "Then get some burlap and clean her up. Mike, you get back over here and let's get this little mama sewed back together."

While she sutured, I sprayed antiseptic. "Don't drown her, for gosh sake," she scolded after I got a little too enthusiastic.

The uterus stitched, Jeanette took up a bigger needle with a thicker gut and began to lace up the hide. When she was half-finished, she said, "Ray, why don't you put in a few sutures? Try to do it like you saw me. Not deep, just catch the hide."

Ray eagerly came over and took up the needle. Jeanette inspected his work and said, "Not bad," which was high praise from her. She took the needle back, finished sewing, tied the thread off, and announced the end of the operation, saying, "Let's see if she'll get up. Mike, go give her a nudge."

Imagine a doc expecting a human female to stand up after a C-section! But Jeanette knew if the cow didn't get up, it would die. I knelt beside the fresh new mama and nudged her but she didn't take the hint. For a minute or so, she just laid there, looking dazed, but then something clicked in her brain and she suddenly got up on her own, staggered a little, her eyes wide and glittery. She looked at me, then at Ray, then at Jeanette, and then started bawling. "She wants her calf," I said.

Jeanette was stripping off her gloves. "Then let her have it. Put them in one of the stalls. We'll let them have a night in the barn. And make sure there's plenty of water. She's gonna be thirsty. Come on you guys. Stop grinning and get moving. I got to clean up in here."

I checked my watch. It had been a little over two hours since I had yelled up at Jeanette as she stood in the window. Nude. That was a hard image to get out of my head. Anyway, she was both a fast and good surgeon. She was also a damn fine boss. I was in love with her, of course, but I wasn't about to let her know that. Too many complications and, anyway, I knew she was never going to get over old Bill even though his ashes had been scattered across the ranch five years ago. Heart attack. At the funeral, a cowboy who'd once worked on the Square C confided to me he was surprised Bill had a heart. Well, he had one and still did. Jeanette's.

Ray and I shepherded mother and child into the barn, picked an empty stall, got them in it, and it didn't take two seconds before the calf was suckling the heifer's teats, a very good sign. I tagged the calf's ear and Ray gave it its shots. When Jeanette came into the barn, we were putting everything up. She said, "Ray, you get back to bed. Did you finish your homework?"

"Yes ma'am, but it's gonna be hard getting to school with all this rain."

"We'll see about that. Mike, I guess I'm done with you."

Ray pulled on his coat and went out. I went back into the surgery and got my slicker. I knew Jeanette wasn't going anywhere. She would spend the night with the heifer and the newborn, just to make sure they were OK. "Well, good night, what's left of it," I said as I passed her.

"You were supposed to check that heifer every two hours," she said to my back.

I stopped but I didn't turn around. "Yeah. Guess I got distracted working on your tractor."

"Cows come first on the Square C, Mike."

Jeanette had me dead to rights and there was nothing I could say so I just nodded and went on outside. The rain had stopped, but there were still distant pulses of lightning, enough to light up my way as I carefully slogged through the mud to my trailer. I kicked off my galoshes at the door, shucked off the slicker and wet clothes, and crawled beneath the blankets on my narrow bunk. There was no sign of the cats. A few hours later, when I woke, it was just starting to get bright outside and a glance out my window told me the storm was done. I could even make out some stars. Montana weather can do that, turn on a dime and leave you nine cents change.

We'd saved the heifer and her calf, I had seen Jeanette naked from the waist up, Ray had gotten to see a C-section, and Montana had scared us all half to death but hadn't managed to kill us. I was content but that was because I didn't know a young man was on his way to us, bringing with him a knowledge of the astonishing creatures that had once walked our land and an ancient and present reality I knew all too well called murder.

2

I FOUND THREE DEAD mice beside the refrigerator, gifts from Rage and Fury. I thanked them, let them out to go back to the barn, percolated some stout coffee, chowed down on some burnt toast well buttered, and then went outside, carrying my second cup of joe. After a rain, it makes for tricky walking because of the gumbo, our black, clay soil that gets hard as a brick when it's dry and slicker than a Hollywood lawyer when wet. Gumbo also has the strange quality of being as sticky as it's slick. Walk on it if you can without falling down and pretty soon you're picking up about a foot of the stuff glued to your boots. Try to drive on it and it builds up on your tires until your truck engine fries itself. Bottom line: It's nasty stuff.

To get up to the barn without busting my tail, I walked along the edge of the road where there was some grass. Along the way, I was joined by Soupy, the Square C's resident black-and-white cowdog. Soupy's real name is Superdog. Like most Fillmore County ranch dogs, he came from a long line of black-and-white canines, had more than a little border collie in him, and took no guff off any cow, yet was always gentle with humans. I respected Soupy and I guess he tolerated me. His true love, of course, was Jeanette, which I understood. She was mine, too.

Soupy and I found our boss lady standing outside the barn jotting down a note in the little notebook she always carried with her. I guess everything that had happened on the Square C during the entire year was in that notebook, every calf dropped, every well fixed, phone numbers of folks she was supposed to call (but probably hadn't), numbers on the cows to sell, number of hay bales off which fields, and so forth. She was bundled up in Bill's ancient canvas barn coat, a coat two sizes too big for her and covered with ranch badges of honor—rips from barb wire fences, tractor grease, and dried cow manure. She loved that old coat. Maybe it made her feel a little closer to her late husband, I don't know.

Jeanette tucked away her notebook and acknowledged my presence with a curt nod. I thought she looked a bit melancholy. She might have been thinking about Bill or maybe the price of beef, there was no way to tell and she surely wasn't about to cry on my shoulder. I stood beside her, had myself a sip of joe, and took a look around. The Square C was soaked but I reckoned if the sun came out, it might dry enough to drive on, a requirement if I was going to go out and finally catch that damn bull that had impregnated our little C-sectioned heifer.

Ray came out with his school backpack and handed Jeanette a mug of coffee. I could smell it and I knew he'd made it strong enough to float horseshoes, just the way his mom liked it. "Fixed you some eggs when you want 'em," he said.

"You driving Bob?" Jeanette asked, referring to the old pickup named after the fellow who'd sold it to Bill a quarter century ago.

"Naw. I'd get stuck for sure. Mr. Thomason got his tractor out. Amelia just called. They're on their way."

"See you," Jeanette said as Ray carefully edged down the road, trying to keep his boots out of the mud. "See you," Ray said over his shoulder. There were never wasted words on the Square C. To translate, what Jeanette and Ray had just said was: "I love you, I will always love you, and I would die for you in a heartbeat." I said, "See you," too, meaning the same to both of them.

The tractor arrived, driven by our neighbor Buddy Thomason, with his daughter Amelia sitting beside him. She was sort of Ray's girl-friend. I could tell because Ray blushed furiously anytime Amelia's name was mentioned. Jeanette and I waved at Buddy who touched his hat to us while Ray climbed up into the cab. Amelia turned her face toward him and gave him a big smile but Ray just looked straight ahead. I thought to myself that maybe I needed to give that boy some advice about women but then, it wasn't my place unless he came ask-ing. Also, truth was I hadn't been all that successful with females myself.

After the tractor ground on down the road, Jeanette and I got to work. She headed inside the house and I went inside the barn to pull on some coveralls and finish the job I'd started the day before on her tractor. One of the lift cylinder seals on the loader boom had blown out. Luckily, I had some extra seals but it was still an oily mess re-quiring lots of pinched fingers and cussing. Throughout the day, I kept checking on the little heifer and her calf and they kept being fine. The sun blazed away all day, too, and by noon, the gumbo had turned hard again and everything was back to normal, if such a thing existed on the Square C.

After I got the tractor fixed, I started working on the case of the errant bull. I'd decided to take what we called the big truck, an an-cient Ford, for my foray into the badlands to chase it down. Heavier than Bob, the big truck would provide extra traction in case there were still some wet spots out there. Before I got too far checking the Ford's fan belts, oil levels, and such, I heard somebody drive into the turnaround. When I stuck my head around the barn, I saw a pickup I didn't recognize. It had probably started out white that morning but the backsplash of red dog and gumbo from Ranchers Road had turned it mostly pinkish-gray. The young fellow who got out of it was wearing cargo pants, a multi-pocketed shirt, and hiking boots, all of which pegged him for a hunter, had it been hunting season. He was also wearing a hat I admired, one of those Indiana Jones-like fedoras with a hat band that had tiger stripes on it. I took right away that this was likely an interesting fellow.

"Howdy!" I called to him, real cowboy-like.

When he turned toward me, I saw he was handsome in a catalog model kind of way, blue eyes that were so blue they were kind of startling, with sandy hair peeking from under his hat. "Is this the Square C Ranch?" he asked.

My response was typical Fillmore County spare. "Yep."

An expression of relief crossed his face. "I've been driving up and down this road all morning looking for you," he said.

"Well," I said, "you're here."

That's when I saw Jeanette, still in her barn coat, coming out of the house. A glance at her face and the way she was walking told me she was not happy. She opened the yard gate and the young man doffed his hat to her, revealing a pony tail tied with a red rubber band. Jeanette stepped up to him and got right to the point. "The answer is no," she said. Before our visitor could reply, she added, "You want to pick up fossils on my ranch and I don't have time to mess with you."

Now, how she knew why that fellow was there, I don't know. Maybe it was instinctive. Anyway, he dug into one of his shirt pockets and produced a folded paper, unfolded it, and handed it to Jeanette. "You're Mrs. Coulter, right? I've been trying to call you for a week but the phone just rang and rang."

I could have told him the reason for that. We didn't have an answering machine and most of the time during daylight hours everybody was outside working. In the evening, Jeanette sometimes simply chose not to answer the phone. It was just her way.

She reluctantly took the paper, looked it over, and said, "I remember this. Ray's homework from about six months ago. How'd you get it?" When I eased in closer to hear everything, Jeanette gave me a warning look, then filled me in. "For English class, Ray wrote a paper about some fossils his father found."

"He included some photographs, too," our visitor said.

Jeanette provided him with the Fillmore County stare, a look that would freeze a man on fire. "I know my son. He wouldn't send this to anyone without my permission. I'll ask you again. How did you get it?"

"Someone e-mailed it to me, an address I didn't recognize. I e-mailed back but got no answer. When I called you and couldn't get through, I decided to come visit. Mrs. Coulter, I'm Dr. Norman Pickford. I'm a paleontologist. The bones described in your son's paper may be very important. That's why I came all the way from Argentina to see them."

Jeanette absorbed this information. "What were you doing in Argentina?"

"Hunting for dinosaurs. It's what I do."

In an attempt to lighten things up a bit, I stuck out my paw. "Mike Wire," I said. "I'm the hired hand."

His grip was satisfactorily manly, even by Fillmore County standards. "Nice to meet you, Mike. I'm called Pick."

"Pick," I said, testing the name. "Sounds like a good name for a man who digs up fossils."

He smiled tolerantly. "I don't dig. I like to say that's why God makes grad students. I just hunt and find. I'm very good at finding." He shifted back to Jeanette. "Mrs. Coulter, those fossils your son wrote about might be important to science. If I could just look at them, I won't take more than ten minutes of your time, I promise."

There was something about Pick that made me want to help him. I was also curious about those fossils. "What could it hurt?" I asked Jeanette.

Jeanette shot me a look, but I could tell she was wavering. I guess she was curious herself. She said, "All right, come on inside. I'll let you have a gander. And you can come along, too, Mike. That way I won't have to explain everything to you later."

"Thank you, Mrs. Coulter," Pick said but it was to Jeanette's back. She was already walking across the yard, her arms crossed, her head down, and I could tell she just wanted to get this over with.

We went inside the house, which was its usual mess. I was a little embarrassed for Jeanette when Pick walked in and looked around her dilapidated living room, furnished with an old sofa, a couple of overstuffed chairs with the stuffing peeking out of them in a couple of places, two mismatched end tables, and an old brass lamp with a tattered, dirty lampshade.

Jeanette led us into the kitchen and pointed at the coffee pot and then the kitchen table, which I guess would have been in fashion when Eisenhower was President. The chairs around the table didn't match. Likely, old Bill had picked them up alongside the road where they'd been pitched. "Mike, pour the man some coffee," Jeanette said. To the paleontologist, she said, "Have a seat. I'll get the fossils."

I did as I was told and silently handed the young scientist a mug of hot joe along with the sugar bowl and some pouches of fake cream Jeanette had carried out of a diner in Miles City. He spooned in a couple dollops of sugar and used all the ersatz cream. Even cut, Ray's coffee was a spine stiffener and when Pick took a sip, he kind of shuddered. I allowed myself a chuckle.

Jeanette returned with a battered old cardboard box with the misspelled word FOSILS hand-printed on its side. She placed it on the table and I moved to look over Pick's shoulder as he reached into the box to pick up a smooth, curiously shaped object that I thought looked like the end of a leg bone. I was disappointed when he said, "This is a sandstone concretion. Not a bone."

"How do you know?" I asked.

"I have a PhD in paleontology and a master's degree in geology, Mike. I know bones and rocks."

Pick rooted around some more in the box and brought out a quarter-sized fragment of yellow rock. "Bone," he said. He plucked out three other such pieces, all about the same size, then put one against his tongue. "A field test," he explained. "If it's sticky to the tongue, it's probably bone. These little pieces are what we call float, a generic term for indistinct bone fragments falling down a hill from an unknown fossil horizon. Your husband has a good eye to find them, Mrs. Coulter."

"I'm a widow," Jeanette replied. "What kind of dinosaur is it?"

"Too small to tell," Pick said, then picked up another fragment about the size of a shot glass "This is the vertebra of a Champsosaur. Notice the hour-glass configuration along the dorsal edge of the centrum? That's the tell-tale clue. Not a dinosaur but a small crocodile-like reptile. This area was mostly floodplain and lake systems during the Cretaceous. Lots of swampy areas. Perfect for crocs."

Jeanette arched an eyebrow. "Sometimes when it rains around here for a few days, it's still a swamp."

Pick gave that some thought, or pretended to, then picked up a chunk of rounded rock about three inches long and two inches in diameter. "This is a portion of a Triceratops horn, likely one of two orbital horns that grew out of its skull above its eyes."

"What's it worth?" Jeanette asked.

"I don't buy or sell fossils, Mrs. Coulter," Pick said, "but I guess maybe twenty dollars at a rock show."

"Is that all?"

"It's not in very good shape. I'm sorry."

She nodded. "How about those bones you called float? Worth anything?"

"Some people make jewelry out of little pieces of dinosaur bone. Earrings, that kind of thing, but I'm against that."

Jeanette narrowed her eyes, always a dangerous sign. "What are you for, Dr. Pickford?"

"Truth through science."

This earned him a mirthless chuckle. "Does truth through science pay your bills?"

Pick thought that over, then said, "I don't need much, Mrs. Coulter. Give me a little food, water, and a place to look for bones and I'm happy."

He took two more pieces of whatever from the box and separated them from the others. "These belonged to a theropod. Theropods were meat-eating dinosaurs."

"They look like chicken bones," I said.

Pick nodded. "We think theropods were distantly related to chickens, only usually a lot bigger and with more brain power. Tyrannosaurus rex is an example of a theropod. You're familiar with T. rex, I'm sure."

"I saw *Jurassic Park*," Jeanette volunteered. Her tone had gone dry. I figured she was about five minutes away from kicking me and our pony-tailed paleontologist out of her kitchen.

"Actually," he said, "T. rex lived during the late Cretaceous, well after the Jurassic. They were one of the last dinosaurs that ever lived. The Triceratops was probably the source of much of its diet. Duckbills, too." When he saw Jeanette's questioning look, he said, "Hadrosaurs, big dinosaurs with long, flat jaws that gave them a duck-like appearance. They were herbivores. Vegetarians."

"Like Mike," Jeanette said, giving away one of my peculiarities.

The scientist looked at me in surprise. "I used to live in California," I said by way of explanation.

"Finish up, Dr. Pickford," Jeanette said before Pick and I could get into a discussion of either vegetarianism or California.

Pick next withdrew from the box a cylindrical rock that was about two inches long and the diameter of a pencil. "This is an ossified tendon from a Hadrosaur. Tendons are like lines in a pulley from muscles to bones. The muscles twitch and the tendons are pulled, thus moving the bones. Ossified means this tendon has turned from collagen to bone. This propensity isn't unique to dinosaurs. Some modern birds like turkeys have ossified tendons."

"What's that little curved piece?" I asked, pointing at something I'd spotted in the box. "Like a hawk's claw."

"A claw, indeed," he said, "but not from a hawk. From a T. rex."

"How come it's so small?"

"It belonged to a baby. So does this phalange." He touched a brown object that looked more or less like a thin twig about an inch long. "By phalange, I mean a toe or finger bone. Although it doesn't fit this particular claw, it could still be from the same animal. These bones are very interesting. A baby T. rex this young has never been found before. We don't know much about them. If the entire skeleton was nearby . . ."

"What would it be worth?" Jeanette interrupted.

Pick had his mouth open to complete his sentence but he closed it, mulled over Jeanette's question, then said, "I don't know. A lot. But to science, well, you can't put a price on it."

Jeanette leaned back against the counter and crossed her arms. "Dr. Pickford, on a ranch like this, every dollar counts. How do I find somebody who'll buy these fossils?"

Pick hesitated, then asked, "Do you lease BLM land?"

Whether he knew it or not, he had just lurched onto a touchy topic in the Montana ranchlands. BLM stood for Bureau of Land Management, the federal agency that owns a great deal of the western states. A rather large portion of that property is leased out to ranches and there is always some consternation about those leases for one reason or another.

"Everybody up and down Ranchers Road has BLM leases," Jeanette replied.

"Did your husband spend much time on your lease?"

"Of course he did. Our cattle graze there. That's why we have it."

"If any of these bones were found on the BLM, then technically they aren't yours. They belong to the government."

Jeanette's face clouded over. "Listen," she said, "the Coulters have been taking care of that damn land for a century. The government can claim it all it wants but our blood and sweat says otherwise."

Pick's reply was gentle. "Mrs. Coulter, I fully understand. I didn't come here to cause any trouble. I have a federal collecting permit, approved by the BLM, but I wouldn't go out there without your permission."

Before Jeanette could reply, he pulled a map from one of his many shirt pockets. I recognized it as a BLM-produced map, which included not only federal land but all the ranches up and down Ranchers Road. The map was a grid of squares, each one representing a square mile. BLM land was identified by a bright yellow color, private property was in white, state-owned land in blue, and the adjacent Charles M. Russell National Wildlife Refuge in a sturdy green.

Pick used the duckbill's ossified tendon to trace a path along a dotted line on the map, which went past a prominent land feature called Blackie Butte to just inside Jeanette's BLM lease. "This is the area I'd like to investigate. Its terrain features indicate to me that it's an outcrop of the Hell Creek Formation. A remnant of the Cretaceous."

"And if you find anything?" Jeanette asked.

"I would take it back to the university for further study."

"Which university?"

"I work through the University of California in Berkeley."

"Bunch of far-lefties out there," Jeanette said.

Pick shrugged. "I'm not political in any way. My mind is fixed on what happened sixty-five to three hundred million years ago. What I like to call deep time."

Jeanette took that snippet of news under advisement, looked up at the ceiling, and then back at our visitor. "If you find something, even if it's on the BLM, I want to know about it."

"Agreed."

Jeanette took another moment, then said, "Mike, I'm going to let this fellow go out there. You get him squared away." In full boss lady mode, she turned back to Pick. "You understand we can't be paying much attention to you. You'll be on your own. How long do you think you need?"

"I don't know," he said. "If I don't find anything, I'll probably be gone in a week."

"You're not going to find anything. I've been all over the Square C and our lease, too. Never saw the first thing that looked like a dinosaur. Likely, Bill picked up everything that was out there."

"You're probably right, Mrs. Coulter." He stood up, his chair scraping on the scarred linoleum floor. "But I appreciate you letting me look, anyway."

"We'll see how it works out," Jeanette curtly replied. She picked up the bones, put them in the cardboard box, and headed upstairs with them while I ushered the young paleontologist out to his truck, opened the gate to the Mulhaden pasture, and pointed out the tire ruts cutting through the grass, which he needed to follow. "Here's a strict rule of the ranchlands," I told him. "You find a gate open, leave it open. If it's closed, leave it closed."

"OK," he said.

He got in his truck and drove through the gate but he didn't get far before I waved him down. There were a few more things I needed to say. "You got a firearm or any kind of weapon?"

"A gun? No, but I have a pick and a shovel."

"It's prime time for rattlesnakes. Watch yourself. Usually, Montana rattlers will just mind their own business but if you get bit, give us a call so we can let the mortuary know. Do you have a radio?"

"Yes. An FM handheld." He opened the glove compartment to show it to me.

"That'll do." I gave him the ranch frequency and he jotted it down in a little notebook. "Set it now and keep it on you. I'll be listening. If I don't answer, climb up on a hill and try again."

He fiddled with the radio, then placed it on the seat beside him. "So I just stay on this track and it will take me out to the BLM?"

"Follow the ruts, stay right at every fork, and go through three gates. The third gate, the BLM's on the other side. It's marked."

"OK."

I gave him my version of the Fillmore County stare. "Listen, there are a lot of ways this country can kick your butt. A little rain, you're down in a coulee, and a flash flood will drown you in a second. Temperatures can spike up to over a hundred degrees by day and then drop below freezing by night. Hell, I've seen it snow in July. I've already mentioned the rattlesnakes. There's scorpions out there, too, and black widows."

Pick was clearly impatient to get going. "OK, OK. I'll be careful."

"Do you have water?"

"Five gallons in a jerry can. There's also natural water out there, right?"

"It's full of alkali. Drink it if you want your guts to explode. How's your sense of direction?"

"Abysmal," he confessed, "but I have a GPS." He again opened the glove compartment and produced a handheld device.

"A tent?"

"Yes, but I'll probably just sleep in my truck."

"Food?"

"Canned stew. Some rice. Coffee. I have a pot and a little gas stove. I don't eat much when I'm in the field."

"Age? Next of kin?"

"Thirty-five. I have a mother in Topeka, Kansas. Why do you ask?"

"If you get killed, the authorities will want to know."

"I'm not going to get killed, Mike. I've lived off the land in Argentina, Mongolia, Africa, all kinds of places."

I figured it was time for me to wave him on so that's what I did, then closed the gate behind him. The track he was following led past Blackie Butte and I was heading out that way pretty soon to catch that damn gimp bull, anyway. I would check on him to make sure he got to the BLM. As I watched him drive away, I was not encouraged. I saw his truck go up the first hill, then reach the fork in the road. He turned left, instead of right. I ran to the barn and got on the radio. "Pick, this is Mike. You went the wrong way."

A minute passed and I called him again. Finally, he answered, "Pick here. I thought you said stay left."

"Stay *right*. All three forks."

"Got it."

"You want to wait for me? I'm heading out that way in an hour or so."

There was no answer, although I tried a couple more times. Now I not only had to find a gimpy old bull and bring it in, I had to look for a pony-tailed paleontologist, too. I allowed a cowboy curse, then got going.

3

THAT EVENING, I CAME rolling in with three heifers and their calves plodding in front of me. At the sound of the big truck, Jeanette came out of the barn. Ray, home from school, rose from behind one of our four-wheelers. The empty cans of 10W-40 on the ground informed me he'd been changing its oil. We take good care of our equipment on the Square C. I climbed out of the truck and opened up the pasture gate and herded the cows through it into the turnaround. They were looking pretty unhappy about the entire experience. Soupy added to their discomfort by nipping at their heels, aiming them toward the holding pen while Ray held its gate open. After weeks on the open range, we would have to give the free-rangers a thorough inspection to make sure they were healthy enough to go back into the general cow population.

Jeanette frowned after the bawling cows and calves, then said, "Mike, I don't see that gimp bull. I guess he's a pretty good hider. Maybe I'll go out there tomorrow myself and catch him. My eyes are better than yours."

I was upset or I wouldn't have snapped at her like I did. "There's nothing wrong with my eyes, Jeanette. I found that damn bull!"

"Well, why didn't you bring him in?" She looked at me and I

looked at her until finally she said, "You gonna tell me about that bull or are we just going to stare at each other the rest of the day?"

I pulled off my hat, a wide-brimmed Stetson I'd purchased in Billings when I'd first come to Montana to learn how to cowboy. I scratched my head, then plopped the hat back aboard. "He's dead," I said.

Jeanette didn't react with much surprise. "The winter killed him. I swear those big old bulls are just overgrown babies."

"Winter didn't kill him. Somebody did." I hesitated, still unable to completely comprehend what I'd found out there. "His throat was cut. Somebody brained him first, looks like, then sliced him open from ear to ear with, I don't know, a hunting knife or something."

Jeanette's expression was one of disbelief. "Who would do a thing like that?"

"A bad man, I figure," I said. "A really bad, bad man." I hesitated again, but there was no way not to tell it. "Somebody also cut our fence. In three places."

Jeanette chewed all this over. "Doesn't make sense," she concluded. "Who could sneak up on that bull to whack it in the head? It's been running loose out there for months without us being able to catch it and, anyway, a bull's got a skull harder than concrete. And who would cut our fences?"

"I'm just telling you what I found, Jeanette," I said.

"When do you think all this happened?"

"The blood looked pretty fresh to me. An hour, two hours, something like that. Flies were just starting to collect."

"You see that fossil hunter out there?"

"Nope, I looked around a bit and tried to call him. No answer."

Jeanette appraised the angle of the sun, then rubbed the back of her neck. Even dirty, I thought it was a pretty neck but I was too tired and upset for that particular fantasy. "Dark in an hour," she said. "We'll wait for morning to track him down."

"You think he did this?"

"No, Mike, I don't think he did it. Or if he did, I've sure lost the ability to judge a man. I peg him for a tree-hugger and a lover of all God's creatures, et cetera. I'm just hoping he doesn't meet up with whoever killed our bull."

"It sure seems a coincidence that this happened the same time that fossil hunter went out there," Ray said, coming over from the holding pen.

"Well, if you hadn't done that paper on your daddy's fossils," Jeanette said, "we wouldn't be worrying about him, would we?"

I could tell Ray had already gotten an earful from his mom about his homework. When he hung his head, Jeanette provided an exasperated sigh, then said, "What's done is done but, hell, I was afraid of this. All the work we got to do and now we got to go look for that fellow."

Ray said, "Nick could use some exercise. I could saddle him and go out tomorrow first thing."

Since the next day was Saturday, Ray had the time, and Jeanette thought his proposition over. "Carry a pistol," she concluded.

Another reason I love Montana so much. Where else does a mother tell her teenager to carry a gun and nobody thinks a thing about it? Nobody but an import like me, that is.

"Anybody who kills an animal like that has to be crazy," Jeanette said, turning to me. "Mike, you ever run across somebody like that in your former line of work?"

The "former line of work" Jeanette was referring to was the twelve years of employment I'd had in the Los Angeles Police Department including seven years as a homicide detective, my career cut short by a bullet, followed by a year of recuperation and three years as a private dick. It was not a time I recalled with much nostalgia. In fact, it was exactly why I was in Montana. I sorted through what I knew, most of which I was still trying to forget. "Lots of murderers get their start killing animals," I allowed.

"Really?"

"Serial killers, especially."

"Oh."

"You might want to lock your door tonight."

She gave that some thought, then said, "It would be the stupidest thing in the world to break into a house out here on Ranchers Road."

Considering everybody on the road had lots of guns and knew how to use them, she had a point. I recalled a sign I'd seen on a rancher's front porch. It featured a cartoon of a pistol with the words: WE DON'T CALL 911. Still, based on my cop years, I knew sometimes things happen in ways nobody can predict. "I don't like the idea of Ray going out there by himself," I said.

"Then go with him," she replied.

"I will."

"I guess I really made a mess of things with that paper and all," Ray said.

Jeanette allowed herself some motherly pride. "It wasn't your fault. I called your English teacher and she said she thought your paper was so good, she put it up on the school Web site. I guess anybody could have made a copy of it. Whoever e-mailed it to that fossil hunter, though, has to be a damned fool. If I ever find out who it was, I'll kick his tail." When Ray and I just stood there, grinning at her, Jeanette said, "You two got work? Get to it."

We got to it, loading the big truck with hay so we'd be ready to feed the cows in the morning.

Ray was in a talkative mood. "It seems like there's us and then there's the rest of the world," he said as we grunted the hay bales onto the truck. "I mean, Mike, how come it seems like we think one way and nearly everybody else thinks different?"

"Like what?" I asked.

"At school, it seems like all I read is where everybody else in the country can't wait for Washington, D.C., to solve all their problems. Out here, we just want to be left alone and look after ourselves. Out there, they murder each other, take drugs, the girls get pregnant without marrying or anything, seems like they're just mad at each other all the time. I think I'd hate it out there."

"Well, it's not quite that bad, Ray," I said. "But I guess it seems that way sometimes on television or in the papers."

"But you were out there, Mike, and now you're here. Why is that?"

I thought about Ray's question before I answered. Finally, I said, "I came here because I was tired of being around people who were messed up, one way or the other. I saw a lot of people dead for no good reason but that was my job as a homicide detective. Then I worked Hollywood and I think that really soured me. I mean there's worse things than murder, trust me. When I started to think my head was just as messed up as the people I was working for, I knew I'd better cut myself loose. That's why I ended up here."

"I'm glad you're here, Mike," Ray said.

"Me, too, Ray."

"Mom says Dad thought the world of you."

"Did she? Well, I thought the world of your dad. Your mom's tops in my books, too."

Ray smiled at me and I smiled back. Then we went back to work. That was the way of the county. Work, always work, and more work. A philosopher I admire said there was no water holier than the sweat off a man's brow. If that was so, sacred water was not scarce along Ranchers Road.

4

WE HAD OURSELVES A quiet night. No serial killers came calling and, though I kept waking up, all I ever heard was the yip of a passing coyote answered quickly by Soupy's warning bark. The sun rose with some wispy clouds hanging around which gave our hills, meadows, and buttes a faded amber glow. I trooped on up to the turnaround. Jeanette came outside, regarded me gazing with pleasure at her property, then said, "Sleep OK?"

"Yep, considering."

I didn't have to say the "considering" was our murdered bull and the cut fences. The Square C was in trouble but what kind, neither one of us yet knew.

"Let's get 'em fed," she said and so we did while Ray slept in a bit. He was a teenager, after all.

We headed into the Mulhaden pasture where we'd brought in our cows during the winter to keep them nearby. This was the last of our hay but, because the winter had stretched on for so long, Jeanette thought we'd best use it and let the grass have a little more time to get going. The pasture was named for a family of Mormons who'd settled the land just after the Civil War. The name was all that was left of their legacy other than a grave of one of their children. It wasn't too far from my trailer and every so often, I tended to its little headstone which was inscribed *Nanette Mulhaden, 1867.* I'd looked her up at the library in Jericho, our county seat. She only had the one year on her stone because she'd only lived three months. Poor little pioneer tyke. We ought to honor those pioneers in this country more than we do. We owe a debt to them that we've mostly forgotten.

Jeanette hooked a bungee cord to the steering wheel and put the big truck in idle, then climbed in the back with me. Soupy trotted behind as the truck made its way and we threw out the hay as the cows and calves got up and crowded in. When I first started cowboying, Bill Coulter taught me to pay attention to what calves did when they got to their feet. Healthy calves usually took a moment to stretch, he said. If they didn't, best look to them. That morning, all the calves stretched, signs that both humans and cow mamas were doing our jobs. On the way back in, I said, "Is there anything prettier than a morning in Montana?"

"Next thing you know you'll be writing that cowboy poetry," Jeanette said, aiming the big truck with one gloved hand on the steering wheel.

"Oh, I could write some," I replied, then fell silent, pretending to be lost in my thoughts although I was really thinking about her and the poem she was all by herself.

"Mike, I forgot about a meeting with the Independence Day organizers this morning in town," she said. "I want you to go with me and pick up some fencing supplies while I'm talking to the committee. I've got a list for you."

"I'm supposed to go out with Ray to look for the fossil hunter," I reminded her.

"Well, I need you more than he does. Ray knows how to take care of himself."

I chose not to argue. When we reached the gate, she braked, I sat, and she looked over at me. I was reminded of the old joke about three cowboys in a truck all dressed the same. Which one is the real cowboy? The answer is the one in the middle so he didn't have to get out and open and close the gates. Well, I was a real cowboy but I was riding shotgun so I got out and opened the gate and Jeanette drove through while I doffed my hat to her. I closed the gate and took my time getting back into the truck. She looked over at me. "You were a little slow," she said. "The big truck probably burned a quart of gasoline waiting for you."

"Take it out of my pay," I said.

"I just might," she replied and I knew there was a fair chance she would. Bandying words with Jeanette was never a good idea, especially when it came to money.

When we got back to the turnaround, Ray was up and saddling Nick with an audience of one, that being Amelia Thomason. Her daddy's truck sat nearby. Wearing jeans, a plaid shirt, cowgirl boots, and a hat with furled edges, she was a teenage cowboy's dream. "Morning, Amelia," I said and she looked over her shoulder and gave me a sweet smile.

"Morning, Mr. Wire. Ray won't let me ride with him."

"Why not, Ray?" I asked.

"Because she'll talk my head off. That's all she's good for."

I made an executive decision worthy of Dear Abby. "Take Dusty," I said to Amelia, nodding toward a gray mare. Dusty was a gentle soul and I knew Amelia had ridden her before. Anyway, Dusty never minded a walk. She was one of those horses quietly curious about nearly everything. I'd seen her one time ponder a herd of antelope for nearly an hour without so much as dropping her head once to munch a blade of grass.

Ray frowned at me, a disappointment considering I'd just made a date between him and the prettiest girl in Fillmore County. "Well, get on in here," he said, finally. "Dusty's not gonna saddle herself."

Since Ray didn't seem prone to do so, I thought it best to fill Amelia in on what had happened the day before. "Whoever did it could still be out there," I concluded.

She looked over at Ray who was fussing with Nick's tack and pretending to ignore her. "I trust Ray to take care of me," she said.

Ray proved it by going into the house and coming back with a pistol. It was a .38 Police Special. He handed it to Amelia who expertly checked it, then tucked it away in a saddle bag. Ranch kids.

"What're you packing?" I asked Ray.

"Granddaddy's forty-four," he answered,

"That ought to do it."

Amelia finished saddling Dusty, then climbed aboard. Ray got on Nick and I opened the pen gate for them, then the gate that led out to Blackie Butte and the BLM. "Take it slow, look around, you see someone you don't know, don't approach him. Observe only," I said.

"What if he's cutting our fence?"

"Pop off a round in the air. Try to chase him off. Then get out of there."

Amelia said, "Daddy would shoot anybody cutting our fences."

"Well, let's not shoot anybody today, OK? I mean not unless you have to."

"I thought you were going with me," Ray said.

"I'll be out a little later. Right now, your mom wants me to drive her into town."

Jeanette came outside. "Mike, you ready?"

"Give me a second," I said. I closed the gate behind Ray and Amelia, and watched as they made their way up the track, looking easy in the saddle, not surprising since both were practically born there.

"Mike," Jeanette said.

"Yes ma'am, right away, ma'am," I said, touching my hat to her.

A minute later, we were headed to town in Bob the pickup. "Road's all dried out," I said as I drove us off the Square C onto Ranchers Road.

"Yep," Jeanette answered, then made a show of opening a folder to study the papers within. We didn't share another word all the way to Jericho, which was nearly an hour away. Well, that's kind of a Fillmore County thing, too. Shut up and drive.

5

FILLMORE COUNTY IS 5,500 square miles of big, or about the same size as the state of Connecticut. That New England state, however, has a population of 3.5 million people while the last census of Fillmore County listed us at 770. I thought that probably included some double-counting of the confusing Brescoe clan. What we lacked in people, we more than made up with livestock, which included, rounding off, 50,000 cattle, 15,000 sheep, 900 horses, 300 buffalo, and 125 pigs.

The county is divided up more or less fifty-fifty into private and public lands, public meaning the state and the feds, mostly the feds. The federal government manages its property through two entities, the Bureau of Land Management (BLM) and the Charles M. Russell National Park (CMR). Of the two, the BLM is the more interesting outfit. It is, in its own opinion, mostly misunderstood. Some locals call it the Bureau of Land Mis-management. Jeanette calls it the Big Lousy Monster. None of the ranchers like it because it controls the land leases they depend on.

Ranchers Road is around thirty-five miles long and runs south to north into a peninsula formed by Lake Fort Peck, a big depression-era man-made lake. The road is the north-south lifeline of the six ranches it connects to the east-west state highway that crosses Fillmore County, a highway otherwise unhindered by any town except the county seat of Jericho. Heading up Ranchers Road, the first ranch reached is the Haxby place, which is owned by Sam Haxby, otherwise known as Sam the Survivalist. Sam's ranch is essentially a fortress. Although I thought the Haxbys were plenty peculiar, Jeanette said she was happy to have them as neighbors. They kept their fences strong, their cattle contained, and their business to themselves. Sam and Ina Haxby had six children over the years, all boys, four of whom had moved away. Jack and Carl, both in their forties, stayed behind to ranch, raise their families, and I guess also to prepare for Armageddon.

The next ranch along the road was us. The Square C was the biggest ranch on the road, although I won't say how big. If you want to tick a Fillmore County rancher off, ask him how big his ranch is, how many cattle he has, and how many guns he owns. You'll not likely get an answer but you'll surely get a steely eyed stare.

The Feldmark ranch, known as the Spear F, lay north of us. Aaron Feldmark was in his early seventies, his wife Flora about fifty-five. They lived alone, not counting all their animals. They had raised a family of three boys and four girls, all of whom had moved away as soon as they graduated from high school. Mrs. Feldmark had arrived here as a school teacher in one of the one-room schools in the county and ended up marrying a rancher. This was not unusual. School marms come out from towns like Billings, single and scared, and before you knew it, some rancher had taken her to a dance, fixed her flat tire, tossed a couple of steaks in her little freezer, and she was here for life.

The Thomason ranch, the Lazy T, was next up the road. Buddy Thomason was a widower, his wife dead from pneumonia when his daughter Amelia was but three years old. It was one of those things.

It was spring, the rains had come, Ranchers Road was one long strip of impassable gumbo, and Greta Thomason, a mail-order bride from Germany who Buddy had picked from a catalog, came down with a terrible cold that turned into pneumonia. Greta passed before anything could be done, leaving Buddy to raise Amelia. Far as I could tell, he'd done a pretty good job of it.

Next up the road was the Brescoe ranch, one of several Brescoe ranches in the county although all the others were south of Jericho. There were more Brescoes in Fillmore County than any other family. At the high school, there were sixty-three students and thirty-eight of them were Brescoes, nearly all of them boys, which I guess made prom night a bit awkward. Julius and Mathis were the Brescoes along our road. They were in their fifties and all their kids, six of them, had grown up and moved away.

Ranchers Road ended at the gate that led into the Corbel place, except the Corbels were long gone, sold out three years back to a Californian named Cade Morgan who some folks said had once been the director of a television show or something. I'd never heard of him even though I'd spent years in Hollywood troubleshooting for some of the big studios. But the television crowd and the big movie people didn't mix that much so maybe that explained why I didn't know him. Anyway, Cade had sold off the Corbel cows and, far as I could tell, wasn't farming, either. What he was doing out there on his ranch, nobody knew, but it was his business. Being able to tend to your own business is what generally attracts outsiders to this part of Montana, including me.

The Fillmore County 4th of July Independence Day organizing committee gathered in the back room of the Hell Creek Bar, Jericho's favorite watering hole and conference center. Although I had my grocery list, I loitered at the door and watched Jeanette sit down beside Sam Haxby and share a couple of words with the survivalist. Sam was one of those little guys built like a fireplug, and about as tough. A quick look around revealed representatives from the other ranches along Ranchers Road. There was Aaron Feldmark, looking like a gentleman cowboy with a big "Hoss Cartwright" hat, black vest, string bolo tie, and striped pants tucked into intricately carved cowboy boots. Sitting a couple chairs away was Buddy Thomason, Amelia's dad, dressed in dirty jeans and old boots spattered with dried mud. Julius Brescoe, his nose stuck in the latest issue of *Western Ag Reporter,* sat behind them in bib overalls. I'd noticed his truck outside with his dogs, a couple of border collies, sitting patiently in back waiting for his return.

I heard some commotion behind me and saw Cade Morgan as he came inside the bar, giving the patrons the high sign and the bartender a wink. Square-jawed, high cheek bones, and curly black hair, Cade Morgan, by any lights, was a handsome fellow. Coming in with Cade was someone I'd never seen before. Tall, bald, about a mile wide at the shoulders, a hawk bill for a nose, and a couple of ears that would have made Dumbo proud, this guy had not only been hit by the ugly stick, he'd been pounded.

Cade saw me, and flashed a grin that showed a full set of chemically whitened teeth. "Hey, Mike," he said. "What do you hear from the City of Angels?"

I'd made the mistake (OK, I was drunk at the time) of telling Cade I'd once been a cop and then a gumshoe for the studios. "Not a thing," I told him. "Which is exactly how much I want to hear."

The big, ugly fellow who was with Cade gave me the once-over. I ignored him until Cade introduced us. "Mike, this is Toby. An old buddy."

Toby and I shook hands. I have big hands but mine was swallowed in his. "This is my first trip to Montana," Toby said and I picked up an accent but not one I could quite place. Eastern European, I thought, or maybe Russian. When I didn't reply to his comment, he added, "I think Montana is very nice."

"It sure is," I replied and left it at that.

Cade swaggered inside the room and Toby followed. When he went by me, I noticed a tattoo creeping up from under the back of his shirt onto his neck. I couldn't see enough to tell what it was but I would have bet money it covered his entire back. Not that I cared, one way or the other. If a man wanted to look like Queequeg, so what? These days, people get tattoos for lots of reasons—fashion, boredom, in search of a personality, or for no reason at all.

Edith Brescoe, aka Mayor Brescoe, aka the wife of the local BLM agent, aka my former paramour—I'll get to that—rapped her knuckles on the table in front to get everybody's attention. The gray suit she was wearing made her look crisp and efficient. She was kind of like that in bed, too. Not passionate. Not romantic. Crisp and efficient.

"OK, people," Edith said. "Quiet down, please." She waved toward the back of the room. At first, I thought she was waving at me but it turned out to be two young men who brushed by me from the bar area. They were dressed in casual slacks, sports coat, and open neck shirts, which meant, pretty much, they weren't from around these parts. Both were thin-faced, had the perfectly combed hair of Ivy Leaguers and, if I wasn't mistaken, manicured nails. I instantly ID'd them as either property developers or environmentalists, both bad news for ranchers. The developers want to subdivide the ranches, the enviros want to knock down the fences and bring back the buffalo. Either way, the ranchers get screwed.

The effete pair walked up front and stood smiling beside the mayor but before she could tell us who they were, Aaron Feldmark stood up and said, "I got something to tell everybody, Edith, and it's damn important."

"Can it wait, Aaron?"

"No. I said it was important. I even put a 'damn' in front of it so you'd know."

Edith was unimpressed by Aaron's cussing. "If you'll indulge me for just a few minutes, I promise I'll get back to you. I want to introduce these two gentlemen who just want to say a few words and be on their way. OK?"

Aaron looked peeved but sat down and Edith went on. "Folks, this is Brian and Philip Marsh. They're brothers and they represent an organization that works to provide habitat for threatened species."

There were groans from the audience because they now knew what they had—environmentalists. The pair shared glances, then Brian said, "Hello everybody. As I'm certain you all are aware, the Environmental Protection Agency has proposed regulations that will strictly control the ecological impact of the raising of large domestic ungulates. My brother and I are here to help you determine the statistical data necessary to comply when these regulations take effect. What we will do is survey your ranches so as to determine the methodology required to bring them to a functioning level of biological diversity. We will do this by determining the biomass consumed and created, including the carbon and methane exhalations from the extant population. Once this is accomplished, we will have the necessary data to provide you with an assessment of pollutants and a methodology for regulatory compliance. Are there any questions?"

The ranchers reacted to this little speech with stunned silence until Sam said, "Yeah Let me make sure I understand. You make your little study and turn it over to the EPA, the government then swoops in, makes a declaration on how we're a menace to society, and we get kicked off our land." He pointed his finger at the two boys. "I tell you before I let you within a mile of my ranch, it'll be over my dead body. I seen your black helicopters. Bring 'em on, buddy. I got some ordnance ready for ya!"

Brian and Phillip looked at each other again, then Phillip said, "We don't have any helicopters, sir."

Sam crossed his arms. "So you say."

"No, really. I mean we just want to—"

Aaron interrupted. "What's the name of your organization?"

"We're from Green Planet, a private non-profit," Philip answered.

"Why you sons of bitches," Aaron growled. "It was you two who killed my heifer, wasn't it?"

"Sir?"

Aaron stood. "They knocked her out yesterday with a sledge-hammer, looked like, then cut her throat. And my fence was cut in two places. I found this note. It's how I know'd it was them." He dug around in his pocket and then produced a folded up paper, unfolded it, and read its contents. It said:

> *This range improvement project brought to you by the Green Monkey Wrench Gang. No Address—we're everywhere. No phone—we'll be in touch.*

A shocked silence ensued while the brothers took on an expression best known as "deer in the headlights." *The Monkey Wrench Gang* was the title of a novel by Edward Abbey about a crew of rowdy, drunken guys raising havoc with private property throughout the west during the 1970s. I'd read it and I suspected most of the ranchers at least knew something about it. The novel had inspired ecoterrorists who specialized in things like spiking trees to cause chainsaws to whip around and kill lumberjacks. They also cut fences, burned homes being built in what they considered eco-sensitive areas, and occasionally killed livestock. In other words, menaces to decent society.

Philip found his voice although it was a bit squeaky. "Sir, we're from Green Planet. We don't know anything about the Green Monkey Wrench Gang."

"And we just arrived this morning," Brian pointed out.

Edith took up for the brothers, saying, "Senator Claggers said these boys would drive in from Bozeman this morning. I saw them pull in. They haven't been here long enough for any mischief."

"Senator Claggers!" This eruption was from Tom Wattles, a rancher from down south. "That old hypocrite? You taking orders from him now, Mayor?"

"It never hurts to be polite to a member of the United States Senate, Tom." Gently, Edith reminded everyone of the sad and sorry truth that made Claggers so important. "Senator Claggers is on the committee that oversees the BLM."

"That don't give him the right to send these two girly-boys over here," Sam said. "But, hell, they look to me like they'd be afraid of a cow. Naw, Aaron. I don't see them doing what you said."

Jeanette stood up. When Jeanette Coulter stood, I don't care what else is going on, folks tended to pay attention. "I had a bull killed the same way," she said. "And our fence was also cut."

"Why didn't you tell us that before?" Sam demanded.

"It was Square C business, Sam," she replied and Sam nodded, getting that.

"If these two didn't do it," Frank Torgerson, the county mortician, said, "then who did?"

I had been watching the brothers. If they were guilty of these crimes, I wasn't getting a vibe in that direction. Sam was right. I doubted either one of them had ever seen a cow up close.

Jeanette nodded to the Green Planeteers. "You'd best leave," she said, quietly.

"Get out of the county and stay out," Sam added. "We catch you around here, I got a rope for a necktie party."

"You'd hang us?" Philip gulped.

"Stretch your neck from here to Bozeman. Now, *git!*"

The Marsh brothers fled the room and, after some grins and winks, the conversation turned to who had done these major affronts to our cow society.

Frank said, "I saw a young fellow in a white truck the day after that big storm. He turned up toward Ranchers Road."

"I know who you saw," Jeanette said and then told them about the young fossil collector. This started another round of talking.

"You let a fossil collector go out on the Square C?" Sam demanded, raising his eyebrows so high I thought they were going to fly right off his forehead.

"He look like he could kill a cow?" Julius asked.

"I tell you somebody's got to look into all this," Sam said.

"Job for the law, Sam," the mayor said.

"Which we don't have," Sam retorted. In fact, the position of county sheriff hadn't been filled for a couple of years after the last one had died peacefully in bed. He was a Brescoe, named Spud. Since there was virtually no crime in the county other than the occasional fender bender outside the Hell Creek Bar on a Friday or Saturday night, the county commissioner, who happened to be Julius Brescoe, Spud's son, had decided to save some money and not hold an election for another one.

"I could call the state police," the mayor proposed, "and see what they say."

Based on the frowns aimed at her, Edith's proposal was not received well. Fillmore County folks never like outsiders to poke into their business and that includes state troopers. After some more discussion, it was decided to let things ride, everybody was to keep their eyes open, and we'd see what we'd see. The gathering then turned to planning the Independence Day celebration and I took my leave. As I walked out, I saw a shiny silver sport utility vehicle, no doubt a hybrid, turning onto the main highway. The Green Planeteers were taking off.

I chased down Jeanette's list, loaded up Bob with barbed wire, nails, and some groceries, then came back to the bar for an early beer. I ordered a Rainier, put my boot up on the brass rail, then drank it with the quiet satisfaction of a cowboy with no present responsibilities.

A dainty foot went up beside mine. The mayor's. Our legs briefly touched and I got a mild thrill although our affair had been over for more than a year. "A Rainier for the lady," I told Joe the bartender.

Joe delivered the beer and Edith and I went over and sat at a table. "You look good," I told her, which was the truth. If I wasn't mistaken, she'd unbuttoned the top button on her blouse since the meeting. I could almost smell the perfume I knew she had dabbed between her breasts.

She appraised me with her gentle, blue-gray eyes. "Thanks, cowboy. You're not looking too bad yourself."

"Why aren't you in the meeting?" I asked.

"When Jeanette's in the room, she takes over. They don't need me. It's good to see you, Mike. I've missed you."

"I've missed you, too. How are you doing?"

Edith picked up her Rainier and took a thoughtful sip. "Ted and I are doing OK these days," she said with no real conviction.

This I took as a signal she had no interest in revving up our affair so I shifted the conversation. "Those two enviro boys could have got hurt this morning."

She smiled a sad smile. "I'm not surprised at the reception they got. Change isn't going to come easy to this county."

"Change doesn't come easy anywhere," I said. "But I don't see the ranchers ever going along with any of this environmental stuff. They figure they're the best environmentalists, anyway, because they take care of the land and all the critters inside their fences."

Edith gave me a hard look. "Mike, the days of ranching in the West are over. All the federal government has to do is change a few rules and every one of those folks in that room would be gone. They have no friends in Washington, D.C., not one."

"How about Senator Claggers?"

Edith responded with a grunt of derision, had herself another swallow of beer, then said, "The ranchers are their own worst enemies. They hunker down here, keeping to themselves, and think they can keep the future away. But it's coming, Mike, and it's going to destroy them. The environmental groups have been shoveling money to the politicians like slop to pigs and now they have lawsuits to glue public land together to create a huge bunch of nothing out here. Monument land will be combined with the BLM and the CMR. Every ranching lease will be canceled. All oil and gas exploration will stop dead. Most of it already has. Let the angels rejoice, it's going to be buffalo and wolves as far as the eye can see. And you know what? I don't much care anymore."

Edith was not a rancher's daughter. Her parents had tried to make a go raising pigs and chickens on a little five-acre farm down in the southern part of the county. When she was in high school, her mother committed suicide and Edith had run away, washing up in Denver as a waitress. Eventually, she'd gotten her GED, latched onto some kind of scholarship that got her a B.A. in Education, and come back to Fillmore County as a grade school teacher. After that, she'd married Ted Brescoe, the local BLM agent, and started dabbling in politics. Now, she was mayor of the county seat. Pretty good for the daughter of a pig farmer in cattle country. I'd always admired Edith, even before we'd started bouncing the bedsprings.

"Do you miss us, Mike?" Edith suddenly asked.

"I try not to think about it," I answered honestly.

"We had some good times, didn't we?"

I recalled them as mostly quick times, me sneaking into her house at night when husband Ted was out of town and I had an excuse to drive to Jericho. Sometimes after we'd made love, she'd weep while snuggling into my arms. I never asked her why because I guess I didn't want to know. Our last time together, she'd pulled away and said we couldn't do this anymore. I didn't argue with her. I just got dressed, kissed her on her cheek damp with tears, and walked out of her bedroom without saying a word.

I looked up and saw Jeanette coming toward us. The meeting had broken up with most of the attendees crowding toward the bar.

"Hello, Edith," Jeanette said. "You after my cowboy?"

"I sure am," Edith replied. "You finished reading *My Dream of Stars*?"

Jeanette and Edith were in a book club that had as its members most of the women in the county. They met once a month at the library a block down from the bar, theoretically to talk about the book they'd picked to read. Actually, it was mostly to gossip and drink wine and not a man begrudged them that little bit of time together. Some of the women had to drive over fifty miles just to get there.

"I read it," Jeanette said. "How about you?"

"Working on it."

Jeanette regarded the mayor for a short second. "Edith, don't you ever bring a couple of jackasses like that near us again. I don't care what that fool Claggers says. Do you understand?"

Edith opened her mouth, perhaps to argue, but then she shrugged and said, "You bet."

Jeanette was done with the mayor. "You ready, Mike?"

I wasn't but I guessed I'd better be. I put my hat on and tipped it to Edith, paid Joe for the beers, then drove Jeanette back to the Square C. About twenty minutes into our drive, I said, "I don't think you should treat Edith like that." Thirty minutes later, Jeanette said, "I treated her better than you did, Mike."

I shut up. That's what you do when somebody has just drilled you between the eyes with the truth.

6

It was nearly two in the afternoon when we got back and Ray and Amelia had not returned which meant they'd been out there alone for over five hours. Jeanette and I carried in the groceries, then I looked in on the little C-sectioned heifer and her calf for a while and Jeanette fed an orphan calf in a separate pen. Jeanette loved that little bum. She'd gone out in a deep March snow to bring him back alive after his mother had died giving birth. Once the calf was fed, she sought me out and said, "I guess we'd better go out there." I could tell she was worried about Ray and Amelia.

First thing I did was to go to my trailer to retrieve my trusty Glock 9 mm, left over from my L.A. days. I packed it into a small backpack, then climbed behind Bob's steering wheel so Jeanette would have to open and close all the gates. She knew what I was doing and said, "Let's take the four-wheelers." We did and she let me take the lead, which meant I opened and closed the first gate. Somehow, even though Jeanette was fearless on an ATV, it worked out she kept dropping back enough I had to open and close all the rest of them, too.

Before we got to the BLM gate, she said, "Show me the bull," and I did.

The dead bull lay in front of a small stand of twisted little juniper trees, one of the few trees that can live out there. The bull's body was swollen, its legs rigid as posts, and it was covered with flies, their excited buzzing like little chainsaws. I made a mental note to bring the tractor out to haul the corpse away and bury it. There was no good reason to let the coyotes get a taste of cow meat even if it's rotten.

Jeanette climbed off her four-wheeler and walked up next to the corpse. The flies clustered on the bull's wounds were too happy to notice. While I held my nose, Jeanette carefully circled the bull, stopping for a while near the junipers. Then she came back and, without another word, climbed on her vehicle and took off. I followed and after we'd gotten some distance away, she stopped and I pulled up alongside her. "It wasn't a sledgehammer that knocked that bull out," she said. "It was a shovel."

"How do you know?" I asked.

"I spotted the working end of one inside those junipers. It wasn't rusty. It also had blood on it."

This made me angry, entirely at myself. If it was there, I should have found that shovel. Why hadn't I poked around in those trees? My experience as a detective had decidedly faded.

We motored on up and over the rolling pastureland. If I hadn't been worried for Ray, Amelia, and Pick, and mad at myself about missing that shovel, I might have enjoyed it more. We found the BLM gate closed but there were fairly fresh tire tracks and hoof prints on both sides of it, which meant to me that Pick likely had made it this far and so had Ray and Amelia. I got off, opened the gate, let Jeanette go through, then got back on my four-wheeler, drove it through, then got out and closed the gate and got back on my vehicle. You see what trouble this is? Even worse, you have to do it all over again on your way back. I've heard of automatic gates but Jeanette, like every rancher in Fillmore County, thought they were too expensive. It's cheaper to let your cowboy do it. That's the attitude.

Some more words about the territory we were entering, and the BLM, which runs it. The Bureau of Land Management is responsible for more land than any other agency, government or private, in the United States and maybe the world. At last count, the BLM was responsible for more than two-and-a-half million acres of land, mostly in the Western states. Since Congress doesn't pay much attention to it, the agency gets only a little legislative pork thrown its way. This is actually fine with the BLM because it makes plenty of money through the sale of gas, oil, uranium, and other energy deposits beneath their lands. It also leases its land to such folks as the owner of the Square C.

This all began with the Taylor Grazing Act of 1934, which allowed leases for private ranchers to graze their cattle on the BLM. Since most of the ranchers had already been grazing cattle and sheep out there for generations, the act simply put in code what was already a fact. The difference was the fee. I suspect the size of that fee is one of those things that Westerners and Easterners will argue about until the end of our republic. Mostly, the ranchers of Fillmore County wished the federal government, or any and all governments, would just go away and leave them to do what they do best, raise cattle and sheep, sell them, then raise some more. As usual, Jeanette had the final word on the BLM, saying it meant well and that was the trouble with it.

Once, a couple years ago, I was in the Hell Creek Bar when Ted Brescoe, the local BLM guy who also happens to be the mayor's husband and therefore the fellow whose wife I'd been in bed with a few times by then, came in. He was already pretty drunk. Ted's a guy who wears a perpetual sneer on his face. When he lurched up to the bar beside me, just to make conversation, I asked him to tell me what he did out on the BLM. "It ain't none of your business, asshole," he said and went back to his booze. Yep, a nasty customer, Ted Brescoe. Although I felt guilty about Edith much of the time we were together, right then I was glad I could give her a little relief from her husband.

So, anyway, there we were on the BLM land which the Square C leased, motoring along on a track that wound through a series of small brown and gray hills, then along the edge of a deep coulee filled with grass and occasional stands of juniper and gnarly limber pine. It was where the coulee necked down near the base of a little hill that we found Pick's truck. There was a tarp in its bed covering whatever was in there. I lifted it up to inspect the cargo, then put it back. What was there, or, more importantly, what wasn't there was interesting but I said nothing to Jeanette about it. Nick and Dusty's hoof prints littered the ground around the truck so we followed them. We had to go a good mile before we found Ray and Amelia. There, we also found Pick.

We drove up to the horses. Nick was looking bored but Dusty was intently watching the three humans who were halfway up a pyramid-shaped hill. I marveled anew how Dusty could be so entertained by herself and her surroundings. Ray saw us and waved. I waved back and we climbed up there. Pick was sitting down, his legs sprawled. Beside him near a pair of leather gloves was a well-used pick, its working end shiny from use. Ray and Amelia were looking at what lay below Pick's boots, which were shapes in the dirt. "Pick says it's a Triceratops," Ray said.

I looked closer and I saw a rock about two feet long that was curved, appeared somewhat cylindrical in shape, and came to a dull point. Its color was only a little different from the dirt around it so I had to look carefully to see it at all. "Tip of an orbital horn," Pick said when he saw where I was looking. "Be careful where you step.

I think there's nearly an entire adult Triceratops here. If you look closer, you can see the edge of its frill, an occipital condyle just starting to weather out, a couple of ribs, and three dorsal vertebra."

"Why did a dinosaur climb the side of a hill to die?" I asked.

Pick smiled. "You have to understand nothing that you see now was the same as it was sixty-five million years ago when this animal lived. This is but one layer of many in deep time. When this layer was on top, it was part of a land of rivers, lakes, and rich, green floodplains. Not too many miles away was a vast, inland ocean."

I had heard something about ancient Montana being a seashore but sixty-five million years was more than my mind could quite wrap itself around. "How do you know how long ago?" I asked.

"We use radiogenic dating," Pick replied. "That means we measure the amount of decay of a radioactive isotope in a sample." When he saw my blank stare, he said, "What's important is what was, still is, or will be. Now, consider this place. What do you see?"

I saw the BLM. I guess so did the rest of us because nobody said anything. "Look at that hill," Pick said, nodding toward a steep cone-shaped mound just south of us. "Do you see the layers like a wedding cake? Each tell the story of life and death in a different age. Your fields, Mrs. Coulter, are composed of sediment eroded from all those ages. In other words, your cattle eat the grass that is produced by deep time."

While we squinted at the hill, Pick led us farther into his vision. "Those narrow bands of gray, yellow, and dark brown near the top are from what we call the Tullock member of the Fort Union Formation. The Tullock was formed after the dinosaurs so what I would find there, if I cared to look, would be the bones of mammals. Nothing big, mostly prairie dog size. But I don't hunt mammals, even ones tens of millions of years old. I hunt and find dinosaurs."

He said the last five words with a great deal of satisfaction, then continued. "Just below the Tullock on this hill is a thin layer of coal. It's easily discernable. It is what we call Z-coal and coincidentally in the Hell Creek Formation it marks the K-T or Cretaceous-Tertiary boundary. That's the famous iridium layer you've perhaps heard about left from a gigantic meteor that struck what is now the Gulf of Mexico. Above that boundary, there are no dinosaurs. Below, we enter the Cretaceous where once creatures such as this big Triceratops flourished."

"I've ridden past this hill a hundred times," I said, "and I never noticed these bones. How did you find them?"

Pick smiled. "I saw what was. That's what I do."

A silence fell over us, the only sound the mewing of the breeze through the little dry hills, and the distant *kee-kee* of a red tail hawk. It was a bit eerie, I'll confess. Finally, Ray broke the spell by saying, "When we found Pick, he was lost. Had no idea where he was."

Pick nodded agreeably. "I get lost easily. As soon as I got out here, I went looking. I found this Trike in the first thirty minutes. There's a Hadrosaur over there, although not much of him. Do you see his bones? There, by those two sandstone boulders that fell down from the top of the hill. When it got dark, I had no idea where the truck was so I just sat out here all night."

"You're lucky the rattlesnakes didn't get you," Jeanette said.

I was thinking of our murdered bull and Aaron Feldmark's cow when I asked, "Did you hear or see anything else?"

"Lights," he said after a moment of contemplation. "And engine sounds."

"Where?"

"I'm not sure. Maybe over there. Or there. I was thinking about something else."

"Dr. Pickford, I really want to know what you were thinking about out here in the dark," Jeanette said.

I'd like to say Pick got a far-away, dreamy look in his eyes but the truth is he seemed to nearly always have that look. He said, "I was thinking about the rivers and streams that led to the pond from which this animal drank, and the forest of conifers from which it emerged, and the vegetation that filled the valley where the pond collected, and the slope that eventually led to the sea. I was also thinking about mud. A swollen river created mud to cover and make this Triceratops immortal. Mud also saved it for me. For all of us."

It was an interesting little speech and I was impressed. I guess we all were. "How did this thing live?" Amelia asked, which caused Pick to smile in her direction. He liked the question.

As Pick described the Triceratops I swear those old bones all but rose from the ground, assembled themselves clad with muscles, sinew, and flesh, and came alive. Then, I noticed a circle of stones in a sandy patch nearby. It didn't look natural and I could see boot prints around it so I asked Pick about it.

"I built it last night to remind me everything important is a circle," he said. "The sun is a circle and so is the moon. The eagle, which many societies consider sacred, flies in a great circle. And when we stand on the tallest mountain, we see a circle where the sky touches the earth. When we build camp fires, we build a circle of stones around it. We do this without thinking. It is our inner selves—psychiatrists call it our subconscious and preachers our souls—that does this. Of that ring you see, Mike, can you tell me where the stones start and where they end? Of course not, because a circle is as much end as it is beginning. That is the way it is with our lives and with the universe itself."

I could tell Amelia was fascinated by all this because she couldn't take her eyes off of Pick. Ray looked embarrassed by such talk, more words than he'd probably ever heard from a man at one time.

Pick, in my opinion, was off the deep end. Yeah, eagles fly in circles but so do buzzards.

Agreeing with me, I think, Jeanette said, "You're a piece of work, boy," then turned to me. "You think we should go looking for tracks to see if we can find what those motor sounds were that Dr. Pickford heard?"

I considered it, then said, "We're not exactly Indian trackers. We'd likely drive over the lip of a hidden coulee as find anything."

"I'm going to dig up this Triceratops," Pick said, ignoring the fact that Jeanette and I were having a conversation. "It's an excellent specimen. If we just leave it, it will weather out and turn to dust in a couple of seasons."

"Well, Dr. Pickford," Jeanette replied, "as you made clear, you have a BLM permit so I guess I can't stop you."

"True," he said, "but it would be easier if I could cross your land with my supplies and equipment. I'll need to call in a couple of my associates for assistance and they'll need to bring their vehicle as well."

I could almost see the picture bubble over Jeanette's head that showed open gates that should be closed and closed gates that should be open. To my surprise, she said, "All right, Pick. Bring your folks by to see me, let me give them the rules, and you can have your Triceratops."

That was when I first realized Jeanette had a favorable opinion of Pick. Since Bill had passed, I'd never observed her giving a fig about any man but maybe it was her motherly instinct. Certainly, Pick looked like the type of fellow who needed a little mothering.

Pick was pondering Ray and Amelia. "Would you two like to help me dig? I can't pay you but you might learn something new."

Amelia immediately said she'd like nothing better. Ray glanced at his mom who raised an eyebrow. "I have a lot of work on the ranch," he said.

"After branding, maybe," Jeanette said. She looked at Pick. "That will be in about a week."

"Excellent," he said.

And so, just like that, in a place where the cycle of ranching and farming was the only constant, something else was about to happen. I thought this was just fine. We needed something to shake up our lives every so often. But then I thought of the murdered bull and Aaron Feldmark's murdered cow and the odd note from some wackos claiming responsibility. We didn't need that kind of change, no.

Once back on our four-wheelers, Jeanette and I drove around for a while, just poking about until I waved her down. "Pick told me he had a shovel in his truck," I said, "I looked and didn't see one. Didn't see one at that dinosaur, either."

"So?"

"So there's a busted shovel by our dead bull."

She frowned. "You think Pick killed our bull?"

"I'm just doing addition, Jeanette. Two plus two equals four."

"I think you'd best leave the math to me," she said and powered on, leaving me to eat her dust.

God, how I loved that woman.

7

AFTER WE GOT BACK on the Square C side of the fence, I let my four-wheeler drop behind Jeanette, planning on telling her my machine was running rough if she asked. She didn't ask, mainly because she never looked back, just kept going until she went over a rise and out of sight. I circled back to where our poor bull was still dead, searched out the busted shovel, found it beneath the junipers where Jeanette said it was, and brought it out into the sun to inspect it. It was well-used, its handle shiny and smooth and the edge of its working end worn. It could be the shovel of someone who dug up fossils for a living, but then I recalled Pick said he didn't dig. But, then again, Pick probably meant the big excavations, not the little digging around a fossil bed like the Triceratops he'd found. And there were sanitary considerations, too. There are no flush toilets on our BLM and number two has to go somewhere, usually a little hole. As for why I didn't see his shovel, I could have missed it among the boxes of supplies in the back of Pick's truck, or it might have been somewhere else. I should have asked Pick about it but I wasn't in detective mode and didn't plan on getting into it any time soon. Just to keep the prairie clean, I strapped the remains of the shovel to my four-wheeler with a bungee cord kept in its storage compartment and motored on back to the ranch, repeating the gate experience several more times. Stop. Get off. Open gate. Get on. Drive through. Get off. Close gate. Get on. And so forth. I bet more than one cowboy quit just to get away from those damn gates.

Back at the house, there was no sign of Jeanette. I did a few more things, then retired to my trailer, there to fix myself a gin and tonic and lounge a bit on the verandah. Yeah, I actually do that. Not every day but it seemed like as good a day as any to relax.

I sat there in my lawn chair beneath my tattered trailer awning and watched a hawk circle lazily in the sky until it made a sudden dive, leveling out before disappearing near an outcrop of sand beside a weathered butte. Likely, a rabbit or mouse was its target. Whether the hawk got a meal, I don't know but I would put money on it. Considering how hard it is to make a living in this country, predators around here don't like to waste energy. That's why they tend to go after sure things.

Which brought me to thinking about our bull. People are different than natural predators. They kill for lots of reasons, not just food, so the purpose of applying deadly force to the bull by a human could have any number of explanations. Consider the little boy or girl with a magnifying glass killing ants. He or she is having fun. Perhaps our bull had been killed just because some warped individual thought it would be a fun thing to do. I started a mental list. Our bull was killed for fun.

Or maybe the bull was murdered because somebody was afraid of it. Fear often causes a human to kill. If, say, a tourist of some sort had been on our property and he was confronted by our bull, could he have panicked, knocked out the bull, then completed the job with a knife? Not logical but feasible so I kept it on my list.

Anger, envy, or revenge were also possibilities. Maybe Jeanette or Ray or even I had done something to irritate somebody and he had taken it out on our bull. This one seemed a long shot. Cows were respected in Fillmore County. You didn't just kill a cow without there being some really good reason and I couldn't think of one. OK, I did think of one. What if, say, a certain husband of a certain mayor found out a certain Square C cowboy had been tapping his wife? As I mentioned, Ted Brescoe was a nasty piece of work but, on the other hand, if he'd done it, then why did he also go off and kill one of Aaron Feldmark's cows and leave that stupid note? That didn't make sense.

Finally, I thought of the possibility that maybe that note wasn't stupid at all. Maybe environmentalists in the spirit of the old Monkey Wrench Gang of the 1970s were not only still around, they were here. In that case, if environmental activists were targeting the cows along Ranchers Road, we were going to be in a world of hurt in a county without a sheriff. The state probably wouldn't do much about it, either. Their troopers were spread thin arresting speeders on the Interstates. As for the federal government, the BLM wouldn't care and any bureaucratic agency higher up on the totem pole likely would side with the monkey wrenchers, anyway.

All this thinking required another gin and tonic and I was also starting to think about supper. Rice, beans, and pasta were on my menu. I'm a vegetarian, as I think I mentioned earlier. I love the work and I love the cows. I just don't care to eat them.

About then, Ray showed up and he didn't look happy. "Want me to fix you a g-and-t?" I asked. It was a facetious question since the boy didn't drink.

"No, thank you," Ray said, politely.

"There's beer in the fridge," I told Ray. "Help yourself."

Ray went inside and came out with a can of cola, as I knew he would. He dragged a lawn chair from where I stored several beneath my trailer, set it up beside me, and sat down. "Amelia gone?" I asked.

"Yes," he answered. "She cleaned up Dusty and took off."

I let that settle for a bit, then said, "She sure is a pretty girl. Amelia, I mean. I mean Dusty's not bad but . . ."

"Don't patronize me, Mike," Ray interrupted.

"I wasn't," I swore, even though I was. "Is there a problem?"

Ray took on the thoroughly miserable expression that only a teen-age boy in love can exhibit and said, "Amelia hates Montana and can't wait to leave. I want to stay. So when I asked her to the Inde-pendence Day dance, she said she'd love to but we don't have a fu-ture. Hell, what does our future have to do with it? I just wanted to dance. What's with girls anyway, Mike?"

"A very good question," I said. "A very, very good question."

When I didn't say anything more for a few minutes, Ray said, "Well, aren't we gonna talk about it?"

"Talk about what?"

"What's wrong with girls!"

"I don't think so, mainly because it wouldn't amount to a hill of beans. They're females, that's all I know."

We sat for a little longer, then Ray said, "What's with that busted shovel?" I had pitched the one that had killed our bull beneath my trailer and I guess he'd seen it when he got the lawn chair out.

"That's the one used on our bull," I said.

"Mom told me about finding it." he said. "Could hitting a big old bull on the head with a shovel really kill him?"

"He died of a cut throat," I pointed out.

"Yeah, but to cut his throat, you'd have to knock him senseless. Could a shovel really do that? Anyway, I didn't see any big dent in his head when Amelia and I stopped to look at him."

I gave Ray's observation some thought, recalling that time when one of our bulls had run head-on into a concrete post. After a shake of his head, he had barreled on, none the worse for wear. "You have a point, Ray," I admitted.

"I know," he rejoined and had himself a swig of cola.

Ray left soon after and I sat there, contemplating that "from the mouths of babes" thing. I also recalled that his mom had made a similar observation when I'd reported the bull's death to her. Our bull could not have been knocked out by that thin-handled shovel unless something else had happened to it first. That's when I knew it was time to get the tractor out. There was more to this dead bull than had yet been seen.

8

THE DAY AFTER WE'D been out to see his Triceratops, Pick drove in, saying he needed to call his crew. Jeanette and Ray were out and about so I let him into the house to make his call. Afterward, he didn't seem to want to stick around so I opened the gate for him and off he went on the rutted track back to the BLM. This time, he turned the correct way.

It was three days before I got the time to go out to bury the dead bull. That morning, after we'd done everything else, I got Ray to help me put the scoop on the tractor. Jeanette saw what we were doing and came over. "What are you doing with my John Deere?"

I answered, "Ray and I are going to bury that dead bull."

She nodded, then said, "I'll follow on a four-wheeler, then go on out to the BLM. I'm wondering about our dinosaur hunter."

"Well, wonder no more," I said, "because there he is."

And there he was, indeed, opening the gate of the Mulhaden pasture to drive his pickup through. He did so, got out, closed the gate, got back in, spotted us, and drove over. "Hello," he said, getting out of his truck. "Have you seen my crew?"

Jeanette said we hadn't and Pick replied, "They should be here today."

"You hungry?" Jeanette asked, which I thought was kind of astonishing. She never asked Ray or me if we were hungry and she rarely, if ever, cooked. Ray did most of it, far as I knew. Of course, I was always on my own. Jeanette roundly disapproved of what she considered my vegetarian quirk. I never told her it had started with the bullet that curtailed my promising LAPD career. It's hard to eat meat when there's a hole in your colon. Maybe I should have told her that was why I stopped eating meat, but I liked being a little "Hollywood" around her, don't ask me why.

Anyway, Pick said that he might indeed be hungry and Jeanette invited him in for breakfast, promising him some scrambled eggs, ham, and buttered toast. All Ray and I could do was gawk and wonder what alien had taken over Jeanette's body.

"We're ready to go out to the bull," I said but it was to Jeanette's back since she was leading Pick toward the house.

Ray and I looked at each other again, then mutually shrugged. "Heck, she don't even know where the frying pan is," Ray said, then dropped the subject.

I wasn't surprised when Amelia arrived in her daddy's truck. "What are you doing?" she asked Ray who was greasing the hinges on the scoop we'd just attached. "Nothing," he said.

"What are you going to do with that scoop?"

"We're going to bury that dead bull," I told her when it was clear Ray was intent on ignoring her.

"Can I go?"

That was, in my opinion, a lovely response. After all, where can you find a beautiful teenage girl who would be thrilled at the prospect of seeing a dead bull buried? Not too many places but Fillmore County. Or maybe, she just wanted to be with Ray.

With Ray driving the tractor, Amelia sitting beside him, and me riding shotgun, we ran on out to the bull. When we got there, we only had to follow our noses to find it. Nothing had bothered it as far as I could tell except the flies and time. I guess it stunk too much for even the coyotes. I took the controls and maneuvered the tractor to get its scoop under the deceased animal but rather than pick it up, I turned it over instead.

"What are you doing?" Ray asked when I got off the tractor and walked up to the bull.

"I need to see its other side," I answered. While Ray and Amelia wisely kept their distance, I got up close and personal with a very nasty corpse. What I expected to see was there. At the base of its neck was a bullet hole. I got out a hunting knife I'd brought along and cut into it.

It was a thoroughly nasty job but eventually, my arms covered with decay, slime, gore, and maggots, I found the bullet. It was a .30 caliber, which didn't tell me very much except that our bull had probably been shot first, then hit on the head with a shovel, then its throat cut. It was only a little more than I already knew.

While I was pondering all this, Ray and Amelia had fixed our cut fences. Then, Ray got on the tractor, scooped up the bull, and trundled over to a coulee not too far away on the other side of the road, dumped the bull, then shoved some dirt on top. He was just finishing the job when a little convoy arrived. It was Jeanette on her four-wheeler, then Pick's truck followed by another pickup with two women in it.

The two women got out. They were young and, by the lights of this old cowboy, good-looking. One was a brunette, the other a blonde. Both were dressed in the same fashion as Pick—hiking boots, cargo pants, multi-pocketed shirts, and flat-brimmed hats with colorful hatbands. I guessed these were Pick's assistants. Pick introduced the brunette to me and Ray as Tanya, and the blonde as Laura. I didn't shake their hands or even get too close. I stunk too much of dead bull. Ray had a grin that just wouldn't go away. Amelia looked sort of doubtful.

Tanya proved to be Russian and had an accent that made me think of Moscow nights on the Volga or something. Laura was a farm girl, probably out of Iowa or Nebraska. She had that all-American beauty and no brains look about her that was quickly dispelled when she said, of our now buried dead bull, "It would be interesting to come back in a million years to study the taphonomy of your bull. I imagine the quality of preservation will be remarkable."

Pick smiled and said, "Laura means the bull should fossilize well."

I took Jeanette aside and told her about the bullet wound. She wrinkled up her nose at my odiferous presence while considering my information, then said, "Then it must have been a hunter who did it."

"Jeanette, we don't have hunters this time of year."

She shrugged. "A poacher, then. Some guys can't wait for the season. You know that."

I showed her the slug I'd dug out of the bull, then gave her a little speech. "Look, that note Aaron found didn't come from a poacher. There's something going on around here and we'd better come to grips with it."

Her expression was cool. "Mike, you're looking so hard at this because you used to be a policeman." She shook her head. "If there's a cow-killer along Ranchers Road, we'll find him and make him wish he never came out this way. Stop worrying. And good lord, you stink!"

Jeanette went back to the group. I did, too, trying to stay downwind of them. They all loaded up, Ray and I got in the back of Pick's truck, and headed off to the BLM. Naturally, I got to open and close all the gates.

When we reached the Trike site, I saw a shovel lying beside it. "That your only shovel?" I asked Pick.

"Yes," he said. "Do you need it?"

I said I didn't, not then, anyway. I noticed Laura looking me over, her nose wrinkled. "I've got a five-gallon jerry can of water in the back of our truck and some dish detergent if you want to wash." I took her up on her offer.

When I'd finished washing, I came back and found Laura down on all fours and sniffing at the Trike site like a border collie. "You've got a good one here, Pick," she said, finally. "Do you want us to start the excavation today?"

"Tomorrow will be soon enough," he said. Then to Ray, "Are you going to be able to dig with us?"

Ray looked at his mother and Jeanette said, "After the branding."

"Can we help with that?" Pick asked. "Branding sounds like fun. I've seen it in the movies."

"Oh, it's great fun," I said, allowing my natural irony to drip.

Jeanette snapped me a look. "Be at the barn Tuesday morning. Come around five."

"In the morning?" Pick asked in an astonished tone.

"Yes, Dr. Pickford. On a ranch, we work early hours. Late ones, too."

"We'll be there," Laura said.

And just like that, we had dinosaur people coming to be cowboys.

Pick directed Tanya and Laura to erect a big hangar-like tent to hold all the stuff required to dig up their dinosaur. I was surprised when Jeanette jumped in and started helping, too. Naturally, Ray, Amelia, and I got busy as well. I noticed Pick carrying a few things, none of them weighing very much. I also saw him tamp down one tent peg but otherwise he mostly supervised. By the time we were finished, I was a little irritated at his laziness, enough that I decided to call him over for a chat about it. Before I could say anything, he said, "I know better than try to do much when Laura and Tanya are around. Part of their job description is setting up camp so they want to do it all. They tell me I just get in the way."

"They do seem to know what they're doing," I admitted.

He grinned. "Wait until you see how fast they dig up that big old Trike!"

I changed course. "Pick, when you came out here that first day, did you see that dead bull?"

He squinted thoughtfully, then said, "I saw it but I just kept going."

"Did you see anybody else?"

He hesitated a tick, then said, "No."

"You told Jeanette you have a BLM permit. Do you mind if I see it? We could get in big trouble with the government if you aren't supposed to be here."

"It's in my truck. I'll show you."

Pick started off in the wrong direction. I turned him around and then led him along the curve in the hill, crossed a small grassy patch, jumped over a narrow crack, then went along another hill. I looked over my shoulder and saw Pick had stopped and was looking up the hill. "What is it?" I asked.

He didn't answer. Instead, he climbed up the slope, mostly on his hands and knees because of its steepness and the loose rock that covered it. Finally, he reached a small ledge, picked up what he was after, then scrambled back down, pebbles and dirt in a little landslide around his boots. He held up his find, a curved brown rock about the six inches wide. When he turned it over, I could see by its striations that it was probably bone. He confirmed it, saying "This is the fronto-parietal dome of a Pachycephalosaurus. A very nice one, indeed."

Before I could ask him what a Packy-whatever was, Pick said, "They were wonderful creatures, like a dinosaur kangaroo with a football helmet. This bone was the top part of the helmet."

"Did they hop?"

Pick blinked at my question. "Hop?"

"You said they were like a kangaroo."

"No, I don't think they hopped. I just meant they looked kangaroo-like. They had large eyes, short front limbs, and muscular hind limbs. Their manus were well-padded but also excellently adapted with a finger-like agility. Their pes had three phalanges, well equipped with ungual phalanxes . . ."

I interrupted him. "I do believe you've lost me."

He took a moment to rethink what he just said, then cleared things up. "Manus are hands, pes are feet, phalanges are fingers, and ungual phalanxes are claws. We paleontologists have our own language."

"So do ranchers. You ought to hear Jeanette and the other owners when they get going talking about things like the estimated breeding value of a bull and the most probable producing capability of a cow. Most folks wouldn't have a clue what they were talking about."

Pick politely mulled this over, then asked, "Do you want to hear more about Pachycephalosaurus?"

"Sure."

"They were odd, even by dinosaur standards. By their size and strength and by those big domes on their heads, you'd think they'd be aggressive but all they had were tiny leaf-shaped teeth, suitable for not much more than chewing on ferns. Their domes were surrounded by pebble-like bumps and prominent osteoderms along the sides of the squamosal that gave them a dragon-like appearance."

"Ostie what on squamie huh?" I asked.

"They had spikes and bony structures covering their snouts and along their mouths. They were also ornithischians, that is to say they had bird-like hips like the Trikes and duckbills. The meat-eaters, by the way, had lizard-like hips, making them saurischians, even though they're much more closely related to birds then lizards. That is a quirk of evolution. Although lay people often think it's confusing, we paleontologists divide dinosaurs into two main groups based on their hip structures."

I let that one ride and Pick went on. "I believe Packys liked to roam in family groups, were cooperative, and ate well. I also think their domes were mostly for sexual display. Some say they used them to butt like mountain goats for sexual dominance but I doubt it. There's nothing in their design otherwise to absorb the shock of using their heads as battering rams. Maybe they weren't particularly good to eat and therefore didn't have to fight very much. Or maybe they had stink glands like skunks. Or even quills like porcupines."

I asked, "Is there more of the Packy-seffy-thing up there?"

"No. The domes were especially suited to survive over the ages but its other bones weren't. This tells us their skeletons were probably not particularly robust. In fact, we've never found a complete skeleton, only ones of similar animals. In China, for instance."

"So you're not sure what they looked like."

He peered at me, like he was pitying my ignorance. Finally, he said, "I have faith in my vision of the Pachycephalosaurus."

This struck me as weird. "Faith? Vision? Is paleontology a science or a religion?"

Pick smiled. "Although I would probably be beat up at the next Society of Vertebrate Paleontology meeting if anyone heard me say this, there is a point in our studies where we go beyond the pedantic and venture forth into the realm of the imagination."

"I do the same thing when I think about sex," I offered.

This made Pick laugh. "Let me turn you into a dinosaur hunter, Mike," he said. "Look around. Within fifty feet of where we're standing, there is a significant dinosaur bone. Find it for me."

I was willing to play his game so I looked around the jumble of rocks, pebbles, scrub pine and juniper, amidst the glaring sun and deep shadows of the BLM. I didn't see anything except exactly what I'd seen a lot of during the last ten years. Mostly dirt.

"Remember those puzzles when you were a kid where you had to pick out something that didn't fit?" he asked. "Approach your search in that spirit."

I gave it another try and still didn't see any dinosaur bones. Finally, he said, "Look at that little drainage over there."

He was referring to a narrow channel that ran from the top of the hill all the way to the base. At the bottom were a jumble of small rocks and pebbles which were brown, red, yellow, and black except for one. I saw now that the coloration of that rock was different from the rest, a pale yellow. When I studied it, I saw that it also had symmetry. "You see it now, don't you?" Pick asked, quietly.

I walked over to the thing and picked it up. It was about the size of my fist, was oval in shape, and there were places on it where it looked like something had broken off. "What is it?" I asked, bringing it back for him to inspect.

"It is the caudal vertebra of a small Hadrosaur. Probably an Edmontosaurus, the most common duckbill found in this formation. Caudal means its tail."

"It sure looks beat up."

"It is. There's only the centrum left. Broken off are the arch that protected the spinal cord and the spines that connected it to the tendons that gave the tail its strength. Every bone has its own history. Mostly that history is one of violence."

"Like getting killed and eaten," I said.

"Yes, predation is certainly a factor. The bones of animals killed by other animals get ingested, stepped on, or strewn around as the skeleton is passed from the top to the bottom of the predator chain, that is to say from the animal that killed it to the scavengers. Or the animal may have been torn apart by a sudden flood, or burned to a crisp by volcanic ash, or maybe it simply fell off a cliff into a river and was ripped apart by rocks and currents. Whatever happened to it, natural forces tend to move skeletons around until the individual bones are far apart or completely destroyed. That's why discovering an intact animal is so rare."

I held up the vertebra. "Can I have it?"

"No. You have to have a permit." He held out his hand and I reluctantly placed the vertebra in it.

Sort of hooked on this finding dino bones thing, I started looking closer at my surroundings. On a little ledge, about a third of the way up the hill, I spotted another rock the same subtle shade of yellow as my duckbill vertebra. I climbed up to it, slipping and sliding, and picked the thing up. About four inches long, it kind of looked like a chicken drumstick. I brought it back down and handed over my find.

Pick admired it which I have to confess pleased me. "Very nice. Where's the rest of it?" This must have been a paleontology joke because he chuckled before saying, "This is a fragment of a toe bone of an Oviraptorid. A theropod. Note that it's hollow? That's the clue we have that it's a meat-eater. Even the T. rex had hollow bones."

I looked around some more while Pick made a GPS reading, jotted something in his little notebook, then said, "We'd best get to the truck," and started walking. Once again, it was the wrong way. I caught up with him and pointed in the correct direction. "Why don't you use the GPS to find your truck?" I asked.

He looked sheepish. "I forgot to mark it."

"You get lost out here, you're going to die."

"I always find my way back, eventually. For a paleontologist, being lost is not necessarily a bad thing. It means I see places I wouldn't otherwise see."

I gave that some thought. "You're dangerous, Pick," I concluded, "mostly to yourself."

Off we went again, this time successfully reaching the truck where he put the Packy dome, my duckbill vertebra, and the ovi-whatever toe bone in a plastic storage box, then opened the glove compartment, took out a folded document, and handed it to me. There were two sheets in the document. The top one was a letter with the official letterhead of the BLM signed by Ted Brescoe. The letter said, in effect, that the names on the attached sheet, all representing Yosemite University, had permission to go on BLM land and collect fossils. When I turned to the second sheet, I saw the names of Dr. Norman Pickford, Tanya Simius, and Laura Wilson. All had the same address: Department of Paleontology, Yosemite University, California. No town. No zip code.

"I'm not familiar with Yosemite University," I said.

"It's up north," Pick replied. "Near Oregon."

"Is it part of the University of California system?"

"Affiliated."

"I thought you said you were from UC Berkeley."

He shrugged. "I was kind of blowing smoke. It sounds better than Yosemite. But I did graduate from Berkeley."

I handed the document back. "OK, thanks."

"Is that all?" he asked, looking surprised.

"That's all."

I looked into Pick's eyes and saw relief. I remembered teaching a rookie cop one time a very important lesson of interrogation: Tell a guilty man you're through with your questions and you'll see relief in his eyes. Every time. He just can't hide it.

9

Shortly after Pick and I got back to the dig site, Montana did its thing. Even though we were into June, the weather blew up cold and started pouring rain, which then proceeded to turn into sleet. Jeanette and Amelia jumped on her four-wheeler and got the heck out of there before they got stuck in the gumbo. Ray and I hoofed it back to the tractor, then drove back to the barn. The last I saw of the three paleontologists was Pick sitting in the girls' truck, safe and dry, while Laura and Tanya were putting up a tent. My guess it was Pick's.

The skies stayed a sullen gray for the next two days and even spat a little snow. We didn't hear a word from Pick and his ladies and we assumed they were hunkered down. Jeanette used the time to pay some bills and ordered me inside to help her. She had an old computer with some accounting software on it, which was hooked to a cranky printer. Of course, I knew the drill. Since Jeanette had never really learned to type, she wanted me to key the receipts and bills into the computer while she sat at the kitchen table and read them out. She also wanted me to listen while she griped about every one of the expenses. We were both very good at these jobs.

I was always astonished at the amount of money required to keep the Square C operating. Electricity, maintenance and repair of the equipment, medicine for the cows, fencing, fuel, insurance, feed—it all added up. The last thing a rancher ever spends money on is himself and I was pretty sure Jeanette had not bought herself any new clothes since Bill had died. Ray got some for school, of course, mainly because he outgrew what he had.

About halfway through the receipts, I remembered I'd forgotten to tell Jeanette something. "Pick showed me his permission to be on the BLM. Ted Brescoe signed it. It said he's from Yosemite University in California, which, according to him, is in northern California near the Oregon border. I never heard of it."

She peered over her half-glasses at me. "Sounds like you don't believe him."

"I don't know why he'd lie about it," I replied.

She tapped her pencil on the table. "What are you thinking?"

I shrugged. "I'm not thinking anything, Jeanette. I'm just telling you what I found out."

Jeanette pondered a bit more, then said, "I like that fellow but I'm not sure why."

"Some men just need a mother, I guess," I said.

Jeanette looked at me, then said, "Maybe that's it."

We went back to work.

On the night before our branding day, the temperatures dropped into the 30s and I half expected it to start sleeting again but then the sun came booming up and it turned into a pretty day. To get the calves in the branding pen, it was necessary to also bring in their moms. Ray, Soupy, and I went out and gathered in the first bunch of pairs. Amelia and Buddy, her dad, were there to help. Then along came Cade Morgan, looking a bit lost, driving up in his Mercedes. Then, Pick, Laura, and Tanya came trundling in from the direction of the BLM. We were going to have quite the eclectic crew.

Ray and I got off our horses and he went over to have a word with Amelia and her dad. I was curious as to why Cade Morgan was there so I walked up to him and held out my hand. Cade was wearing crisp, clean jeans, a white shirt, expensive running shoes, and a straw hat. Bill Coulter always said never hire a man with a straw hat because he'd spend all day chasing it.

We shook hands and I asked, "You come to help us brand, Cade?"

The Californian gave me a two-hundred-watt grin, the kind a man gives you when he's after your wallet or your girl. "I just came to watch," he said, then added before I made a comment, "Jeanette said it was OK."

I was in the mood to give Mr. Cade Morgan a little bit of a third degree. "Have you seen anything strange out your way?" I asked. "People you've never seen on the road or trucks, four-wheelers, anything?"

"I'm at the end of the road," he said, accurately. "You'd see them before me."

"Maybe," I said, "On the other hand, we're working and you're not."

"Oh, I work," he said.

"Doing what?"

"Screenplays."

"Any film I'd know?"

Cade's grin faded. "Why the interrogation, Mike?"

"One bull and one cow dead with cut throats and a note from the Green Monkey Wrench Gang. You know anything about that?"

Cade shook his head. "You going back to being a detective?"

"Maybe. How's Toby?"

"Gone. Decided to scout locations in South Dakota. He's a director."

"He ever direct a movie I might know?"

Cade squinted at me, then said, "Mike, I wouldn't be surprised," then walked away, leaving me thinking I needed to find out more about Cade Morgan and Toby whatever-his-name was.

Jeanette fired up the propane branding pot and pointed one of the Square C brands at me. "Mike you gonna just stand around scratching your butt?"

I touched my hat to my observant boss, stopped scratching my mental butt, and got after the work at hand. The first chore was to separate the calves from their moms. Ray and Amelia did this job on foot, sending the calves through an alley into the branding pen. Jeanette told Laura to pair with Tanya, and me with Pick. We have a calf table which is the easiest way to brand but Jeanette likes to do the first few calves the old-fashioned way. Sizing up Laura and Tanya, Jeanette said, "Let me show you gals how to do it. Come in here, Amelia."

Amelia climbed into the corral. "That one," Jeanette said, pointing at the largest calf. Amelia nodded and then she and Jeanette tackled the chosen calf, Jeanette grabbing a rear leg and Amelia a front leg and, in unison, flipping the calf on its side. I advanced with the branding iron and pressed it against the struggling calf's flank. There's no way to brand a calf fast. It takes a while to penetrate through its hair into the hide so I held it until an acrid smell told me I'd reached flesh. The calf gasped, I pulled back, and Buddy moved in, his task to vaccinate. He had the needle in and out of the calf before it knew what happened. If it had been a bull, we'd have put bands on its balls but this was a heifer so off she went, kicking and bawling for her mom which answered with a long, withering groan on the other side of the fence. Cows are such good moms.

"Ladies," Jeanette said to Laura and Tanya, "you're next. Try that one."

The two dino girls didn't hesitate. Laura tackled the front of the calf and Tanya the rear and was abruptly rewarded for her choice by a fine spray of manure in her face. Sputtering, she fell back and then the calf, too strong for Laura alone, broke free. "Don't just sit there," Jeanette yelled at the two women. "Get her down!"

Laura and Tanya got up and went after the calf again, this time successfully. I advanced, the hide crackled, Buddy vaccinated, and the calf took off. I was pleased to see Laura and Tanya were laughing with excitement and success. But now it was time for me and Pick to try our luck. I handed the iron over to Jeanette and went over to the paleontologist. "You ready?" I asked.

"I don't know if this is my thing, Mike," he said.

"You take the back of that little bull, I'll take his front."

He considered that. "Do you mind if I take the front?"

Well, that showed the boy wasn't a complete idiot. But I answered, "Yes, I do mind," and went after the calf, grabbing its front legs and tossing it down. Pick clutched the wriggling calf's hind legs and when a little excrement got on his face, he sputtered like he'd been hit by a brown tidal wave. Still, he hung on while Jeanette and Buddy moved in and did their thing.

Jeanette seemed satisfied that her calf catchers had been tormented enough and ordered the calf table activated. A calf table is a wide steel plate on which there are two rails, which form a chute. You push the calf between the two rails, push over a lever to clamp them against the calf, then pull the whole contraption over, which lowers the trapped calf on its side. After that, you can do pretty much whatever you want with the animal, in our case branding and vaccinating. Laura and Tanya took care of most of the calves for the rest of the day, herding and pushing them onto the table. Pick went over and sat at one of the picnic tables we'd set up in the turnaround for lunch. He didn't look very happy.

When lunch time rolled around, at least half of our calves were branded. We were doing well. By then, the noise was deafening. The calves inside the branding pen were crying to their mothers and their moms were responding by bawling hysterically. It was enough to break my heart but at least I knew there would be a happy reunion at the end of the day.

Aaron and Flora Feldmark had a little side business of providing lunch during brandings. As I came out of the branding pen, I noticed Mayor Edith Brescoe had driven in and was helping the Feldmarks. After I got my plate filled, she sat down beside me while I ate my salad, beans, and macaroni and cheese. "Don't you ever crave a good steak, Mike?" she asked.

"All the time," I said. "Why be a vegetarian if it's easy?"

"You're a nut," she replied with a smile. Then, she said, "Did I make you happy, Mike?"

"Sure." What else was I going to say?

"I'm glad. It's good to be happy."

She got up and went to help Aaron and Flora, leaving me to wonder if I'd made her happy, too. If so, she hadn't mentioned it.

After lunch, I traded places with Ray for a while. Amelia and I were putting some branded calves back with their mamas when one of the calves, for no apparent reason, turned around and started running back into the branding pen. I blocked its way, then pushed it at the shoulder to turn it around. The calf bawled its unhappiness and its mom, hearing this, decided I was required to pay for this affront. She came running, knocking down the other cows between me and her like bowling pins, threw herself into the air, turned halfway around, and kicked me square in the nuts. I went down in a crumpled heap while she flounced off, her head held high and the other cows cheering. Yep. Like Bill Coulter used to say, things can get a little "western" out here.

After I limped over to the fence to lean against it for three seconds of rest, Jeanette swung by long enough to remark, "Lucky she didn't kick you anywhere it mattered."

I almost replied, "I adore you." I know, I know. I was sick when it came to Jeanette Coulter.

Edith also swung by. "You hurt, honey?" she asked.

"Yes."

She whispered in my ear. "I hope the best part of you didn't get itself bent."

She sidled away while from the corner of my eye, I saw Cade Morgan slither out of the shadows (actually, he was sitting at the picnic table drinking lemonade). Edith walked past him and I almost missed what she did. A flick of her hand, just trailing for an instant across his shoulder. Now, what the hell did *that* mean? I might have walked after her to ask but my balls hurt too much.

Ray came by. "Need anything?"

"Ibuprofen and two weeks off."

"I can get the pills," Ray said, "but you'll have to ask mom about the time."

A couple of hours later, when all the cows and calves were happily reunited and released to pasture, I lounged at the picnic table, gone to beer and ibuprofen with the prospect of a g&t later on. Jeanette was touring Pick, Laura, and Tanya through the barn. Edith had left in her pickup, and Aaron and Flora had finished their catering chores, cleaned up, and likewise departed. Amelia had also left with her dad, leaving Ray so depressed he was changing the oil on his mother's tractor even though it didn't need it. Cade Morgan was still around, for no good reason that I could discern, although he was entertaining Jeanette's bum calf, reaching in its stall and allowing it to chew on his fingers. This surprised me. I would have thought him more squeamish than that. He gave the calf a pat on its head, then nonchalantly strolled in my direction, got a beer out of the cooler, and sat down at the table across from me. He took off his fancy straw hat, wiped his brow with his shirt sleeve, and said, "I learned a lot today. Maybe I'll get me some cattle yet."

"Around here, Cade, we say cows, not cattle," I instructed, adding, "Red angus. They're small, they're docile, and they market well."

"I'll try to remember that," he said. "Or maybe I could just hire you to buy them for me."

"Sorry. I already have a job."

"Working for peanuts for Jeanette and living in a rented trailer without a telephone?"

"Or a computer or the Internet," I added. "But I do have a refrigerator and a microwave."

"And probably a lot of good books," he said.

"Yes. A lot of good books. It's all a man really needs."

"Some men." He took a long swig of beer. "Me, I need my comforts."

This comment from the Californian kind of interested me. "Then what the hell are you doing at the end of Ranchers Road?"

He smiled. "I have a nice place."

"Yeah, but it's not the Ponderosa."

"Close enough."

There was a burr under my saddle that I didn't even know was there until it came out. "What's between you and the mayor?"

Cade smiled. "What do you mean?"

"She's not as strong as she makes out to be, Cade."

"I don't know what you're talking about."

"Yes, you do. I was there, where you are now."

This made Cade think and I could tell he didn't like what he was thinking. Finally, he said, "What I like about Montana, Mike, is we all mind our own business."

He had me there. I guess we had run out of things to say because for the next few minutes, we both just sat there, drinking our beers. Then Jeanette, Pick, Laura, and Tanya, finished with their tour of the barn, trooped up to the table. Jeanette threw open the cooler and handed out more beer. "When do you think you'll start digging up your dinosaur?" Cade asked Pick after they'd all settled down at the picnic table beside us.

Laura said, "We've already begun."

"Mind if I come watch?" Cade asked.

"I don't think that's a good idea," Pick replied. "It's best to minimize the number of people around a dig. You could contaminate it."

"Too bad," Cade said.

"Well," Tanya said, "it's just a lot of dirt, anyway."

Cade nodded, retrieved the keys of his Mercedes from his hip pocket, and stood up. Even though there was a trash can only a few feet away, he left the empty beer bottle on the table, confident, I suppose, that someone would take care of it. Like me. "Guess I'll be off," he said and when no one said or did anything to stop him, he made good on his plan.

Laura was shooting eye-daggers at Pick. "Pick, what's wrong with you? The man was offering to help."

Pick ignored her and looked over in my direction. "Mike, I appreciate you volunteering to work with us."

This was news to me. Jeanette said, by way of explanation, "I volunteered you, Mike. The cows are all where they need to be, things have slowed down on the ranch, and I figured you'd enjoy it."

"I was thinking about going to Vegas in a couple of weeks," I said, which happened to be the truth. Every so often, I still needed a bright light or two.

Jeanette didn't think much of my vacation plans. "I'd appreciate it if you helped Dr. Pickford," she said, pointedly.

"Then I guess I'll do it," I answered, the Las Vegas strip blinking off in my head like a busted street light. I sometimes surprised myself with how eager I was to please the queen of the prairie. Every man has to have a weakness. Of course, I had no idea it would almost get me killed and I guess Jeanette didn't, either. I'll give her the benefit of the doubt on that one.

10

I DIDN'T GO OUT to Pick's camp for another four days. Jeanette might have said we were caught up but I knew even as she said it, it wasn't true. The Big Man in the Sky had turned off his faucet. The Square C was drying out, which meant we needed to stir the cows around to put them on some pastures that hadn't been grazed for a while. This fell mostly on me and Ray, Jeanette worrying over the plans for the Independence Day celebration.

Then word came of another murdered cow, this one south of Jericho on one of the Brescoe ranches. The *modus operandi* was the same, right down to the note from the Green Monkey Wrench Gang, which, come to think of it, we didn't receive with our murdered bull. I wondered if maybe the note had blown away or maybe the cow murderer hadn't come up with the idea of writing us a missive when he was on our land. When she heard about the new dead cow, Jeanette worked the phone, talking to the mayor and folks up and down the road on whether the state police ought to be called. I asked Jeanette what the consensus was and she said, "They'd send some kid up from Billings who wouldn't even know where to start. We've decided we can handle things just fine."

I started to remind her of my police background but shut my

trap. Jeanette had not asked for my help, which was tantamount to her saying she didn't need it. So I told her I was heading out to the dinosaur diggers. At the time, she was sitting at her kitchen table with a legal pad full of notes, a ledger, a calculator, and a telephone. "I'm glad somebody gets to have fun around here," she said as if going out there was my idea.

I went back to my trailer and packed a cooler of veggies, then grabbed two bags each of beans and rice from my stores, a couple bottles of gin and tonic water, and the usual toiletries. I scrounged around until I found an old duffel bag and stuffed it with underwear, socks, work shirts, T-shirts, an extra pair of jeans, old running shoes, and a bandana. I found the old tent and sleeping bag Bill Coulter had given me when I'd first arrived on the Square C for the infrequent times I needed to stay overnight out on the far fringes of the ranch. I also retrieved a five-gallon water can from beneath the trailer and filled it. I loaded my favorite four-wheeler with all my stuff and headed out. Ray opened the gate that led to the BLM. "I'll be out there pretty soon," he said.

"How about Amelia?"

He shrugged. "Who cares about her?"

"You do."

He frowned, then shook his head and said, "You're right. What do you think I ought to do about her, Mike?"

"I'd kiss her if I was you, Ray. And tell her how you feel."

"But I don't know how I feel. Not exactly."

"Well, just kiss her, then. It'll do for now."

My advice to the lovelorn accomplished, I drove straight to where the bull had been killed, thinking to look around for a note just in case the wind had blown it somewhere. The odds of finding it, even had it existed, were slim and I knew it. Sure enough, I poked around, found nothing, and gave it up and drove on out to the BLM.

When I arrived at their camp, I saw Pick and his ladies had constructed quite the complex. There were three of what I took to be personal tents, and two big canvas wall tents. Not only that, there was a windmill atop an aluminum tower about thirty feet tall. No one was around so I peeked into the wall tents to see the secrets of professional paleontologists. The first one contained bags of plaster, jerry cans of water, a variety of potions and chemicals, and also picks, shovels, trowels, saws, hammers, ice picks, and other standard tools. The other wall tent held cans of food, breakfast cereal, flour, corn meal, powdered milk, and rice in plastic containers. It also had a refrigerator with room for not only my veggies but my tonic water. I followed its cord outside and found that it was attached through a box to the windmill.

I unloaded the rest of my traps off the four-wheeler, then motored on to the Triceratops site. No one was there but there was evidence it had been worked over based on two piles of dirt heaped at the base of the hill. There was also what I took to be bones contained in three foot-locker-sized lumps of white plaster sitting in a small meadow of sparse grass beside the women's truck. I went over and pushed on one and it didn't move. Getting these things on the truck, if that was the plan, was going to take some heavy lifting.

Carefully so as to not disturb anything, I climbed up beside the dig. Littered around were ice picks, paint brushes, trowels, knee pads, and small plastic bottles containing an amber liquid. Looking closer at the dig, I could see the outline of what appeared to be a bone, brown as tobacco. Whatever the bone was, it was big. I looked back at the trucks and the three big plaster casts and wondered how it was possible to get a bone like that out without busting it up.

"Halloooo!" came a yell and I spied Pick climbing out of a drainage. His shirt was soaked with sweat and his pants were filthy. "Come to help at last!" he said as he reached the trucks.

"Just tell me what to do," I replied.

He got a bottle of water from the back of his truck and drained it. "Laura will do that," he said. "She's in charge of the dig."

"Where is she?"

"I gave her and Tanya a little time off," he said, "so they went prospecting. That's what paleontologists most love to do, look for something new."

"Have you found anything new?"

"Well, when they get back, we'll ask them," he said, leaving unanswered whether he'd found anything. I didn't push him about it.

Pick sat in the shade of the truck and I joined him. "This is the life," he said. "This is what I live for, the thrill of digging into the past, the anticipation of what might be found, and every day something new and wonderful."

"I went to Bozeman one time," I said, "and stopped in at the Museum of the Rockies. They have a couple of Triceratops skeletons there as I recall. What good does it do to dig up another one?"

Pick looked shocked at my question. "What good does it do to read another book if you've already read a couple?" he demanded. "We're dealing with more than sixty-five million years, Mike. Those Trikes in Bozeman may have been separated by a thousand generations and evolutionary pressures may have changed their design a great deal. We learn something new with not only every skeleton but every bone if only we care to look. I'm one of the few paleontologists who really, truly looks at every detail of every bone. A lot of them just go for the big picture but not me. I hold the bone and study it until I know the animal. It talks to me. Sometimes, it even comes to me in my sleep, tells me of its life and its death."

I didn't know what to say to that, which to tell the truth sounded genuinely squirrelly, so we sat quietly for a while until he said, "This big old Trike. I think it was a bull. That means it was a defender of the herd and fought all its life against predators. There are growths on his bones that indicate battle scars."

Pick didn't say much more, mainly because he soon fell asleep. I sat with him, relaxing, reflecting on the ancient animal that lay quietly above us, listening to the gentle wind, watching a hawk scouting for rabbits, and a rabbit with only its head out of its hole, watching for hawks. There was the smell of fresh sage in the air. I discovered I was enjoying myself immensely, sitting beside the dozing paleontologist while cottony clouds floated across the vast sky.

This was Montana, I thought. The real Montana.

Before long, the women arrived. They were wearing backpacks which looked to be heavy and I wondered if they were filled with bones. I stood up as they rounded the back of the truck. They were wearing the same kind of multi-pocketed shirts Pick favored, plus cargo shorts, snake gaiters, and hiking boots. I noticed Laura had nice legs but Tanya's were spectacular. In fact, she oozed sexuality like so many young Russian women.

"Wondered if you were coming out," Laura said, stripping off her backpack and putting it in the back of the truck. Tanya provided me with a shy smile as she unloaded her pack on the truck beside Laura's. Both women were careful not to disturb Pick who was still snoozing. "He is like a little boy," Tanya said.

"Mike, do you want to know what we do on a dig?" Laura asked and I told her I would be happy to be educated. She drained a canteen, removed a salt shaker from her backpack, sprinkled some in her hand, licked it off, and gestured for me to follow her up to the site. We settled around it on our haunches and she got busy telling me in some detail how a dig was photographed, mapped, and everything collected, even the smallest scraps. "You'd be surprised how some of those wizards in the lab—we call them preparators—can fit scraps of bone together like a jigsaw puzzle."

Laura glanced down at Pick, still sleeping, and Tanya who was removing some plastic zipper bags from their packs and placing them in a large plastic storage box. It occurred to me that maybe Laura was in the business of distracting me. If she was, I couldn't imagine why. I didn't much care what they found.

Laura started up again, explaining how her specialty was crafting an excavation plan and how the Hell Creek Formation was pretty easy to work in comparison to some where jackhammers were required.

"How about a backhoe?" I asked. "Or dynamite?"

She considered my question. "A backhoe would definitely help if the bones were deep," she said. "I've never used dynamite but some of the old-time dinosaur diggers did. Barnum Brown, maybe the most famous of them all, was quite happy to use it. He found the first T. rex, by the way, about thirty miles from here in 1906. Just think of it. No one knew there was such an animal. To see that skull come out of the rock and mud must have been astonishing. I sometimes wish I'd lived in those times. There were virtually no laws or regulations about digging and the ranchers didn't care. In fact, they helped Brown a lot by taking him to sites they knew about. He dug up the bones, carted them away to New York, and nobody said a word. Maybe because there wasn't a lot of money in it back then. In fact, hardly anyone would give a cent for dinosaur bones. Everything was done in the name of science."

"Have you ever sold bones?" I asked.

"No," she said, "I wouldn't do that, even if I was starving."

"How about Pick?"

"Only to support his research. I've forgiven him for it. Once you get to know Pick, you realize he's a genius even though he's got his peculiarities. There's nobody like him when it comes to finding dinosaurs, that's for sure."

Laura looked down at Pick who had come awake, yawning and stretching. Tanya was sitting beside him, quietly talking, then she offered him water. He accepted her canteen, licked salt from her hand, then pulled his hat over his eyes, and settled back against the tire. "Is Tanya his girlfriend?" I asked.

"No, and neither am I," she said. "Pick is never in the moment, if you know what I mean. He's always a million miles away, or I should say sixty-five-plus million years away. He mostly lives in deep time."

I'd heard that phrase a couple of times now. "Explain 'deep time,'" I said.

"Well, think of it this way," she said. "The more we understand time, the more we realize how connected it is. It's like a deep ocean. The water at the bottom is the same as at the top except they're in different places. But there's nothing to keep the water from changing places and sometimes it does, usually because of temperature or salinity changes or the pressure of the overlying water. Anyway, the important thing is that it goes from water we can see and touch to water beyond our reach. That's like present time turning into ancient time and vice versa. It's all connected. Pick sort of lives closer to the bottom of the ocean of time than we mere humans."

"OK," I said. "All this is too deep for me."

Laura laughed. "And for me. Maybe Pick will explain it to you. He's better at it than I am. I probably screwed it all up."

Laura showed me how to use the ice pick and trowel to carefully work around a bone and how to use the amber liquid in the plastic bottles, which was a glue called vinac, to harden the bone before it was removed. "If we have a stable bone, like a horn or a claw," she explained, "we just wrap it in aluminum foil and number it. If it's fractured, we apply a plaster cast. If it's a big enough bone, we dig around and under it, leaving just a little pedestal for the bone to sit on. Pedestaling is what the technique is called, as a matter of fact.

We wrap it with aluminum foil and wet paper towels, put strips of burlap in plaster, and lay them across the bone at a variety of angles to give the cast strength. After it hardens, we can flip the bone over and finish up. After that, it's ready for the lab. Of course, getting it there, heavy as the bones and the jackets are, is always a chore but we get it done, one way or the other."

"Where is this skeleton going?" I asked.

Laura gave that some thought, then said, "I don't honestly know. Somewhere where it will be appreciated, that much I can tell you. Pick sees to that." She pointed at a bone still in the ground. "That's a toe. Its shape indicates it was used for digging."

I looked at the bone which was about six inches long and shaped like an arrowhead. "What did it dig?" I wondered.

"We think Trikes liked to eat ferns. Maybe they needed to dig around the other vegetation to get at them or maybe they dug up the entire plant. They had a beak, like a big parrot, which I suppose was effective at chopping plants. Their molars were a little like a cow's or camel's."

"Did they eat grass?"

"There was no grass, at least not the kind we have now."

"You're kidding! No grass? I thought there was always grass in Montana."

Her eyes grew distant, a trait I'd noticed was common for paleontologists. "The world the Triceratops lived in, Mike, was a far different place than this one. Although the theropods, the meat-eaters, could probably live today—meat is still meat and I guess they could eat your cows—the plant-eaters would not survive. Vegetation and the seasons have just changed too much. Maybe that's why the theropods live on through the birds while there are no descendents of the plant-eaters. It's sad, really. Can you imagine the millions of years it took to evolve a creature like this, just to have it disappear?"

"What killed them, do you think? I know you only care about how they lived but you must have a theory on why they disappeared."

"Oh, I think environmental and evolutionary pressures are the likely culprits. We also think there's less oxygen in the atmosphere now so maybe it just got too hard for them to breathe. Anyway, whatever it was, I don't think it was anything so dramatic as a meteor or comet, although something like that may have pushed them over the edge. Maybe a virus, even. I just don't know. No one does, no matter what they say."

I glanced down and saw Pick was awake again and peering into the box where Tanya had placed the plastic sample bags. He took one of the bags out, pondered it, then put it back. The way he held it, I couldn't see what was in it, not that I would have recognized what it was, anyway.

"What did you find this morning?" I asked.

"Just odds and ends," Laura replied. "You ready to help dig up this old boy?"

"Sure thing."

Laura called Tanya and she climbed up beside us. Pick wandered off and then things got quiet for the rest of the morning as the three of us dug and scraped. It was hard work and my fingernails, knees, and back took a beating. I looked up once and found both women smiling at me. "What?" I asked.

"You'd make a good grad student," Laura said. "You work hard and you don't complain much."

"I like that in a man, too," Tanya said, giving me a dazzling smile. I confess my heart sped up a beat.

After a while, Tanya got up from the dig, got her backpack off the truck, dropped in some water bottles, and went off in the direction Pick had gone. I sat back, swigged some water, and appreciated her trim little figure until she'd disappeared around the hill. "Where's she going?" I asked.

"To find Pick," Laura said. "He'll be lost by now. She'll try to track him down or give him a call on the radio to figure out where he is. He never goes far. He always finds bones and that slows him down."

We dug, picked, scraped, and glued for a bit more, then Laura squinted at the sky where the sun had taken up station, seemingly not moving and just blazing down. "We need to put up an awning," she said.

We walked back to the camp and she got out a tarp and some poles, ropes, and pegs. It wasn't easy on the side of that hill but we managed to get the tarp up to provide some shade. When we were finished, Laura pronounced the working day over. "When you get too tired, you start to make mistakes on a dig," she said. "Want to go prospecting?"

That sounded like fun so I said OK. She filled a pack with water bottles and I did the same. She handed me a small digital camera, a pocket-sized notebook, a pencil, some plastic lock-type sample bags, a permanent marker pen, a two-way radio, and a handheld GPS. After a quick lesson on the GPS, she showed me how to write up any finds I might make, then pointed at a low line of wedding-cake shaped hills. "Those hills look to have some Hell Creek Formation," she said. "Ever been on them?"

I had not, even though they weren't that far from the Square C. "They're on Haxby BLM," I said. "I wouldn't even think about going over there without permission."

"But we have a BLM permit," she said. "And we won't cross private land getting to it."

"You don't know the Haxbys," I replied.

Laura looked at the hills longingly. "I'm sure we'd find some good bones there."

I gave it some thought, mostly focusing on Laura's unhappy expression. "All right," I said, finally. "But if anyone comes around, let me do the talking."

This suited her so we hefted our packs, tested our radios, and off we went, first crossing a field of grass that stopped abruptly at a deep coulee that had been invisible until we were right on top of it. The badlands can fool you that way. What you perceive to be an expanse of flat land can suddenly drop a hundred feet straight down. More than one cow, trundling along, has lost its footing along one of those coulees and taken the tumble of death. We were more careful, clambered down inside it, then walked along its narrow bottom. There was a layer of cracked mud studded with some low reeds, clinging to life. Laura spotted a grayish outcrop of dirt and walked over to it, bent over, and plucked out a bone. She showed it to me. "Theropod toe bone, probably Ornithomimosaur."

Quoting Pick, I asked, "Where's the rest of it?"

"That's always the question, isn't it?" She gave me a grin, which was nice. Even though we'd just spent all morning digging up bones and erecting an awning in the hot sun, and were now walking in the hottest sun of the day loaded down with packs full of water, Laura was cheerful. I have always believed cheerful is a fine trait in a woman. I reflected that Jeanette was hardly ever cheerful but I didn't care. I still loved her. Love is weird that way, ain't it?

We found a way out of the coulee and continued across the field until we reached the hills, which proved to be steeper than they looked from a mile away. "I'll go that way," Laura pointed, "you go the other. See that first step? I think if there are any bones, they will be at that level. It's a bit too steep for me to try to go along there so what I like to do is walk around the base of the hill and look for float at the bottom. If I see anything that looks interesting, then I'll climb the hill up to the step to see what's there. You might try the same strategy or just make up your own. There's no right or wrong way to find bones."

Although I wasn't certain it was a good idea for us to split up, considering that we were on Haxby BLM, I went along with it. I went off in the direction she wanted me to go and before long, I was thoroughly enjoying the pleasant stroll at the base of the hill, which was actually several hills with low saddlebacks. I soon came across some float, clambered up to the shelf Laura had suggested, and was rewarded by a pile of shattered bones. There was nothing in the pile that had any shape, just irregular scraps, but there was enough of it to fill up several backpacks. I settled for logging the GPS coordinates in my notebook, photographing the site, taking a sample, and moving on, feeling very much like a true paleontologist. I searched all along the base, finding more float and scraps here and there. Though I climbed up to the step, I found no more piles of bones, just scraps including something that looked like a claw, although the tip was broken off. No matter that I had probably found nothing of importance, I had still discovered the remains of creatures, which had lived very long ago. I sat down on one of the steps and just looked out at a land which should have been familiar to me but now seemed alien, as if I'd been plucked up and set down not only far away but long ago. Maybe I was getting a sense of deep time, I don't know.

I was startled by the *clip-clop* of a horse at the base of the hill and, when I looked down, I saw an equally startled rider. It was Carl Haxby, Sam's youngest son. "Hello, Carl," I said.

Carl finally found his voice. "What are you doing up there, Mike?"

"Looking for dinosaur bones. There are quite a few of them on this hill."

Carl briefly scanned the exposed brown dirt, the ancient gray mud, and the sagebrush of the hill, then shook his head. "All I see is Haxby property," he said. "Are you lost?"

It would have probably saved us all some grief if I had answered that I was indeed lost and would get my tail back to the Square C first thing but, instead, I said, "No. I know exactly where I am. I should have asked you before coming out here but I'm working with some folks who have a BLM permit and . . . well, here we are."

"We?"

"On the other side of this hill is a young lady. She's a professional paleontologist. She's just looking for bones, Carl. No reason to get upset."

But Carl was upset. "I'll thank you to leave our property, Mike," he said.

He didn't curse, he didn't say he was going to climb up there and whup my ass, he didn't threaten to go burn down my trailer, he just said what he said, most calmly. He was also armed. There was a rifle, a .30-06, slung next to his leg. I climbed down until I was eye level with him and opened my backpack, showing him the fragments of bone I'd picked up. "This is all I'm doing," I said.

"You found those on our land?"

"On BLM land." I sat down on a rock. I had learned in my past life in the thin blue line that sometimes sitting down while talking to someone in a tense situation tends to have a calming effect. "I'll say it again, Carl. I should have asked before coming out here and I apologize. But, technically, BLM is not your land."

"I'll have to tell my dad," Carl said. "He's going to raise hell."

I took off my hat, wiped the sweat from my brow with my sleeve, and plopped it back aboard. It was hot and getting hotter and I needed to get going and probably so did Carl on whatever business had brought him out here. "All right," I said. "But be sure to tell him I apologize for not asking him first."

Carl backed his horse up, then swung it around. He nodded toward the plastic bags. "Could I look at that bone again that was sort of like a claw?"

I stood up and handed it over. He studied the bone in his big, calloused hand. The Haxbys worked hard, all of them, and Carl's hands reflected that. "Looks like a broken bird claw," he said.

"Yep. Dr. Pickford—he's the lead paleontologist—says there were a lot of dinosaurs with claws out here. Sharp teeth, too."

"Then why does it look like a bird claw?"

"I don't know, Carl."

"Maybe there were big birds that didn't get on the ark," Carl offered.

"Could be," I said.

Carl cocked his head. "How did you get into this, Mike?"

"Jeanette volunteered me."

"You do what she says?"

"She's my boss."

"But you'd like her to be more," he said, smiling for the first time since he'd found me. When he saw my expression, which wasn't happy, he added, "Sorry. The Haxby wives gossip. I sometimes listen."

"Tell them I said I'm in love with her. That'll give them something to talk about for a long time."

He rubbed his jaw, then shook his head. "I'll do no such thing."

"I'll get off your land, Carl. Right now. I'll find the girl and make her leave, too."

He nodded, then said, "No need. As far as I'm concerned, you just asked for permission. Have fun picking up bones."

Carl rode off and I waited until he disappeared around the hill. Although I was relieved at the way things had turned out, I still felt like shit. The Haxbys had their ways and I didn't agree with all of them but they'd always been good neighbors. Now, I'd thumbed my nose at them in the worst way I could do it.

Wanting to get off the Haxby BLM as soon as possible, I crossed the hill at one of the low saddles. Laura wasn't in sight as I came over but I did spot some bones. They were horn chunks, probably Triceratops. I wrote them up in my log, and collected them. Then I slid down the hill and walked along it for a while before spotting Laura on one of the benches. She was sitting there, looking at something with binoculars. I turned to see what it might be and saw that she was looking toward Blackie Butte. "What do you see?" I asked.

Startled, she hastily put down the binoculars. "Nothing. Just looking," she said.

I climbed up beside her. "May I?" I asked, indicating the binoculars and she reluctantly handed them over. I looked at Blackie Butte and saw two people standing on a ledge about halfway up it. "Is that Pick and Tanya?"

"Yes," Laura said. "I'm glad Tanya found him. Lost as usual."

Laura had lied to me. She had definitely been watching the pair but, if so, why hadn't she said so? My first guess, me being a man, is that she was jealous that Tanya was alone with Pick.

"Look," I said, "one of the Haxby brothers caught me and he wasn't too happy about us being here. Let's go back."

"We have a permit," she said.

"Yes. That and permission from the rancher who leases the BLM is all that we need to hunt fossils on this land. We have one but not the other."

Laura looked at me. "Did you find anything?"

I showed her my plastic bags. Nothing interested her except the claw. "Nice," she said. "Where's the rest of it?"

I smiled. "I don't know."

HOMER HICKAM

"OK. Let's go back. I'm kind of tired, anyway." She rubbed her shoulder and winced.

I crouched beside her. "I used to know how to give a decent shoulder rub." When she didn't say anything, I took it as permission to proceed. She was muscular and some of those muscles were in knots so I had my work cut out for me. She leaned back into my hands.

"That feels good," she said and took off her hat and dropped her head forward to let me at her neck, which was also in a big knot. I kept going until she said, "Thank you" and stood up. "Ready to go back?" she asked.

"Sure." If I expected any kind of reciprocity, that clearly wasn't going to happen. I reached for the binoculars, planning to see what Pick and Tanya were doing now but Laura quickly stuffed the binoculars in her pack. She headed down the hill and I followed her, wondering what it was she didn't want me to see but pretty sure she wasn't going to tell me if I asked. So I didn't. Sometimes, things just have to come out on their own.

11

WHEN WE GOT BACK to camp, Pick and Tanya hadn't returned so Laura suggested a snack. I suggested snacks with drinks. When I told her I had the ingredients for a g&t, her eyes lit up. I followed her into the cook tent and to the refrigerator. When she opened the door, she saw my veggies. "I'm a vegetarian," I said and she stared at me in shock. "No kidding," I added.

"OK," she said, stretching out both letters, "I guess now I've heard everything. A vegetarian cowboy." She eyed my other traps, especially the duffel bag which had the logo of the Los Angeles Police Department on it. "I heard you used to be a policeman."

"I heard the same thing. So did a bad guy who shot me." When she raised her eyebrows over her lovely baby blues, I told her a condensed version of how I was just standing there minding my own business when some fellow popped me. Actually, I had just beat up his buddy and tossed him through a plate glass window but never mind.

"What brought you to Montana?"

"A truck," I said. "I sold it to Bill Coulter for one dollar. He sold it for five hundred."

She let my evasion slide and asked, "Who's Bill Coulter?"

"Jeanette Coulter's husband. He died five years ago."

She nodded, then poked around in the fridge until she found some crackers and cheese spread. "This OK? How about fish? I have some tuna salad."

"Works for me. Eggs are OK, too."

"Got it," she said. "By the way, I tried being a vegetarian once but I kept having strange dreams."

"What about?"

"That I wanted a steak and couldn't have one."

"I have that dream all the time," I confessed. "Then I go out and help a heifer have a calf and I forget it."

"You help a heifer have a calf? Cowboys are really that lonely?"

I chuckled. "Maybe I could have put that a better way."

"How about my drink? Get a cup from that box. Mine is that red one on top of the fridge."

The indicated box held plastic cups. I used my pocket knife to slice a lime on a folding camp table, added ice from the little freezer compartment, and made two g&t's with a lot more *g* than usual. I felt we deserved it. I also hoped it might loosen Laura up so she would provide more information about . . . well, I didn't really know but my antenna was starting to go up. Something was going on that wasn't exactly clear.

Beneath the awning of the tent, Laura had another table set up along with two unfolded folding chairs. She had emptied some crackers in a plastic bowl and taken the top off two plastic containers, one with a creamed cheese something, the other the tuna salad. She stuck a white plastic knife into each. I subsided in one of the chairs and handed over her g&t. Cocktails were served.

Everything was pleasant. The sun hid behind a big puffy cloud, a little breeze came mewing over us, and no mosquitoes, flies, or gnats chose to bite us. Laura confirmed the obvious. "This is nice," she said.

"Agreed," I replied.

"The drink is excellent."

"Some people would say it's the gin that's important, or the tonic, but actually it's the lime."

"I would say all three ingredients are important," Laura replied. "The lime keeps scurvy away, the tonic is a preemptive strike against malaria, and the gin is an ancient tranquilizer, good for the heart."

Laura had bested me and I acknowledged it with a nod of my head, saying, "Well, anyway, I was glad to see the limes in the fridge since I forgot to bring any."

"I bought them in Bozeman," she said. "Little natural foods shop downtown."

"Bozeman's nice," I said.

"Yep. I went to school at Montana State. In a way, you might say I was one of Jack Horner's protégés. You know who he is, right?"

I did, mainly because I loved Michael Crichton's books and the movies made from them. I said, "*Jurassic Park* advisor, Crichton's model for the paleontologist in the book, an author in his own right, and so forth?"

"Well, those are a few of Jack's attributes. Actually, he's important to paleontology because he changed the way we think about dinosaurs with his study of Maiasaura, a duckbill he named and described. Its name means 'good mother lizard' and Horner showed by his excavations how Maiasaurs took care of their nestlings. For the first time, somebody was talking about dinosaurs as social animals that parented their little ones. Without that insight, we might have been stumbling around in the dark for years about these animals. His insights gave other paleontologists a platform to build on. Now, we can infer that nearly all dinosaurs led complex, interesting lives, much like the animals of today."

"What's the word for when you think of animals like people?" I asked.

"Anthropomorphic," she instantly answered, cocking an eyebrow. "Perhaps Horner and the rest of us are a bit guilty of that but I don't care. Animals feel a lot of the things we feel. They get afraid like us, and sometimes they panic and do stupid things, just as we do. They sleep, they drowse, they even ponder. Have you ever seen a squirrel stare at one of those bird feeders designed to stop them? They figure out a way to get at it, eventually. This is not by trial and error. They *think*, Mike. More importantly, many animals, and Horner showed this included some dinosaurs, feel a type of love, love of their children, love of their mates. Oh, I'm sure Jack Horner would argue he didn't say anything like that at all, but was only describing the methodology used to perpetuate the species, but I believe the emotion they felt was very akin to what we think of as love."

"It's hard to imagine they had time to do anything but avoid getting eaten by T. rexes," I observed.

She sipped her drink, then allowed herself a moment before answering. "Maybe things weren't quite as horrible in their world as we think. Maybe, in fact, they would think our world is the horrible one, what with all our rushing around, our polluting, our broken families, our terrible reliance on mind-altering drugs—your excellent g-and-t, of course, gets a pass here—and on and on."

"Well," I said, "the next time I'm in Bozeman, I might just go shake Dr. Horner's hand. You said you were his protégé. Why aren't you still with him?"

"A higher calling named Pick Pickford. It was an emotional

decision, I'll confess, not an intellectual one. Luckily, I already had my master's degree before I met him at the annual SVP conference. That's the Society of Vertebrate Paleontologists. I heard him speak, saw the results of his work, and asked him if I could help. He said he had no money and I said that was no problem. I had a little and it was his if he'd take me on his next expedition. Been with him ever since."

"Happily?"

She shrugged. "Most of the time. We've found some important stuff together."

I decided to be blunt. "What else out here have you found besides this Trike?"

Again, she gave her answer some thought. In fact, she gave it so much thought, she didn't answer at all. So I prompted her by saying, "Pick said he was mostly interested in finding a baby T. rex, matching the bones Bill Coulter found years ago."

"That would be grand, wouldn't it?" she said. "But maybe you ought to ask Pick."

I didn't respond, mainly because our little moment with our snacks and drinks was really too pleasant to spoil. "I enjoyed myself today," I said. "Being a dinosaur hunter is fun."

"Nothing like it in the world," she said. "It astonishes me that everyone doesn't want to do it. I mean, being outside, breathing fresh air, digging up the past, having a drink with a vegetarian cowboy and all that. It's the best way to live."

"Cowboying is a bit like that, too, except there's cow manure involved," I said.

She smiled. "Wait here," she said, and jumped up and went behind the cook tent where her own tent was pitched. She brought back a plastic sample bag, opened it, and handed me part of its contents.

I handled what appeared to be a brownish-gray lump of crumbling rock. "What is it?" I asked.

"T. rex poop! Isn't it beautiful?"

I looked it over. Now that I knew what it was, I could see by its shape, sort of a tubular blob, that it was indeed poop except it appeared to be made out of rock and dirt. "How do you know it's T. rex?"

"Well, it's big and, if you looked under a microscope, you'd observe crunched bone. T. rex is the obvious candidate."

Based on my expression, I think she could tell I was suitably impressed. "You paleontologists sure are interesting," I said.

She smiled, but then took the T. rex manure away. "We call this stuff coprolite."

"Why?"

"It's Greek. It means 'shit rock.' "

"Ah, the Greeks," I replied.

She carried her dino-doo back to her tent, then returned just as Tanya and Pick arrived, all sweaty and with their packs full. They did not offer to show me what was in them. Instead, with Laura helping them, they put the packs away and joined us for our hors d'oeuvres. I inquired about drinks for the two and both agreed that would be just fine. I could tell my gin wasn't going to last long with this crowd.

We lolled around the table, everyone being quiet. Finally, Pick said, "I heard you and Laura had a productive day."

"I learned a lot," I answered. "I also found a claw or at least a partial one." I showed it to him and he took a moment to admire it.

"Ornithomimosaur," he said, confirming Laura's estimate. To my disappointment, he put it in his shirt pocket. "You put down in your log where you found it?"

"I did."

"Good. I might want to go have a look around there. Ornithos were interesting animals. They were theropods without teeth, just beaks."

Tanya said, "I'm the cook tonight. Thought I'd grill some hamburgers."

"Mike's a vegetarian," Laura said, which, based on Tanya's expression, surprised her.

"Good for you," Tanya finally said.

"Don't worry about me," I said. "I can feed myself."

"I'll fix a big salad," Tanya offered. "And we have lots of rice. How about saffron rice? Would you like that?"

"Sure. I brought along rice and beans to add to your stock."

She smiled at me. "Mike, you are an interesting man." This made me happy. I mean how often did a beautiful Russian woman declare that I was interesting?

Laura wanted to document our Trike dig some more so I went along to help her. She took photographs, jotted notes, and directed me to brush off the exposed bones. When we returned, dinner was served around the same table where we'd had our drinks. The salad and saffron rice were excellent and before long, we were all stretching and letting our tiredness be known. Soon, we'd wandered off to our respective tents. When I crawled into my sleeping bag, I knew I wasn't going to last long and I didn't.

Tanya, who apparently was always assigned cooking duties, had breakfast ready first thing in the morning. Scrambled eggs, bacon (not for me, of course), toast, and several kinds of breakfast cereal. I was feeling downright pampered. "Back to the Trike," Laura told me.

"I'm your cowboy," I said.

"Giddyup," she replied, smiling and giving me the eye. I liked both of Pick's ladies. They seemed to like me, too, which was kind of nice.

Pick and Tanya said they were going to go prospecting again so Laura and I dug, photographed, measured, and packed bones away until just before noon when a distant drone told us company was coming. It proved to be Ray and Amelia on four-wheelers. "We came to help," Ray said.

"Can we?" Amelia asked, eagerly.

"Yes," I answered before Laura could say a word, "but first I'll have to explain what we're doing here and why."

Laura laughed and said, "Mike is already an expert dinosaur digger. Come on up. Let him teach you what you need to know."

They parked their vehicles and came up and I essentially repeated the lecture Laura had given to me. Laura added some instruction on the careful use of the tools, assigned them a large bone to work on together, and then let them settle down to it. After a while, Laura said, "If you get hungry, food's in the mess tent. Fix what you like."

Over the next week, we fell into a rhythm of up early, breakfast; Laura, me, Ray, and Amelia at work on the Trike; Pick and Tanya going off somewhere and returning in the evening with full packs. They seemed as tired as we were at the end of the day, so cocktails for those who wanted it, dinner, and to bed after a little conversation around the fire pit which we'd dug to burn cedar in to chase away the mosquitoes.

Of all of us, Amelia seemed to be having the most fun. She loved it all, the picking, scraping, and brushing. She overflowed with questions on our Triceratops and Laura patiently answered them all.

One night around the fire pit, Amelia said, "I've decided to be a paleontologist."

Pick said, "I think you'd be a good one. But I have to tell you there's not much money in it."

"I don't care," Amelia replied. "I like it. Anyway, it'll get me out of this place."

"What's wrong with this place?" Ray demanded, then said, "Never mind. I've heard it all before."

"What's wrong with this place," Amelia said precisely, "is that it's like living inside a cage. We're stuck, Ray. Can't you see that?"

"All I see is this ranch, which I think is a fine place to live. I don't think I'm in a cage at all."

"Well, good luck," she answered. "I'm out of here after graduation."

"Sure. Good luck to you, too," Ray grumped.

Laura and Tanya, recognizing a lover's spat when they heard one, stayed out of it. Pick wasn't so smart. "I can give you recommendations," he said to Amelia. "There are several excellent institutions you could attend, including Montana State."

"Thank you," she said, smiling at him. I looked over and Ray was gritting his teeth. I felt sorry for him but there was nothing I could do. Ray sat there for a few more minutes, just staring at the fire, then got up and went to his tent. Amelia pretended not to notice. Before long, we all made our way to our sleeping bags. I slept like a rock except I was awakened once by a distant grumble of an engine. It sounded too guttural for a four-wheeler but sound can play tricks in the badlands. I would have thought about it more except I couldn't keep my eyes open. My last thought before I went back to sleep wasn't the odd engine noises but Jeanette. What was she doing back on the ranch? Did she miss me? I knew in my heart she didn't, except for the work that wasn't getting done, but I wondered just the same.

The second week didn't change much except I ran out of gin. That meant beer in the evening. Nice, but not the same. Ray, Amelia, and I dug out the Trike with either Laura or Tanya supervising. We had exposed a femur and a tibia and a number of vertebrae. Laura said she was sure we were going to find a sacrum. Part of the skull had also been exposed, including the frill but Laura had decided to go after it last. "The rest of this animal we can move bit by bit," she said. "But the skull is going to be huge. I have no idea how we're going to move it."

Mostly, I loved the evenings. Tanya, Laura, Ray, Amelia, and I shared cooking duties, our meals simple but nutritious. Afterward, we retired to the fire pit, drinking beer (Ray and Amelia got soft drinks) and talking. Both Laura and Tanya were full of stories—mostly with Pick as the hero—of their expeditions in Mongolia, China, Argentina, and Tunisia. In almost every story, they arrived at their foreign destination, were escorted to the happy dinosaur hunting grounds, realized they had been taken to a place where it was all hunted out, and Pick went on to make a dazzling find. At the end of one such story, told by Tanya and featuring an adventure in China where they had given their escorts the slip and discovered a new feathered dinosaur only to have it taken away before they could present it to the world, I asked, "Tanya, what's your story?"

"What do you mean?" she asked.

"I mean, how did you become a paleontologist?"

She looked a bit flustered, then said, "I am not a paleontologist, Mike."

"She's a first-class digger," Pick chimed in, "and a great assistant."

"I am Russian," she said, quietly. "I have a green card. I will apply for citizenship."

"I didn't mean to snoop," I apologized.

"It is all right," Tanya said and gave me a small smile.

Of course, eventually the talk turned to me and I gave them my quick spiel. I had been raised all around the world, with my father being in the Air Force. When Dad retired, he took a job in California and we settled in. Eventually, I joined the army, and afterward, went to junior college, then joined the force as a rookie cop. I rose to detective but a bullet from a bad guy shortened my career. After that, I spent three years being an investigative gofer for the major film studios and a couple of Indies. In between all that, I married a couple of times to good women who, after a time, wised up to my bullshit and threw me out. I had come to Montana to escape life in general and met Bill Coulter who agreed to make me into a cowboy. That had been a decade ago and I had not left since except for brief forays to Las Vegas.

We also talked about dinosaurs and what they were like and why they were so fascinating. When Ray asked what killed them, Laura, Tanya, and Pick said, almost in unison, "We don't care. We only care how they lived." It seemed a mantra they had settled on.

Summer in Montana means long hours of daylight but when the sun finally set, the full glory of the sky was ours to admire as we sat around the fire pit, the twisted little cedar sticks turned to glowing embers. Not only the stars, planets, and the edge of our galaxy were on full display but multiple satellites as well. One flew over every few minutes and from all directions. They were fascinating to watch. Laura, it turned out, was a space buff and could accurately predict the arrival of the Hubble Space Telescope and the International Space Station. The latter looked like a gigantic, sparkling city passing overhead and all we could do was watch with open-mouthed awe. "I wish I could go up there," Amelia said after a dramatic pass.

"Is there anything you don't want to do?" Ray demanded. "I mean other than stay around here?"

"Ray," Laura said quietly, "let Amelia be what she wants to be."

"Who am I to stop her?" Ray griped, then got up and went to bed.

Sometime into the night, I woke, hearing once more a low, almost moaning engine sound. I climbed out of my tent and listened. It was far away, whatever it was, but seemed to be getting closer. I put on my clothes, boots, and some leather gloves then climbed the hill in front of the camp. Everything was immersed in a milky light provided by the moon. The way up wasn't easy, the dirt and rocks slippery, but I took my time. At the top of the hill was a layer of sandstone. I carefully ran my gloved hand over it, checking for snakes, then pulled myself up and over. From the top, which was a small plateau, I could look across a great expanse. A sliver of Fort Peck Lake could be seen, the moon glittering on it. The sound of the machine, whatever it was, continued for only a few seconds, then went abruptly silent. I strained my eyes but could see nothing. Then I wondered if maybe the noise was coming from the lake and what I was hearing was a boat of some kind. I'd never seen anything on the lake bigger than a medium-sized houseboat but Fort Peck was large enough for a small cruise ship. I waited, hoping the sound would start up again but it didn't and I climbed back down. Near the bottom, a rattlesnake buzzed a warning and I jumped about six feet, fell, and landed on my butt. Sore and a little shaky, I climbed back into the sack.

The next morning, over a breakfast of pancakes, I asked Laura if she'd heard any noises. She said she hadn't. No one else had, either. I was beginning to wonder if it was just me.

12

ONE NIGHT, SITTING AROUND the fire pit, Pick said, "Sometimes, I tell a little story about the bones we find according to the evidence. I hope I won't be boring you if I tell one now, will I, Mike?"

"Sounds good to me," I said. By then, I had a couple of beers under my belt and was ready for anything.

Pick leaned back in his chair. "I think our Triceratops—let's give him a name, Big Ben is what I'm thinking—was probably a bull, old for his species, tired, and, based on the gnarly growth I have observed in his joints, painfully arthritic. As he grew ever older, he slept a lot. We can't say how Trikes slept but most likely, like cattle and other herbivores, he slept standing or kneeling. I am certain Trikes never rolled onto their side to sleep or rest. Much too heavy for that. Their heads were especially heavy and made up nearly half the length of their bodies so, most likely, they let their heads droop to touch the ground. So, let's say, old Ben one day went to sleep, his beak immersed in a meadow of sweet-smelling ferns."

Pick looked at me. "Grass, Mike, wouldn't be invented for another million years."

Since Laura had already told me that, I knew it but I let it pass, not wanting to knock him off his story. Pick continued. "When Big

Ben woke up on the day he died, he looked around for his herd but found himself all alone. Trikes, we are certain, were herd animals and to be alone is the worse thing that can happen to a creature that depends on others for protection and has the herd instinct. You know that with your cows. Around the pasture was a forest of conifers—pine trees—and angiosperms—flowering plants like maples, oaks, and magnolias—the latter introduced during the late Cretaceous of the American West. Big Ben raised his heavy head and pondered his loneliness. His neck hurt. Probably he hurt all over. Big Ben, alone and frightened, would have called out, hoping to receive a response from his herd. What did he sound like? I think a bit like an elephant. High-pitched screeches and snorts. But there was no answering bleat on that day from a fellow Trike. There was, however, another sound, the hiss of released breath from something very big, something even bigger than Ben."

Pick stopped his story and looked around our little group. It was very dark, the fire in the pit only glowing embers. Overhead was the river of stars known as the Milky Way. Pick was, in a way, telling a ghost story and, I confess, it was pretty spooky.

He went on. "Ben knew what animal made that sound. It was the enemy he had hated and feared all his life. But now, he discovered he neither hated nor feared it. He welcomed it. He was in pain. He had trouble breathing. He could no longer distinguish the taste of the different varieties of ferns or reach the succulent vegetation on the low limbs of the conifers. The females no longer paid any attention to him. He knew instinctively there was a time to live, and a time to die. He was done. His life was over."

Pick leaned forward, his face aglow from the fire pit. "Now, he heard its heavy footsteps crunching through the dry pine needles and then going quiet as it came out of the forest onto the soft ferns of the pasture. Big Ben did not try to run. He did not even turn to see his fate coming on two clawed feet. He chose, instead, to look for his herd. Then, through bleary eyes, he saw them far away, and moving placidly, and without fear. Big Ben felt good and warm to see his herd safe."

Pick took a deep breath and fell quiet, as if he was himself the old Trike, waiting, waiting . . . "The pain," he said, "was sudden and it jolted Ben to his knees. Ben cried out but the pain would go away, as happens for many prey. They have programmed in their brains to go into shock at the death bite, to give up, to fall away, to go to sleep, and travel to the other place forever. Except," Pick paused dramatically, "Ben didn't. He was still alive, in shock, yes, but still alive. His attacker, a fully grown adult T. rex, had been distracted after the first bite." Pick squinted into the fire pit, as if searching for answers. "I saw the bite mark, not healed, on his pelvis. That can only mean one thing. The T bit him there, then released him. Why, do you suppose?"

I'm sure I didn't know but Pick thought he did. "I think another T. rex came upon the scene. Maybe a couple of them and they challenged the first T. This was unusual. We are fairly certain that Tyrannosaurs, like most predators, established hunting territories, which were normally respected by others of their species. After all, if every time you went out to hunt, you also had to fight off a number of your own species, you're not going to catch much prey and you're going to be beat up. So what this indicates is that there was a rogue presence and probably not just one rogue, but more like two. Since there are no more bite marks on the pelvis, just the one, I think the attacking T had to go instantly into fight mode. How much of a fight? Probably mostly mock charges, feints, and so forth. Predators don't like to fight other predators. There's no value to it except to get themselves wounded or even killed. Whatever happened, Big Ben was left alone. This was not a blessing. He'd been bitten severely and was dying. Ben lived near the sea and there were swamplands.

He went there, where the watery mud supported his great weight, where he always felt better. And there it was he died, bleeding to death in the mud. Around seventy million years later, this is where I found him, still asleep, waiting patiently for all these years to be found."

The story had apparently come to an end. Laura asked, "Pick, do you think—?"

"Yes," he said. "I believe there is something terrible about to happen."

Laura and Tanya nodded thoughtfully while I puzzled over what he'd just said. I looked over and saw Amelia and Ray were both asleep in their chairs. We sat there a while longer, then Pick got up and walked away in the wrong direction before turning around and going to his tent. I woke up the kids and we all turned in. That night, I kept turning over what Pick had said. Something terrible was about to happen. In deep time or in the present? Or, with Pick, was it all the same?

Uninvited visitors started to arrive. The first one was Cade Morgan and his buddy, Toby, who was obviously not scouting locations in South Dakota any more. They motored in on four-wheelers to the Trike site, got off, and looked up at us as we looked down on them. "Hello," Cade finally called out. "What are you doing?"

"Digging for gold," I called back. "Are you here to jump our claim?"

Cade thought that was pretty funny and laughed out loud. Toby didn't laugh. He only stared up at us, then started climbing. Cade stopped laughing long enough to follow. Towering over us, his big shadow almost heavy on my back, Toby asked in his light accent, "What is it?"

Tanya was supervising our work. "It is a Triceratops," she answered, then said something to him in Russian.

Toby glared at her, but didn't reply. Cade had worn himself out climbing but finally caught his breath long enough to inquire about the Triceratops and Tanya took a moment, actually several minutes, to patiently explain what the big animal was or had been, long ago.

Amelia added, "Ray and I have learned so much out here already. This is the most fun I've ever had in my life!"

"How about you, Ray?" Cade asked him.

Ray put down the brush he'd been wielding and sat back. "It's been OK but I need to get back to the ranch."

Amelia sat back, too. "You'd leave me alone out here?"

"You wouldn't be alone. You'd have everybody, especially Pick."

"What are you trying to say?" Amelia demanded.

"You're in love with Pick."

Amelia put down her trowel. "You take that back, Ray Coulter!"

"I will not!"

"Where is Pick?" Toby suddenly demanded in an angry voice. This stopped the lover's quarrel and was also a surprise to me. I didn't even know he knew our dino hunter.

Tanya answered in Russian and Toby glared at her again. Cade said, "I don't think I caught that."

"He is out there," Tanya said.

"Where?" Toby insisted.

Tanya waved her hand. "Out there. He hunts dinosaurs. That's what he does. This is one he has already found."

"Has he found anything else?" Cade asked.

"He always finds dinosaurs," Tanya answered. "Wherever he goes."

I stood up. "I didn't know you were into dinosaurs, Cade."

Cade pointed at the four-wheelers. "I'm not. Those are my new toys. Just thought this would be a good place to try them out."

"Did you ask Jeanette if you could cross the Square C?"

"Sure did."

"How is she?"

"She looked fine to me. You missing her?"

"Shut up, Cade."

"Listen to him," Cade said, grinning. He cut an eye toward Toby. "Did you know Mike used to be a private dick in Los Angeles? Now, he's a dick, only in Montana."

"Mister Morgan," Ray said, "I wish you wouldn't use that kind of language in front of Amelia. Or Tanya."

Cade nodded. "You're right, Ray. I'm sorry."

I glanced at Amelia and she was looking at Ray. She had a little smile on. Toby said, "Los Angeles is too hot and crowded for me."

"How about Moscow?" I asked.

Toby didn't answer. He just frowned. I was pretty sure I had him pegged. Certainly, Tanya thought so, even though she hadn't been able to squeeze a Russian word out of him. There are only a couple of reasons why a man would try to hide that he was Russian, neither of them good. One was that he was ashamed of his heritage but Toby didn't look the type who got ashamed about much. The other was that he was dirty, meaning he was either illegally in the country or in the country being illegal, if you get my drift.

Cade said, "We need to see Pick. Would you please tell him, Tanya?"

Tanya didn't answer and I said, "We need to get back to work."

"Be our guest," Cade answered, looking put out. Toby just looked like Toby, which meant he looked dangerous.

They climbed back down the hill. Toby lit up a cigarette, then they both climbed aboard their four-wheelers and puttered off.

The next of our uninvited guests were, to my astonishment, the two Green Planet environmentalist brothers, Brian and Philip. They stumbled around the hill and collapsed at the base of it. I was busy pedestaling a tibia at the time but heard a thump and looked down and saw them, sitting next to their packs. They looked sunburnt and generally unhappy. Laura was supervising that day. "Hello," she called down before I told her who they were.

"Can you help us?" Brian asked. "We're out of water."

Laura rolled her eyes, then got up. "Amelia," she said, "let's see what we can do."

Even though she hadn't asked me to help, I went down the hill to see what was up with these two, leaving Ray to scrape, chisel, and brush on his own. He didn't seem to mind. In fact, in the last couple of days, he'd seemed almost cheerful. Mostly, he and Amelia weren't talking, which maybe was helping his attitude. Or not. I couldn't figure those two out.

Laura squatted beside the brothers, felt their foreheads, checked their pulses, and said, "You're both into heat exhaustion. Can you walk a bit farther? You need to get in the shade and cool down."

Numbly, both boys nodded their heads and staggered to their feet. Amelia and Laura led them back to camp with me pulling up the rear with their backpacks. When they rounded a curve and were out of sight, I set the packs down and opened them. Inside were BLM maps, empty water bottles (only two small ones per pack, the saps), a couple of half-melted granola bars, and notebooks. Philip's note-book was blank except for some phone numbers. Brian's was a daily log and what was in it gave me a chuckle. Apparently, the two were going from block to block on the BLM, counting cows and cow pies. One entry, pretty much typical, said:

No cow seen on this grid. 14 cow excrement documented. Especially large and smelly. See GPS chart.

These guys were a hoot. If they wanted to see cow doo, I could have helped them out. I knew where a lot of it was. Why they wanted to see it I guessed had something to do with them trying to document that we ranchers were fouling the people's land with our nasty old cows. Yeah, right.

Laura and Amelia had the two brothers lie down beneath the cook tent awning, then gave them water and salt. Brian subsequently started screaming about having cramps. He grabbed his legs and rocked from side to side, his eyes slits of pain. Philip similarly groaned. "The cramps will pass," Laura said, fanning them with a magazine. I sat there and looked at these two doofuses and reflected that they represented so many indoors environmentalists—filled with a fantasy of what the outdoors was really like but, once out there, pretty much disasters to themselves and the environment. Brian proved this by pooping in his pants.

"Whoa," I said, wrinkling up my nose at the smell.

Laura allowed a grin. "Another symptom of heat exhaustion," then pulled off Brian's pants, got a basin of water, and helped him clean himself up. Brian kept moaning, then seemed to lapse into a coma. I worried about him until he started snoring, which I took as a good sign. I made a GPS reading, then retrieved Brian's log from his backpack and made a note, doing my best to copy his printing style:

1 *Human excrement documented. Especially large and smelly. See GPS chart or look in my pants.*

I knew it was stupid but at least it made me laugh. "What are you laughing at?" Laura asked and I showed her the notebook. She called me a goofball.

There was something I needed to know so I asked Philip, "How did you get here?"

"We rented a pontoon boat at the marina," he answered, "and

came across the lake. Then we hiked into the BLM. We had no idea the terrain was so rugged."

"Do you have a rifle? Any firearms?"

"No. You mean like to kill bears?"

"There are no bears out here but there are cows. You ever kill one?"

Philip closed his eyes while a wave of pain shuddered through him. "I'm really sick."

I didn't care how sick he was. "Have you ever shot a cow out here?"

"No. Of course not."

"You're telling me you never shot a cow, or cows, out here and left a card behind calling yourself the Green Monkey Wrench Gang?"

"Man, this has to be a bad dream," Philip said, then curled up into a ball.

"Brian, how about you? You shoot any cows?" Unhappily, Brian was spreadeagled on the ground, still unconscious. "Brian?"

"Mike, for God's sake, leave them alone!" Laura admonished. "What are you talking about, anyway?"

"I'm suspicious of these guys. Somebody's been killing cows out here. Shooting them, then cutting their throats. They were already under suspicion when we let them go." I told her about the meeting in town where they'd shown up. "So why are they still here?"

"Well, they're not up for interrogation in their condition," she said, then shooed me away.

I went back to work at the Trike site where I was surprised to discover that Pick and Tanya had shown up. "This is going to be one of the most complete Triceratops specimens every recovered," Pick gushed. Then he said, "Mike, a word, if you don't mind."

Pick and I went down the hill. "I've found something," he said.

I asked, "The baby T. rex?"

This astonished him. "How would you know that?"

"Because that's why you're here. At least, that's what you told Jeanette the first time we met you."

He pondered that, then said, "There's a problem. Maybe a big problem."

I waited but he just stood there, staring at me. Finally, I asked, "OK, Pick. What's the problem?"

"Is Blackie Butte on the BLM or your ranch?"

"I believe part of the north side of Blackie is on BLM," I said.

"But the fence goes around it," Pick said.

I tried to remember something Bill Coulter had told me once about that fence. "The BLM built the fence," I said, the memory coming back. "I think they went around it because it was easier that way."

"How much of the north side do you think is on the BLM?"

"Most of it, I think, but I'm really not sure. You'll have to ask Jeanette. Believe me, she knows exactly where her property line is."

"We found something interesting on the south side of Blackie."

"Then you'll most definitely need to talk to her," I said, adding, "Maybe I ought to go take a look at what you've found."

He considered that, then said, "OK, but not now. I need to get in the shade for a while." This comment allowed me to bring up the Green Planet guys. "Where are they?" he asked.

"At camp, nearly but not quite dead of heat exhaustion when I saw them last."

"How did they get here?"

"By boat across the lake."

"What did they have with them?"

"Backpacks and two liter-sized bottles of water apiece."

"In this heat? Are they idiots?"

"Why, yes, Pick. I believe they are."

"I'd better go see them," he said and stalked off.

When he got to the end of the hill, he hesitated and just stood there, looking. I called Ray down from the Trike. "Go show Pick how to get to camp," I told him.

"Done," Ray said and was on his way.

This left me and Tanya alone, which was fine by me. I clambered up to the Trike and helped her plaster the femur we'd uncovered. We worked quietly for an hour and then I said, "Pick told me what he found on Blackie Butte."

"Yes? It's very exciting, don't you think? We never expected there to be so many."

Her response was confusing. So many what? Baby T. rexes? We worked a little longer. When I came across a metatarsal—a foot bone—Tanya said we should wrap it in paper towels and aluminum foil. This we did and then I asked, "What do you think of the stuff on Blackie Butte?"

"Well," she said, "it's amazing. But I think it will be hard for us to get everything out during the summer. Pick told you that we need more people, yes?"

"Yes," I lied. "But not how many."

"Well, not so many. Maybe just a few. And maybe some machinery. You know, like that thing you used the other day?"

"The tractor? Yes, I can see how it might be useful to move dirt."

"As long as one is careful. These bones are very fragile. And, of course, there are the possibility of eggs."

"Pick didn't mention anything about eggs."

She didn't look surprised. She said, "Maybe it is because the eggs are not the most important thing. It is the story, all of it put together, of how these creatures lived. And, in this case, how they died, too. I imagine Pick is having to deal with that as well."

I kept probing. "Has there ever been anything like this found?"

My question amused her in a quiet way. "No, Mike, this is a wonder. How could you imagine otherwise?"

"I'm not a paleontologist," I reminded her, as if she needed reminding.

She reached out and took my hand. This was startling but also very nice. "Mike, you are a very funny and nice man. I like you."

"I like you, too," I said which, of course, was true.

"You should see me when I am not so stinky as now. Maybe someday you and I will talk after I've taken a bath."

I provided her with what I thought was as insightful a thing I'd said all day if not all year. "Tanya, there are many rules for this land. Leave the gates the way you found them and so forth. Another one is there is nothing sexier than an intelligent, dirty girl. I like you just the way you are."

Tanya laughed and squeezed my hand before letting it go. "I think we will dance when we are in town," she said and I felt, well, thrilled.

I might have stayed thrilled a little longer, had Amelia not showed up at that moment. She climbed up beside us, squatted down, and started back to work without saying a word. When Tanya and I just sat there, kind of enjoying the glow of our flirting, Amelia finally stopped picking and brushing and looked up at us. "What?" she demanded.

"Nothing," Tanya said.

"Nothing," I said.

"Did I interrupt something?" she asked.

"No," we both said in unison.

She frowned at us, then smiled. "I think I did." Then she gave me a compliment that I could have done without. "Mike, I think it's really nice how you can still act young sometimes."

"Thanks," I said while Tanya laughed. When she winked at me, I winked back.

"Ray acts so old all the time," Amelia went on, oblivious to our flirting.

"He is a very nice boy," Tanya said.

"Yes, but that's all he is. A boy," Amelia said, not noticing or caring that she had just contradicted herself.

We dug on in silence until we'd dug ourselves out and headed back to camp. That evening, after dinner, I found myself sitting alone before the fire pit. I was feeling a bit blue, don't ask me why, but then Tanya appeared with two highball glasses, which clinked with ice and held a clear liquid. My spirits immediately rose. She handed me one of the glasses and sat in the chair beside me. She raised her glass and said, "Cheers."

"Cheers," I replied and we drank. It was, unless I missed my guess, a vodka tonic. "Tanya, I think I'm in love."

"With me or my vodka?" she asked, winking to show she knew I wasn't serious.

"Where did this come from?" I asked.

"What Russian girl does not keep a stock of vodka on hand?" she asked. "The tonic is Pick's. He likes to keep a store of it around because he says it keeps away the malaria he caught over in Africa. He hides it but, of course, I know where it is."

"Well, God bless Russian girls and stealing from Pick, too." I took a deep breath, and caught a whiff of Tanya. She smelled good. "What's that perfume?" I asked. "It's delightful."

She preened. "Ivory soap, my dear."

"You've bathed!"

"Well, I did my best from a bucket of dishwater."

I took another deep inhalation. "Surely, there must be more. I detect the hint of an intoxicating fragrance that is familiar, yet I can't quite identify."

"Ah, you have a discriminating nose, Mike. Yes, the scent you detect is one hundred percent pure Diethyl-meta-toluamide."

I took a wild guess. "You sprayed yourself with DEET."

"Yes, my dear. I am not only clean, I have my mosquito armor on like a good little dinosaur girl. Another vodka tonic?"

I gulped mine down and held out my glass like a cowboy Oliver. "Please, ma'am, can I have some more?"

Oh, we had a fine time that evening, drinking up her vodka and Pick's tonic, and solving the world's problems if not our own. The others joined us briefly, even the two Marsh brothers, but everybody seemed tired and slipped away to bed early, our guests given lodging in the cook tent.

After a while, a dreamy mood overcame Tanya and me, and we just sat there and watched the moon rise and the Milky Way blink on and the satellites crossing over. When, toward the end of the evening, she assured me that she had a "very great deal" of vodka tucked away, I began to understand how really special this woman was. Of course, Tanya and I went to our respective tents alone. We were playing the flirty game and, so far, that's all it was.

That night, I again heard the strange engine noises. I stayed in my tent and listened. There was no way I was going to climb that hill again to see what I could see. I went to sleep, waking to what sounded like a small avalanche. I got up. Everything was quiet except for the brotherly snores coming from the cook tent. I started to climb back into my tent when I heard the sound of a rock rolling down the hill. It smacked the sand at the base with a solid thump. Or someone? I got out my heavy duty flashlight from my tent and shined it up the hill. All I saw were rocks, dirt, and the layers of deep time.

13

THE NEXT DAY, WE had more visitors show up. I was beginning to think we were at the crossroads of the world. This time, it was Mayor Brescoe accompanied by her husband, nasty Ted of the BLM. They arrived on foot, without water or anything else, having left their truck somewhere nearby, a suspicion soon confirmed when Edith crawled up beside us and said, "I'm bushed. Ted made us walk from the gate. Hello, Mike, Amelia, Ray. I'm sorry, I've forgotten your name."

The name she'd forgotten was Tanya's. I reintroduced them and they both smiled at one another, though not particularly warmly.

Ted climbed up beside us. He was in jeans, a white T-shirt that said BLM in black letters on the back and a blue hat with yellow letters that also spelled out BLM. If I hadn't known it already, I would have guessed he worked for the BLM. He looked over our dig, then said, "This site will be returned to a natural state after you're through here."

"Of course, sir," Tanya replied in a most sincere manner. I took her response as more or less genetic. If you were Russian, when one of the Czar's or Stalin's minions showed up on the farm, you did as you were told and tried to appear grateful while doing it.

Having grown up in the U.S.A. where we don't much care for government stooges, I came forth with a challenge. "Are you kidding?" I demanded. "This hill is just a pile of mud and rocks. Maybe we'll throw a few shovelfuls of dirt in our hole."

Ted ignored me and spoke to Tanya. "I will be inspecting this site after you're finished. When do you expect that will be?"

"That is difficult to say," Tanya answered. "Much will depend on how much of the animal we find. You should speak to Dr. Pickford."

"Where is he?" Edith asked.

"On a walkabout," I answered before Tanya could. We exchanged meaningful glances, which, upon reflection, was probably not lost on anybody. To change the subject, I told them about our two sickly environmental wackos wallowing back at camp in the cook tent.

"They have a permit to be out here," Ted said, "but not to collect fossils. I should inspect their packs."

"I've already done it. They had two completely empty plastic bottles of water and that's about it."

This made Ted angry. "Out here in this heat with only that small amount of water? What idiots! If they died, it would be my ass."

For Edith's sake, I didn't start an argument with her husband although I could have observed how shitty it was that Ted only seemed concerned about himself, or that he must be a bigger idiot than the Green Planet brothers because he was out here with *no* water. I offered Edith my canteen. She took it, drank, and, without my leave, handed it over to Ted. Now I would need to boil that canteen. He handed it back to Edith who handed it back to me whereupon I discovered Ted had guzzled every drop. I should have kicked his butt right then. I still regret that I didn't.

About then, Pick and Laura showed up. Ted yelled, "Hey, you, I want to talk to you!" and scrambled down the hill and took Pick aside. Laura listened in for a moment, then rolled her eyes, and headed in the direction of camp. I didn't know what Ted and Pick were talking about but Ted seemed to be doing most of the talking. I supposed it might be about Pick taking good care of the BLM, which had been eroded, beaten down, crushed, and flooded by Mom Nature for over 65 million years. We humans can be such idiots about this planet. We think it's fragile. In fact, we're the ones who are fragile. We screw up our world, it'll kill us, and go on as if we never existed.

Edith interrupted my thoughts, "Can I help you dig, Mike?"

"Sure," I said and gave her the standard introductory course on the proper etiquette of fossil excavation. She took up an ice pick and said, "OK, I'll dig. You brush." And that's what we did for the next hour. When I raised my head, I noticed that Pick and Ted were gone off somewhere. I hoped Ted wasn't expecting Pick to lead him back to camp. On second thought, I hoped he was.

Edith uncovered some big vertebra and Tanya said we were getting close to the sacrum. "That will be a huge, complex bone," she said.

"How long will it take to dig out?" Edith asked.

"Two days," Tanya answered, "maybe three."

"What part of Russia are you from?" Edith asked.

"Saint Petersburg, actually," Tanya replied.

Edith nodded. "I went there one summer while I was in college. I was on a tour of Europe and Saint Petersburg was on the schedule. It is a beautiful city."

"*Da*," Tanya answered, "for all but those who must live there."

"I'm sorry," Edith said. "I suppose after the Soviet Union fell, it was a difficult time."

"I was but a child then," Tanya explained with a shrug. "But being an orphan is difficult at any time."

"I imagine it is," Edith replied. Then she asked the question every American wonders about when we meet someone born elsewhere who has come to our shores, apparently to stay. "How was it that you came here?"

"I was sent here to work," Tanya answered.

"Work on what?" Edith asked.

"Just work," Tanya said.

Without skipping a beat, Edith asked, "Were you a prostitute?" and the entire world, or so it seemed to me, went silent except for the wind through the grass.

Ray and Amelia were looking shocked at Edith's blunt question but Tanya remained perfectly composed. "Yes," she said. "That was what they wanted me to do. But I had other plans." She narrowed her eyes. "What gave me away?"

"Well, you're lovely, for one thing. But, as Mayor of Jericho, I receive FBI bulletins about how criminals over here promise Russian women that if they come, they will work as nannies or maids but are instead forced into the life. We're supposed to report any suspicious activity. I'm glad you were able to escape."

"I escaped because I had a dream and that was to be a paleontologist. Someday, that is what I will be."

"Yes, well, good for you."

Edith went back to digging and then, one by one, the rest of us did, too. Afterward, after Ted returned without Pick but with the two Green Planet brothers, Edith stood up, brushed herself off, and said, "I guess it's time to go. Good luck. I hope you find all of it."

"Oh, we will," Tanya said. "If all of it is here."

"Bye-bye, Mike," Edith said.

"I'll walk you down the hill," I told her and I did. Halfway down, I stopped her and asked, "Why did you say what you did to Tanya?"

"Mike, I knew what she was and she knew I knew."

"But she isn't anything. She might have been brought over here for that purpose . . ."

"Please, Mike," Edith interrupted, "I thought you used to be a cop. Where's your antenna for this kind of thing? Of course she worked as a prostitute. Probably for a few years. They hook these girls on drugs. You know that."

In fact, I did. I had been called to take home more than one strung-out Russian girl procured by a studio boss who was having second thoughts. The girls were hooked by their pimps, then had to keep working to pay for their addiction, a vicious cycle. Tanya had broken free, somehow, which made me respect her all the more.

"Don't be cross with me, please, Mike," Edith said. "I am in no way condemning this girl. She is obviously very smart and very brave. She did what she had to do, then got away. I hope you two enjoy each other. I just wanted you to know what she was before you got too far."

I wasn't cross before but I was now. "I don't think I need you to protect me from women, Edith."

"A couple of marriages would say otherwise," Edith replied.

"Yeah, well, how about Cade Morgan?"

This surprised her. "What about Cade Morgan?"

"You two, you're . . ."

She darted her eyes toward Ted who was looking at his watch. "Just shut up, Mike. Just shut up."

"Listen . . ."

"We have nothing more to say."

Edith climbed down the hill where she had to catch up with Ted who was already walking back toward wherever they had left their truck. The Green Planet brothers were trailing behind him. I guessed they were going to catch a ride into town. Edith had to run to catch up with Ted but he never looked back. A great guy, that Ted.

That night around the fire pit, Pick made an announcement. "I want to wrap up the Trike tomorrow. I know we have a lot of work to do on it and we'll get to it, eventually, but for now I want to move to the Blackie Butte site."

This upset Amelia. "But I hate to leave Big Ben!" she cried.

"Do you think he'll be lonely without us?" Ray sniped.

"Shut up, Ray. I'm going to miss that old thing."

Laura was sympathetic. "It is not unusual to begin loving the animal we dig up. They become very real to us. That's why almost always we give them names. It hurts when we find a broken bone or some other evidence of a violent end."

"It's just an old pile of bones," Ray groused.

"That's because you don't have any feelings or imagination," Amelia accused.

"I do, too. I feel that my mother needs me to stay here and help her run the ranch. I also imagine you're a nut case."

Well, if we wondered how our two teenaged love bugs were doing, that answered that. Ray and Amelia started sulking and Pick said, "Laura will be in charge of wrapping up the Trike site. Mike, would you help her? Ray and Amelia, you'll go with Tanya and me to Blackie Butte and help carry our tools and equipment over there. We'll also be moving our camp site."

"If you're going to move off the BLM onto the Square C, I think you'd better have a talk with Jeanette," I said.

"I'll go over there tomorrow," Pick promised.

And that was that. The Trike dig was over and we were on our way to Blackie Butte for whatever was there. I couldn't wait to find out what it was.

14

Laura and I closed down the Trike site and spent the day plastering the bones already pedestaled and wrapping paper towels and aluminum foil around a variety of exposed vertebrae, horn chunks, toes, and other bones too fragmented to immediately identify. Then, we picked and shoveled until everything that remained was covered with at least six inches of dirt. Laura said she hoped Ted Brescoe was going to be satisfied with our clean-up of the site. I told her to not worry about it. In fact, I was thinking maybe I might yet go and kick his butt for no other reason than it would make my day. Then I thought of Edith and let it go.

The base of the hill was littered with plaster casts filled with Trike bones. "What'll we do with them?" I asked.

Laura shook her head. "I'd like to move them to our old camp site. That way a truck could get to them when we're ready to take them out. Any ideas on how to do that?"

"Well, we could leave them here and I could use the tractor to make us a road but I don't think Ted Brescoe would like that very much. Maybe we can use the four-wheelers."

Laura thought about that and said, "I'm a pretty fair field engineer. Let's go see what we can figure out."

We filled our packs with some of the smaller foil-covered bones and hiked back to camp, where, after giving it some thought, Laura came up with the idea of using a wheelbarrow attached to a four-wheeler. For that, I said we'd need to do some welding and Laura said, "We don't have time for that. We need to move those Trike casts today. I think Blackie Butte's going to eat up all the time we have left this summer."

I scratched my head after taking my cowboy hat off, then said, "OK, let's do this."

My suggestion was crude but, oddly enough, it worked. We called Pick on the radio, asked for Ray and Amelia, and met them at the Trike site. We grunted each big bone onto the back of a four-wheeler (thank God for young backs), strapped it on with ropes and bungee cords, then, with Amelia or Laura at the wheel and me and Ray walking on each side to keep the four-wheeler balanced, trundled them all, one by one, slowly and carefully back to camp. It required a lot of sweat but we got her done. We had to take a day doing it and Pick managed to wander back to camp that night, frustrated that nothing much had been done on the move to Blackie Butte. "Did you go see Jeanette?" I asked.

He confessed he hadn't so I climbed a hill and used the handheld radio in an attempt to contact her. Happily, she answered. It was good to hear her voice. I told her what was up, and she said, "I'll be out there first thing in the morning."

"Meet us at Blackie," I said, and resisted telling her I'd missed her. "How's the ranch?" I asked, instead.

"Your work's building up but I guess it'll be waiting for you when you get back."

"You sent me out here," I said, defensively.

"And you were more than willing to go!" she shot back.

"Listen . . ."

I heard a double-click of the transmitter, meaning she had nothing more to say. Frustrated, I stared at the radio. Couldn't she at least have said something like, "The ranch just isn't the same without you, Mike," or something other than my work was waiting for me in a tone that sounded like I was just out here having a good time? Well, that was Jeanette.

That night, Pick came off as a nervous wreck. While the rest of us, not counting Ray and Amelia who went for a walk to continue their various arguments, sat around the fire pit and drank Tanya's vodka mixed with Pick's tonic, Pick was pacing back and forth. He just couldn't sit still. Then he started complaining about losing stuff. It started with his logbook and he tore up the camp looking for it. When Laura finally got up, went to his tent, looked under his inflatable mattress, found it, and handed it over, he said he'd also lost his GPS. Laura found it rather quickly, mainly because it was hanging around his neck. It continued on, the two women finding everything that Pick was certain he'd lost forever, including his socks, and then segued into complaints about how much food had been eaten, how much water had been drunk, how much glue, plaster, and aluminum foil had been used on the Trike, and so forth. Finally, back in their chairs with highball glasses in hand, Laura and Tanya exchanged glances when Pick griped some more, then together in perfect unison, the two women chorused, "Pick, shut the fuck up!"

Pick stomped up to them. "Listen, you two, I'm not made of money!"

Laura and Tanya re-exchanged their glances, then provided a very similar response to the one just given. In fact, it was the same one. Pick glared at them, then said, "I'm going to bed."

"Good," Laura said.

"Good," Tanya said.

"Good night," I said.

Pick pointed at me. "Mike, at least you understand," he said, then wandered off in the opposite direction of his tent, caught himself, and crept back past us. I tried not to laugh but wasn't entirely successful.

Laura looked over at me and said, "Sometimes, even geniuses can be assholes."

"I'm sure I wouldn't know," I responded. "But whoever fixed this v-and-t is a genius."

"That would be me," Laura said.

"I provided the vodka," Tanya said, "and the recipe."

Maybe I was being a little too full of myself, but I caught a hint that these two lovely ladies were sparring over me. I wondered if they'd hang up on me like Jeanette had done and concluded neither would be so rude.

We enjoyed a couple more drinks, watched the satellites fly by, admired the moon, and then a sudden reality settled on me. "This weather is entirely too nice," I said. "We're going to pay for it."

"In what way?" Laura asked.

"Montana will figure it out."

Neither woman seemed inclined to worry about the weather at that point and instead said they were getting sleepy. I was, too, truth be told, and after Ray and Amelia got back, this time hand in hand (go figure), off we went to sleep under the stars and, in my opinion, the entirely too clear skies. My sleep was restless though I didn't hear the mysterious engine noises.

The next morning, Pick, Laura, and Tanya acted like nothing had happened the night before. In truth, it hadn't been much, just a little dustup between friends and colleagues. Pick said, over his breakfast cereal, "We need to load everything up on the truck and four-wheelers this morning. Mike, what route should we take, do you think?"

I consulted a BLM map and pointed at the network of roads on the ranch. "Best thing is to go back onto the Square C, drive to this Y in the road here, turn left, and follow the trail. It will take us to Blackie."

"Is it a good road?"

"It's not really a road. Just a cow path. But I think our trucks should be able to cross along it. We just need to go slowly."

"Then that's what we'll do," Pick said.

And that's what we did. By early afternoon, we'd broke camp, loaded everything up, and transited over to Blackie Butte. We left the big plastered Trike bones behind, Pick saying we could pick them up later. Heavy as they were, I didn't see anyone stealing them.

I was burning to get up on Blackie and see what had been found but first things first, and that meant re-establishing our camp. This we did, me driving the last tent peg in just as Jeanette rode in atop Nick. Ray saw her and good son that he was went over to say hello. She got off and they spoke. There were no hugs. Amelia, however, provided a hug, which Jeanette received with obvious joy, meaning she didn't flinch. She also patted Amelia on the back, which, for Jeanette, was like she had smothered her with kisses.

Jeanette came over as I put down the sledgehammer. "How's your bum?" I asked, reflecting that only on a cattle ranch would that question to a woman be received correctly.

"He's fine. I let him out in that little fenced section of the Mulhaden. The heifers and calves next door have been coming over and paying attention. He seems to like that."

"What are you going to do with him?"

"All I'm planning right now is seeing him get fat on good Square C grass."

"How about our little C-section heifer and calf?"

"She's been accepted by the other girls. Her calf's loading on the pounds. Do you like being a fossil digger?"

"I like it a lot but I like being a cowboy more. Don't fire me just because you figure I've got another gig."

She shook her head. "Mike, just before he passed, Bill told me I was to keep you around as long as you were willing to stay."

"Bill gave good advice," I said.

Her answer inordinately pleased me. "Yes, he did."

Pick called everyone over. "We're going up to the site now. I want everyone to start being very, very careful about where you step. All dig sites are fragile but this one is especially so. Just follow in my footsteps and I'll point where I want you to go. Before we begin, it's important you understand what we know we have and also what we think we *may* have. OK?"

We all nodded and off we went, climbing the south side of Blackie Butte. I could tell by the trail already leading up to it that we were heading up to the third terrace, which was about twenty feet below a layer of coal, perhaps the famous "Z" coal Pick had told us about, which marked the boundary created by the famous dino-killing meteor.

Pick stopped and indicated we should fan out around the terrace, which was covered with several big blue tarps. Laura and Tanya slowly and carefully removed the tarps, revealing an area of disturbed dirt about thirty feet square. I thought I could see the hint of something that was curved just beneath the dirt but I wasn't certain. Pick knelt near it. He had a paint brush and whisked some of the dirt aside. The curve turned out to be a series of vertebra. "This is the articulated tail of an adult Tyrannosaur," he said, then whisked away some more dirt, revealing a large bone. "Based on its size, I believe this is the tibia of another adult," Pick said.

I knew enough to know this was kind of breathtaking. Laura

had told me only about thirty-five T. Rexes had ever been found and here were two. Pick added to the breathtaking quality of it by saying, "We have also found other bones that indicate there is a juvenile Tyrannosaur here."

"Why so many?" Jeanette asked.

Pick smiled a tight smile. "I believe this is a T. rex nest, Mrs. Coulter."

Laura held up a glass jar. "These are a few bones from the juvenile. Actually, it's a baby. We think maybe it was only a few weeks old."

"This site could reveal more about how Tyrannosaurs lived than any other since modern paleontology began," Pick said. "But it is very much a challenge. It could cover much more than this terrace. That means we've got to remove all this stuff to get to it."

I realized that Pick was talking about taking the top off Blackie Butte. There was at least fifty feet rising above the step we were on. I shook my head at the enormity of it. Pick saw me and said, "What is it, Mike?"

"I was just thinking about what it would take to move all that dirt."

He smiled and said, "I hope we don't have to do that but I intend to follow wherever the bones lead me."

"Well," I said, "you either dig into the side or take off the top. I don't see any other way."

"Let's cross that bridge when we get to it, Mike," Pick said.

"Dr. Pickford," Jeanette said. "Blackie Butte is a prominent feature on my ranch. I'm not sure I want it dug up to this extent."

Pick looked surprised by Jeanette's remark. I had told him he needed to talk to her and now maybe he understood why. "Let's take a break," he said. "Be careful where you step, please."

We all carefully dispersed while Pick and Jeanette took a walk. Actually, they climbed to the top of the butte. Just as I was thinking about going down to the tents, Jeanette called, "Mike, would you mind coming up?" I didn't mind. "I wanted you in on this," Jeanette said while I caught my breath.

Pick said, "This is an amazing find, Mrs. Coulter."

For some reason, they were both being very formal with each other. "I'm sure it is, Dr. Pickford," Jeanette answered. "But Blackie Butte has been a landmark on the Square C for a very long time. How would you feel if I came to your house and chopped down an old tree in your yard?"

"I don't have a house," Pick said, "but if I had a tree that would provide major scientific dividends if it was chopped down, I would cut it down myself. Besides, even in the worst case, I don't think we'd have to take the whole top off this hill, just a portion of one side."

Jeanette considered that, then asked, "How much do you think these skeletons are worth?"

Pick looked unhappy, then said, "It's impossible to put a price on them. They could very well revolutionize paleontology."

"Then they must be worth a great deal," Jeanette said.

Pick looked at me but all I could do was shrug. He was on his own. "We need to come to terms," he said at last.

"Indeed we do," Jeanette answered. "This is my land. That means those bones belong to me and I don't want you to dig them up unless the Square C gets something out of it."

"I won't sell these bones, Mrs. Coulter!" Pick declared.

"Then who will?" Jeanette calmly asked. "Tell me and I'll call them."

Pick turned pale, evident even through his tan. "Mrs. Coulter, you can't let anyone know about this! If you did and it got out, we'd be covered up with the media. There might even be people who would try to steal the bones."

"Then what do you suggest?" Jeanette asked.

Pick took a deep breath. "Look, I'm not sure what's here. I only have my suspicions. For all I know, there's only the bones showing now. Can't you wait until we uncover more before we worry about what to do with them? I promise you this. I'll keep you apprised every step of the way and not remove a single bone without your approval."

Jeanette took off her hat and tapped it against her leg. "I am a sequential thinker, Dr. Pickford. I see a great deal of work ahead that will result in plastered bones coming down my hill. I see those plastered bones stacking up. Then I see them going somewhere, perhaps when I don't know it, but where would that be?"

"I will need them to go a lab where I can study them properly."

"Where? Yosemite University?"

"Probably not," Pick said. "It doesn't have the facilities I need."

"I'm sure it doesn't," Jeanette said, tapping her hat harder against her leg, "since it doesn't exist. I checked."

"It exists wherever I am," Pick said. "I am Yosemite University."

"It's a scam, Dr. Pickford, as I suspect you are."

Pick pursed his lips, then said, "Not a scam. A cover. I have a wide academic background but I can't really tie myself down to only one institution."

"When you first came on my ranch, you told me you were from UC-Berkeley."

"I got my doctorate there."

"That's not what you said. You said you were *from* there, meaning implicitly that you worked there. And then Mike saw your BLM permit and it had on it this mythical Yosemite University."

Pick took a moment to gather himself, then said, "I already explained that to Mike. Didn't he tell you? Anyway, I'm sorry about that. Sometimes, it's easier to kind of talk in a shorthand way, rather than try to explain everything."

"In other words, sometimes it's easier to lie," Jeanette said.

Pick shrugged.

"So," Jeanette went on, "who do you work for, Dr. Pickford?"

"I work for myself," he said.

"So," Jeanette said again, "who do you work for, Dr. Pickford?"

Pick frowned, perhaps thinking Jeanette hadn't heard or misunderstood the answer he'd already given, but then the light came on. "I suppose I work for you."

"That's right. Anyone who works on the Square C works for me. Anything recovered off the Square C belongs to me. Nothing will be removed from this ranch without my approval. Do we understand one another?"

Pick absorbed that, then said, "Yes, as long as you understand my position. I am here for science, not profit."

"I think we can both get what we want," Jeanette said and put her hat on. "Dr. Pickford, you may proceed. How long do you think it will take to excavate the site?"

"The rest of the summer, I think," Pick said.

"Then let's get on with it."

"Since you've offered, I need a few things," Pick said. "Jackhammers, a supply of water for plaster, food and drink for our crew, about a dozen chisels, picks, shovels, pry bars, and ice picks. Also a variety of paint brushes and brooms. I can make up a complete list for you if you like."

Jeanette gave Pick a hard stare, then said, "Give me your list. I'll see what I can do."

"I need the jackhammers right away," Pick said.

"All right, Dr. Pickford," Jeanette replied testily, then put forth her hand. "Let's make an agreement. Shake."

Pick grasped her hand. "What are we agreeing to?" he asked.

"We're agreeing to a ten to ninety percent split to any proceeds made from this enterprise," Jeanette said. "My hand is my bond."

"Well . . ." Pick released his hand. "Who gets the ten percent?"

Jeanette chuckled. "You do, Dr. Pickford."

"That doesn't sound very fair," he said.

Jeanette was still smiling. "I've done my research. The courts have always sided with the property owner on fossil disputes. So it's my call what you get. I might increase it if I think you've done a good job. I'm not one for signing contracts and getting lawyers involved so you're just going to have to trust me as I've decided, against my better judgment, to trust you. We'll work it out but, for now, you will be rewarded one dollar out of every ten if you can successfully dig up and guide me to the proper marketing of these creatures. Deal?"

"I'm a scientist, not a marketer!" Pick sputtered, but then hung his head, recognizing finally that our boss had him well over her barrel. He allowed a sigh, then said, "All right, Mrs. Coulter. It seems I have no choice on any of this. We have a deal. Please don't forget my jackhammers and the other things on the list I will provide before you leave."

Jeanette's eyes narrowed. "Don't worry about the jackhammers. You'll get 'em." She turned and climbed down the hill without another word.

"That is some woman," Pick muttered and I could tell he was shaken by his encounter with the queen of the prairie.

"You don't know the half of it," I said and followed Jeanette down the hill. Pick stayed behind, I guess to study the horizon or maybe wonder what he'd got himself into.

I saw Laura climb up and confer with him, then she followed us. "If you'll give me a minute, Mrs. Coulter," she said, "I'll get you that list."

Jeanette was willing to give her the minute and together we waited for her. Jeanette said, "These women—what do you think of them, Mike?"

"Very smart. Hard workers."

"Have they been friendly toward you?"

"Yes. Tanya even shares her vodka."

"I don't trust them. I don't trust Pick, either." I had nothing to say about that so she said, "Keep an eye on them for me. Will you do that, Mike?"

"You're the boss," I said.

Her hand had been absently stroking Nick's neck but at my comment, it stopped. She leveled her gaze at me. "You think I'm wrong for wanting to get something for the Square C? Every year we just squeak by. I can't allow something like this to just be given away."

"Sometimes," I said, "there are things more important than money, Jeanette. This might be one of them."

She gave me one of her dirty looks that, as I looked her in the eye, turned thoughtful. "I am who I am," she said at length. "The Square C, it's all I've got."

"It's all I've got, too," I said before I could stop myself.

"That certainly is not true," Jeanette replied, then held out her hand, not for me, but for the list that Laura had brought.

"This is most of it," Laura said.

Jeanette glanced at the list, then handed it to me. "Mike, you know where the credit card is. You and Ray get on down to Miles City and buy the heavy stuff, then come back to Jericho and buy the food. I like to support the local folks where I can. The water for the plaster, you can get from our pump. Use those old drums behind the barn to put it in. Be sure to mark them non-potable. For drinking water, see if you can find a suitable container and fill it up in Miles

City. I think our Square C water would give some of these folks the runs. Get going on this right away. That suit you, Miss Wilson?"

"Yes, ma'am."

Jeanette swung up into the saddle with fluid grace. "Ho, Nick," she said when the stallion stamped a little. Jeanette looked toward the top of the hill where Pick was still posed. She frowned up at him, then clicked her tongue and aimed Nick toward home. I sought out Ray, told him our orders, and we got on our four-wheelers and headed after her.

15

Ray and I stopped off at our respective domiciles long enough to take showers, then got Bob and headed for Miles City where we bought out the place, pretty much. As I suspected, the heavy equipment we needed couldn't be found so we drove on down to Billings where, after some searching around, we located some used jackhammers, compressors, and tools. Luck was on our side as to a water tank as well. In a Billings junk yard, we found an old army water tank on wheels. We scoured it out, filled it with Billings water, and drove back to Jericho where I needed to stop for a cold one at the Hell Creek Bar. There, to my surprise, I found parked outside a shiny silver hybrid SUV and, within the bar, the Marsh brothers, sitting at a table looking forlorn. They brightened up at the sight of me and Ray, and invited us to sit.

"Can we help you dig?" Brian asked after I told them we were working on a different site.

"Why would you want to do that?" Ray asked. "I thought you just wanted to count cow pies and cause us trouble."

The brothers looked at each other, then shrugged. "We think we'd rather be paleontologists than environmentalists," Philip said.

"Yeah. It's more fun," Brian added.

"Besides, we got fired by Green Planet," Philip went on. "They said we weren't sufficiently motivated."

I gave it some thought, then said, "Follow me." The worst that could happen, I figured, was Pick would send them back. They didn't look particularly strong but I guessed digging could fix that.

We headed to the Square C. By then, the day was over and we spent the night at home, the brothers sleeping in the living room on the floor. Somebody knocked on my door after I'd gone to bed and I got up, pulled on a terry cloth robe, and found Jeanette standing outside. I opened the screen door for her.

She looked around and then had a seat in my easy chair. I sat down on the only other chair which was a folding picnic chair. Jeanette opened with, "Mike, I can't believe how much you spent today."

I knew where this was going and also knew there was no use arguing about it. "Ray and I did the best we could," I said.

"That may well be," she said, "but I was still shocked."

"Some of the stuff we can sell after we're done with it like the jackhammers, compressors, and water tank," I pointed out. "Anyway, I guess you have to spend money to make money."

Jeanette received my homily with something less than enthusiasm. "That's bullshit," she said, but added, "I know where you're coming from. I hope you didn't offer to pay those brothers."

"No, but if Pick thinks he needs them, I guess we'll have to feed them," I said, adding, "we'll go into Jericho tomorrow to get the food."

"No, I'll do that. You and Ray need to get that equipment out to Blackie Butte. Use Bob and my John Deere. Be careful with both, you hear?"

"Yes ma'am."

"But you don't need to keep Bob out there. Bring him back, you and Ray, and take the four-wheelers."

"Yes ma'am."

Jeanette had her hands on her knees and her fingers were tapping a tune on them. "Wonder what Bill would think about all this?"

"He would have never let Pick cross your land," I pointed out. "So he wouldn't have had to deal with it."

Her tapping stopped. "You're right, Mike. Bill would have kicked Pick off the ranch so fast his head would've spun right off his neck. I've really opened us up to something, haven't I?"

"Yes you have," I answered. "But I don't guess there's any reason to beat yourself up over it."

She didn't take my comment well. "You should have spoke up, Mike. Instead, you acted like a little school boy with all his talk about dinosaurs. I could have used better advice."

"I don't recall you asking my advice."

"Well, that's a given."

I started to defend myself, but my better angels said to let it go. "I'll try to do better."

This made her smile, which, of course, I was glad to see. "I swear, Mike, you tell me to go piss down my leg with fewer words than any man I've ever known." She got up. "Well, you need your sleep and so do I."

"Sure you won't stay for a drink?" I boldly asked. "I was so tired when I got back, I forgot to have one."

She hesitated, looked me in the eye, then said, "It's best to keep my head clear around you, I think."

I wondered what the hell *that* meant but before I could ask, the screen door was slapping behind her and she was gone into the night. I sat there for a little while, then went back to bed, there to dream not of Jeanette but of Blackie Butte. I saw Pick, Laura, and Tanya climbing up and down it, carrying big bones in their arms. They were giving them to somebody but I couldn't see who it was. I also heard the low, guttural engine noises that had interrupted my sleep out there. That woke me up and I listened carefully but heard nothing but the hum of my window air conditioner, which soon lulled me back to sleep. I had no more dreams, at least none that I recall.

16

Ray and I were greeted with enthusiasm by Pick, his ladies, and Amelia as we rolled into camp early the next morning. Laura and Tanya, especially, were like kids on Christmas morning going through all the equipment we'd brought from Miles City and Billings. "These are great jackhammers!" Laura cried, practically swooning at the sight of the heavy, dirty things. "And look at these compressors. Woo-hoo!"

How many women in the world get excited about heavy construction equipment? If they only knew, it is nearly a direct path to a man's heart.

Tanya loved the water tank. "Where did you find this, Mike?" she bubbled. "I have never seen such a lovely tank before!"

"Got something else for you, too, darling," I said in my most manly tone. "Got your name on it. Look in the back of Bob. That would be the truck."

She looked, saw the cardboard box with her name on it, climbed in, opened it, and yelped in almost orgasmic ecstasy. "Vodka! Oh, Grey Goose! A dozen bottles!"

"There's tonic in that other box," I said, hoping to hear another orgasmic cry.

Instead, Tanya jumped down from Bob and gave me a big hug and a kiss on the lips. My knees went a bit wobbly. Before I could respond, Laura came running over. "Tanya, they bought brand new chisels! Hardened steel! Come see!" and together these two dream gals went scampering off to look at tools.

Ray swung by. "I saw you got a kiss," he said, a bit sour.

"How about you?"

"Amelia said she'd been thinking and had decided she was too young to get engaged. What does that mean? I never asked her to get married! I just wanted to, you know, make out and stuff."

"How does she feel about that? Making out and stuff, that is."

"Who knows?" he replied. "Best I ever got was a little kiss."

"Well, Ray, I guess a little kiss is sometimes all you need."

"Boy, it's been a long time since you were a teenager," Ray pointed out and went on his way.

Pick came over. "Mike, how long do you think it will take to hook up those jackhammers?"

I looked over to where Laura, Tanya, and the two former Green Planet brothers were already hooking the jackhammers up to the compressors. "About as long as it takes to carry them up to the top of the hill," I said. "I take it you've agreed to take on Brian and Philip."

"Sure," he said. "Willing backs who work for nothing but food? Every paleontologist's dream."

The chatter of a compressor began and Laura attacked a boulder at the bottom of the butte with the thirty-pound jackhammer. She knew what she was doing and, within a minute, the sandstone rock gave it up and fell apart. Laura handed the jackhammer over to Tanya and raised her hands in victory. Pick looked at the spectacle and smiled. Tanya assaulted another boulder.

After everyone took a turn on the jackhammer to get the feel of it—everyone but Pick who suddenly had a need to work on his journal—Laura called for a break and detailed her plan to move the equipment where it needed to go and how we were going to take down the butte. When she finished, I had to point something out. "It's July one," I said. "The Independence Day celebration in Jericho is a big deal. Ray and I are on tap to do some work on it and Jeanette's one of the prime organizers. I suggest we go in on the evening of the third and enjoy the day. Jeanette always has a few rooms reserved in Tellman's Motel for the occasion."

Laura gave that some thought. "A break would be good," she said. "And I look forward to a shower."

"I do as well," Tanya said, giving me a suggestive glance. My heart sped up.

"OK. We'll go in on the evening of the third to enjoy the fourth," Laura said. "But the next couple of days, I want to see some work done."

This was received with good cheer. We were all serious dinosaur diggers, after all. While Ray and I took Bob and the tractor back to the ranch and returned on our four-wheelers, Laura directed the move of equipment. Then, she realized she'd forgotten something. The BLM fence, which ran along the bottom of Blackie's north side rose like a thin net to catch all the debris we were about to send down on top of it. "We should move that fence, Mike," she told me.

I considered it, then agreed but explained it would mean another delay because to move it meant lengthening it and we didn't have either extra wire or posts.

"Then just take it down," Laura said. "We can put it back later."

Since none of our cows were out this way, I agreed and went after Ray and Amelia who knew what to do. Within an hour, we had the fence down and it wasn't more than a minute later that Laura had the rocks tumbling off the butte.

The rest of the day was spent with the hot and dusty task of taking down what was essentially a mountain. Even Pick climbed up and helped pry loose a couple of huge slabs of sandstone, which, when they broke loose, slid and rolled with ponderous majesty down the back side, crashing at the bottom with a jolt that I could feel even standing on top. That night, the v&t was needed just to dull the ache in my bones and I didn't last long around the new fire pit. I crept to my tent and was out cold almost instantly.

Sometime in the night, I woke, hearing the same low engine noises I'd heard at the Trike site. It didn't sound nearby so I let it go. The next morning, Tanya came to me while I was eating my break-fast of cold milk and cereal. "Mike, I think I heard those sounds you keep talking about. What could be making them?"

"I have no idea," I confessed.

"I think it came from the direction of the lake."

"Yep. That's what it sounded like to me, too."

"Will we be near the lake on the fourth of July?"

"There's a dance at the marina that night. Fireworks, too."

She smiled. "I would enjoy a dance."

My heart did its little flutter. "Then I'll see you there."

The day boiled on and Blackie got a little shorter. Jeanette showed up driving Bob, which was filled with groceries. She watched the activity for a while, then called me down to talk. "I hate what you're doing to my butte," she said.

"It's just dirt, Jeanette. And we don't come out here that much to look at it. Nobody does. Not even that many cows."

She sighed. "You know what I mean, Mike. You, of all people, know."

"It's too late to change it now," I said. "Let's just go with it."

She nodded but actually bit her lip, the first time I'd ever seen her do that. I knew what she was thinking. Bill Coulter would have never allowed a major landmark on the Square C to be destroyed.

Pick came over and he and Jeanette walked off together. I climbed back up on the butte and took my turn on the jackhammers. When I looked back, I saw Pick helping Jeanette carry the groceries from Bob into the cook tent. When they were finished, Jeanette climbed up to our ersatz quarry, got a shovel, and started using it with gritty determination. The young people—meaning Ray, Amelia, and the Marsh brothers—stopped briefly and just watched her go. Blackie Butte, now that Jeanette Coulter was there with her mind made up to take off its top, stood no chance.

Then Ted Brescoe showed up in his official white BLM pickup. "What the hell are you doing?" he screamed as soon as he climbed out. "Stop this. Stop this now!"

From the passenger seat stepped Edith, out here for no apparent reason. I surely couldn't believe it was because she liked being with her husband.

"Stop nothing," Jeanette said to the others and climbed down to confront Ted. I followed just in case I got orders from the queen of the prairie to beat up the representative of the Big Lousy Monster.

Ted was in a state that bordered nearly on out of control. He was stomping around, screaming obscenities. When he saw the fence was down, I thought he was going to blow an artery. He rushed over to Jeanette and shook his finger in her face. "You will be fined! You will be fined!" he screamed.

"You shut up, Ted Brescoe," Jeanette replied. "This is my land and my lease. The Coulters have taken good care of this property for a hundred years. What we are doing here is my business and not yours. You calm down or I'll have Mike run you off. Hell, I'll do it myself."

Ted's finger folded and he brought it down but he was still clearly enraged, his eyes bugged, his jaw clenched, the sinews in his neck standing out. "That lease may not be yours much longer," he threatened. "And I'll tell you something else. I'm going to get a surveyor out here to check the BLM line. I've always suspected all of Blackie Butte is on federal land."

"Only you, Ted, would say something so stupid," Jeanette retorted.

"We'll see," he seethed.

"Ted," Edith said, "why are you so worked up? It's just an old hill. There's ten thousand of them out here."

Ted turned on her. "Shut up, Edith. I gave these idiots a permit to look for bones, not dig them up. And they sure didn't have permission to knock down that fence. Anyway, this has nothing to do with local politics. This is a federal matter."

I took this as an interesting comment, primarily because it was from a husband to a wife but it sounded like a dustup between two bureaucrats, one a lowly local, the other a lordly federalista.

Edith retorted in kind. "It is my responsibility to see my constituents represented."

"Jeanette doesn't live in Jericho," Ted pointed out. "This falls under my purview."

At least, their little turf struggle had calmed Ted down. "Ted, why don't you do a bullet chart and present it to us at our next meeting?" I asked.

Ted glanced at me, his expression filled with contempt. I guess he didn't like my idea. He turned back to Jeanette. "Until the BLM completes its survey, I am hereby ordering you to cease and desist. If you don't, I will find a federal judge to issue a ruling to make you stop. And I'm not kidding about that fine. You destroyed federal property when you knocked down my fence."

"I'll build you a better fence, Ted," Jeanette said. "There's no reason for any of this."

Ted drew himself up. "I have a duty here to oversee anything that occurs on the BLM and, by God, that's what I'm going to do. Cease and desist, Jeanette, cease and desist."

"Ted?"

"What?"

"Go fuck yourself."

It was rare when Jeanette used the F-word, but I guess Ted Brescoe was able to bring out the worst in anybody.

"We'll see about that," Ted said, and stomped to his truck.

"I'll talk to him, Jeanette," Edith said, giving me a cool glance. I just shrugged. She rolled her eyes and followed her dear husband.

Laura, Tanya, and Pick had gathered nearby to hear all this. Jeanette turned to them. "It's all right. Everything is all right. Go back to work."

We went back to work but when we took breaks, most of the talk was about the BLM agent. The consensus was he was an idiot, which, of course he was, but he was also a powerful one, at least on federal property. I hoped Edith would talk some sense in him. I also hoped he wasn't right about the boundary lines of the BLM.

17

WE KEPT TAKING OFF the top of the butte and, to my surprise, Jeanette stayed out to help. She said she'd asked Buddy Thomason to look after the Square C for a few days and she was ready for a little vacation. She chose to be quite sociable, joining us for our drinks, telling a few funny stories about ranch life and, more seriously, how she'd met Bill Coulter, twenty years older than she, and how they'd taken the Square C from a struggling, backward little ranch into the twenty-first century of animal husbandry. Of course, it was still struggling, she said, but at least she was working with the very latest information provided her by Montana State University and other institutions of higher learning in the state.

"Some day," she said, wistfully, "we'll start turning a consistent profit and we'll prove to the other ranchers they also need to upgrade their methods."

"It sounds like you nurture the land, Mrs. Coulter," Brian said.

"I do my best," Jeanette replied. "All ranchers in Fillmore County do the same."

"I have to say I have some reservations about tearing this hill down," Philip said.

"I do as well," Jeanette responded, "but I've been assured the scientific value is the greater interest here."

I have to say I had never heard Jeanette be so pedantic. I, for one, was impressed and so, apparently, were the brothers who just leaned back with their v&t's. When she wanted to, Jeanette could charm anyone. Anyway, I think those greenies wanted to get charmed, else they might have asked her about the greater interest called the profit motive. Actually, I think they were enjoying knocking down Blackie Butte and it *was* fun, make no mistake about that. It made me think of my trip to Delphi in Greece with the second wife. Delphi is a mountain of ancient Greek monuments that are somewhat battered. What had battered them? Our guide said after the classical period, probably goatherds on top of the mountain with nothing better to do than to roll rocks and chunks of monuments down the hill just to see what they'd do. In short, it was fun to make stuff roll down hills and the Marsh brothers were having the time of their lives.

As to Pick, he was apparently shaken by Ted Brescoe's threats. He had gone very quiet and somber around the fire pit. To cajole him out of his funk, Laura and Tanya were being extra solicitous with him, getting him another drink, making sure he had his favorite food (a cheeseburger), telling stories about what a great dinosaur hunter he was, and urging him to tell some stories of his own. Finally, toward late evening when the rest of us were thinking about our sleeping bags, Pick seemed to snap out of it. "I've been thinking about what's up there," he said, "and I think I understand part of it."

Laura and Tanya smiled at one another and sat back. Seeing their reaction, I did, too. Pick was about to tell a story as he had of Big Ben. The others, including Jeanette, waited politely.

"We have a family," Pick said. "The bones tell me that much. But something happened, maybe more than one thing. I'm studying more than the bones. I'm studying the dirt."

He let that hang, although Laura cocked her head. Pick went on. "Understand where they were. They lived by a tributary of a vast, inland sea. There were islands, beautifully green like emeralds in the bluest ocean you can imagine. The air was filled with oxygen, more than we have now. Every breath provided streams of energy to all the creatures who lived. The meadows of ferns were an extraordinary green. There were many open spaces. The Triceratops and Hadrosaurs saw to that, eternally grazing on endless pastures, overlooked by rolling highlands. A shallow river ran through the countryside. Butterflies flitted in the ferns and the bromeliads and orchids that coated the land. It was a splendid place for a family of Tyrannosaurs to live."

"You make it sound like paradise," Philip said.

"It was," Pick said, "except, even as big and thick-skinned as these Tyrannosaurs were, they needed always to be wary of creeping things with teeth and poison."

"I can't imagine anything could threaten them," Jeanette said.

"Oh, there were many threats, Mrs. Coulter," Pick replied with a significant look. "And among them would have been other T. rexes. Rogues. I think there were rogues."

I noticed Jeanette was now watching Pick with intense interest, almost as if it was the first time she'd ever seen him.

Pick went on. "The mother of this family would have been a big dominant female. We haven't found her bones and maybe she isn't here. What we have found is evidence of two adult males and one juvenile or infant. But let me speak for the moment of the mother T. Tyrannosaurs, I believe, had a matriarchal society, the females leading each family. I've seen her clearly in my thoughts and dreams and, for that reason, I think we will find her. She must be under Blackie somewhere."

Laura said, "I notice you've been reading Robert Bakker again, Pick."

"I have," Pick replied. "He makes a great deal of sense to me."

Laura looked around our little group. "Robert Bakker first postulated that dinosaurs were fast, smart, adaptable, and warm-blooded. He also did some groundbreaking work on nesting Allosaurs demonstrating parental care."

Jeanette leaned forward in her chair. "What was the mother T. rex like, Pick?"

Pick regarded Jeanette for a long second, maybe thinking that if there ever was a matriarchal society, it was the Square C. Then he said, "The mother T would have been bigger than the males. When she walked, it was on her tip-toes, three phalanges on the ground with long curved claws that could tear through armored hide an inch thick. Her teeth were shaped like serrated steak knives and her jaws were strong enough to crunch massive, heavy bones into swallow-size chunks."

Amelia shivered and said, "She sounds so scary."

Pick nodded, then said, "To us, she would have been. But to her family, she was the symbol of security. This much I think is true. Although she was fearsome to behold, I think she had the capacity for love. And joy. She could also feel pain and sadness. Her intelligence even allowed her to mourn, the curse of the evolved predator's mind."

"I hope she was happy sometimes, too," Amelia said.

"Oh, yes," Pick replied. "There were a few simple things I'm certain made her happy. She liked to drink cool water from the river. She liked to squat in the meadow on her pubis bone and rub her belly across the smooth ferns. She liked when the birds jumped down from the trees and pecked along her back for the beetles that burrowed into her skin. And I think she liked to rub her neck along the neck of her mate. We think Tyrannosaurs could make a humming sound and I bet she made it when she was happy. When he hummed back, she would close her eyes and perhaps her heart sang. But I think most of all, she liked to look at her children and delight in their existence. That was the love she felt."

"How did she give birth?" Amelia asked.

"She laid eggs, as birds do, and reptiles," Pick answered. "I'm hoping we'll find evidence soon of egg shells. If Tyrannosaurs nested like other theropods, I think the eggs would have been laid in a circular pattern, two by two, each egg arranged around the center like petals on a flower."

He looked out past us, into the badlands. "I have built another circle of stones out there," he said. "I did it last night. The circle is the universe's signal to us that there is no beginning and there is no end. The natural world loves the circle and reproduces it whenever it can. If any of you like, I will take you to it. You may want to make your own circles with the stones we've cast down from Blackie Butte. These are powerful symbols and will help us in our quest to understand how this family lived."

"But why did they live?" Brian asked. "For that matter, why do any of us live?"

We all turned as one to Pick for the answer, as if he had one. It's amazing to me how smart a little alcohol can make a philosopher.

Pick leveled his gaze on Brian. "Oh, that's been answered to my satisfaction, Brian," he said. "They lived because they could. Nature, God, the Creator, whatever we may call Him, Her, or Them, had the blueprint of life and desired to use it. But when it comes to humans, we are the more complicated question in terms of why *we* exist."

"Wait, what are you saying?" Philip nearly exploded. "It sounds like you believe in God! How can a rational scientist believe in a supernatural God? What about evolution?"

"I am giving you a philosophical answer to a philosophical question," Pick said, "and therefore open to many explanations and interpretations. The truth is as you deem it to be, and that's the way it will live in your soul. But I must warn you. Believe in nothing and you will be nothing."

"I believe in Mother Earth," Philip said, drawing himself up in his chair.

"And not the universe?"

"I can't protect the universe. I can only protect my planet."

"Then by all means do so," Pick replied. "But know this: We are on the leading edge of deep time. That which you see now will pass away because nothing can resist the clock. This, of course, gets us back to my answer concerning why we humans exist. What's interesting about us is that we have more intelligence than we need. For instance, here we sit in this circle talking philosophy. Any animal that can talk philosophy rather than using its intelligence to feed itself, or procreate, has too much brainpower. Therefore, the only conclusion is we are smarter than we need to be. There is but one possible reason for that and that is we are what we are, established at this time and place to look back over deep time and understand it, and marvel over it. In other words, we are observers, sharing our observations with ourselves and anyone or anything that will listen. Maybe the authors of the Bible had it right. God was lonely and wanted to share His universe with someone, anyone, even such low creatures as ourselves. He wanted to be appreciated for what He'd done."

There settled over us a thoughtful silence. Jeanette was looking into the fire pit. Amelia's eyes were glued on Pick and Ray was surreptitiously watching Amelia, no doubt torn with jealousy. Laura and Tanya had leaned back during Pick's discourse and I think both of them were lightly napping. They'd heard it all before, of course. Brian and Philip wore tense expressions as if trying to force feed themselves Pick's words and reject them all at the same time. Doubtlessly, they were both impressed and distressed. I was, too. In my opinion, I'd never heard such utter and total bullshit so well spoken.

Of course, maybe it wasn't bullshit but most likely it was. I mean, who knows what any of this means? It's fun to think about but tomorrow it wouldn't move a molecule of dirt. We'd have to get our butts up that hill and take it down, rock by rock, by the sheer grit of our determination. Then, I thought, maybe that was Pick's point. Why were we willing to do that? Why sweat and grunt and bleed and tear our muscles and bruise our skin if not for knowledge of deep time? Then I thought, *Wait a minute!* Jeanette is doing it to make a buck. Instantly, I felt better. That was a motivation I understood. I was still understanding it, I guess with my eyes closed, when Laura gently prodded me on my shoulder. I blearily looked around, surprised to see all the other chairs empty.

"Time for all sleepy cowboys to go to bed," she said.

"Let's go," I replied, still half asleep.

She chuckled. "Not tonight. My bones are creaking. They don't need to be jumped on."

I hadn't meant it that way but I was pleased that at least she'd entertained the thought. I stood up and got a hug and a kiss on my grizzled cheek.

I was thinking pleasant thoughts about dirty dino girls on the way back to my tent. To get there, I had to pass Bob and saw that Jeanette had rolled out her sleeping bag in the back. "Good night, boss," I said but she didn't answer. She wasn't asleep, I didn't think, but maybe she was. Funny thing, when I crawled into my sleeping bag, I was thinking about that, whether Jeanette had deliberately ignored me, and not all the marvelous philosophy Pick had spouted or the fact I'd been kissed earlier by a young and very pretty woman. "You sure are perverse," I told myself and myself agreed but only briefly because I was soon asleep. No low, guttural engine noises from the far BLM woke me up, either. Maybe I was getting used to them.

18

After another morning of doing our best to knock off the top of old Blackie Butte, we headed for town. Jeanette drove Bob, Amelia sat beside her, and Ray and I rode in the back. Laura drove their truck with Pick sitting beside her, Tanya and the Marsh brothers behind to hunker down from the wind and dust. I pondered the sky as we careened down the road to Jericho. It was crystal clear. Not even a wisp of a cloud in it. I felt more foreboding. Montana was being entirely too nice to us. What was she up to, I wondered.

Once we were in town, I checked in at the Tellman's Motel, which was owned by Mori and Titus Philips, Mori being a Tellman. Mori met me in the tiny office that was actually a back room of her house with a separate door. The sign on the door said IF YOU WANT A ROOM, SORRY WE'RE ALL FILLED UP PLEASE HAVE A NICE DAY. It was too impolite in Fillmore County to just say NO VACANCY.

"You look like you need a shower, Mike," Mori said while I filled out the cards for the rooms. "Jeanette rationing water at the Square C these days?"

Mori was a fine young woman who made a habit of winning the walleye tournaments held annually on the lake. Nearly all Fillmore County women hunt and fish and look good doing it and Mori was decidedly no exception. She had big brown expressive eyes that just looked inside a man, right down to his soul. I was kind of hiding my soul these days so I kept my head down and focused on the card I was filling out. I did answer her, though. "Been dinosaur digging these past weeks. Severe lack of showers out in the BLM."

Of course, she already knew that and said, "Yeah, I was just teasing ya. I heard that Ted Brescoe went out there and caused a big stink. What are you going to do about that?"

I took the three keys she had placed on the counter. "Nothing for me to do," I told her. "I'll leave that to Jeanette and the dinosaur hunters."

"We all got a big laugh about it here in town," she said. "There's nobody more puffed up than Ted. When he doesn't get his way, his lower lip starts to tremble, then he cries. Of course, I'm remembering him that way from grade school."

That was another thing about the county. Most of the folks out there of the same age had gone to school together from the first grade through high school. Ted Brescoe apparently had been a whiny brat. This did not surprise me.

I asked Mori about Titus and the children, then picked out a room and went in and took a shower. Refreshed and wearing clean clothes I'd brought with me—jeans, plaid shirt, boots, and my town cowboy hat—I sought out Laura to give her a key to one of the rooms. I found her holding court with Tanya in the Hell Creek Bar, both of them knocking back beers as fast as Joe the bartender could deliver them. There were a half dozen empty Rainiers on their table and one each in their hands. Both Laura and Tanya gave me surreptitious winks when I handed over the key for the room they were to share. I thought I might be in trouble—too-many-women trouble—but it was kind of thrilling trouble so I sat down, had a beer with the ladies, then went looking for Jeanette.

I found her where she said she was going to be, in an upstairs conference room of the county courthouse with the other Independence Day organizers. The courthouse was built of stone around the turn of the last century and it's quite an impressive structure, reflecting the certainty of that era of a solid future based on cows and petroleum. Only the cows were still around, the oil fields played out, so the courthouse was now a monument to another time. Pick's ideas of deep time rattled a bit through my brain as I climbed the steps of the now mostly empty building. It represented a busy, prosperous future the men who built it had expected but that had not occurred. In their heads, they had gone to a time that did not exist but was very real to them, else they wouldn't have bothered building such a fine and expensive courthouse. In our time, we saw they were wrong but since they never knew, what difference did it make to them? They had enjoyed our time, in effect, a lot better than we were.

Anyway, I found Jeanette in a conference room, naturally sitting at the head of a table and running the show. Edith was there, too, and gave me a bland smile and a nod. Jeanette accepted the motel key to her room and kept talking. She was holding forth on the subject of vendors and where they were going to set up. She looked across the table, her eyes landing on Al Cunningham who had once been a professor at Montana State University but now owned a ranch on the far eastern border of the county. "Al, I hope you've got the signs up so the vendors know where to go," she said.

"All taken care of, Jeanette," Al said and I escaped before Jeanette thought of something for me to do.

In fact, I had something to do but it didn't have anything to do with the Independence Day celebration. I walked across town and stopped at the county library, a wood-frame building built back in the 1950s but kept in tip-top condition, mostly by volunteer book-lovers in the county, meaning just about everybody.

I went inside and inhaled one my favorite scents, that of hard-cover books. Fillmore County had a good collection of them, both new and old, and there ordinarily was a steady stream of customers. This being the day before the big celebratory day, however, every-one was apparently staying home and resting. The only person other than me in the library sat at the reception desk. She was Mary Dutton Parker, the librarian and the wife of a rancher down south where the grass was greener and lusher than along Ranchers Road. It didn't make the ranching any easier but it did allow for fatter cows, always a good thing.

Mary was also one of those pretty Fillmore County girls, though she was actually born and raised in an adjoining county where they made them about the same—that is lean, pretty, in this case blonde, and perfectly capable of kicking my butt when it came to cowboy-ing. I'd seen Mary on a horse one time when Jeanette and I visited the Parker ranch to consider a tractor they had for sale. While we talked to her husband, Wade, Mary was out on her horse working the cat-tle. I saw her cut into the herd and she and her horse moved those cows around like they were on wheels and glued together. Me? I cut into a herd and they scatter in every direction until I wise up and let the horse do the work. More wisdom from Bill Coulter: When in doubt, let your horse do the thinkin'.

Mary gave me a smile. "What can I do for you, Mike?"

First, I asked about her kids, a boy named Angus and a girl named Maggie who were very cute and very smart. They were fine, she said, Angus being pure boy and the little girl a true princess. She was doing fine, too, as was Wade and also the ranch was getting along "although we could use some rain."

"Your computers up?" I asked.

"This one is," she said, nodding toward the one on her desk. "Want to use it?" I did and she very nicely got out of her chair to let me sit down. "Need help with it?" she asked.

"I need the Internet," I said and she leaned over my shoulder, clicked the mouse a couple of times and a browser appeared. "I think I've got it, Mary," I said. "Thanks."

"No problem," she said and went into the back to give me some privacy.

I had several reasons to do some research on the Internet but the top one on my list was to find out something about Cade Morgan. I typed in his name in the browser's search engine, and got back a number of hits although none of them seemed to be about our man. One was for a baby in Iowa named Cade Morgan, another a fireman in Massachusetts with the same name. I doubted either of them was my Cade Morgan so I typed in "Hollywood" beside his name and searched again. Nothing came back. Whoever he was, Cade wasn't a Hollywood player, at least not under that name. I considered the possibility that he produced or directed under a different name. Thinking about this, I tried Cade without the Morgan and also "producer" and "director." Interestingly, a "Morgan Cade" came back. Mr. Morgan Cade, it turned out, was both a producer and director for Shock and Awe Film Studios in the San Fernando Valley. A quick search gave me a return I expected based on the location of the studio. My work for the majors had included a few visits to one or more of the myriad porn studios out in the valley. Most of the people I met out there were nice folks, trying to earn an honest living in their own peculiar way, but there were some fly-by-nighters out there, too. They were run by, shall we say, unsavory characters? Yes, we shall. I had never heard of Shock and Awe Studios and clicked on their Web site, only to have it refused. A little embarrassed, I sought out Mary and asked her, "Is there a filter on the library's computer?"

Mary gave that some thought, then said, "I don't think it will let you look at naked girls, if that's what you're trying to do."

"I'm not," I swore, holding up three fingers in the Boy Scout manner. "But I am trying to look at the site of a Hollywood studio that makes, well, I guess you might say stag films."

Mary's eyebrows went up at that but then she said, "Is it true you used to be a police detective in California?"

"Yes," I said. "In Los Angeles but I did some work in Hollywood, too. I was private, then."

Mary cut to the chase. "Are you being a detective now, Mike?"

"Yes, and for a good cause," I told her. I hoped it was true.

She sat down at the computer, did a few things to it, and said, "Try it now." She got up and retreated to the back of the library again.

I tried the browser and up came the Shock and Awe Web site. It was pretty basic and so were the women shown on the covers of its DVDs. Basically naked, that is. I was glad Mary had not stuck around. A quick search around the Web site revealed a photograph of a producer-director named Morgan Cade who looked an awful lot like the owner of the old Corbel place. Mr. Cade, the Web site said, was a producer-director of many fine films and a winner of a number of adult film industry awards. There was no mention of him being retired and gone to live among the cows and conservatives of Fillmore County although I did notice that the last of his productions, a flick titled *Dancing with the Stark Naked,* had been released over five years ago. Apparently, Shock and Awe didn't get around to updating its site very often, or maybe it was coasting on its past successes or maybe these kinds of films had an endless shelf life.

Having discovered at least something about Cade Morgan, I went after his buddy Toby, which I knew was bound to be more difficult as I only knew his first name. I also suspected it was fake or at least a nickname. I looked around the Shock and Awe site, hoping for at least a photograph of his ugly mug at a party but had no luck. I went back to the search engine and broadened my search, trying as many combinations I could think of that included Toby, director, producer, pornography, and so forth. Nothing came back that made any sense. I called Mary. "I think I'm through here," I told her.

She came back to her desk, sat down as I vacated her chair, and tapped the necessary keys to, I suppose, put the computer back in a safe mode for the ranchers and the families of Fillmore County. "Did you find what you were looking for?" she asked.

"Yes and no," I said.

"Tell me what you're trying to do," she said. "Maybe I can help." I hesitated and she said, "I can keep a secret, Mike."

She was looking at me with her sincere, and very blue eyes and, so of course, I melted. "You know Cade Morgan? Well, I was trying to find out more about him. I found some stuff but I was wondering about his friend Toby who's been hanging around for the last few weeks. No luck there."

"Cade Morgan made X-rated movies before he came here," she said. "And Toby is a Russian national who invested in his films."

I'm sure my astonishment played across my face. "How did you know that?"

"Mike," she said, "the women in this county know everything."

"Do you know who cut the throats of those cows?"

"No," she confessed. "We've been leaving that one up to the men. Do you think Cade and Toby did it?"

I told her something I hadn't even told myself. "I think they may have had something to do with it. That's only a suspicion. I don't have a thing on them."

"How about those two brothers from Green Planet?" she asked.

I had actually given Brian and Philip a pass, just as all of us had that first day we met them. Now that Mary had brought them up, I gave those boys a good think, conceding, "It would make a kind of strange sense, I guess." I added, "But I've been working with them out on the BLM and I don't think either one of them could use a knife without cutting their own fingers off. I also don't think they're the cow killer types."

She nodded. "And Cade and Toby are?"

"I don't know, Mary. Let's just keep all of this between us, OK?"

She mimed a zipper with two fingers across her pretty face and said, "My lips are sealed."

I left the library and headed back to the Hell Creek Bar. On the way, I considered asking to use the phone in the bar to call some pals I still had in Hollywood to ask them what they knew about Cade. On the other hand, I again reminded myself none of this was any of my business. When I arrived at the bar, Laura and Tanya were not there. Joe said, "They went to the motel to get washed up. Want a beer?"

I did but I had some other things to do. Like all cowboys in town, I needed to visit the hardware store, not to buy anything but to talk to the owner, a man named Normal (not Norman but Normal) and yet another of the Brescoe clan although his last name was Packer. Normal Packer's mother was a Brescoe so that still made him one. "Hi Normal," I said, after pretending to shop along the short aisles of his store. "How's business?"

Of course, that's the wrong question to ask a small businessman in a place like Jericho so it was fifteen minutes later before Normal had finished his discourse on the state of his economic situation, which was naturally not good and never had been. "Well," I said, "maybe things will pick up."

"We'll see," Normal said. "So what's up with you, Mike?"

"This is kind of off the wall," I said, "but you being a Brescoe and all, what's the latest on the mayor and Ted? They doing OK?"

Normal considered me, and said, "As a matter of fact, I think they are. I haven't heard anything, anyway. Why?"

"I always liked Ted and I just wondered."

"You like Ted? I'd say you were about the only one. I don't like him and I don't know anybody in the family who does. He's right much a prick."

"I guess I've always rooted for the underdog," I said, lamely, and made my escape.

I'd pretty much done downtown Jericho since I'd hit the bar, the motel, the library, and the hardware store so about all that was left was the mortuary and fortunately I didn't have any reason to go there. I headed back to the courthouse, catching Jeanette on the steps as she walked out with an entourage of county leaders. They fanned around her and kept going, apparently with their Jeanette "to do" lists.

Jeanette waved me over. "Mike, go on over to the fairgrounds and help the vendors set up. The rodeo folks will also need assistance figuring out where to put their trucks and what to do. You helped last year so you know the drill."

"OK, boss," I said, even though she'd just given me enough work to burn through the entire day and probably most of the night, too. Because I was feeling a little silly, I said, "After I finish that, what else do you want me to do?"

Jeanette didn't take my question as silly at all. She thought about it, then said, "Help the folks putting up the decorations on the main drag. Have you seen Ray?"

I hadn't, nor Amelia, now that I gave it some thought. They had friends in town, though, and I figured they were hanging out with them so that's what I told Jeanette. "Find him and find her," she ordered. "Take him with you to the fairgrounds to help you. Send Amelia to me. I've got work for her to do."

I clicked my heels and saluted with a stiff arm and a *Heil Jeanette*. Actually, I said "OK, boss," and headed back to the motel to consult Mori who knew everything that was happening in town and would probably know the location of the two kids.

Along the way, I ran across Laura and Tanya who were strolling along the sidewalk taking in the sights of Jericho. The ladies seemed to be heading in the direction of the gas station, which was also a restaurant. They confirmed that by saying, "We're going for lunch. Want to come along?"

"Jeanette's got me on a mission," I said. "But how about ordering me two six-inch subs, one veggie for me, one turkey and all the fixings for Ray, and I'll pick them up in about an hour."

They agreed to this and I kept going to the motel. I rang the bell on the office in the back and Mori opened the door. "I'm looking for Ray and Amelia," I said. "Got any idea where they might be?"

"Sure," she said. "They're in room number twelve."

Two teenagers, one male, one female, both in love with each other whether they admitted it or not, were in a motel room together. This was not good. I thanked Mori and abruptly departed, heading for room number twelve which was the room I'd assigned to Laura and Tanya. I hesitated in front of the door, then pounded on it. "Ray, open up!" I cried, a little frantically. Jeanette was going to kill me if what was happening in there was what I feared it was.

It was Amelia who opened the door. She was fully clothed, she didn't appear flushed or out of breath or anything, but when I looked past her, there was Ray lolling on the bed and it looked a bit rumpled. "What's going on?" I asked, knowing full well what had been going on.

But on my second look, I saw the reason for Ray on the bed and the rumpled appearance of it. There was a Monopoly game in its center. Amelia went back to the bed, took up station cross-legged in front of the board and said, "I am killing Ray."

"She is not," Ray said. "I just bought Boardwalk."

"Well, that's all you've got," she said, "and it took nearly all your money to buy it. You're cooked."

What was I thinking? This was Fillmore County, which is to say it was 1950s U.S.A., and teenagers alone in a motel room were more likely to play Monopoly than literally screw around. But I knew that could change on a dime, considering that Ray and Amelia were, after all, the real deal so I said, "Ray, your mother wants you to go with me to the fairgrounds. The vendors always need a lot of help. Amelia, Jeanette wants to see you as soon as possible."

Amelia hopped up. "I'll beat you later, boy," she said.

Ray and I headed to the gas station/restaurant where our subs were waiting for us. We got some cold drinks, chatted briefly with Tanya and Laura who were enjoying the air conditioning, then departed for the fairgrounds via Bob, eating our subs on the way. There, predictably, a Chinese fire drill was going on (as we used to call confusion and turmoil before we all became politically correct and the Chinese bought our country) and Ray and I waded in to help sort everything out. It was midnight before he and I got back to the motel. We were both tired and hungry but more tired so he went to the room he was sharing with his mother and I went to mine. I didn't know where Laura was or Tanya, either. I considered going down to the bar to see if they were there but instead I stretched out on the bed and fell pretty much instantly asleep. This was getting to be a habit and maybe it was time to admit I was getting old. Either that or stop working eighteen hour days.

19

JERICHO WAS BUZZING WITH excitement the next morning when I arose, which was around five in the morning. Brian and Philip were sharing the room with me but I hadn't heard them come in. Brian was on the other bed, asleep on top of the covers and Philip was asleep on the floor in a sleeping bag. They were lightly snoring and I didn't do anything to wake them up. Instead, I stepped outside to a bright white sun already rising and skies so clear I could see all the way to the moon, which was also hanging up there, the man in it apparently enjoying the view of Fillmore County on its biggest day of the year. Every crook, crevice, and alley in town had a pickup parked in it and people were out and about. It was sort of like a family reunion, everyone in the county related by ranching, if not genetically, and come to town to enjoy the day. I spotted clusters of men, their hats pushed back on their heads, mugs of coffee in their hands, standing around telling lies and laughing. A few women were out, too, most of them on the way somewhere. Both the library and the bar were already open, their doors swinging open and closed as patrons went in and out. The parade wasn't supposed to start until ten o'clock but already the fire truck and the floats were lined up. It looked like Jeanette was going to have a tough time keeping them from starting early.

I headed to the gas station/restaurant and joined a throng of folks for breakfast. Laura, Tanya, Ray, Amelia, and Jeanette were there although she was just leaving as I came in. She was wearing jeans, a somewhat frilly blue sleeveless cotton blouse which showed off her lovely arms, and cowgirl boots. She also had her hair down which is the way I like it, not that she cares. "Did you get the vendors squared away?" she asked as I held the door open for her.

"Sure did."

"More will be coming this morning. Go up there and make sure they get set up."

"OK, boss. Do I have time for breakfast?"

"Yes, if you make it fast. And Mike? I want you to look after those fossil hunters today. Especially Pick. There are people around here who might try to play tricks on him. You know what I mean."

"OK, boss," I said, mentally tacking one more thing on my work list. Look after Pick. Great.

Jeanette left and I went inside, nodded to the Blackie Butte crew, which I realized was missing our intrepid dinosaur hunter. Once I loaded my plate with eggs and biscuits, I sat down with Ray and Amelia, there being room at their booth, and looked over my shoulder where Laura and Tanya were sitting. "Where's Pick?" I asked them.

"He won't be up until noon," Laura said. "He loves his air conditioning."

I was tired enough I didn't filter my next question. "Where is he sleeping?"

"With us," Laura said.

"In the other bed," Tanya added.

This made Amelia giggle. "And where did you sleep, young lady?" I asked, recalling she was supposed to bunk with the dino gals.

"With Ray," she answered, sweetly.

"In the other bed," Ray said, shooting eye darts at Amelia. "Mom stayed with Aunt Ophelia."

I was aware that Jeanette had relatives in town, specifically an aunt. But that was a never mind. "Did she know you and Amelia were sleeping in the same room?"

Ray didn't say anything, which was an answer. "Come here, young man," I said and stood up and went over by the ice maker.

He joined me. "Yeah?"

"Listen, did anything happen?"

"Yeah. She beat me at Monopoly."

"You'll call me sir and don't give me that. You know what I mean."

"Nothing happened, Mike, I swear. Sir."

I looked Ray in the eye and could tell he was telling the truth. "Look, pardner," I said, "a thing like this could get out and hurt Amelia's reputation. You wouldn't want that, would you?"

"No sir, but—"

"There's no but. Tonight, she sleeps somewhere else. I don't care where but not with you. OK?"

Ray nodded. "OK."

I clapped him on the shoulder. "Hurry up and eat. We've got work to do."

We went back to our breakfast, choked it down, and headed out for the fairgrounds, running into the Marsh brothers going inside. "Can we help?" they asked.

"Yes," I said. "Stay out of trouble. And don't say a damn thing that might be perceived as environmental to one of these cowboys. You got that?"

"Can we talk about the dinosaurs?" Brian asked.

"No! Don't say anything at all."

Ray and I took off, arriving at the rodeo grounds to find not a

Chinese fire drill but a full-blown Chinese disaster, not that the Chinese had anything to do with it. Vendors were squabbling over their locations, there was an impromptu roundup going on since a couple of bucking bulls had escaped, and the sun was already beating down. As soon as everyone spotted me, they lined up in a polite queue, each telling me their problems and allowing me to sort it all out. Actually, we were ignored but Ray and I charged in, anyway, and did our best to help.

We worked until we were sweaty messes and we didn't make the parade although I understand it was pretty grand. There was the volunteer fire department fire truck, two floats, one featuring the girls basketball team at the high school and the other sponsored by the mortuary, which had, appropriately enough, the owner and his family members dressed up like Montana pioneers (they're all dead, you see). There were also some rodeo contestants riding their fancy horses, and a red convertible containing a local beauty queen, a Brescoe, of course, her sash reading MISS WALLEYE, which referred to, I believe, the fish and not any imperfection of the young lady. I also heard Pick was part of the parade, not because he was supposed to, but because he got lost going to the gas station/restaurant for breakfast and found himself in the middle of main street between the two floats. When people started to cheer, he started waving. That's our Pick.

After the parade, the pickups filled up with folks and headed for the fairground, disgorging ranchers, their ladies, and their kids to swill on hot dogs, soda pop, and popcorn; peruse the horses, calves, pigs, sheep, and rodeo riders getting ready for the competition; and visiting with each other as the movable Fillmore County family reunion/Independence Day celebration continued, only at a slightly different location.

I spotted the Haxbys or, more accurately, they spotted me and the next thing I knew I was being confronted by Sam, Jack, and Carl, which was a lot of Haxbys to be confronted by. "Heard you took a walk around my place," Sam said, and by the tone of his deep voice, I knew he was not pleased by my little sojourn on his lease.

I cut my eyes toward Carl, hoping for a twinkle in his eye meaning I was getting teased, but it wasn't there. I said, "I apologized to Carl for that, Sam, and I'm apologizing to you, here and now. I'm sorry and I mean that. I should have checked with you first."

"Carl told me all that, Mike," Sam replied, "but I have to say I'm completely surprised and disappointed in you. I know you're still new out here but I thought ten years was enough for you to learn a few of our rules. A man could get shot, he wanders where he's not supposed to go."

This irritated me. I don't like to be threatened, especially after I had sincerely apologized for something I didn't have to apologize for. "If a man could get shot, Sam," I said, "another man could go to prison for a very long time."

Sam scowled at that. "Around here, we don't send people to prison who defend their property from trespassers."

"I was on BLM, Sam, under a BLM permit."

"You were on land that we Haxbys have tended to for over a century. How would Jeanette like it if I and my boys started trespassing on her BLM?"

"You'll have to ask Jeanette," I said. "But I don't think she'd shoot you."

Sam had another gripe. "You got those damn fossil hunters and those damn green wacko brothers out there on the Square C. You tell Jeanette we think she should kick them all out."

About then, someone came to my defense although it was the last person in the world I wanted on my side. Ted Brescoe. "You don't own the BLM, Sam Haxby, not one square inch of it," he said, stepping up after a bout of eavesdropping. "And I'll tell you something else. I've contracted with a surveyor and we're going to see exactly where your property line runs. I think you've been moving your fence twenty to thirty feet every few years, encroaching on the BLM. If I find out you've been cheating, your lease won't be renewed. I'll have the FBI on you, too, trust me on that, and maybe I'll have them out to see what you've got hidden away on your ranch. Wouldn't surprise me if you had an atom bomb."

Ted's discourse left us all a little breathless, including Ted. To my surprise, Sam actually seemed deflated and didn't argue back. Maybe it was because the FBI is both respected and feared in these parts and it was at least conceivable a BLM agent could bring his big federal brothers to kick over some cans. "Come on, boys," Sam said, and he and his two sons went off without another word.

Ted watched them go, a tight smile stretched across his ugly face. "You have trouble with them again, Mike, you come to me." This was a nice thing to say, which was unlike Ted so he salvaged his reputation by adding, "That surveyor's gonna also look at the Square C fence. Jeanette's lease might be canceled, too."

"Ted, we know the fence is wrong. Your agency put it up wrong so it wouldn't have to work so hard stringing it across Blackie Butte."

"Maybe so," Ted snorted, "but then you tore it down. That's destruction of government property. You could end up in jail."

"Have a real nice day, Ted," I said and got out of his sight. In fact, I decided to get out of all their sights, even Jeanette's, and enjoy myself a rodeo. I figured I'd earned it.

20

THE RODEO BEGAN AND, for the most part, it was a normal Fillmore County Independence Day Rodeo, which was pretty fine. There was the pig chase, the mutton busting (kids riding sheep, no lie), the calf roping, the barrel race, team roping, and the bull riding and bronc busting. The audience was as knowledgeable as any that ever watched a rodeo, a gathering of ranchers who made their living with cows and horses, and therefore were all the more appreciative at what they were seeing. I didn't go up in the stands where there was shade, being too dirty and sweaty to sit beside anybody, so I just hung around at the beer garden and sucked down some brews. The garden was up on a berm so I had a pretty good view of the proceedings. I'd seen Laura, Tanya, and Pick come in earlier and they'd gone off somewhere. Then I'd seen Pick by himself, down by the hot dog stand, but I didn't see where he'd gotten himself off to after that. Anyway, there I was, minding my own business watching the bucking broncs toss off their riders when Ray came running up. "The Haxbys got hold of Pick!" he said and I dropped my beer and went chasing after him to see what was what.

Ray led me around the corral where the bucking horses were

kept. I saw, to my astonishment, Pick climbing up on one of the chutes, the Haxbys—father and sons—urging him along. Even more astonishing, Pick seemed intent on climbing aboard the horse in the chute. I yelled at him and Pick looked up and grinned and waved. He looked like he was in charge of the world. Of course, he wasn't in charge of anything except getting his neck broke. The three Haxby men were looking like the proverbial cats who'd eaten the proverbial canaries. "Don't get on that horse, Pick!" I cried. He looked over at me, cocked his head, and gave me another big, proud grin.

"Stop him!" I yelled at the Haxbys just as the announcer announced: "Ladies and gentlemen! Now, a special treat. As you know, Fillmore County has been invaded by dinosaur hunters!" There came a smattering of applause and boos.

"No-o-o-o-o-o!" I yelled and started climbing up on the fence to make my way to the chute.

The announcer kept going. "Now, in chute number three, we have Dr. Pick Pickford, one of the greatest dinosaur hunters ever known, riding a saddle bronc today to show us how to do it. His horse is Tornado!"

"Not Tornado!" I cried while Sam, Jack, and Carl laughed and slapped their legs. Then Pick climbed into the saddle, clutched the lead from the halter, the gate opened, and Tornado lived up to his name.

Looking back on it, I don't think Pick was actually on that horse for more than maybe a quarter-second. Probably less. Tornado sent him flying into the air pretty much before the paleontologist/horse combination got all the way out of the chute. Pick went up and up, flailing. Then he did a very stupid thing. He allowed himself to fall down on top of Tornado. The bucking bronco right away let Dr. Pickford know that this was not a good idea by indulging in a couple of stiff-legged hops followed by throwing his back hooves straight up toward the sky. Technically, this maneuver is known as sunfishing, don't ask me why. Anyway, it was good enough to send Pick flying like a rag doll through the air until he plowed face down into the churned-up dirt and not a small amount of horse, calf, and sheep manure in the arena. Tornado kept bucking until he saw his rider in the dirt. Then he stopped as if to savor his victory. I swear I saw an evil grin cross that horse's face. Oh, yes, there are some horses who are evil.

Anyway, I don't know how I got over that fence. Maybe I jumped over. I found myself running over to Pick who was just lying there, looking pretty bent. I knelt beside him. "Pick! Are you all right?"

Pick had his eyes open, which I thought was a good sign unless, of course, he was dead and couldn't close them. But then his eyelids fluttered and I knew everything was going to be OK unless, of course, he was paralyzed or dying. Either way, I knew Jeanette was going to kick my butt.

The Haxbys opened one of the gates and strolled over. "We were just having a little fun, Mike," Sam said.

"We asked him if he wanted to do this and he said he sure did," Carl added. "Hell, what were we supposed to do? He's an adult."

"He's not an adult, you rat bastard!" I yelled. "He's a paleontologist!"

"Can we help?" Jack wondered, his thumbs stuck in his pockets.

"You've done enough," I growled and the Haxbys took the hint and skedaddled, waving to the cheering crowd as they went.

The next thing I knew I heard the outer gates of the arena open and the *beep-beep-beep* of the county ambulance backing in and then there were two hysterical women on top of us, namely Laura and Tanya who, ignoring the paramedics' entreaties not to move Pick, clutched him into their arms, rocking him to and fro, his head wobbling like a broken doll's. "Oh, Pick," Laura sobbed, "don't die."

Tanya was wailing and crying something in Russian. At last, Pick seemed to come around. He blinked a couple of times, then his eyes landed on me. He allowed a crooked grin. "Hi, Mike. What did I do wrong?"

"You trusted the Haxbys," I said. "And you got on the wrong horse. Hell, with you, that would be *any* horse."

Our next arrival, stiff-arming the paramedics who still hadn't managed to examine Pick, was Jeanette. She pushed in, observed the situation, and announced, "He'll be all right. You boys take over." That meant the paramedics and they finally did their thing, loading Pick into the ambulance. The crowd reacted with polite applause while the announcer encouraged everybody to visit the beer garden and the 4-H concession. The ambulance sped off somewhere, probably just out of sight since Fillmore County didn't have a hospital.

While Laura and Tanya continued to bawl, Jeanette drew me aside. "Didn't I tell you to look out for Pick?"

I did my best John Wayne, hoping to amuse myself out of trouble. "Well, pilgrim," I said, "the Haxbys got the drop on me."

Jeanette spotted Sam and his sons looking at us from the fence. They raised their beers. "It was a joke, Jeanette," Sam called.

"Sam Haxby, I'll take care of you later!" she yelled. She looked at me. "Sometimes, Mike, you disappoint me more than my heart can stand."

So much for amusement. I rallied as best I could. "I didn't know I was supposed to hold his hand all day."

"That's a lame excuse and you know it. I trusted you!"

I started to mention the hours of labor (most of it free and above and beyond the call of duty by any standard of humanity) that I'd put in since we'd come in to Jericho but I let it pass. Once again, I hadn't done my boss's bidding and I knew it. I just shrugged and let her glare at me until she got tired of it and stomped off. Laura and Tanya had already gone somewhere, which left me standing alone in the arena. "Mike," the announcer said, "you want to clear out so we can get on with the show?"

I sought out the announcer, gave him a one finger salute and then strolled on out through the gate, taking my own sweet time and feeling the fool, which, of course, I was.

Figuring Ray would get a ride, I gathered up Laura and Tanya and took them into town in Bob, finding the ambulance sitting in the motel parking lot. Along the way, neither woman would spare a single word in my direction. I guess everybody was blaming me for Pick's little adventure. The paramedics were coming out of one of the rooms. "He's going to be fine," one of them said. "No broken bones, no sign of concussion, just some contusions and hurt feelings." Laura and Tanya leaped from Bob and ran inside the room.

I wandered on over. Pick was stretched out on a bed and his ladies were seeing to his comfort and health. When Laura looked up, I saw her face was streaked with tears. She said, "Why didn't you take care of him? Jeanette said you would." Tanya shot eye darts at me and I took that as my cue to leave, closing the door behind me.

I went to my room, stripped, took a long shower, and then stretched out on the bed until I thought to myself, "I should get drunk." I dressed in some fresh duds and headed for the Hell Creek Bar to make my thought a reality, only to see that the crowd from the rodeo was now descending on the bar for the annual Fillmore County Independence Day Barbeque which always follow the annual Fillmore County Independence Day Rodeo. This, now that the schedule was coming back to me, would be followed by the annual Fillmore County Independence Day Dance held at the Hell Creek Marina on Fort Peck Lake, some twenty miles north of us. We were just warming up, folks.

I decided to spread my drunk out, although it was still my firm intention. I went inside and caught Joe's eye and gave him the OK sign, which was my signal for a g&t and then two fingers, which meant I wanted it strong. Joe accomplished my request, putting my drink in a plastic go-cup, and I gulped down half of it, then wandered back outside where the steaks were a-cookin'. There were some good sides being served as well so I got in line with some other cow-boys, most of whom I recognized but a few were either rodeo riders or Texans since they were wearing huge, ornate belt buckles. If you ask a Montana cowpoke, he'll tell you we don't sport those things because if you have to do that much advertising, you're probably trying too hard to sell the product. Deep in my heart, though, I kind of wished I had one of those buckles.

I made small talk with a hired hand from down south. He worked on a Brescoe ranch, he said, and was from Kentucky by way of Iraq where he'd been deployed out of his reserve unit four times as a ma-chine gunner on a Humvee, which I took as dangerous work. "I didn't leave no forwarding address this time," he told me. "I think I done my part."

I agreed with him. Four times in a combat zone, the war gods just have to take notice and want to rub you out. Or maybe that was the gin that was talking, I don't know. I finished it off.

I told the nice lady who was taking the money for the food I didn't want a steak, just the sides and she looked at me like I was crazy. "What are you?" she asked. "A vegetarian?"

"Yes ma'am," I said and her expression changed to one of shock.

She took my money, anyway, and sent me on my way. I got maca-roni salad, cole slaw, green beans, mashed potatoes, and a couple of homemade whole wheat buns and sat at one of the picnic tables.

Joe swung by and put a brimming plastic cup beside my plate.

"You look like you need this," he said and kept going. It was another g&t, just as stiff as the last one. I silently thanked him.

Well, this was pleasant and pretty soon, stomach full and mildly intoxicated, I became an observer of the human condition, rather than an active participant. I sat at the table, my chin resting on my hands and just watched Fillmore County do its thing. What I saw of greatest interest was Sam Haxby, his two boys, and Ted Brescoe. Ted was up on his toes delivering a lecture and Sam and sons were listening and didn't appear to like what they were hearing. I guessed Ted was giving them another what-for about their BLM. Then, I saw none other than Cade Morgan, or maybe Morgan Cade, appear or, as I liked to think of it, slither into view accompanied by good old Toby. Now that I had a moment to think about it, I decided Toby looked like Mister Clean's evil twin. He even had the gold earring.

Cade and Toby looked around, took note of Ted and the Haxbys, took two steps toward them, then unfortunately noticed yours truly and came over and sat down across from me. "A great day, isn't it, Mike?" Cade asked me. Toby didn't say anything. He just stared at me, sort of menacingly, which he was very good at.

When I didn't reply, Cade continued, saying, "So, how are things out at the dino dig?"

"We haven't found anything," I said, hoping to make him go away. "A dry hole."

"I do not believe you," Toby said.

"We might come out to see for ourselves," Cade said.

"You already did," I pointed out, "and you know we're digging up a Triceratops."

"What about the Tyrannosaur?" Toby demanded. "This is what we would like to hear."

"Tyrannosaur?" I spotted Joe and raised my cup. "I don't know nothing about no stinking Tyrannosaur."

Cade said, "You know, Mike, I really don't know much about you. I mean, your economic situation and all."

"I know all about you," I said, letting the gin do the talking. "Shock and Awe. But is your name Cade Morgan or Morgan Cade?"

Cade or Morgan didn't seem bothered that I had checked up on him. He smiled. "Well, it paid the bills, Mike. You do what you have to do. In Hollywood, I was Morgan Cade. Here, I'm Cade Morgan. I hope you'll keep my little secret. No use getting the folks upset. I want to be a good neighbor."

Joe swung by, left another cup, took my empty one, and disappeared. "How about you, Toby?" I asked after another swallow of the transparent miracle drug. "What's your real name? Ivan? Yuri? Sergei? Are you a member of the Russian mob? Just wondering."

"My name is Toby," he said with a look that could kill. I was glad it was just the look. His muscles could probably do the real thing.

"Toby is Russian," Cade said. "But part of the mob? Does he look like a criminal to you?"

"Why, yes, Cade, he does," I said.

"Well, looks are deceiving," Cade replied, amiably. "Now, let's talk money, OK? All you have to do is let us know the progress of the dig. What was found, what Pick says about it, that kind of thing."

"OK. How much?"

"Twenty bucks a day."

I whistled. "Hello, big spender."

"Fifty," Toby said.

"How about a hundred?"

"Done," Cade said.

"I'll take the first hundred days in advance," I said. "Ten thousand dollars. Pay up."

This provoked Toby, don't ask me why. He crashed his huge fist on the table, rattling my plate and nearly tipping over my drink. I caught it just in time. "You are not serious!"

"Toby, you are absolutely correct," I confessed. I looked him in the eye and then did the same with Cade. "You want me to be a spy. What I can't figure out is why?"

"It's nothing sinister, Mike," Cade said. "We're just interested. If there's a valuable dinosaur on Jeanette's property, maybe there's one on mine. If so, I'd like to hire Pick to come look. That's all. Just idle curiosity."

This I doubted but I didn't get to express it because Ted Brescoe swung by, apparently through threatening the Haxbys with me next on his list. He was feeling his oats that day, I guess. "I got more to say to you, Mike," he said.

I made my regrets to Cade and Toby, who looked properly chagrined that I was leaving their company to consult with our local BLM agent. "What's going on out there?" Ted asked. "What have you found?"

Maybe they all thought the gin would loosen my tongue, I don't know, but it seemed like everyone thought I was the dinosaur gossip of all time. "Ask Pick," I said, "or Jeanette. I'm just a hired hand what don't know nothin'."

Ted gave me a sour look. "I know you know this much," he said. "You know how to screw another man's wife!"

I realized that Ted was drunk. I guess it takes one to know one. I also realized the last thing he'd uttered had been in the twelve decibel range because everyone around us stopped talking and just stared. "Let me buy you a drink, Ted," I said.

Ted was having none of it. He gave me an evil glare and stalked off. Ray came by. "You sure are causing trouble," he said.

"Innocent of all charges," I maintained. Ray laughed and suggested perhaps I was drunk. "Not drunk enough," I replied. Still, I thought I'd better get out of Dodge so I went back to Tellman's and fell into bed. There I snoozed until Ray let himself inside. I guess Mori had given him a key. I opened one eye when he said, "How come you're not ready to go?"

"Go where?"

"The dance."

I got up because I felt like dancing. I was also confused and still intoxicated as I fell into Bob's passenger seat. Ray was driving. "Where's your mom?" I asked.

"She and Mayor Brescoe decided to go out to the marina together."

"Really? Since when are they such friends?"

"I don't know. I'm just a kid. Nobody tells me anything. Amelia went with them, too. I guess they had girl talk to talk."

"How about Ted the aggrieved husband?"

"I saw him in his own truck."

"OK. Let's go down the list. Pick, Laura, Tanya, Brian, Philip?"

"Pick's truck. Pick and the girls in front, boys in back. Anybody else you want to know about?"

"Cade Morgan and his buddy?"

"Don't know about them. You ready?"

I was ready and so off we went along the twenty miles of dirt road to the Hell Creek State Park and the Hell Creek Marina for the annual Fillmore County Independence Day Dance. Overhead, the moon was out, bright and luminous in a clear, starry sky. It was a gentle, peaceful evening, which, even through the gin, reminded me that Montana was probably up to no good.

21

THE DANCE AT THE marina was nice. The owner had strung Japanese lanterns and other cheerful and colorful lights around the dancing deck, which was behind the little A-frame office/restaurant/bait store that had burned down twice and been built back during the ten years of my life in the county. There was a cowboy band, playing the latest cowboy dance tunes, and those ranchers who had wives or girlfriends who'd nagged them enough to make them learn how to dance, were out doing the two-step with their ladies.

There was a nice breeze coming off the lake, cool and refreshing. There were more steaks on the grill and hamburgers and hot dogs, too. I settled for a bag of chips, which tasted just fine. There was the hum of pleasant conversation as an undertone to the dance band. The only discordant note was the yelping noise of Ted Brescoe who had moved his unhappiness to the marina. He was now busily crabbing at Brian and Philip. In fact, he was giving it to them with both barrels. "You morons!" he screamed. "I gave you permission to do your idiotic study and you betrayed me! Well, you're out there illegally now. I'll have you both in jail before this is over. There will be a big fine, too. Just wait!"

Brian and Philip, plucky lads, were giving it back to him. They were both a little drunk, just like Ted, and were raising hell about the BLM and how it was an outlaw agency that needed to be reined in. "You sell the people's land to the highest bidder!" Brian shrilled, revealing his pinko, left-wing, Socialist leanings. Otherwise, I thought he was a fine fellow, a pretty fair digger, and a secret Republican because he and his buddy had attacked Blackie Butte so arduously. But, under pressure, they had both reverted to type and there they were, screaming lefty epithets at our federal man. Philip even punched his finger into Ted's chest and said, "You be careful, you be careful, or I will hit you."

I will hit you? That's what he said. Philip wasn't very good at threats. Anyway, somebody asked them to move their fight away and they stalked off in opposite directions. For a little while, things got back to normal, everybody having a fine time.

I was pleased to see Ray and Amelia dancing. Since I can two-step with the best of them, I walked up to Laura who was chatting with Aaron and Flora Feldmark and asked her to dance. I halfway expected her to slap my face because of my failure to protect Pick from himself but she smiled and said, "Of course, Mike" and took my hand.

As we coasted around the platform, I asked her, "Have you forgiven me yet?"

"For what?" she wondered.

"You know. Pick and his bucking bronco adventure."

"Oh, that. I was just upset. I was never really mad at you."

"Good. How's Pick?"

"Good enough to come to the dance," she said. "You see? He's right over there."

He *was* right over there, beneath a string of Japanese lanterns, and pretty much cozied up to Miss Walleye who was looking at him like he was the second coming. I guess she'd never seen a golden-haired California dino-dude before.

"I think he might get lucky tonight," Laura said.

"How about me?" It was the gin talking, of course.

"You never know. Which is it to be, me or Tanya?"

I gave that some thought for about as long as Pick stayed aboard Tornado. "You. Of course."

"Well, Tanya likes you, too, and I reckon we're both ready to bounce the bedsprings with somebody."

I was thrilled beyond belief. It sounded like a twofer, not that I'm into that, but that's what it sounded like. Of course, I thought there was a possibility she was kidding. I also didn't much like the way she put it, "bounce the bedsprings with *somebody*," like I was just convenient or something. "You and Tanya want to flip a coin?" I asked.

She laughed. "Did you think I was serious?"

Crushed, I said, "Well, I hoped you were."

"Maybe I was," she said. "Let me think about it. Buy me a drink."

"I'll buy you three drinks."

"Ah, the old get-her-drunk strategy."

"Candy's dandy but liquor's quicker," I said. "Shakespeare."

"Yeah, Shakespeare Ogden Nash," Laura said, endearing herself to me. I mean she knew who Ogden Nash was! I was impressed.

The band played on, Laura and I two-stepped until Tanya tapped her on the shoulder. "Me, please," she said, fluttering her long Russian eyelashes.

Laura gave away graciously and I took Tanya in my arms, pleasantly astonished at how small her waist was. It felt like I could put my hand around it if I tried. She was also a good dancer. In fact, I said, "You're a good dancer."

"I studied ballet," she said, "before I came to the United States."

"It shows," I said. "Can you do the two-step on your toes?"

Tanya laughed and spun out of my arms. She moved into the center of the platform and did a pirouette and a couple of other fancy ballet moves. When she was done, everybody applauded. I happened to look over toward a dark corner and caught Cade and Toby standing there. Cade was applauding but Toby wasn't. He looked pissed but what else was new? I waved at them and Cade waved back. Toby sent me air kisses. Yeah, right.

Tanya gave a little bow with her legs crossed and came back to me and we started the two-step again. Her eyes were bright. "I love Montana," she said. "It is so nice here and the people, they are nice, too."

"I agree," I said. "That's why I'm here."

This was all lovely but then here came old Ted again. He stomped up to Mayor Brescoe who was sitting alone on one of the benches that ringed the dance floor. "Stand up!" he yelled.

"Ted, please," she said, but she stood up whereupon to the astonishment of just about everybody, he slapped her hard in the face. She abruptly sat down, her hand to her cheek, while he called her a whore and a couple other ugly names.

Naturally, Ted was jumped by about a dozen cowboys who dragged him off. I was one of them. We carried him into a little copse of woods behind the marina and slapped him around a little. Not too hard, just enough to make him cry. The Haxbys were with me, so was Brian and Philip. So was Cade and Toby, for that matter, although they were just gawking. We left Ted slumped against a tree although he cried after us, "I know who you are, every one of you! I'll get you for this, don't think I won't!" Ted was such a sweet fellow.

I returned to the dance floor but Tanya was nowhere in sight. Laura was dancing with some Texas cowboy and she looked pretty happy. I'd missed out there. I looked around until I spied Jeanette. I still had enough gin in me to ask her to dance but before I could, Pick, leaving Miss Walleye for the moment, asked her. They danced, then he deposited her back on her bench and took up again with the game fish beauty. I guess I was feeling pretty sorry for myself because I hit the bar again and this time I did the drunk thing absolutely proper. I had bought a bottle of gin, screw the tonic. Screw Jeanette. Screw them all. Well, I wanted to screw somebody but it wasn't going to happen so I screwed myself with my gin.

I sat down on one of the picnic tables out in the grass and admired the moon glittering on the lake until Edith, of all people, came over. "Have you seen Ted?" she asked.

"You mean since we beat him up?"

"I'm sorry you fellows did that. It was between him and me."

Intoxicated as I was, I was still prepared to set her straight. "Any time a man hits a woman, it's no longer between him and her."

She shrugged. "Well, maybe he had the right, Mike, I don't know."

"I'm telling you, Edith. No man ever has the right to hit a woman."

"If you say so."

"I say so. Do you want to have sex?"

She laughed. "I love you, you big jerk."

"No, you don't. But I appreciate the thought."

She gave me a hug, then went off somewhere. My next visitor was Jeanette. "Have you seen Ted Brescoe?"

"Not since I helped the others beat him up."

"Well, he's missing."

"How can you tell?"

"Don't be an idiot, Mike." She peered at me. "Well, I do believe you're drunk."

"How can you tell?"

Jeanette went away. I kept hitting the gin and admiring the

moon. Sam Haxby came over. "Mike, tell Edith I don't know where Ted is. She thinks I did something with him."

"Where is she?"

"Over there."

"What did you do with him?"

"Nothing, I swear."

"Have her come over here and I'll tell her."

She never came over and, anyway, I was feeling pretty sleepy. Then Ray asked me if I was ready to go home. At the time, I was lying on the picnic table looking up at the stars and the satellites go over. OK, I was unconscious but I woke up long enough to consider Ray's question and suggested that perhaps he should go away and leave me the hell alone. Later, he came back to tell me he was going back to town but he was leaving me Bob to drive in after I'd sobered up. He also told me everybody had given up looking for Ted and, even though his truck was still in the parking area, the consensus of opinion was he'd caught a ride into town with somebody because he was too drunk to drive.

"Who would give Ted a ride?" I asked and then faded to dark.

Morning comes early in summertime Montana, which I think I've already mentioned, I woke to shouts out on the water. I sat up. Well, I actually rolled off the table and threw up, almost the same thing. I pulled myself back aboard the bench and listened to the shouting. Finally, I managed to squint enough to see there was a bass boat out there and they were yelling something about something being in the water. I looked around to see a more responsible person than myself and saw no one at all. So I staggered down to the dock. Pretty soon, the bass boat came roaring in. It contained two Canadians identified by their ball caps emblazoned with Calgary Stampede logos. Another clue was their T-shirts which heralded, no lie, *Canadians Do It More Often And Find It More Appealing*.

Anyway, one of them said, "There's a body in the water out there."

I absorbed that and said, "Describe it to me."

"I think it's a man," the other one said.

"Well, that narrows it down," I said.

"It does?"

Actually, it did because I knew exactly who it was. "Take me out there," I said, tiredly.

I climbed aboard their boat with shaky legs, then tried to gulp in as much fresh air as I could while they were taking me out to the body. When we got there, I held my head and kept my eyes closed against the glare of the sun richocheting off the lake. "Pull the damn thing in," I said.

The Canadian fishermen were thinking by then they'd asked the wrong person to help them. One of them said, "Are you somebody, like, official?"

"Yeah," I responded, still holding my throbbing head, "I'm the law. Haul him in."

They hauled the body in. It wasn't easy from the sound of it. A lot of grunting and then I heard them get the thing in which flopped like a big dead fish on the deck. I wanted to look at it but I didn't, fearful I might toss my cookies on top of it, which probably wouldn't have been considered professional by my fishermen who were convinced I was the "law."

"Take his pulse," I said.

They did and the report came back there wasn't one. Then one of them said, "He has his throat cut."

"Ear to ear," the other one said.

"Looks like somebody whopped him on the head, too."

That explained the no pulse thing. "Back to shore," I ordered and we sped back to shore and I crawled off the boat. By then, the owner of the marina, a man named Earl Williams, and his two adult sons were down there.

"Where should we take him, Mike?"

It looked like everybody wanted to keep me in charge so I said, "Lay him out on one of your picnic tables." I figured if it was good enough for me, it was good enough for Ted Brescoe who, of course, was the dead body. "And call the state police. Tell them they don't need an ambulance. A pickup will do."

Earl went off somewhere while his stout sons carried Ted to one of the tables, there to lay him down. One of the fishermen came over to me where I was sitting on the grass, my head down. "You gonna be OK?" he asked.

I raised my hand and waved and he went away. After a bit, I managed to get to my feet. It was time to take a closer look at Ted. But before I could study our BLM agent's remains, I was intercepted by Earl. "I called the state, Mike. They said they'd send somebody from Billings. They said it would take at least four hours to get up here so they're sending the paramedics in Jericho to pick him up."

"All right," I said. "After I look at Ted, put him somewhere cool until they get here."

Earl gave me a funny look. "Ted? This isn't Ted. I don't know who it is."

Well, that fried it. What we had was some drunken cowboy or fisherman who'd pitched off the dock in the night. But then I thought, wait a minute, didn't those fishermen tell me his throat had been cut and his head bashed in? As I got closer, I still didn't know who our body was until at last I saw his shaved head and the gold earring in his ear. *Toby!* "Man," I said, "I figured you to be the killer, not the killee."

Toby didn't answer but his sliced throat told its own story. I lifted up his head and observed the back of his skull, which had a dent in it. It looked like maybe a hammer was the weapon. Lowering his head, I searched his pockets, finding his wallet. His driver's license, issued by the state of Nevada, identified him as Sergei Tobovski and gave his address as a street in Reno. Even his photo on the plastic card looked threatening. "Now, who would dare attack you?" I wondered, then kept searching. There wasn't much, just some car keys. I looked in the parking lot and saw a white Hyundai sedan, probably a rental car and probably Toby's. I looked some more and found a folded up and very soggy paper. When I unfolded it, I discovered it was actually a notice that read:

> *This range improvement project brought to you by the Green Monkey Wrench Gang. No address—we're everywhere. No phone—we'll be in touch.*

Earl was watching me. "You didn't kill him, did you, Mike?"

"No, Earl," I said, "and I don't have a clue who did, either. The only person who deserved killing last night was Ted Brescoe. That's why I thought the body was his."

"Ted's in room thirteen," Earl said. He looked at me. "You're not going to beat him up again, are you?"

"I didn't beat him up before. Well, not by myself, anyway."

I walked over to the motel, which was actually a string of doublewides. I climbed up on the deck attached to unit number thirteen and knocked on the door. To my astonishment, Tanya opened it. "Mike," she said. She was dressed in a white terry cloth robe.

It took me a moment to gather myself. "I was told Ted Brescoe was here," I finally managed to croak.

"And here I am," came the answer from the couch. Ted Brescoe, alive and well, stood up and strutted to the door.

I looked at Tanya. "Well," I gulped, stupidly. "What do you know?"

She raised an eyebrow, but remained silent.

"Need a word, Ted," I said. "Outside."

Tanya moved out of the way. Ted came outside and I asked, "Where were you last night?" It was a dumb question but it was the best I could do, considering the circumstances.

"Who wants to know?" he asked.

"A man was murdered last night," I said, dully. "You know anything about that?"

"Why would I?"

I ignored that for now. "It was Cade Morgan's friend, a man who called himself Toby."

"Don't know him. Ain't got no business with Cade Morgan. He gave up the Corbel leases as soon as he bought the property." He studied me. "Hey, you don't look so good. You upset because of this Russian whore? Shit, Mike, a hundred dollars is all it takes. Go ahead. You can have my sloppy seconds."

I hit him. I hit him real hard. I hit him so hard I knocked him clear off his feet and he went down like a sack of potatoes. Then I kicked him. After that, I reached down and picked him up and knocked him down again. Tanya opened the door and dragged me off him. "Get me a knife, Tanya," I said. "I'll cut his throat and throw him into the lake. Maybe they'll think there's an epidemic."

"No, Mike, please. It's OK. Really."

"What do you mean?"

She stood up and walked to the edge of the deck. I came over and put my hand on her shoulder. She didn't move. Instead, she said, "Once a whore, Mike, always a whore."

I took my hand away and sat down in one of the deck chairs and just went kind of numb.

22

WELL, WHAT'S A COWBOY to do when his gal who isn't his gal bounces the old bedsprings with as nasty a creep who ever drew breath? I had beat up Ted which was nice but it seemed like I should do more. What that should be I wasn't sure so I just sat there, feeling miserable and maybe a little unnerved because of Toby, not that I much cared he'd been murdered. I mostly hated that murder had come to the place where I'd retreated to get away from murder. It had taken ten years but now the ugly things people do to other people had finally caught up with me even in deepest Fillmore County.

Tanya had gone inside room number thirteen and closed the door. I continued to sit until Ted came around. His lip was split and he had a black eye. We'd been easy on him the night before, just cuffing him around the shoulders and such, but this time I had done a pretty good number on his face. It didn't make me happy. It made me feel ashamed. So what I did was go to work like the homicide detective I used to be. That meant asking the suspect questions, not busting his chops.

Ted wasn't interested in cooperating. When I asked him if he knew anything about Toby being murdered, he said, through swollen lips, "You're gonna be sorry about this."

"I already am," I told the federal agent and asked him the same question again. This time, his answer consisted of a series of obscenities so it didn't look like I was going to get far with Ted.

The only hard evidence I had was lying on one of the picnic tables so I walked back to it. Toby was still there although someone had wrapped him in a sheet. Only his big feet, clad in wingtip brown leather shoes, were sticking out. I sought out Earl who was in his store, selling bait to a trio of walleye fishermen who, if they noted there was a dead man on one of the tables just outside, thought less of it than getting advice on catching fish. "I thought I asked you to move that body to a cooler place," I said.

"Just a sec, Mike." Earl replied then calmly finished his sale, gave the fishermen an advisory on where to find walleye, and turned to me while his customers took their leave. I like a man who has his priorities straight and I guess Earl did. Walleye fisherman were his customers while cowboy detectives were pretty rare. "I had my boys wrap it in a sheet," he said.

"I know. I need to get it unwrapped. Then we need to at least get it in the shade."

Earl used a handheld radio to whistle up his sons who met me at Toby's picnic table. I supervised by sitting down and holding my throbbing head while they unwrapped him. He was still dead, his head was still knocked in, and his throat was still cut. Yes, I know as a homicide cop veteran, I should have known better than to mess with the evidence but this was Fillmore County and who knew when a state trooper would show up to investigate? Anyway, what I wanted to see was beneath his shirt, which was a garish Hawaiian print. It wasn't easy to strip him of it as Toby was one heavy dude but the Williams boys managed. As I expected, when I finally stood up, ol' Toby was covered with tattoos. I studied them, recognizing them for what they were, symbols of the Russian mob, or *bratva* as it is called. The word meant "brotherhood" but I knew there was little of that in the loose confederation of gangs that had formed around the world after the disintegration of the Soviet Union. Rather than brotherhood, there was competition, i.e., killing each other at the slightest provocation or no provocation at all.

I was no expert on Russian mob tattoos but I knew enough to know Toby was a long-term member of these very bad guys because of the combination of blurred blue tats and some that were very fine and black. The blue ones were most likely done in prison where homemade inks and snips of guitar wire attached to an electric razor were used. The fine-line skin drawings looked fresher and were probably done professionally. The biggest tattoo on his back was the Kremlin with the silhouette of a wolf on the largest onion dome. As I recalled, a tat of the Russian capitol meant Toby was once a guest in a Communist prison. The wolf, I suspected, represented the *bratva* branch Toby was a soldier for. Below the wolf were Cyrillic letters, which I thought might be the name of the organization. Stars on Toby's shoulders told me he was a high-ranking member of the mob. Russian churches, five on his left breast, four on the right, meant Toby had spent nine years in prison, all hard time because there is little else in Russia. Men who spent a lot of time in Russian prisons and came out sane were rare. Most of them would kill you over breakfast and then go on eating. All the other symbols continued the same theme. Russian mobster, a very bad guy, and a killer, our Toby. He was also Cade Morgan's buddy.

But now this very dangerous man was dead, murdered in Fillmore County. Somehow, I didn't think that was a good thing. Russian mobs don't like outsiders killing their members. They prefer to do that themselves.

We were about to wrap Toby back in his sheet when Tanya walked up to the table. When she saw him, she didn't look much surprised. "He was a man born to die," she said.

"We are all born to die," I said. "But not like this."

Her eyes were swollen and I could tell she'd been crying. "Stop looking at me like that," she said.

"Like what?"

"Like you know."

"Did you have anything to do with this?"

"Do you think I would tell you if I did?"

I rolled Toby on his side and pointed at the letters below the wolf. "What does that say?"

She read the script, then said, "It says kill or be killed."

"Nice. I thought it was the name of his organization."

Tanya studied the myriad of tattoos and said, "He was a member of the *Volk*. The Wolves. I know this group. They are all brutes. They have to kill to be accepted."

"Are they the ones who brought you here?"

"No. In fact, that mob was destroyed by this one. It is how I was able to escape when everything was in disarray. They specialize in prostitution, pornography, extortion, kidnapping, and especially murder. They are also loan sharks, as I think you say."

A light bulb, somewhat dim, went on in my head. Cade Morgan was probably somebody who'd get mixed up with a loan shark. "What a delightful bunch to attract to Fillmore County," I said.

"This is not my fault, Mike. I have nothing to do with this man."

"How about Morgan Cade, sometimes known as Cade Morgan? Have anything to do with him?"

"No. Nothing." She took her big blue eyes off Toby and rested them on me. They felt good. It made me hate Ted all the more. "What do you do now?" she asked.

It was a good question. In fact, for the umpteenth time, I reminded myself this was really none of my business. I was not a cop. I was a cowboy, a simple hired hand of Jeanette Coulter on the Square C Ranch, temporarily assigned dinosaur bone-digging duties. I gave it some more thought. So far, I was free and clear. There was no reason for the Russian Wolves to come after me. I could just walk away from Toby, let somebody else sort it out. Yep, that's what I could and should do. Or not.

Earl's boys wrapped Toby up and I instructed them to move him to a picnic table shaded by an old cottonwood. Then I took Tanya by her arm and walked her down toward the marina. We stopped when I saw Ted come out of cabin number thirteen and head for his truck. He didn't look around, just climbed in and drove away.

"Nothing happened between us," Tanya said. "But when I saw you believed Ted, I wanted to hurt you."

I wasn't buying this. "You spent the night with him and nothing happened? Then why do it?"

"Oh, Mike," she said. "There are not explanations to everything, you know."

"There has to be one for this."

"I don't want to talk about it. Will you give me a ride back to town?"

I could tell by the set of her pretty mouth that she was done talking. "OK," I said. "But I want to wait until they come for Toby."

"Why? This has nothing to do with you."

In that I agreed but I knew I couldn't just drive away, no matter how much I wanted to. Tanya shrugged, then went into the marina store. She brought out one of those cardboard carriers with two cups of joe and two peanut butter cookies. I took one of each and thanked her for breakfast. She shrugged, then walked to a far picnic table and sat down on it. I didn't join her. I needed to think.

When the ambulance arrived, it was crewed by the same paramedics who'd taken care of Pick. I led them to the body and they unwrapped him, whistling at the bashed-in skull, the cut throat, and the tattoos. Paramedic number one, whose name was Charlie according to his nametag, said, "Man, this is one bad-looking dude."

Paramedic number two—Henry according to his nametag—wondered, "Who woulda taken this monster on?"

"He was hit in the back of his head with what I bet was a hammer," I said. "That was enough to kill him or at least put him down for a good, long while. I'd also be willing to bet his throat was cut after he was struck. An ambush, maybe."

"Still, it would take some guts to hit this guy," Charlie said.

I couldn't argue with that. After they loaded him up, I asked, "Where's he going?"

"We figured the Jericho mortuary," Henry said. "Mr. Torgerson's eyes are gonna pop out when he sees the tats on this guy."

"Good idea," I responded. "Tell Frank to send the bill to Cade Morgan."

Charlie wrote that down and then he and Henry took Toby for a ride into town. I sought out Tanya who was still sitting on a picnic table. She was staring at the lake. "I'm ready," I said.

She pitched her coffee cup and the cardboard thingy in the trash can and off we went in Bob. Tanya said nothing on the way and neither did I. When we got to Jericho, I checked the parking lot of Tellman's. None of our trucks were there but Mori was, playing basketball with her kids. "They all checked out this morning," she said when I asked her about Jeanette, Ray, Amelia, Laura, Pick, and the Marsh brothers.

"You need not bother with me, Mike," Tanya said. "Laura will come back to take me to camp."

"I think you should stick with me," I said. "Anyway, I'm heading back to Blackie Butte."

"I thought you would not go back there. I thought you were done with us."

"I work for Jeanette," I said. "She told me to dig bones so that's what I'll do until she tells me to stop. But before we go out there, I'd like to have a word with Cade Morgan."

Tanya had no problem with the extra stop. When we turned out of the motel parking lot, I saw a State Police car rolling by. It turned toward the Hell Creek Marina so I drove Bob after him, flashing my headlights. The trooper pulled over and I waited for him to approach me.

As I expected, Billings had sent us up a kid cop. He looked all of eighteen, although he was probably in his early twenties. He walked up to the front of Bob and peered at me through chrome sunglasses beneath a Smokey the Bear hat. "What can I do for you, sir?"

"Are you going out to see that body at the marina?"

He studied me, then said, "Yes. Do you know something about that?"

"The body is in the Jericho mortuary. That's on Main Street, across from the Hell Creek Bar."

He withdrew a notebook from his shirt pocket and jotted something down. "Your name, sir? And can you tell me your interest in this?"

I gave him my name, address, and the Square C phone number and told him I was one of the guys who'd pulled the body out of the lake. When I asked the policeman his name, he said he was Trooper Philpot and I let drop that I was a brother, more or less, i.e., a retired cop. "Do you have any credentials to that effect, sir?" he asked.

I didn't. "You can check with the Los Angeles Police Department. They still send me a disability check."

"All right, sir. Thank you for this information."

"Look," I said, "I think this guy was a member of an organization that kills people and loves doing it. If this hits the newspapers, more of them might come here looking for revenge. I think you should talk to your superiors about the situation."

Trooper Philpot's eyes were heavy-lidded. "Sir, we have procedures for every case. I see no reason to talk to my superiors, as you say."

"Trooper Philpot, these people will come after you and, just for the fun of it, cut off your head and use it for a soccer ball."

"I believe I have all I need, sir," he said. "Anything else?"

There was nothing else. Trooper Philpot got back in his car, turned around, and headed for the mortuary. Tanya saw my worried frown and said, "What are we going to do?"

"Visit Toby's best friend," I said and aimed Bob out of town, to Ranchers Road, and on to the end of it where the old Corbel place was, and also Cade Morgan.

23

CADE HAD NO GATE at the entrance of the dirt road that lead into his place. There was, however, a cedar-and-wrought iron arch over it, which read MORGAN'S MESS. Well, we had a mess, all right, and Cade had identified whose mess it was. After all, he had brought Toby to Fillmore County and, for all I knew, had taken him out of it, too. The three main reasons for murder are, so the detective handbooks say: jealousy, revenge, and money. Based on my truncated cop career, I would also add insanity, passion, stupidity, and just because. In Cade's XXX business, there was plenty of every one of those motives.

Cade's house had been remodeled into a California-style split level, which was very nice and modern and therefore looked completely out of place on a Montana ranch. His pastures were overgrown with knapweed and leafy spurge, which were living testament to his ignorance. These were villainous plants, which, unhindered, could spread across the ranches of Ranchers Road like wildfire, choking out the good grass. I wondered if Cade had any idea of the threat his neglect was causing the rest of us. Most likely, he thought letting nature do what it wanted to do was environmentally friendly. For his neighbors, even if he'd killed Toby, this was his worst sin.

"Stay here," I told Tanya who nodded and curled up on Bob's

seat, closing her eyes with a sigh. She was pretty as a picture, that girl. It was hard to imagine her with a hammer and a knife but at this stage, anything was possible.

Cade's Mercedes was parked in his paved driveway. I walked by it and knocked on his door. After I knocked a couple more times, the door opened and there stood Cade, dressed neatly in jeans, a checked shirt, and running shoes. There was some cool jazz playing in the background. He smiled and asked, "To what do I owe the pleasure, Mike?"

I came inside. Cade, or whoever had decorated his place, had good taste. Leather chairs and sofa in a great room, modern paintings on the wall, expensive Persian rug on a hardwood floor, and so forth. It was cool, the hiss of the central air conditioner as subtext to the jazz. "I came to ask you about Toby." Since Cade was not a true rancher, I saw no need to go through the usual discussion of the weather, price of beef, and whatnot before getting down to cases.

He waved me to one of the leather chairs. "Can I get you a drink?"

"No, but thank you."

Cade sat on the sofa across from me. "I'm sorry Toby acts the way he does. He's an odd duck."

"No, Cade, he's a dead duck. He was fished out of the lake this morning."

I saw the blood drain from Cade's face. It's hard to make that happen so I assumed my news was news to him. That was kind of disappointing. It would have been far better for all of us if Cade was the murderer. We could chalk it up to California craziness and go about our business.

"What happened?" Cade croaked.

I gave him the run-down, then said, "When did you see Toby last?"

Cade thought it over, then said, "He was interested in the Russian girl. You know, one of the dinosaur diggers. He said he wanted to talk to her. I told him to leave her alone but he had his mind made up so I said to hell with him and drove home. He had his own car. You should talk to the Russian girl if you want to find out what happened to him."

"I will. What was he doing here?"

"He was an investor in my movies. This was years ago. What? You don't believe me? You worked in Hollywood, Mike. You know how porn flicks get made. Somebody has to put up the money and men like Toby have plenty of it. Over the years, we became friends. He liked to come out here to get away from the stresses of his life." Cade provided me with a wan smile. "As you can imagine, he had a great deal of it."

"Why were you and Toby so interested in our dinosaur dig?"

Cade's smile grew into a grin. "You pretend to be a cowboy but, boy, the cop in you just can't stay hidden, can it? I already told you. I was interested in having somebody look for a dinosaur on my ranch, too. Toby was used to intimidating people to get what he wanted so that's why you saw the side of him you did. Actually, he could be a sweetheart, at least for a Russian who'd spent time in prison." He chuckled. "I told him how everything was low key here but he just never understood."

I absorbed Cade's story. It was slightly plausible but I wasn't convinced. "Pretty soon, Toby's buddies are going to wonder where he is. I suspect they'll be calling."

Cade shrugged. "Well, I don't know any of them. I only worked with Toby. If they have a beef, I guess it will be with whoever killed him. That Russian girl, like I said."

"Tanya hit him in the back of the head with a hammer, then cut his throat, then dragged him to the lake and threw him in. That's what you think happened? She weighs maybe one-hundred-and-ten pounds. What was Toby? Two-eighty?"

"You sure you don't want that drink?"

"No, Cade, but you look like you could use one. Say hello to the Volk for me when they arrive."

"The Volk?"

"The Wolves. They're Toby's subset of the Russian mob."

"Never heard of them."

"Good-bye and good luck, Cade," I said and stood up to leave.

Cade stood up, too. "I've always liked you, Mike," he said. "That job I offered, it's still open."

"Sorry. I prefer a boss who doesn't have a target on his back."

I went outside and got in Bob. Tanya was napping and I woke her up when I closed the door. She blinked sleepily at me and smiled. I did not smile back. There was nothing to smile about. I drove us through the arch back onto Ranchers Road and asked her, "You're sure you didn't kill Toby?"

"Where would I get a hammer?" she replied.

"I don't know, Tanya. There's a tool chest in the back of every pickup truck in Fillmore County. There's even one in Bob. Should I stop to see if there's blood, hair, and brains on it?"

"Do not be crude," she said. "I did not kill him."

Her answer didn't send me any truth vibes nor did she sound like she was lying, either. "Cade said Toby wanted to talk to you last night. Did he?"

She looked at me for a long second, then said, "Yes."

"What did he say? Come on, Tanya. Tell me what happened."

"We are Russians. If you were in Russia, wouldn't you want to talk to a fellow American? And what would you talk about? Just ordinary things."

I still didn't get a truth vibe, one way or the other, so I dropped my questions and reminded myself one more time, none of this was any of my business or my responsibility. I drove to the Square C and

THE DINOSAUR HUNTER

parked Bob beside Buddy Thomason's truck. Soupy came out of the barn to greet me and it was sure good to see him. He looked lonely. I asked Tanya to give Soupy some attention and went looking for Buddy, finding him in the pen, feeding the horses. His hand, a cowboy named Delbert, came out of the barn. "They're out at that dinosaur dig," Buddy said when I asked about Jeanette and Ray. He nodded toward Delbert. "Delbert's looking after the place for your missus. We were just talking about where he should stay. How about your trailer?"

I told Buddy that would be fine. Delbert was generally a nice fellow and I didn't think he had any bed bugs. I went over a few things with them on the care and feeding of the Square C cows and horses, then went inside the house. I was surprised, to put it mildly, to discover the old couch was gone as were the tattered easy chairs, replaced by new ones in the Southwestern style with a nice Navajo print. I shook my head. If somebody killing Toby was strange, Jeanette Coulter buying new furniture was downright weird. Did I have another mystery to solve?

I looked on the mantel, perusing the framed photos of Ray as a baby and a playful child, and Bill Coulter in his paratrooper uniform, and Jeanette and Bill on their wedding day. She was wearing a pretty bridal dress with lots of lace and beads while he was in a severe, dark suit. She was smiling tentatively. His mouth was a grim line. Both were posed, looking like they couldn't wait to get it over. Well, at least they'd got along well enough to produce Ray.

I looked around the kitchen. Nothing new there, just the same old scratched table and dented chairs. I climbed the stairs and looked into Jeanette's bedroom. I'd never been in there before. I found a big, old fashioned bed with a faded quilt pulled over it, a couple of pink pillows and that was it. Her furniture was basic, a chest of drawers, a table beside the bed, an old ceramic lamp with a shade that was ragged around the edges. I went over and picked up one of her pillows and smelled it. There was no perfume but there was a scent, one that I recognized as Jeanette, sort of like wild sage.

I realized my heart was beating fast and I sat on the edge of her bed to get control of myself. I loved this woman so much and I had no idea why. What was there about her that was lovable? I'm sure I didn't know. I guess there wasn't anything except everything. That's the way it is. Thank you, Walter Cronkite wherever you are.

I came back downstairs and went to the gun cabinet where I got four handguns, a hunting rifle, and all the ammunition for them I could find. The handguns I chose were a .38 Smith & Wesson Police Special for Amelia, a .357 Magnum for Jeanette, his grandfather's .44 for Ray, and a .22 short-barreled pistol for either Laura or Tanya, I hadn't decided. The rifle was a standard .30-06. I packed a box of ammo for each of the pistols and three boxes for the rifle. I put the ammo in a plastic bag, then wrapped up the little arsenal in a gunny sack from the barn and strapped it all onto the front of the four-wheeler. I still had my Glock, of course, which was in my backpack. Tanya, at my invitation, climbed on the four-wheeler behind me. "You have one duty," I told her.

"What is that?"

"Open and close the gates."

She laughed. "To get back to the dig, anything."

Anything it was. We waved good-bye to Soupy, she held onto my waist, pressed her breasts against my back, which felt nice, I gave the four-wheeler some gas and away we went. As far as I was concerned, my investigation of Toby's murder was over. I silently wished Trooper Philpot my best.

24

At BLACKIE BUTTE, THE work to flatten the hill was proceeding at full speed with jackhammers rattling, shovels shoveling, picks picking, and slabs of sandstone crashing down the back side. I sought out Jeanette, finding her with Pick studying some bones in the cook tent. When I walked in, she didn't seem particularly ecstatic to see me but Pick lit up. "Mike, come here and see what I've found."

On a white towel covering a camp table were three tiny weirdly shaped bones. "These are the ilium, pubis, and ischium of a baby T. rex," he said. "I dug them out while the others were working on the hilltop."

"Where's the rest of it?" I asked.

Pick chuckled. "I think we're going to find the rest of it this time, Mike. But, look, just these bones are incredible. The question that rises in my mind is why weren't these bones ingested by the animal that killed this juvenile? Something very strange happened here."

"Something very strange happened at the marina last night, too," I said and told them about Toby.

Jeanette listened, then said, "It sounds like someone should talk to Cade."

"I already have. He says he doesn't know who did it."

"He would say that, wouldn't he? Anyway, it's just as well. A man like that Toby character has no place in Fillmore County."

Pick had gone quiet. He picked up one of the bones and put it back down, which I took as a nervous gesture. I said, "Jeanette, you don't understand. The people who sent Toby here are going to be very unhappy. They may come to find out who did it."

"Let them come. We don't have anything to hide."

I absorbed that, then said, "I have some ranch business I need to talk to you about."

Jeanette and I walked outside the tent. Before I could say anything, she looked toward the top of the hill and said, "I see the Russian woman is back. You two spent the night together, did you?"

"No, we did not," I answered. "And her name is Tanya."

"Yes, that's right. I remember now."

"Look, I want to make sure you understand how serious this is. Toby was a member of a very violent fraternity, possibly the most violent in the United States."

"You think one of his own killed him?"

"Not likely. I think we would have noticed another tattooed Russian mobster at the dance."

"Then who did?"

"I don't know but the note on him means he had something to do with our dead bull and the other murdered cows."

"Or," she posited, "the murderer put the note on him to throw us off."

"Off what?"

"I don't know, Mike. You're the detective."

"No I'm not. Right now, I'm a dinosaur digger until you tell me to do something else."

This earned me a smile. "What if I tell you to be a detective?"

"Then I would tell you to go to hell."

This earned me the unhappy Jeanette face.

"Please understand," I said, "who killed Toby isn't as important as who comes from California to see about it. If they think it was someone on this dig, then they might come here. There's nothing to stop them. The only law in this county . . . well, there is no law in this county. The state trooper that came up here is probably already back in Billings drinking coffee and telling his fellow troopers about the antics of the crazy ranchers in Fillmore County and some tattooed freak drifter who got himself murdered."

"Well, I don't see what we can do about it," Jeanette said.

Actually, I didn't, either, except to be well armed, which, considering the weapons I'd brought with me, I guess we were. "I just wanted you to know," I said, then told her about the little arsenal strapped to my four-wheeler.

"Bringing the guns out here was a good idea," she said. "I'll take one of the handguns. Give Amelia and Ray one. You're the best shot so you keep the rifle with you."

Since that was already my plan, I said, "Agreed."

She went on. "On a happier note, Pick says those little bones all by themselves are worth a fortune. Of course, he's still not thrilled by the idea of selling them. He never misses an opportunity to tell me about how important they are to science."

I surprised myself by what I said next. "I think he's right. They belong in a museum to be studied, not on the auction block. Jeanette, you're doing OK. You're not rich but you have a fine ranch and a great son in Ray. I think maybe you've got your head screwed on wrong about this one. Why don't we just go back to ranching and let Pick and his girls do their thing out here? We could also do a better job of watching what might be coming up Ranchers Road at us."

Jeanette was not pleased by my little speech. In fact, I could tell she was steamed. "Those bones are on the Square C and they belong to me and Ray. I don't understand why that doesn't mean anything to you."

I didn't reply to her accusation, mainly because I thought it was obviously ridiculous. Hell, who worked harder for Jeanette and Ray than me? Now I was the one getting steamed. I nodded toward Blackie Butte. "OK, boss lady, have it your way. I'm going back to work."

"You have my permission," she said while raising a challenging eyebrow.

There was not another woman in this world I would take such crap from. But Jeanette . . . Even I didn't understand the hold she had on me. I started to go but then an old question bubbled up inside of me. "Jeanette, just curious. How did you know I was having an affair with Edith?"

Jeanette smirked. "Every woman in the county knew it, Mike. We thought it was good for her and we thought it was good for you."

"But how?"

"It came up in book club."

I was incredulous. "*In book club?*"

"Well, the wine does flow there, you know. Edith started talking and nobody thought to tell her to shut up. We all swore later to keep it to ourselves."

Feeling like I was about to explode, I took myself on a walk straight out across the badlands. I just stomped along, muttering to myself about how stupid I was for even liking Jeanette, much less being in love with her, kicking at clods of dirt, yelling at a startled rattlesnake, then about a mile out, turned around and stomped back. Calmer now, I went to the four-wheeler for the guns, then called Amelia and Ray down from the hill. They were looking happy, tanned, and fresh. Ah, youth. "Just keep these close by," I said after explaining the reason for the weapons. Neither of them seemed upset that bad men might be coming our way. They were both hunters, though being hunted isn't nearly the same.

Carrying Jeanette's Magnum and the rifle wrapped in the tablecloth, I headed to my tent to change into my digging clothes. When I crawled out, Pick was waiting for me. He appeared upset, a worried frown creasing his forehead. He ran his hands through his golden mane, and bit at his lower lip. "I just talked to Tanya about that Russian guy getting killed," he said.

I corrected him. "As I told you, Pick, Toby was murdered, not killed. A subtle but important difference."

"Tanya said he was found in the lake," Pick said. "Couldn't he have just drowned?"

"An interesting theory," I replied. "Do you think he drowned before or after he had his throat cut and his skull punched in? Didn't you hear a word I said?"

He grimaced. "I guess not."

"Pick, you've got to climb out of deep time occasionally to see what's happening in real time."

Our boy paleontologist nodded. "So . . . who killed Toby?" he asked after looking down at his boots for a long second.

"I have no clue."

"But you'll find out, right?"

I shook my head. "Pick, I'm going back to tearing down Blackie Butte. When would I find out?"

"Well, you used to be a detective."

" 'Used to be' are the operative words here."

"But couldn't you . . . I mean . . . shouldn't you . . . ?"

There was something decidedly weird going on in Pick's mind, not that this was entirely unusual. "OK," I said, allowing a short sigh of exasperation. "Let me start detecting with you. Did you murder Toby?"

Pick went wide-eyed. "Me? Why would I do that?"

"Maybe you knew him before you came out here."

"How could that be?"

"Beats me." I made a check mark in the air. "OK, that's one suspect found innocent. I think I've detected enough for today. I'm going to go pick and shovel." I reached back inside the tent to get my backpack with the Glock and Jeanette's big pistol. I left the rifle wrapped in the tablecloth. When I stood up, Pick was still there staring at me like he had something else to say. Instead, I said, "Pick, I'm done with you. Get out of my way."

Pick got out of my way. I found Jeanette sitting in a camp chair studying a BLM map. She accepted the .357 Magnum without comment, placing it on the table beside her. She never even looked up. I wanted in the worst way to give her some grief about her general attitude but decided it wasn't worth my energy. In fact, at that moment, I decided I was through with Jeanette and the Square C, too. There were other ranches that needed a seasoned cowpoke like me. I thought maybe Mary, the librarian, and her husband, Wade, would take me on and maybe even give me some respect. My decision made me feel a lot better. Yep, that's exactly what I was going to do. I could scarcely wait to see the expression on Jeanette's face when I told her. But first, I had a mountain to take down and some dinosaurs to find.

I climbed up the hill. Laura was on one of the jackhammers but handed it over to Brian and came over. Before she could say anything, I led her about halfway back down the hill to get away from the noise and asked, "Did you kill Toby?"

"That Russian guy? Is he dead?"

"Tanya didn't tell you?"

"Tell me what?"

And here I thought women shared everything with their

women buds! Once more, I went through the litany on how I found Toby and his various wounds. "I'm surprised Tanya didn't tell you," I concluded.

She looked over her shoulder to where Tanya stood, shovel in hand. She was watching us. Laura turned back to me. "Did you and Tanya spend the night together?"

That was a sore subject and I may have winced. "No. How was your Texas cowboy?"

"Married. His wife showed up during the last dance and took him away."

"Too bad."

"Well, too bad about you and Tanya. I'm surprised it didn't work out. We drew straws for you, by the way."

"I'm afraid to ask. Did she win or lose?"

Laura laughed. "Won, silly." She looked me over. "You look pretty stressed."

"I am. Some very bad guys may be on their way to Fillmore County."

She gave that some thought. "Most likely, they'll visit Cade Morgan first."

"That's what everybody thinks. I think so, too. But he could send them here."

"Why would he do that?"

I shook my head. "I don't know, Laura. None of this makes any sense. Is there anything you can tell me?"

She pondered my question, then looked over at Brian and Philip who were trying to lever loose a big slab of sandstone. "How about those two? I didn't pay much attention to them at the dance. They came back with Jeanette, I think."

I considered the brothers, then shook my head. "Maybe they only act like idiots. Maybe they aren't even brothers. Who knows?"

Laura touched my arm. "I'm worried about you, Mike. You need to take better care of yourself."

"What do you mean?"

"Just know that I care," she said and then went back to work.

As I watched her go, I noticed that Brian and Philip, resting on the sandstone slab, were looking over in my direction. So was Tanya, still rooted in the same spot she'd been when I climbed the hill. When I looked at the brothers, they suddenly got engrossed in sharing a canteen, then got up to lever at the huge slab some more. When I looked at Tanya, she gave me a cheerful smile. What the hell did that mean? I thought about going over and interrogating the brothers and maybe Tanya again but then decided nobody was going to give me straight answers. Hell, maybe there were no straight answers. Sometimes, things are just the way they are. For all I knew, maybe Pick was right. Maybe Toby bashed himself in the head, cut his own throat, staggered down to the lake, and fell in. Worst case of suicide I'd ever seen.

I got busy, taking on the big jackhammer to break up the sandstone the Marsh brothers were trying to move. It was hot, sweaty, bruising work and I needed it. At least, something was getting done, something I could see, feel, and even taste considering the dust that jackhammer raised. All day I hammered, shoveled, picked, and levered. That night, Laura, Tanya, and I cooked dinner but we did so without anything much past polite conversation. Afterward, there was no camaraderie around the fire pit. We just took to our tents. The next day was much the same except that night, Ray woke me up, saying, "Do you hear that, Mike?"

I crawled out of my tent. It was that same stupid engine noise. I was pretty much convinced now it was coming off the lake and said so. "I don't think that's right," Ray said. "I think it's not more than a mile away."

"Nothing we can do," I said, stretching and yawning.

"We could go out and look for it."

"Ray," I said, "whatever is out there has been out there for at least a month. It doesn't seem interested in us. Let's just let it be."

Ray took my advice and went back to bed. But I looked out in the darkness, listening and thinking. If there was a two plus two to add up, I couldn't figure out what it was. I wearily climbed back into my tent. My sleep was restless, my dream a nightmare. I found myself back on that night of the storm when Jeanette cut open the little heifer. Instead of a calf, only entrails spilled out of her, nasty and flopping and hissing like snakes. When I looked over at Jeanette, she wasn't there. Instead, it was old Bill Coulter. He looked at me, held up his bloody scalpel, then nodded back at the heifer. When I looked down at it, it wasn't the heifer at all but Toby grinning at me with two grins, one below his chin.

25

It took us the rest of the week but we got most of the top of that butte down to just a few feet above where bones had already been found. When we got there, we all stood around, covered with dust and sweat, looking for all the world like soldiers who'd just finished a battle. In a way, I guess we were the veterans of the battle of Blackie Butte. Finally, the story of what had happened to these creatures lay just below our boots. At least, that was the hope. The only way to find out was to dig some more, this time without the jackhammers. Laura said this had to be much finer work, digging one scoop and one scrape at a time because the baby bones were so tiny. I could see days were going to tick by before we got everything uncovered, days that might give Toby's people time to get here if they were coming. It was a big if and there was nothing I could do about it, anyway. If they did—well, we had the guns. If they didn't, then we'd bag our dinosaurs and get the hell out of the badlands. After that, I would tell Jeanette I quit and go cowboying somewhere else. I would miss Ray but that was about it.

So we scraped and scooped and scraped some more until we found more bones. And what incredible bones they were. There were both big and small bones, the smallest of them—Kentucky

Fried Chicken size—were exhumed and folded inside paper towels and tissue paper and then wrapped in aluminum foil. The larger bones, the tibias, femurs, pelvises, and caudal (tail) vertebrae of two adult Tyrannosaurs were exposed. Then we slowly followed a trail of dorsal vertebrae of one of the adults. These bones were big as coffee cans and Laura was excited to find them articulated, meaning they were lying there in the same order they had been in life. We also found ribs. Our digging revealed that the other T. rex disappeared beneath the one we were working on. Laura called them the superior and inferior T. The one on top was superior.

"Why is one lying on top of the other?" I asked Laura but it was Tanya who answered.

"We don't know, Mike. Maybe their skulls will tell us why they are in these positions."

"I heard Pick say skulls were often washed away," I recalled. "Something about the neck attachment."

"That's true," Laura replied. "For most dinosaurs, we have hundreds of specimens but just a very few skulls."

"I think we're going to find these skulls," Tanya said, then revealed a surprise. She held up what looked like a brown tusk, then handed the thing to me. It had to weigh a couple of pounds. "What is it?" I asked, somewhat in awe.

"It's a T. rex tooth. I've found six so far," she said, patting a cloth bag on her hip.

Laura said "Tanya is very good at finding teeth," then went on to tell us a few things about the T. rex dental plan. "Their teeth were serrated with razor-sharp edges," she said, "and were biggest in the middle of the maxillae and dentaries. The teeth in the premaxillae—that's the front teeth, Mike—were smaller, probably for scraping bones." Most likely, she said, the T's ate meat by the chunk, swallowing it whole like sharks and lions. The teeth in the

upper jaw were also especially sharp and pointed, in effect a combination of butcher knives and daggers. Laura said, "Tyrannosaurs
also had an endless supply of teeth. When one was lost, another
grew back in the socket. We think they changed out all their teeth
at least once a year."

All this, I thought, was pretty cool. "Did they eat anything besides meat?" I asked. Me being a vegetarian and all, of course I'd
wonder about that.

"We don't think so," Laura answered. "They were what we call
hypercarnivores, on an exclusive meat diet. Oh, another thing
about their teeth. They were more conical than most theropods like
the raptors or even Giganotosaurus. Since conical teeth are best for
crushing bone rather than ripping flesh, that's one of the reasons
Jack Horner hypothesized that T. rex was mostly a scavenger. Nobody knows if that's so but it's interesting, nonetheless. We love to
argue about things like that at SVP conferences."

Pick called down from his perch. He had taken to sitting over us
on a slab of sandstone like some potentate overlooking his kingdom.
"They were both predator and scavenger," he said, then disappeared
back into deep time or wherever he went when he was watching us
work. Laura chuckled.

Tanya took the tooth back from me and put it in her hip bag.
"Are these teeth from the top T or the bottom T?" I asked.

"Probably the superior T," Laura answered. Then glanced up at
Pick. "Pick will figure it out. He sees everything we do. He will make
sense of it."

After another day of work in the heat, which climbed into the low
one hundreds, most of us came down the hill, our bones creaking, our
muscles feeling like they'd been torn into little, bloody shreds, our
eyes filled with grit, and our fingernails torn and raw. Pick stayed
up there, studying the day's results. Laura and Tanya took turns

carrying him food and water. Even after dark, he was there, study-ing with a flashlight what we'd revealed. I wondered if he was tell-ing himself a story made up from the bones.

The next day, we reached the neck vertebrae and cervical ribs of the superior T. We also found the same bones of the bottom T mixed in which made for a confusing jumble. Pick called a halt to our digging and said we'd best jacket the bones we'd exposed and move them down the hill. This took another week of backbreaking work. Then Montana, after so many hot but otherwise calm days, decided to be Montana, just as I kept fearing she might.

Our beloved state first revealed her plan with a clap of thunder. I was in my tent, having just gone there after dinner and our usual nightcaps. Everyone else, except Pick who was at the dig, were bed-ded down, too. I waited for more rumbling skyward but that was it. I took that as very strange, then heard the *pok* of a raindrop on my tent. Then, another *pok* and another and another. The drops of rain increased until there was a steady staccato of them. I relaxed. This was not going to be a big storm, just a nice little rain. Maybe, I hoped, it would cool things down. I slid off into dreamland, waking a couple of hours later. The staccato of rain was still there, neither increasing or decreasing. That was when I knew we were in trouble.

I pulled on my clothes and crawled outside into our campsite or, as it might more accurately be called at that point, a swamp. I stood up, took a step, and fell down, the dirt beneath the grass already well on its way toward gumbo. I sat there, quietly cursing, and con-sidered the other tents. I neither heard nor saw movement within any of them. I guess they were probably enjoying the gentle sound of the rain on their tents, just as I had until I realized Montana's little game. It was called a gentle rain, a very long, drowning gentle rain. I had seen them go on for days.

I woke up Laura and Tanya. "I'm going up to check on Pick," I told them after explaining about the rain. Then I crawled up the hill to the dig site and found Pick beneath a tarp that Laura had rigged for him. He was in his sleeping bag between two big slabs of sandstone. He was gently breathing, apparently unaware of the disaster unfolding below. I shook the paleontologist. "Pick, wake up. We have a problem."

He blinked awake. "What is it?"

"It's raining."

"So?"

"I've seen this before. It's going to rain all night and probably all day, too."

Pick grasped what was about to happen. "Mike, we have to protect the dig. Let's shovel dirt over it, then put tarps on."

I will say one thing for Pick. He could work when he had to. Beneath the steady rain, we shoveled dirt fast and furious. Then Laura and Tanya came crawling through the gumbo and rock to help us. They had brought tarps and after we'd put as much dirt over the bones as we could, spread them over the site, using sandstone blocks to weigh them down. After that, there was nothing to do but slip and slide down Blackie Butte to the camp. We looked like mud people when we got there.

It rained all night. Then it rained all day and the gumbo swamp got deeper, which meant a lot of falling down. By the next nightfall, we were all coated with the nasty stuff and thoroughly miserable and stayed that way until Tanya said, what the hell, and broke out the vodka. By then, even Ray and Amelia needed a little v&t and Jeanette gave them permission. In the mess tent, we huddled together for warmth and began to sing old campfire songs and Tanya, in a nice voice, sang some Russian folk songs. Her voice wasn't that great but she sure did look good doing it. I thought to myself that at least nobody was going to be able to get to us in this gumbo. Not until the place dried out, anyway. This was a comfort.

When the sun finally burned through the clouds, and the gumbo firmed up enough for us to walk on it, we had a look around. We were like dazed survivors of a slow-motion flood. Everything that was in our personal tents was soaked so Ray and I rigged up some clotheslines. Pretty soon, the Blackie Butte camp looked like the base camp of Mount Everest with all those colorful flags fluttering. Our flags, however, were not tributes to the gods, just our laundry. But I thought all those flapping clothes kind of made the place look cheerful.

It took another day before we could dig again because the ancient mud just refused to dry. We used the time to inspect and repair the jackets of the plastered bones, check their field numbers against what Laura had logged, and generally spiff up the camp. By the way, every bone, even the smallest one, was labeled with its own field number and location on the quarry. They were also photographed *in situ* and a notation made in Laura's field notebook. We had also done that with Big Ben, our Trike.

Hauling plaster and water up that hill was killing work but we did it, one bag and one bucket at a time. By the time we had plastered and moved the collective tails, tibias, and femurs of both dinosaurs, and a partial pelvis and the dorsal vertebrae and ribs of the T. rex on top, we were a bunch of exhausted puppies. I went to Pick sitting above the work, musing over what lay below him, and occasionally reaching down to sift the soil through his hands. "Pick, we need a day in town to clean up and get a good night's sleep."

Pick gave my suggestion approximately one millisecond of thought. "There's no time for that. We can't leave this dig for even a minute."

"We're worn out," I insisted.

"No. I will not leave this dig."

I went to Jeanette and gave her my idea. She was on her hands and knees at the time, helping Tanya plaster a long thin bone Laura said was an ischium. "Here at this juncture," Tanya said when I knelt beside them, "is where the femur—the upper leg bone—fit. There was a big triangular sheet of muscle that was attached to the ischium, the pelvis, and the femur, which made the upper leg very powerful."

"Great," I said. "You ladies ready for a day in town?"

Both women, dirty, sweaty, eyes heavy-lidded with fatigue, sat back. "I would give anything for a shower," Jeanette said.

"You're the boss. You could make it happen."

Jeanette glanced up at Pick who was furiously writing something in his journal. "I saw you talking to him. What did he say?"

"He didn't like my idea."

Jeanette mused a bit, then said, "What would Bill do, I wonder?"

I was tired enough that I reminded her again that her late husband wouldn't be facing this particular problem. Then, I said, "But I recall him saying one time that a tired man will make ten times the mistakes a rested one will."

She studied me. "Did he really say that?"

He hadn't, but I said, "Yes, Jeanette, he did."

She glanced back at Pick, then said, "I'll have a word with him."

Just as she promised, Jeanette had that word. She and Pick were in the supply tent and the rest of us were moping around in our camp chairs and could hear every word. The last words were, of course, Jeanette's. "We're taking a day and a night off. That's it."

Pick stomped out of the tent. Jeanette came over to us. "We're going to take tomorrow off." She collapsed into one of the chairs. "Mike, you got a v-and-t for me?"

I did and we all had one ourselves except Ray and Amelia who were sitting beside each other, holding hands. Jeanette saw them. "What's going on?" she asked.

"We've agreed to disagree," Amelia said. "He's hardheaded and stupid but I've decided to forgive him."

Ray shrugged. "She's not so bad for a girl."

Pick chose that tender moment to come back from wherever he'd been pouting after getting his orders from our lady boss. Apparently, he was reconciled with her decision. "I think I know a little more," he said, sitting down while we all leaned forward to hear his story.

He said he was going to tell us a story of a rogue. He reminded us that Big Ben, our Trike, had escaped after being bitten by a T. rex adult. That meant, he said, that another T. rex must have scared or distracted the attacking T away. Since the baby bones indicated an apparent nest, Pick said he believed the mighty Tyrannosaurs were homebodies of a sort, which staked out a territory. In this, he said, he thought the analog for a T. rex family was that of a modern set of predators, namely lions.

"Lions work hard to keep their families intact," he said. "They nurture their young and devise their feeding strategies to ensure everyone gets plenty to eat. It is a patriarchal family, an alpha male lording it over the females and the other males. With T. rexes, how- ever, we paleontologists think those roles were reversed. All the evidence to date indicates female T's were larger than the males. The T. rex brain was also quite large, the largest of all the dino- saurs, nearly as large as the human brain and as complex in their own way. There is proof across all vertebrates that the brain that is used more develops more. As an aside, this is why young humans need to study mathematics and the sciences, not because they may necessarily use that knowledge for anything practical, but simply because it makes their brains a better functioning organ."

All this was very interesting but I sensed Pick was diverging from his story so I drew him back to it. "What about the rogue?" I asked. Subtle, ain't I?

"Ah, the rogue," he said. "In lion prides, the alpha male eventually drives out the junior males. Some of them go off and form their own prides but others become rogues. I think this was true with the T. rex except the rogues would have been female. I believe the superior T up on Blackie Butte is a rogue female. The inferior T is smaller and, I'm sure when we study it back in the lab, we'll see that it was a male. Their positions indicate to me a struggle. Both are aimed in the same direction, I think toward a nest. We may be on the cusp of the most important discovery ever made in paleontology, proof that Tyrannosaurs had nests and that they defended them, even against a titanic rogue."

Laura asked, "But Pick, isn't it possible what we're seeing is simply two T's who died together? Or even were washed together by a river after they died?"

Pick shook his head. "There is absolutely no evidence of our dig being in a stream or river bed, no smooth stones, nothing. This nest was probably on the top of a hill or perhaps a big ledge."

"I don't know, Pick," Laura said. "You're making a lot of assumptions."

Pick tapped his forehead. "I see it all here," he said. "I know what is true."

When Laura stayed silent, Pick went on. "I've been studying the mud around these bones. I think it was transported by a huge flood carrying a great deal of silt from the adjoining highlands. It must have been very sudden, tsunami-like, catching them in a snapshot of time. Sort of like that storm that hit us last week, only much bigger."

"But why would these T's stay?" Laura erupted. "Why wouldn't they try to run away the moment the water started to rise?"

"Maybe," Pick said, "there was something of interest to them that was greater even than survival."

"What would that be?" I asked.

"Perhaps the strongest emotion in the universe," Pick answered. "Love."

It got very quiet around the fire pit. Pick finally broke the silence by saying, "I must find out if what I believe is true. I'm certain it is but I need evidence. That's why we can't stop digging."

Jeanette remained firm. "Only one day and one night, Pick. A tired man will make ten times the mistakes of a fresh one."

"That goes for a tired woman, too," Laura said, earning her a sharp glance from Pick.

Philip said, "My crotch is rubbed raw with grit. I've got to get it out."

"Don't get it out around me!" Brian exclaimed.

The rest of us hooted. "Well, that settles it," Jeanette said. "Tomorrow morning, we'll get out of here." When Pick started to object, Jeanette said, "But not into town. We'll all go to the Square C, get washed up there, and spend the evening indoors. I don't have beds for everybody but I guess you can camp out well enough in the living room and such." Jeanette held up her hand. "That settles it, Pick."

"I won't leave this site," Pick said.

"Suit yourself," Jeanette replied, and that was that.

26

Ray, Jeanette, Amelia, and I hopped on our four-wheelers and the others followed in the trucks. The Square C had never seen such a sorry caravan as that which finally reached the turnaround in front of our barn. The four-wheelers and the trucks were coated with dried mud and so were their passengers. Soupy came running through the gate to sniff everybody and then jumped into Ray's arms. It was quite the homecoming. While the women and Ray went inside the house, I sent Brian and Philip to my trailer to take showers while I had a talk with Delbert. Delbert was in the barn, cleaning the stalls and the horse tack. "Pretty quiet," he said. "Cows are good, horses are good, Superdog is good, all is good, I reckon. I been spending some time just cleaning some things, greasing what needs to be greased. You keep a nice tight ranch here."

"We do our best. You want a job, I've been thinking about quitting."

Delbert laughed. "You leave the Square C, Mike? I don't think so."

This irritated me but I didn't let it show. "Anybody been here to visit?"

Delbert rubbed his grizzled jaw, then said, "That fellow Cade

Morgan was looking for Mrs. Coulter. I told 'em where she was. He didn't say anything else. Just left."

"Was he by himself?"

"Yep." Delbert thought a bit more, then said, "T'other day, there was a funny car that came up and turned around. Big, black limousine-like thing. I came out of the barn but it never stopped. It just swung around and went back down to the road."

"Could you see who was inside?"

"Nope. Had those tinted windows. License plate was Arizona."

I had no way of calculating the odds of a lost Arizonan limo ending up on the Square C, or even the significance of it, but it added to my worry.

"Oh, Ted Brescoe and the mayor were out here, too."

I was beginning to think maybe the entire county had visited us. I resisted being sarcastic toward Delbert about dribbling out the information. Instead, I asked, "Were they together? Ted and the mayor?"

"Yep. His truck. BLM, you know."

I knew.

"You staying long?" Delbert asked and I told him the plan.

"OK. You care if I go help Buddy for a day or two? The fort's held down pretty good here, I'd say."

I agreed with that and told Delbert he could go but only for tomorrow. We'd leave plenty of food and water for Soupy and the horses but I didn't like the idea of more than a day going by without someone here. Delbert said that was fine. I added, "Would you keep a radio on you, Delbert? With our ranch frequency? We might need to get in touch with you while we're out there."

"Sure thing," Delbert said, then got in his truck and left while I considered what next to do.

What to do, I decided, was to visit Cade Morgan again, this time without knocking on his door. I pitched my backpack with the Glock into it on Bob's front seat, climbed in, and took off. About a mile before I reached Cade's ranch, I pulled off onto a side road, drove down it a little, then parked. I tucked the Glock in my belt, walked back out to Ranchers Road, listened for traffic, then ran across and climbed over Cade's fence. I slipped through the wild grasses, circling around until I reached a small hill that overlooked Cade's house. There was a black limo parked in the driveway along with Cade's Mercedes. There was no movement outside or in and, though I waited and watched for a couple of hours, I didn't see anyone.

I went back to Bob, put the Glock back into the backpack, and drove home. I went to my trailer and checked to see if the Marsh brothers were still there. They weren't so I showered, got into some clean clothes, and sat on my veranda with a nice fresh g&t. Tanya soon joined me and I fixed her one, too. As the evening sun faded and the stars came out, nobody came to visit. It occurred to me this was by design. "I have some macaroni and cheese," I told her. "And I can whip up some fresh biscuits with butter."

"You know how to spoil a girl, mister," she said and our evening was planned.

A gentleman does not kiss and tell but I guess it doesn't matter now. There was some kissing and there was some telling each other how much we liked each other, and there was some bedspring bouncing and it was all really, really good. Tanya was an amazing lover. She made this old heart sing. I hope I provided some songs, too. Her lyrics, as I recall, were all vowels. That's always a good sign.

The next morning, I was alone, Tanya slipping off in the night I guess to sleep on Jeanette's living room floor. I rustled up some coffee, warmed up a few of last night's biscuits, and had myself a nice little breakfast. Then I walked on up to the turnaround just like old times. Rage and Fury were there, each with a mouse dangling from their mouths. I praised them, then went inside the house where I found Ray and Tanya cooking breakfast. Tanya gave me the shy eye and I provided her with a grateful smile. If anyone was aware of our pleasant time together, nothing was said. After breakfast, everyone started to pack up to go back to Blackie Butte. Laura said, "I called Pick every hour on the hour last night but he didn't answer."

"That doesn't mean anything," I said. "There's hills between us and Blackie Butte and the radios don't reach out that far, anyway. But trying to check was a good idea."

"Should I have checked on you, too?" she asked.

I smiled. "No. I was OK. Better than OK."

"So I hear," she said, returning my smile. "Well, maybe Tanya and I can draw straws again some time."

I didn't know what to say to that so I didn't say anything, which was fine since Laura sashayed away. Dinosaur girls are pretty wonderful, all in all.

I next visited Jeanette, catching her feeding her bum calf. "I'm going to take Bob and go into town to see Ted and Edith," I informed her. "They came out here to see us. I want to find out what they wanted."

"Why don't you just call them on the phone?"

"I need to buy some more rice and beans, too."

She studied me, then shrugged. "All right, Mike. Whatever you think is best."

It just popped out of me. "Jeanette, I've been thinking about going to work for the Parkers. You know, Mary and Wade. They always need a good hand."

She studied me anew. "Whatever you think is best," she said, again.

"I think that would be best."

"Bill would have been disappointed," she said, then turned on her heel and walked back to the house.

I swallowed hard, then climbed into Bob and headed to town. I found Mayor Brescoe in her office. She looked a little stressed when I walked in, then rallied with a smile and an outstretched hand across her desk. It felt really strange to shake the hand of a woman I'd once made love to but Edith was a politician and I guess that's what politicians do. There are a couple of ways that can be taken, I suppose.

I sat. "You and Ted came out to see us. Anything you need?" I asked.

"Ted wanted to know the progress of the dig," she answered. "BLM work, you know."

"And you?"

"I wanted to know, too. If you've found something special, this could be big news for Fillmore County."

I will confess it occurred to me at that moment that what I should do was to tell Edith, "Why, yes, Mayor. We've made a spectacular find. Please go forth and alert the national news media of this wonderful event so hundreds of reporters can descend on us, thus perhaps keeping the Russian mob away." Foolishly, I didn't. Instead, I said, "Well, we're sweating a lot. And we almost got washed away by that storm a couple nights ago."

"We wondered if that hit you," Edith answered. "So, come on, Mike, you can tell me. What's been found?"

"Maybe you should call Ted and have him come over so I can tell you both at the same time."

"He's gone to Billings," she replied. "Come on, cowboy. Give."

I sat back in my chair and gave her a long Fillmore County stare. "Edith, are you mixed up in something?"

"Like what?"

"Like anything having to do with Cade Morgan."

She licked her lips, then shook her head. "Honestly, Mike. You saw him touch my shoulder and you've blown that up in your head until it's crazy. No, I'm not mixed up in anything with Cade Morgan."

"You're sure?"

"Absolutely sure."

The phone rang, as it always does in a politician's office, so I took my leave. I went to the grocery store, got my rice and beans and a ribbon for Tanya's hair—I know that's an old west thing to do but I was feeling like an old westerner—and carried it all out to Bob. That was when it hit me. I would have smacked myself in the head had it not been for the rice, the beans, the ribbon, et al in my arms. I put the groceries in Bob and went off to make a call. Since the world had not ended, the Hell Creek Bar was open. I went inside and asked Joe if I could use his telephone. He allowed it, I dialed the number, waited until it was picked up and said, "This is Mike. Meet me at your gate in an hour. It's about the IRS investigation."

I thanked Joe, thought about a beer, thought it best to keep my head clear, then purchased a Rainier, anyway. It was hot outside and Bob didn't have air conditioning. I drove up Ranchers Road, enjoying my beer, and stopped at the steel gate of the Haxby ranch. Sam, Carl, and Jack, leaning against a truck inside the gate, were waiting for me. I pulled into the entrance and the gate opened automatically but Sam motioned me to stop. "Get out and approach the gate," he said.

I did as I was instructed. "Hidy boys," I said.

Sam studied me. "What's this about the IRS?"

I feigned ignorance, something I'm pretty good at. "IRS? Oh, you mean what I said to Jack? I told him 'I are ess-tremely needin' to talk to you.'"

The Haxbys were not amused. "You got ten seconds, maybe less," Sam growled.

"All right," I said. "I've been thinking about who killed Toby. You know, the big Russian guy out at the marina? I'm sure you know all about it. In fact, after I gave it some thought, it occurred to me there was only one man, or men in this case, who had not only motive but the balls to do it. That would be Sam Haxby and his boys."

The Haxbys did not blink an eye. "That's bullshit and you know it," Jack said.

"Look, I'm not criticizing you. Somehow, you figured out he killed our bull and those cows and thought he had it coming. I happen to agree."

Sam cocked his head. "You wearing a wire?" he asked.

I took off my shirt, throwing it onto Bob's hood. "Does this look like I'm wearing a wire?"

"Take your hat off. Your pants, too."

"Sam, nobody ever put a wire in a man's hat or his pants."

"Your underwear, too," he said.

My purpose in all this was not to crack the case and send the Haxbys to jail. No, indeed. I just wanted to find out if my hunch was correct. I thought it over, then took off my boots, my pants, my underwear, and my hat in that order, putting them on Bob's hood. This, as fortune would have it, was just as Flora Feldmark came trundling along in her old truck. She raised her hand to us and the Haxbys touched their hats. I just waved. Flora's eyes went as wide as saucers but she kept going. I tell you, Whoever made this planet and put humans on it sure had a sense of humor and still does.

Anyway, I picked up my hat and used it to cover my privates. Not that I was shy, I just didn't want to get little big Mike down there sunburned. "OK," I said. "Clean as a whistle. So, how about it? When did you find out Toby was the killer of cows?"

"Hell, that's news to me," Sam said.

"Come on, Sam," I wheedled. "Did he say something? Or did you see that Green Monkey Wrench Gang note in his pocket?"

Sam chewed that over, and said, "So you think we did it. Well, go right on thinking that, Mike. Guess it was a good thing it got done."

"So you're saying you did it?"

The Haxbys laughed, then, without another word, walked back to their truck. I guess one of them had the remote in his pocket because the gate started to close. Then they drove away. I watched the dust cloud of their truck rise behind them and considered what I'd just learned. They had confessed that they had killed Toby. Or had they? I turned around to get my clothes just as Flora came trundling back. She stopped her truck and rolled down the window. "Mike, you having some trouble?"

"Doctor says I have a Vitamin D deficiency, Flora." I pointed abstractly at the sun. "As much skin exposure as I can get, he says."

"Oh," she said, then turned around and headed back up the road. After I got back into my clothes, I went in the same direction.

I was surprised to see Pick's truck in the turnaround. The only other two vehicles were my four-wheeler and Jeanette's. I looked in the barn first, then went up to the house, knocked on the door and no one came to it so I let myself inside. I thought I heard someone talking and went into the kitchen but there was no one there. I went back into the living room and that's when I heard Pick's voice. I couldn't hear what he was saying, but it sounded vaguely urgent. I also realized it was coming from upstairs. Then I heard a groan but it wasn't Pick. It was Jeanette. I almost tore up the stairs, thinking my worst nightmare had come true, that the Russian mob had arrived and were attacking Pick and Jeanette. But something stopped me. I realized the Russian mob wasn't my worst nightmare, not by a country mile. My worst nightmare was happening upstairs in Jeanette's bedroom. A few more vowels from Jeanette and Pick and everything was confirmed.

I went out on the porch, closing the door gently behind me, then

I turned around and considered kicking it in. I must have turned around three or four times before I found myself through the yard gate and halfway down the road to my trailer. Once there, I didn't know what to do with myself. I drank a glass of water, I turned the radio on, then off. I opened the refrigerator, then closed the door. I operated the microwave, just to hear its hum and the ding of its timer bell. None of that may make sense but when you're crazy, what else are you going to do?

I sat down in my easy chair and looked at my watch. I tapped my boot on the floor. I got up and looked out the window. I went back through the routine I'd just accomplished. I was going to wait an hour. I made fifty-five minutes.

A lot can happen in fifty-five minutes. When I walked back to the turnaround, Pick's truck was gone and, to my surprise, I found Jeanette with a cow in the holding pen. Seeing me approach, she said, "Oh, hi, Mike. That stupid Delbert. He brought this lady in to doctor her and then didn't get around to it. Look at her. She's got foot rot in her right hind leg. Come on. Help me get her into the surgery."

Well, this was something of an emergency and I guessed my poor broken heart could wait. We pushed and prodded the limping cow into the surgery, then clamped her in the chute. "Get the antimicrobial salve, a syringe of penicillin, a bucket of water, and a sponge," Jeanette ordered and I complied. When I brought them out, she took the salve and the bucket and said, "I'll doctor the hoof, you give her the shot. You need the practice."

I waited until Jeanette knelt to inspect the affected hoof and then jammed the needle into the cow's shoulder. Hard. I mean *really* hard. The cow jumped while simultaneously providing Jeanette with a full blast of sick bovine poop in her face and hair. I would have laughed except then Jeanette would have thought I just did what I did on purpose. Which, of course, I had.

I pulled out the needle and peered around the cow to where Jeanette was kneeling and glaring at me through manure-coated eyelashes. "What's wrong?" I asked, in all innocence.

"What do you think? Thanks to you, I'm covered in shit!"

This was very true so I had no comment.

"Why did you stick that cow while I was still down here? You know better than that."

"I apologize," I said, flatly.

"That's all you have to say?"

"That's all I'm saying."

She pondered me for a couple of long seconds and then I saw a little light register in her eyes. She asked, "When did you get back?"

"About an hour ago."

"How was town?"

"Wonderful. How was fucking our favorite paleontologist?"

She didn't skip a beat. "That's none of your business."

"You're absolutely correct."

She glared at me but then her features softened. "Mike, sometimes a heifer . . ." She hesitated. "Well, you know how a heifer sometimes . . ."

"Spare me, Jeanette. You're not a heifer. I don't know what you are."

"All right, Mike. Sometimes an *old cow* sees the heifers, sees the young bulls going after them but not her, feels her insides all dried up. But then, somehow she catches a young bull's eye. He looks at her and then he gets interested. He walks up next to her and the next thing she knows she . . ."

"Leave it to you to tell a story about screwing using cow euphemisms. My God, Jeanette. You are a piece of work." I walked out of the surgery.

"Where are you going?"

"To kill Pick."

"Why would you want to do that? I slept with him. What's it to you? You slept with that Russian girl, didn't you? And what's that to me?"

I turned around. "What's it to me? What's it to you? I don't know, Jeanette, except for this. I love you. I have always loved you. I loved you from the moment Bill first introduced me to you. Sometimes, when I'm around you, I think my heart is going to tear itself right out of my chest. When a day goes by and I don't see you, I think my soul dies a little. If there wasn't you, there wouldn't be me. Not the same me. Some other me. Some sad, unhappy, poor in spirit, poor in life me."

She glared at me, but then her eyes softened "I never knew," she said.

I reentered the surgery and went down on one knee beside her, grabbed her, and kissed her full on the mouth. "Now, that's love, honey," I said. "Ask your dino hunter to kiss you when you're covered with shit."

27

When I got to camp, I saw Pick was back on his sandstone perch over the dig, looking for all the world as if nothing had happened. I considered the best way to kill him and determined there was no best way, only the most fun way. That was going to my tent, getting the .30-06 rifle with the scope, propping it on a boulder, and picking him off like a prairie dog sitting on the lip of his burrow. Like the prairie dog, Pick would fall into his hole or, in this case, on top of his damn dinosaurs. Oh, there would be some consternation and some wailing from Laura and Tanya and maybe even the others but, what the hell, I would have saved us all from Pick's stupid concept of deep time. Then, maybe we could just dig up the damn bones, sell them legitimately or on the black market, make some money, and go home. Of course, I might not have a home. Likely, I no longer had to quit because I was fired. Then I thought, since I was going to murder Pick, home might not be a problem for me. State Prison in Deer Lodge. That's where Montana keeps its death row.

Thinking of Deer Lodge and the executioner gave me some pause. There weren't yet enough Californians in Montana to keep the good and gracious citizens of the Big Sky state from occasionally extracting a life for a life. So while I was pausing, I took stock. I looked up where Pick was sitting and realized he might have had sex with Jeanette but to him it probably didn't mean that much The only thing that meant anything to him was back in the Cretaceous.

So, instead of killing Pick, I did the next best thing and got myself a beer and sat on one of the lawn chairs around the fire pit and silently talked to myself. It's sad when you need to talk to someone you can trust and the only person who falls into that category is yourself. But that was my situation and I needed to think through all that had happened and all that I had uncovered to see if there was anything I had missed. It also kept my mind off Jeanette and our dinosaur boy wonder.

I started with Toby. According to the evidence of the note in his pocket, Toby had killed our bull and the cows. This was for reasons unknown but OK, I could believe he was the cow killer. So, ergo, if Toby was the cow killer, then Cade Morgan knew it and maybe had helped. Why? I didn't know but they were both idiots so maybe Toby did it because he needed to kill something every so often and, when Cade thought it might be him, Mr. Morgan suggested, "Hey, Toby, why don't you kill that bull and those cows?" Yes, I know that didn't make sense but, as I said, I was trying to come up with the motivation of idiots.

If I accepted Toby as our cow killer, then what? Somehow, probably, maybe, perhaps, the Haxbys found out about it. How was that? Well, Toby got drunk and talked, or maybe the note in his pocket fell out and somebody saw it, or maybe Cade let it slip. There were a lot of ways Toby's guilt could have been exposed and, in Fillmore County, you didn't murder cows without someone getting even. So why the bashed head and slit throat? Well, the Haxbys were decidedly an eye-for-an-eye, tooth-for-a-tooth bunch so it would be just like them. Of course, there was nothing in the history of the Haxbys to suggest they were cold-blooded killers but that was true of most cold-blooded killers. Yes, all right, OK, I decided the Haxbys had done ol' Toby in, probably in that little copse of trees behind the marina, then dragged him down to the lake and tossed him in. That made me wish I'd searched that little copse of trees but never mind. I reminded myself for the umpteenth time I was no longer a detective and I had no business investigating this or any other crime. So why was I going through all this in my mind? Well, why not? It beat dragging my tired butt up that hill and, like I said, thinking about Jeanette and Pick. I needed another beer.

Now I came to thinking abut Tanya and Ted Brescoe. Why had they spent the night together at the marina the night of the dance and Toby's murder? And who was right about what happened? Ted or Tanya? At least a certain part of me believed Tanya because, after all, I'd taken her to my bed last night without a thought of Ted. This, I believe, is not normal behavior for a male human being. If another man has been with a woman, a certain amount of time has to pass before we male creatures consider the woman clean enough to screw. OK, that probably has a direct correlation with a man's age. Teenage boys would mate a knothole, no lie, even if King Kong had just finished with it. We older guys get a mite more discriminating or so we like to think.

So, OK and anyway, why had Ted and Tanya been together that morning and was that somehow tied in with Toby's death? If the Haxbys had done it, and I had decided they had, then no, it didn't. Basically, to clear this up, I needed to ask Tanya. But if I did, I might hurt her feelings. I was sure she wanted to put that night behind her. The truth is, I did, too. Another beer. That's what I needed.

Now I needed to think about Cade Morgan. What was up with Cade? He had visitors at his ranch who came in a dark limousine. Dark limos did not necessarily mean Russian mobsters. Since he made skin flicks, maybe he had brought in a bevy of gorgeous girls. In fact, I hoped he had but that's also a never mind. My working theory was the limo passengers were connected with Toby. For all I knew, maybe ol' Cade had been exterminated by now and the boys in the limo had departed the county. I could only hope.

Then there was Edith, our fair mayor. Was she connected to all this? I just didn't know. And what about Jeanette? And Pick? After all, most everything Pick had told us had been proved a lie. And now he and Jeanette were lovers. Was there something I was missing? I shook my head, finished the beer, and tossed the bottle into the fire pit on top of the others. The truth was I hadn't solved anything. My conjectures on the cow murders, Toby's murder, the Haxbys, and Cade Morgan could all be wrong. I got up and, carrying my pack with the Glock in it, climbed the hill, got my ice pick and trowel, and went back to work on the Cretaceous. Deep time was all that made sense on Blackie Butte.

Jeanette didn't come out until the next day. I was glad she'd come, mainly because I got to studiously ignore her, which I did with a vengeance. By then, we had most of the exposed bones of the top and bottom T's jacketed and carried or slid down the hill. All of us, even Brian and Philip, were getting to be very good at digging, pedestaling, and jacketing. We had almost made an assembly line job of it. A few more tiny baby T bones were found, a femur, Laura said, and a couple of vertebras, so tiny they were almost missed. "What we need to do when we're finished with these big ones," she said, "is to bring in a screen and go through all the spoil matrix to find the rest of this little guy." Great. That sounded like hot, back-breaking work, just like all the other work on the dig.

So now it was time to see what remained of the front parts of the two big T. rexes. What we found first was the upper neck of the top T. This part of the neck of a Tyrannosaur, it turns out, is a very complex series of bones. The neck bones themselves were each about the size of the fist of a professional heavyweight boxer. Attached to each on opposing sides were sharp prongs that reminded me of tent pegs. These were the neural spines and below them was the neural arch or pathway of the spinal cord. Atop this arrangement were somewhat rectangular-shaped bones that acted as stops to keep the neck from bending too far. According to Laura, this whole crazy combination of bones in the neck allowed it to be flexible. "Although," she said during a rest break, "the neck of the T. rex, if we just look at the bones, is much too thin to support their massive skulls."

Ray asked the salient question. "Wouldn't that mean they would be walking around with broken necks?"

"Don't be silly," Amelia countered. "If their necks were broken, they wouldn't be walking around."

"You know what I mean," Ray shot back.

"I *never* know what you mean, Ray Coulter," Amelia spat.

It was nice to see the kids were still getting along.

Anyway, Laura cleared the mystery up, explaining that the neural spines were attachment points for extremely powerful muscles that stretched all the way to the back of the skull. She also said that as we approached the skull, we would see some long rib-like bones that nearly wrapped around the throat. These, she said, were to provide places to connect muscles and also probably to protect the windpipe although why such protection was needed, she didn't exactly know. What creature in the late Cretaceous would be able to or want to bite a T. rex neck?

Having watched plenty of science-fiction movies, I thought I had the answer. "Another T. rex," I said.

Pick, who I thought had fallen asleep on his perch, suddenly opened his eyes and said, "Mike, you are exactly right."

The next day, we found more teeth mixed in with the top T's

neck vertebrae and ribs. This meant, Laura said, another T, probably the one below, had locked on its throat. The next thing we found was a short, heavy bone that Laura said was the humerus of a Tyrannosaur arm. It was so small I had trouble believing it really belonged to the massive skeleton but Laura shrugged, saying, "Growing bones and muscles takes energy, you know, and life is inherently lazy."

"What do you mean by that?" I asked.

"Just what I said. To evolve away from some physical characteristic takes work at the cellular level, maybe even below it. Unless there's some compelling reason to do it, the animal will stay the same. In this case, the T. rex got bigger because it needed to be bigger to eat the animals it ate. Its arms, on the other hand, just stayed the same size because they weren't useful. Anyway," she waved her hand in a dismissive gesture, "we don't know why their arms were so small. They just were."

Then we found our first skull or at least part of it. It was, based on its size, the bottom T's lower jawbone which was missing some teeth. Then we found the upper jaw and other bones of the skull. Laura explained T. rex skulls didn't come in a unit but were a complex maze of bones and hollow spaces. "We'll jacket them in their matrix," Laura said. "Otherwise, they could get damaged."

Laura found an exposed socket in the jaw and tried some of the teeth we'd found in the top T's neck. One of them fit perfectly. Pick came down and knelt over our find and we all waited for him to make his appraisal. "They were fighting," he said, "and the inferior T got a good bite onto the superior's throat. But I don't think it killed him. Keep digging and we'll find out what did."

"We must map everything first," Laura insisted.

Pick sighed. "Of course, you're right. Map, map, map."

"And jacket."

He waved his hands tiredly, not that he had done any real work. "All right. Jacket."

We mapped and jacketed, then dug like crazy people. Yes, we were careful, but we dug as fast as we could. I forgot all about Toby and the cows and all the rest of that mystery, which seemed unreal compared to the mystery we were solving right before our eyes. Then we found the other skull. It was oddly posed, the neck contorted, the head thrown back. Laura said this was the classic death posture of dinosaurs. As rigor mortis set in, tendons tightened and pulled the head backwards. "Why isn't the other skull like that?" Ray asked.

"Because its teeth were embedded in the neck of the superior T," Pick answered from above.

We gathered around our latest find. This skull was gigantic, thick, and yet, as we exposed it from the gritty dirt of Blackie Butte, we observed that parts of it were shattered, others parts punctured. And in one of those punctures on a bone that Laura said was the nasal bone, we found a hole too big to be made by the teeth of the smaller T. We also found the animal's sinus cavities and palate had been crushed into splinters. It looked like a sledgehammer had been used.

Pick came down and inspected the damage done to the skull. "I think while the inferior T held this T's neck, another T clamped its jaws on the superior's head until the bones in the skull were crushed and death ensued." That was a clinical way of saying the big T had been bitten on the head by something even bigger. And meaner, I presumed.

"How do we know this skull wasn't crushed postmortem by the pressure from the burial?" Laura challenged.

"Mud doesn't puncture bone like this," Pick replied. He stood up and fastidiously wiped the dirt from his pants. "When we dig deeper, I think we're going to find broken ribs. By the posture of the inferior, it had to be beneath the superior's feet which were equipped with extremely sharp claws. Those claws would have done enormous damage. While the inferior T held onto the superior's neck, the superior would have been tearing the stomach and intestines out of the inferior. The flow of blood must have been like a river. Yet, this smaller T hung on, giving another T, a big one and probably female, time to provide the death bite."

"You're saying the inferior Tyrannosaur sacrificed his life?" Laura asked.

"I'm certain of it," Pick replied.

Laura was dubious. "Assuming it had the mental capacity for sacrifice, what would be its motive?"

"I already told you," Pick replied. "Love."

"A nest," Amelia said. "She was protecting her nest. And her babies."

Pick nodded his head vigorously. "Or *his* babies. And mate."

Tanya said, "Then the little skeleton we found was probably a chick that got stepped on during the battle." Tears began to streak down her dirty cheeks. "That poor little thing. It was just trying to get out of the way."

"I think you're right," Pick said.

I looked around. There were lots of tears. Even Jeanette's eyes were wet. Ray looked away until Amelia's hand found his and held it tight. Tanya was too far from me to take her hand but I wanted to. Laura was writing in her journal, stopping to wipe her nose with the back of her hand. The two brothers of Green Planet were openly sobbing. Me? Well, I felt sorry for the little tyke but it had been a long, long time ago. Pick soon reminded us of that fact.

"The way I read the dirt," he said, "I think this happened in the late Cretaceous, around sixty-five or seventy million years ago. So the question is why have we found them so well preserved?"

"You're already told us," Laura said. "They were covered with mud."

"That's how," Pick replied. "But my question is why?"

"I don't understand," Laura said.

"OK, let me put in a different way. Why are we finding these creatures now? Why was deep time flipped on its head to bring them to the surface at this moment?" When Laura shrugged and the rest of us reacted with querulous frowns, Pick said, "I believe it is because the time has come that we—meaning our civilization— learned the lessons these bones can teach us."

This was too much for Laura. "That's crazy, Pick! You're talking like there's a big God in the sky who left us a note by arranging these bones this way. I totally reject your hypothesis. Why are these bones here and so well preserved? It's simply the random result of millions of years and the death of millions of animals. This is just what happens to be. The result of a cosmic roll of the dice."

"Einstein said God does not play dice with the universe," Pick replied.

"He later refuted that," Laura growled. "You're going too far."

"If you're right, Pick, what is the lesson?" Jeanette asked, cutting to the chase.

"I don't yet know," Pick answered. "But we're getting close." He pointed at the unexcavated dirt. "The answer lies there."

We crept forward—our shovels, our ice picks, our trowels at the ready. "No you don't," Laura said. "We pedestal and jacket the rest of these bones before we move a teaspoon of any more dirt."

"That will take days!" Tanya protested.

"It will take what it takes," Laura said as Pick regally climbed back on his perch.

28

We were up at first light and, as soon as we got some coffee and breakfast under our collective belts, went back to work. As we pedestaled and jacketed and moved the bones down the hill, I kept marveling over the crushed skull of the big T. rex that lay atop the smaller one. Stuck in it was a tooth over a foot long. Whatever animal had planted that tooth through three inches of solid bone had attacked with enormous force, energy, and passion. But why? Self-defense was my instinctive answer but Pick was hinting it was more. The answer, as always in paleontology, was in the dirt.

Blackie Butte was more than the pyramidal peak we had taken down to a stump but actually several connected outcrops, smaller hills, and peninsulas. When we eased up for lunch, Tanya asked me to meet her on a narrow dirt bridge which had several small cedars perched on it. I agreed, making a detour by my tent for something I wanted her to have. Well, two things. I settled beneath one of the cedars on the earthen outcrop and enjoyed the view until she arrived with peanut butter and jelly sandwiches and sports drinks, the latter to replenish the lost salts caused by our labor. She also had a salt shaker and suggested that I sprinkle some on my hand and lick it off. Of course, I would have preferred to lick it off her hand, as I'd seen Pick do once, but I did as I was told. We sat there quietly, enjoying our meal. When we were finished, she put her hand on my knee. "Thank you for our night together, Mike," she said. I thought it was me who should thank her and was about to say that very thing when she said, "That night Toby was murdered, I am ready to tell you about that now."

"You don't have to tell me anything," I said, even though I was eager to hear it.

She smiled. "I think you have a great passion for the truth. Yes, I will tell you this." She took my hands in hers. "The night of the dance, Toby found me sitting on one of the picnic tables. I was enjoying the music, looking at the lake, and, I must admit, thinking of you."

She gave my hands a squeeze, I squeezed hers back, and she kept going. "Toby said he knew I was a whore but since he was a fellow Russian, he did not think he should have to pay me for sex. He said I should go with him into the trees and take care of his urges. When he grabbed my wrists—he was so strong, Mike—I told him I did not understand why he wanted me. There were many men at the dance and I was sure one of them was who he really wanted. If we have sex, I told him, he would only be closing his eyes and thinking of a man. This made him very angry but he did not deny it, either."

She was squeezing my hands so hard they hurt but I didn't say anything. I needed her to keep talking and she did. "When he walked away, I watched him and before he got far, a man came from behind the marina building. They stopped and talked and then they walked into the trees. It was the government man. Ted Brescoe."

This, as they say, was a jaw-dropping moment. "Say that again," I said.

"Ted Brescoe and Toby went into the trees together."

Well, that at least cleared up why Ted and Edith's marriage

wasn't exactly made in heaven. Tanya fell silent, so I prompted her by saying, "But the next morning, you were in Ted's room."

"Oh, Mike. It wasn't his room. It was mine! I had reserved it, hoping you might join me that night." She took her hands away. "But I saw at the dance that you only had eyes for Jeanette. I am not blind so I went to my room alone."

I saw no need to deny my love for my lady boss. I put my brain in fast rewind. What had Earl, the marina owner, said when I asked him about Ted? He'd said, "Ted's in room thirteen." He didn't say it was his room, only that he was in it. A good cop would have asked a follow-up question or two. Of course, I'm not a good cop, not anymore, anyway. "But the next morning Ted was in there with you," I said.

"When I came outside in the morning—the mist coming off the lake was so beautiful—I found Ted curled up on the deck. He said he'd slept there all night. He was filthy and his clothes were torn. I knew nothing about Toby's death so I let him come in to wash himself and go to the bathroom. I swear, Mike. That's all that happened."

"So . . ." I let the word hang for a long second but I didn't have a finish for it. So *what?* Had Ted murdered Toby? But, if so, why the knock on the head and throat cut the same way the bull and the cows had been killed? Would Ted do that and did that mean he'd also killed our bull and the cows? He was an unpleasant fellow, make no mistake, and him murdering the Russian wasn't entirely impossible, but killing cows? A Brescoe from Fillmore County? And what about the fact that Ted's truck was in the marina parking lot all night. Why hadn't he just driven home? "Curiouser and curiouser," I said. Then, I actually asked a cop-like question. "That morning, when you let him into your room, did you see any blood on Ted?"

"No. Did you?" I confessed I hadn't until I'd beat him up, and she said, "Later, I asked myself did Ted kill Toby? My answer is I don't know."

I pointed out the obvious. "Ted was the last man seen with Toby before he turned up dead."

"As far as we know," she said.

"As far as we know," I agreed.

Well, this was all a fine howdy do. Even with these revelations, I didn't know much more than before. It didn't even prove that Ted and Toby had decided to play kissy-face or kissy-whatever in the woods, only that they'd gone into them. For all I knew, they went in there to discuss the latest stock averages and whether the Yankees were going to win the pennant. Then again, Toby had next been found floating face down in the lake. Then again, Ted curled up on the deck of the marina motel the next morning didn't indicate a strong need to run from the scene of his crime. Then again, why didn't Ted drive home that night, in any case? Then again, Ted was an idiot. Then again, I still didn't have a clue who had done what to whom. Then again, why did I care?

The answer to that last one was I still had a suspicion that a load of coprolite (so to speak) was about to be dumped on all our heads because of Toby's murder or maybe for some other reason I had not yet discerned. "What are we to do?" Tanya asked.

"Wait for further developments," I said. This turned out to be a stupid answer. What we should have done was jumped in our trucks and four-wheelers and run like hell. But who knew? I should have but I didn't. Maybe I thought we were so well armed we could handle anybody who wanted to do us harm. Or maybe I was just too stupid and tired to think straight. Probably a little bit of both. This, folks, is how things like the Alamo or the Titanic happen. So far, so good, and then, well, you know. Here come the angry Mexicans or the iceberg.

Anyway, I opened my backpack and gave Tanya my presents, the ribbon I'd bought her in Jericho and Ray's short-barreled .22-caliber pistol. She loved the ribbon but wasn't sure about the gun. "This little pistol probably won't kill anybody," I told her, "but it might stop them long enough for you to get away."

"Mike, you're scaring me."

"Good. Sometimes, being scared is what keeps us alive."

She took the pistol and I gave her a quick basic course which was pretty simple like the gun itself. It had a safety and a trigger. It was already loaded. Keep the safety on until time to use it. Then aim and pull the trigger. Nothing to it. Tanya put it in one of the voluminous front pockets of her cargo pants and I felt compelled to remind her once again about the safety.

We went back to work pedestaling, jacketing, and hauling. It took us two long days but the rest of the bones of the two T. rexes were removed from the dirt and carried or slid down Blackie Butte. To get the giant leg bones and skulls down the hill, Ray and I rigged up a pulley system using the winch on the tractor to inch them down. We had a few pinched fingers and toes but, otherwise, the work was done without mishap. Of course, there were strained muscles, damaged backs, and a variety of abrasions and contusions but, as Laura said, that's why God made ibuprofen. When we laid them all out, the big white jackets reminded me of tombstones in a cemetery.

When the top T's skull, which required a block of plaster the size of a refrigerator, was lowered, we stood around it feeling a sense of awe at what we had accomplished. Inside its jacket was not just the bones of the skull but quite a bit of the matrix in which it was found. The thing had to weigh at least a ton. Pick said preparators in the laboratory that would work on the skull preferred to include the surrounding rock and dirt because they could use their specialized tools to remove it without harming the bone. This made sense but it also raised the question (to me at least) as to where the two T. rexes and the crushed baby T were going after we finished our field work.

I found Jeanette sitting in the dirt of Blackie Butte, her back braced against a boulder of sandstone, her eyes closed, and her brow knitted in pain. This was the prevalent rest posture of dinosaur diggers. I picked a nearby boulder to sit on and waited patiently until she at last opened one eye and took note of my presence. "So," she said, "you deign to speak to a fallen woman?"

"I was just wondering where these bones are going?"

"Pick said we ought to move them to our barn after we finish," she said.

"I guess we can make room."

"We? Are you still working for the Square C?"

It was the perfect opportunity to make my quitting official but, to my disappointment, I found I couldn't do it. "I don't know. Am I?"

"What would I do without you, Mike?"

"For one thing, you'd have to hire a cowboy and pay him some decent wages."

She thought that over, then said, "How about a ten percent raise if you stay?"

I felt the urge to tell her where she could put her 10 percent raise but instead, I said, "Sounds good. So, the bones are in the barn. What then?"

"Well, Pick says we can negotiate with a university or museum or maybe even the Smithsonian to take the bones and prepare and study them. He'd work with them, of course. After that, the bones would be ours to sell. It would take a few years but he thinks we're looking at several million dollars."

I gave Jeanette a hard look. "Laura says if any of the bones end up in private hands, their value to science will be lost forever."

"Well, that's why they'll go to the Smithsonian or somewhere like that first." She looked at me. "Mike, these are my bones. Just drop it."

I had done my best for science. I don't know why I was arguing about it, anyway. Hell, for that matter, I didn't know why I had agreed to keep working for the Square C. I was a pretty confused puppy at that point. And tired. That was it. I took a breath, then said, "OK, but how about this? To keep your bones safe, maybe we ought to go ahead and take them to the barn. I could bring in the big truck and load them up with the tractor and then Ray and I could go back and forth until we got them moved."

"I suggested that very thing to Pick," she said, "but he said he doesn't want to take the time now. He says it's best to forge ahead."

I didn't think that was the best strategy and said so but Jeanette was also tired and waved my objections away. "I'll sit Pick down and talk to him about this later," she said. She studied me for a moment and then said, "Mike, I want you to know what you said in the surgery about how you feel about me, well, that meant a lot."

"I'm glad it did, Jeanette," I said.

Since I didn't want to talk about that, I stood up and took a step down the hill, stopping when I heard her giggle. It was a giggle that turned into a laugh. In fact, she started laughing so hard there were tears curling through the encrusted dirt on her face.

She looked at me looking back at her in shock. "Oh, Mike, I'm sorry," she said, wiping her eyes with the back of her filthy hand. "But kissing me with that cow shit on my face . . . every time I think about it, I can't help but laugh."

"Well," I said, "I guess I can't be too mad. I'm always saying you don't laugh enough."

She chuckled a few more times, then her smile faded. "I never loved Bill Coulter," she said, "but I respected him. I decided early on to become the woman he deserved." Her eyes turned soft. "He never loved me, either, but he knew he'd found a woman who could help him build the Square C into a profitable, modern enterprise. When we had Ray, we knew we had a partnership that only death would end. Still, I confess sometimes I missed being loved. Until you said it, Mike, no man ever told me he loved me. I'm sorry it happened on the day it did. You should have told me earlier."

"What was the point?" I asked, my voice small even in my ears.

She pondered my question. "Maybe it's this heat or maybe because I'm so tired or maybe it's because I've been listening to the crazy things Pick says but here's what just popped into my mind. Could it be that everything that's happened, from the moment Pick arrived, was so you'd have to tell me you loved me? Does that make sense to you?"

"No," I said. Then, after a moment of reflection, I said, "That would be something, wouldn't it?"

"A domino falls so that all the other dominoes fall, too. But there are dominoes we can't even see. All leading to love."

"I wouldn't try to float that one at the next Cattleman's Association meeting, Jeanette."

She nodded. "Anyway, Mike, thank you."

A man expressing love to a woman who replies with an expression of gratitude is not going to be happy. That was me at that moment. Although I knew she was through with me, I had another thing to say. "What would you think if I had someone move into my trailer?"

The surprise on her face was palpable. "Tanya?" she asked.

"Yes. If she wants to. I don't know that she does."

"I don't think that would be a good example for Ray."

"You're right," I admitted. "Maybe I can get a place in town."

"That would be a long drive and I wouldn't have you to help me at night." She gave it some more thought, then said, "Have you considered marrying the girl?"

"Not really."

"I think . . ." She gave herself a moment, then said, "I think you need to discover how you feel about Tanya before you take the next step, Mike. When you know that, we can talk."

"Fine," I said and walked down the hill.

29

THE NEXT MORNING, THE mayor of Jericho arrived, wearing a wide-brimmed hat, jeans, shirt, and field boots. Edith walked among the tombstone-jacketed bones, having herself a good look, then climbed the hill. There she found us tunneling into the embankment. No one greeted her. We were too busy. She watched silently while Ray and I shoveled and picked. Behind us, Tanya crept forward on her hands and knees, sifting through the disturbed matrix to find any little bones that might be hiding there. Occasionally, I would catch Tanya's eye and she would smile and I would smile and then we'd go right back to work. Above us, Laura, Jeanette, Brian, and Philip were removing another layer of sandstone. Jeanette finally took note of Edith and walked over to her while the rest us of took a break. At Jeanette's greeting, Edith said, "Ted's sick so he asked me to come out and represent the BLM. My purpose is to observe, not to interfere."

Jeanette said, "This is Square C land, not BLM."

"Yes, of course," Edith answered. "But Ted says until the survey is done and the map is updated, the BLM boundary is unclear. I have to support my husband on this, Jeanette."

Jeanette, ever agreeable, replied, "Get off my property, Edith."

Edith didn't budge. "The old BLM line is right over there. If I went there, I could still see what you're doing."

Jeanette absorbed that, then waved her hand. "Be my guest."

"Please be reasonable," Edith said. "Ted's very sick but he has a job to do. I promised him I would do it." Her eyes sought me out. "If you'll let me stay, I'll help you dig. Would that be all right, Mike?"

The way Edith looked at me, so beseechingly, I couldn't help but feel sorry for her. All right, I'm an old softy, especially when it comes to a woman who had clawed her way up from being the poor daughter of a detested chicken-and-pig farmer to mayor of the county seat. Inside, I sensed she was still that frightened little girl who'd run away from home. Also, of course, she had always been decent to me. "I guess that would be all right, Edith," I allowed. "But it's up to Jeanette, not me."

"Please, Jeanette," Edith implored. "Let me help you dig. I won't be any trouble."

Before Jeanette could answer, Pick said, "We can always use another hand. I think we may have more rock to move than I thought."

Jeanette glared at Pick, then nodded down the hill, a gesture which meant she and Pick should meet and discuss the situation and then she would tell him what he was going to do. Pick gave up his catbird's seat and joined her below. They disappeared inside the cook tent. To this day, I'm not certain what Pick told her but, to my surprise, when Jeanette came back, she said, "All right, Edith, but if you're here, you're here. You have to stay until we're finished with our work. Did you bring what you need?"

"I have everything in Ted's truck including a tent."

Jeanette said, "OK." And Edith responded with a grateful smile.

For the rest of the day, we dug. Edith pitched her tent, and then climbed up to us to join Amelia, Laura, Brian, and Philip on the sandstone cap. She worked so hard during the next hours, I heard

Laura caution her to slow down or she would go into heat exhaustion. That was one of the things I really admired about Edith. It didn't matter the job she took on, she worked diligently to see it through.

For all our work, nothing was found and Pick finally called it a day. We dragged ourselves down the hill and collapsed in various poses of exhaustion all over the camp. I stretched out beside my tent until the ants started to bite, then sprawled in one of the chairs around the fire pit. Gradually, everyone gathered there. Edith showed up, her face coated with dirt and dried sweat. "I brought beer in my cooler," she said. "Enough for everyone."

"Bless you," I said to her since every drop of gin, vodka, tonic, and beer was by then drunk up. Edith went off with Brian and Philip to carry the cooler. After a while, she returned with a bottle of Rainier for me and told the others that cold ones were waiting for them in the cook tent. Off they went, leaving me and Edith alone. We clinked our bottles and I considered just going with the flow but what remained of the detective inside me made me ask, "What's wrong with Ted?"

"Just a bug. Don't worry."

"I'm not worried. I think you know I don't give one fig about your husband. It's you I can't figure out. Why are you really here?"

She didn't reply to that and we silently drank our beers as the others filtered back to the fire pit. Tanya came over. "Mike, if we don't cook the steaks tonight, I'm afraid they could spoil."

"Steaks!" Ray cried. "I could sure use one of those!" Others around the fire pit also cheered the prospect of eating the juicy tenderloins Laura had stocked. My muscles ached and my bones creaked but, for the morale of the troops, I was willing to be the cook even though it meant I would be preparing something I couldn't eat. Being a vegetarian was never so hard as that evening when I smelled those steaks cooking over the charcoal. Fortunately, while Tanya and I barbequed, Laura and Amelia made biscuits and some fantastic potato salad, and Jeanette tossed a green salad so I had great food to eat, too. Ray, Brian, and Philip set up the tables and chairs. Edith, of course, supplied the beer. We were a good team. Pick was somewhere wandering. I didn't much care if he got lost. He apparently was learning his way around, however, as he showed up in time for dinner.

After the meal, everybody else went to bed but I sat with Tanya at the fire pit. I really enjoyed her company. We talked about this and that, but then I asked her, "After this dig is finished, where do you go from here?"

She looked me over. "Where do you want me to go, Mike?"

My heart fluttered, then demanded to speak. I let it. "Wherever I am."

She leaned over and kissed me. "I love you, you know," she said.

I checked with old brother heart and he gave me a thumb's up. "I love you, too."

Suddenly, everybody appeared out of the shadows and cheered. Someone had fireworks and they shot them into the sky, showering us with bazillions of brilliant and flaming colorful sparks. The moon popped out, milky and brilliant, and the sun posed on the horizon, turning the sky a bright pink and the clouds scarlet. A skywriter appeared and traced out a heart in the sky and two rabbits and a prairie dog linked arms and did an impromptu cancan dance.

Actually, none of that happened. Tanya and I just gazed at each other, realizing that we were always going to be together from that moment on. It didn't matter if three hundred million years passed, our part in the timeline would be there, affecting everything that was to come. Time, at that moment, was in our hands. Deep time never seemed quite so real.

Edith appeared, breaking our little spell. "Mike, could I have a word?"

I was willing to provide a word. She had, after all, brought the beer. I demurely pecked Tanya on the cheek and followed Edith to the base of Blackie. I sat down on a sandstone boulder and she sat on another. "Tanya is a beautiful girl," she said.

"She is," I replied and left it at that. Talking about a new lover with a past lover, I suspected, was not real intelligent.

Edith studied me. "You look beat," she said. "Maybe you should take a break. Why don't you take a few days off, go back to your trailer, get cleaned up, and get some sleep?"

I thought she was kidding so I chuckled and said, "Thanks, but I'll stick it out."

Even though the temperature was still in the low 90s, she shivered and wrapped her arms around herself. "Get away from this place, Mike," she said.

I realized she was serious. "Why would I want to do that?"

"Jeanette has no loyalty to you. She just wants to work you like a dog."

My shrug was one of those *what else is new?* gestures.

"You owe her nothing. Why work so hard? She's just being greedy Jeanette as usual." She nodded toward the field of jacketed bones. "Everything belongs to her. Even these damn bones. Nobody gets anything but Jeanette."

"It's her land," I reminded the mayor.

"That's right." Her tone turned hard and sarcastic. "She owns the land. She owns everything. All these ranchers own everything. What's left for the rest of us?"

"Edith, you're losing me. What are we talking about?"

She gave me a disgusted look. "Well, I tried," she said.

I'd had stranger conversations but I couldn't recall when. Anyway, she just sat there, looking all defeated, and I said, "The night Toby was killed . . ."

"Don't ask me about that. Don't ask me about anything."

"The last person seen with Toby was Ted."

"How do you know that?"

"Somebody saw them."

Edith seemed to be studying her boots, then she shook her head. "What do you want from me?"

"Do you think it's possible Ted killed Toby?"

Her laugh was harsh and bitter. "Ted doesn't kill men. He loves them."

I wasn't too surprised that she knew this. "Maybe a lover's quarrel?"

"Just don't go there, Mike." When I opened my mouth to say something more, she waved me off and said, "I'm just not going to talk about this." Then she stood up and walked back to camp.

I watched her go until she went inside her tent. Ted's truck was parked on the other side of the field of bones and a thought occurred to me. I strolled nonchalantly to it and took a look in the back. Besides some rope and a shovel, there was a tool box. Just about every truck in Fillmore County has one so this was no surprise. I opened it and examined its contents, finding the usual dirty wrenches and screw drivers. There was also a hammer. In fact, it was a ball-peen hammer. When I took it out to examine, I saw it wasn't dirty like the other tools but clean. In fact, it was so clean, it gleamed in the light of the setting sun. I put it back and considered the ramifications of a clean tool in a box of dirty ones.

I went back to the fire pit where all the chairs were empty. I chose my favorite one, sat down, and tried to make sense of what I had discovered. Ted had driven his truck to the marina the night of Toby's death. His tool box was available to lots of people while it was parked there but if his hammer was the murder weapon, it was another nod toward Ted being Toby's killer. Unfortunately, before I could think too deeply about this, I dozed off. When I woke, I saw someone moving in the direction of the bones. Quietly, I sneaked through the shadows and saw it was Edith. She walked a little outside camp, a telephone to her ear. It was news to me that a cell phone would work this far from Jericho but I'm not up on the technology. Although I couldn't hear her, she talked for a few minutes, then walked back to her tent and went inside.

So who was she talking to? And did it matter? I had no idea about that or much else. I went to my tent and crawled inside. A hand covered mine, then arms took me in. "Hello, cowboy," Tanya said.

Later, I woke up because I think I'd programmed my brain to hear that particular sound. There it was, that strange engine noise, far out in the darkness. I started to wake Tanya to see if she could make sense of it but she looked so peaceful, I left her alone. The next thing I knew, it was morning, and Tanya was in my arms again. She kissed me. "Good morning," she said. "I love waking up next to you."

"Any morning with a beautiful Russian woman in bed with me is bound to be a good one," I answered.

"Just any beautiful Russian woman?" she teased.

"No, dear," I said. "Just you." And, what do you know, I meant it.

30

Pıck gathered us outside the cook tent. "People," he said, "I'm an idiot."

When no one disagreed, either because they were too tired to argue or they thought his assessment was spot on, he continued. "The T. rex family would have gone out to meet the intruder. Therefore, the nest must be somewhere else."

"What about the little bones we found?" Laura asked. "That indicates a nest."

"Not necessarily. Those bones could belong to a chick, which followed its mother."

He spread out the BLM map on a field table and stabbed his finger on the eastern end of Blackie Butte. "I looked over there yesterday. An excellent outcrop of the Hell Creek formation, the right elevation, and on the other side of what was a small stream from the battle."

"The chick couldn't have crossed a stream," Laura pointed out.

"It was just a little stream, not very deep. There were rocks that the chick could have hopped on to cross." He looked up, squinting at the hill. "The mother T would have gone back to the nest after the battle, leaving the bodies of the dead rogue and the little male, which was probably her mate. It was at least a day later that the rain came and the flooding began that would preserve everything including, if we find it, the nest. Of course, the mother T would have left when the water started to rise but a nest, perhaps with eggs or egg shells, would be an amazing find all by itself."

When we all just stood around, scratching our bug bites and massaging our sore muscles, Pick said, "The bottom line is we need to move the dig."

This announcement prompted groans and whining. Laura let them play out, then started organizing everything. I was keeping an eye on Edith. When she walked away from the rest of us, I sneaked between the tents so I could watch her. She went into her tent, came out with a telephone in her hand, and walked over to Ted's truck and went behind it. In a couple of minutes, she returned to her tent, then came out without the telephone.

As our little army climbed painfully up the hill to fulfill Laura's plan and Pick's vision, I pulled Edith over. "I didn't know cell phones worked out here."

She hesitated, then said, "It's a satellite phone. As mayor, I need to be in touch with my office."

"Who were you talking to?"

"Oh, office personnel."

"You don't have any office personnel," I pointed out. "Did you talk to Cade Morgan? Last night, I'm pretty sure I heard you say his name." I hadn't but it was a stab in the dark.

She looked exasperated, and then said, "OK, Cade and I have a thing going. He's funny and makes me laugh. That's why I called him. Anyway, with Ted the way he is, what did you expect?"

I ignored that. "Did Cade mention visitors? Say, in a black limo?"

Edith shrugged. "Toby's relatives came to pick up his body. They needed a place to stay so Cade let them spend a few days at his ranch."

"Do you mind if I call Cade on your phone?" I asked. "And Ted?" The latter was because I was curious about Ted's illness, which seemed somehow convenient.

"Yes, I mind very much," Edith said with some heat. "And I mind that you're asking me all these questions. It's like you're accusing me of something. I think, Mike, you and I are no longer friends."

"Edith, I'm on your side. I always have been."

"I know," she answered, softening. "That's what makes this all so hard."

Edith kept climbing after the others and I went back to my tent and got my backpack with the Glock. I told Ray and Amelia to carry their pistols, too. I caught Jeanette drinking her second cup of coffee in the supply tent, told her about Edith and her sat phone, then said, "She and Cade are up to something. I don't know what it is." I then told her about the black limo. "My guess is it hauled some of Toby's friends here."

Jeanette considered this and said, "I still don't see why they would care about us. We didn't kill Toby and we're just a bunch of nuts digging up bones."

"These bones are worth a great deal of money," I pointed out.

She considered that, then said, "Tell you what. You work on Edith, try to find out what she knows. I'll let Pick know he's got three days and then we're going to pack up our bones and go home. We need to be thinking about getting in our hay, anyway. Is that OK?"

"Yes, except let's go in tomorrow."

She shook her head. "Look, even if Cade has designs on these bones, this is the Square C. Nobody's going to bother us here."

"Jeanette, you grew up in Fillmore County so you have a powerful belief in the sanctity of private property. Believe me, Cade Morgan doesn't operate from that perspective."

"Well, Edith does."

"Edith? I wouldn't depend on her."

"I'll give it some thought," she promised but I could tell she had her mind made up. We were stuck out here for three more days.

Pick's new site didn't look like much, just a step of ancient black-and-gray mud on the side of a fifty-foot-high peninsula, capped by a seam of rotten coal and a layer of sandstone. Above and to the right of the step was a cave. I knew that cave from my rides out by the butte and had even gone inside it just to see what I could see. It wasn't very deep, likely formed by water seeping down from the top. I'd seen rabbits in there but otherwise it was empty.

Laura appraised the site and concluded it was good matrix to dig. It wasn't too hard and or too soft, she said, and began to lay out where she wanted us to start and how we would proceed. Start we did and within a few hours, Amelia, on her hands and knees working with an ice pick and a brush, found something. "Bone!" she cried.

Laura carefully crawled over to the find. "Everybody back up, please," she said. Then, after a quick appraisal, she added, "It's bone all right. Good work, Amelia."

Amelia grinned. When she stood up, Ray was beside her, telling her how proud he was of her. She fell into his arms and right there in front of God and everybody, kissed him full on the lips. "I love you, Ray Coulter," she said.

Ray took off his hat, threw it in the air, and let out a mighty whoop followed by, "I love you, too, Amelia Thomason!"

While the rest of us were watching Ray and Amelia, Laura was focused on the bone. She scraped around it, then whisked off more dirt. Whatever it was, it was big. "It's the ilium, two paired bones," she finally announced. "But this is the top of them, not the side. That's unusual." She dug into the dirt around the twin bones and found more bone. "I think this is the end of a femur that fits into the pelvis," she said, then dug and whisked on the other side of the iliums.

"The joint of the other femur," she announced, then sat back on her haunches and whistled. "Somebody get Pick. *Now!*"

Philip went running and within minutes, brought Pick back. Pick went down on his hands and knees to inspect the bones. "What do you think it is?" he asked Laura.

While we all strained to hear, Laura said, in a voice tinged with awe, "I believe this is a Tyrannosaur standing upright. Every T. rex ever found has always been on its side."

Pick nodded. "You're almost right, Laura, but this animal is not standing. It's sitting. Or, I should say, *she* is sitting."

"On her nest," Laura said, understanding what he was getting at. "She's protecting her nest."

"Even with a torrential rain pouring down on top of her, she is nurturing her chicks. Yes, I think so."

Pick crawled off the site, then went over to a slab of sandstone and sat down, his chin resting on his palms. We all waited while he thought over whatever he was thinking. Finally, he said, "We can't expose this skeleton from the top down. The articulation would probably fall away and we would lose knowledge of her posture. I propose we come at her horizontally and expose only one side."

"In effect, a bas relief," Laura said.

"Yes. It may be that we'll have to leave her that way to be studied. We'll also have to build a structure over her for protection. Great care must be taken to preserve everything we find. Laura, I leave it to you to make the necessary plans to make this happen. No paleontologist has ever tried this, not with a creature as big as this one, but I know you can do it."

Pick's confidence in Laura was well-placed. A couple of hours later, she presented us with the plan. Essentially, it meant starting off to the left side of the T. rex, using our picks and shovels to remove all the dirt down to the probable level of the animal's feet, then shaving off the matrix trowel by trowel, ice pick by ice pick, brush by brush until we found bone again.

We attacked the site like maniacs, tons of earth moved, the spoil piling up below. It was nearly ten o'clock that night when we were done slicing off a nearly rectangular step in the side of the peninsula. We were ready to start moving toward the T. rex but Laura stopped us, telling us to get some rest and we'd start again at first light. There was no one to fix us dinner since we were all at the new dig site. All but Edith, that is. I don't know where she was during all this, maybe on her fancy sat phone for all I knew, but I saw her when we staggered back into camp. She was in one of the chairs around the fire pit, looking glum. I hoped she was thinking about leaving. Tanya and I ate some crackers, drank a sports drink, and crawled into my tent. If the strange mechanical noises occurred that night, I didn't hear them. I don't think I would have heard an atom bomb.

The next morning, we all made a run on the cook tent to grab food, mostly cereal and bread. Nobody was willing to wait for a cooked breakfast. Ray and Amelia already had the coffee going, dark and stout. It never tasted so good. "Today," Pick said as we prepared to trek to the new site, "we may make one of the most important discoveries ever made in the history of paleontology."

Pick knew how to motivate the troops, I'll give him that.

We toiled through the day, revealing more and more of the extraordinary creature. We stopped when Laura ordered us to stop so she could insure there was enough matrix to support the bones. This meant no pedestaling. We revealed only enough of the bone to see what it was, then left it in place. Gradually it began to take shape. The big T. rex's tail drooped, her legs were drawn up along her rib cage, and her neck was down. And around her was a set of small bones, snuggled against her leg. A chick maybe a yard high, still sixty-five million years later struggling to get closer to its mother for protection from the rain, just as our calves do with their moms in the pasture during storms. Of course, from the mudslide cascading down on this baby, there was no protection.

When we found the young T, Amelia couldn't take it. She retreated to a boulder for a good cry. Brian said, "Ray, you've got a great girl there."

"Don't I know it!" he exclaimed. "And you know what, she can be anything she wants to be. If she wants to be a veterinarian, then that's great. If she wants to be a paleontologist, that's fine, too. We'll figure out a way to be together."

Laura responded to this pretty little picture by saying, "Get back to work, you guys." But she said it with a smile on her face.

I pointed out some clouds on the horizon. "I think we've got rain coming our way."

Laura studied the clouds with me. "We'll keep tarps handy. That's all we can do for now." She looked at me and caught something in my expression. "What?"

"Do you believe in karmic events? I mean, we just found these dinosaurs killed by a rainstorm. Are we going to get punished for that by the rain gods?"

Laura took my observation seriously. I could tell by the way she rolled her eyes, then said, "Cut the bullshit, Mike, and get back to work." I got back to work.

The digging kept on until we reached the last vertebrae in the mother T's neck. There was no evidence of the skull. Pick came down to investigate. "I'm sure it's here," he said.

"I don't think so," Laura said. "The flood likely carried it away."

"No, Laura," Pick said quietly. "Don't you feel it? Her spirit is still here. She will be here forever to protect this nest."

"Spirit and skull are not the same," ever-practical Laura said. "I'm telling you, Pick. We're not going to find her skull. It's gone."

"Her skull is here," he replied. "All of her is here. Her love for her family would not let any part of her leave. She has defeated deep time. Don't you understand? She is watching us, trying to decide if we're worthy. When she is ready, she will let us see her face."

Laura smiled. "Pick, for a genius, sometimes you say the damndest and dumbest things. We could be making the same mistake, only in reverse, that was done for years with the Oviraptor."

At our blank expressions, Laura explained that an Oviraptor was a theropod about the size of a large dog. When paleontologists first found a partial skeleton of one in China, it was lying beside a nest with eggs. They assumed that it was raiding the nest of an unidentified herbivore and named it Oviraptor or Egg Thief. The name stuck for decades until another skeleton was found, this one nearly complete, sitting on a nest. There were Oviraptor embryos in the eggs, which sealed the deal. Rather than being an egg thief, the Oviraptor was an example of a good dinosaur parent. Laura's point was, with only this one T. rex nest found, Pick could be misinterpreting what he was seeing.

Pick, of course, was having none of it. "My vision of what happened here will be accepted by the Society of Vertebrate Paleontologists," he said.

"Maybe," Laura snapped, "but they also accepted the original Oviraptor story, too."

"I think we should celebrate," Tanya said, interrupting the esoteric discussion between the two paleontologists. "Laura? Don't you have some champagne tucked away?"

Yes, indeed, she did, Laura allowed, kept back for just such a discovery. And so we trooped into camp, the bubbly was broken out, and tired, sore, and dirty, we nonetheless held our plastic cups high and drank to our find. However it might be interpreted by scientists, at least it was certain that this was something very special.

As night fell, Pick couldn't stand being away from the nest and proposed that we troop over there. We were all tipsy enough with the champagne on our empty stomachs so off we went. It was as happy a bunch of dinosaur diggers I guess as there ever was.

We stood at the base of the hill. With our flashlights playing over the outline of the mother T. rex and her baby chick, Pick stood next to it. He said, "What you have done here will echo through history. One of the most fearsome creatures on this planet has been revealed to be a good mother, so good she was willing to lay down her own life to protect her chicks and her eggs. Just a hundred yards from us are two T's who fought to the death. One of them, the larger one, I'm certain, was a rogue. The smaller T killed the larger one with the help of another Tyrannosaur. So who was the smaller T, the one we so wrongly call inferior? I believe he was the mate of this mother T. These were his chicks, his eggs, his progeny. He had to know to take on an adversary so large and fearsome would be suicide, yet he did it. He and his mate fought as a team."

I began to visualize the scene as I think all of us did there in the dark beneath the billions of stars strewn across our big sky. The rogue approaches with stealth. The mother T smells it before she sees it. She rises from her nest and makes a cry for help. A little away, her mate answers and comes running. They see it now, the giant rogue. It intends to take over. It will murder the chicks, smash the eggs. It gets cloudy here. Is the rogue male or female? Its purpose is to begin a new family and so, depending on the sex of the rogue, it will kill the mother or the mate. No matter. The mother T and her mate are prepared to fight. They gather at the nest, then splash together through the stream to do battle. One of their older chicks follows them, hopping from rock to rock across the stream. The rogue does not hesitate. It is a killer. It charges, knocks the male off his feet, and slams into the female, meaning to force her to retreat while it deals with the smaller male. She staggers back but her mate clambers to his feet and goes after the only vulnerable part of the rogue, the underside of its neck. As the rogue tries to throw him off, the chick is trampled. The mother T shrieks. Her chick is dead and her mate is being ripped apart. With every rake of its claws, the mate's stomach and intestines are torn out of his body. There is a river of blood erupting from the guts of the little male, yet he hangs on, pulling the rogue down until the mother T rises above. She opens wide and snaps her great jaws on the rogue's head. Again and again, her huge teeth smash and stab, puncturing and splintering bone. With a terrible roar, the rogue struggles to rise but the little male just won't let go. Finally, the mother T makes the killing bite. One of her teeth punctures the rogue's brain cavity and the battle is over. The rogue T collapses into the mass of intestines and blood of the little male. Together, they die, forever joined, tooth and claw.

Pick went on, his voice echoing across the tortured land. "The mother T was not wounded much by the battle. All the breaks and cracks on her bones have bony masses covering where they healed. Still, she was old and her wounds would have hurt. She limped back to her nest, there to be comforted by her surviving chicks, and also because her latest eggs were still safe. She settled down on the nest. She had just a few more days at most to live."

We could all imagine it. Miles away, there was a crack of sudden light and long thunder. A massive storm was upon the land. Down came torrents of rain on the mother T but she would not leave her eggs or chicks. Then came a distant rumble that grew ever louder. Still, she stayed. A gigantic wave of water was racing toward her, traveling at hundreds of miles per hour. It struck the hill she and her nest was on, then swirled about, tearing away huge boulders and ripping huge trees out by their roots. Still, she stayed. Above, a great cliff, already loosened by the torrential rain, came loose and slid down, a tidal wave of mud. It covered everything including the mother T, her chicks, her eggs, and her nest. The great blackness of deep time began for her and her progeny. Later, more floods came to cover the nest and everything was sealed and protected.

"And so it happened," Pick said, "that all this was preserved for us to discover, to see, to contemplate, and, at last, to understand. For this is nothing but confirmation of the ultimate victory that is love. We weep for this creature as we must weep for ourselves. She and her mate have taught us lessons that we as a civilization should already know. There is no greater gift than to lay down your life for those you love. The family is holy and eternal. Nature, God, the Great Being, or Event that created life on Earth put those truths inside even this most fearsome creature. When we reveal it to an anxious world, I think there may well be a revolution of spirit everywhere."

It was a pretty speech but I couldn't help but feel that perhaps Pick was making way too much of it. By their expressions, Tanya, Amelia, Ray, and the Marsh brothers were enchanted by all this. I looked over at Jeanette. She was frowning and I think a little embarrassed by what Pick had said. Edith just looked perplexed. Laura's expression was one of doubt. Well, I guess philosophers, or even slightly nutty paleontologists, expound truths and we either accept them or not. All I knew was, at that moment, my heart went out to that Tyrannosaur family and I felt like they were right there, still alive.

31

THE NEXT MORNING, WHILE we were eating breakfast and preparing for another long day with the mama T, Cade Morgan arrived in his Mercedes followed by the black limo. Cade got out his car and four men got out of the limo. The men were dressed in loose slacks, Hawaiian print shirts, and wingtip shoes. Their heads were shaved. Across their shirts were leather straps holding holsters with the butts of pistols protruding. They were, in other words, armed Russian bully boys, almost certainly soldiers of the Wolves. My backpack with my Glock was sitting on the ground beside me. I knelt and removed the pistol, then tucked it under my belt in the small of my back.

Cade was all smiles. "Hallooo," he called. "This is quite the complex. And all those big white things. Are those the bones? Pick, where are you?"

The Russians lined up behind him as Jeanette came out of the supply tent. She was holding a mug of coffee. "What are you doing on my property, Cade Morgan?" she demanded.

"Well, hello, Jeanette," Cade answered in a cheerful voice. "This may be your land, but those are my property." He nodded toward the jacketed bones.

"What are you talking about, you fool?" Before I could stop her, Jeanette walked up to Cade. "What the hell is this?"

I glanced at my tent where my rifle was and judged it too far away. Then I saw Ray coming around the cook tent with his pistol in his hand. I caught his eye, gesturing with my chin for him to get back out of sight. As he did, I caught a glimpse of Amelia behind him. Laura, Tanya, Brian, and Philip came out, attracted by the raised voices. Cade looked past Jeanette to the others. "I don't see Pick. Didn't I ask for him? I'm sure I did."

Jeanette jabbed her finger in Cade's chest. "Leave, you idiot! Now!"

Cade frowned. "Aw, Jeanette, you always make things so hard. By the way, we shot your dog as we came in. He didn't like us on your ranch for some reason."

"You killed Soup?" Jeanette yelled and reared back and threw a punch at Cade.

Cade dodged and laughed. "Well, we shot him. I don't know if we killed him or not. We didn't have time to check." He nodded toward Tanya. "The Russian girl," he said and one of the men walked over and grabbed Tanya by her arm. He had taken his pistol out of its holster.

I drew my Glock and pointed it at the Russian. "Leave her alone."

The Russian, a huge brute who had to weigh three hundred pounds, looked at me and laughed. Then, faster than I could react, he jammed his pistol into Tanya's hair and pulled the trigger.

The way I remember that moment is like this. It was as if the very plane of life had turned into one of those curved mirrors that reflect reality in a distorted way. Tanya's face expanded grotesquely as the bullet traveled into her skull and out the other side. Before she fell, I fired for the Russian's heart and my bullet sped straight and true. He staggered, then fell on his back, his short, thick legs flung up, one of his wingtip shoes flying off. He was wearing white socks. It's odd what you remember when you shoot a man in the heart.

Before I could turn toward Cade and the other Russians to shoot them, I was bowled over. Two Russians piled on top of me and one of them wrenched the Glock out of my hand, then jerked me to my feet. To my everlasting disappointment, the Russian I'd shot was sitting up. He was also laughing; his teeth ugly, broken, and yellow. He unbuttoned his shirt and pointed at the body armor covering his chest. He found his shoe, put it on, then stood up and walked over to me and punched his huge fist into my stomach. I doubled over, fell, and he kicked me in the back. I expected a bullet next but it didn't come. They simply walked away. I rolled into a sitting position as Pick made his appearance, looking wide-eyed and scared. He saw Tanya lying in the dirt, the blood leaking from her horrible wound. His reaction was to gasp, his mouth falling open in shock.

Cade walked over and slapped Pick hard in the face. "We had a deal and you're going to see it through," he said as Pick choked back a sob.

I heard Edith's voice. "Get over there with the others." I saw Ray and Amelia walk from behind the cook tent with Edith behind them. Edith was holding two pistols, a .38 and Ray's .44. Ray was holding Amelia at her waist, his hand on the small of her back as if urging her along.

"Sorry, Mike," Ray said as they walked to stand with the others. "I thought Mayor Brescoe was on our side."

I climbed to my feet. Jeanette walked over to stand beside me. Edith confronted us. "I told you to leave, Mike."

"Tell me what's going on here, Edith," I said, grateful she'd put herself between Jeanette and me and the Russians. They hadn't killed us yet and I wasn't sure why. What was certain was I needed to kill them.

"We just wanted the skeleton of the little dinosaur Bill Coulter found," Edith said. "Pick made this all so damn complicated finding all these other bones."

"Edith, shut up," Cade said. "Everybody shut up."

Jeanette ignored him. "Pick, what is this? You tell me."

"I did everything for science," Pick replied, looking miserable.

"For money, you fool," Cade said. "You knew that."

The Russian I'd shot kept eyeballing me like he couldn't wait to tear me into little pieces. The other three were standing around, nonchalantly holding their pistols. I guess they were waiting to find out who to kill next. It appeared Cade was in charge and I suppose wholesale slaughter wasn't his way although I had no doubt that would be the end result. It was either them or us. The scene of what was going to happen played itself out in my head. First, Cade was going to berate Pick for not doing what he was supposed to do. Pick, I understood now, worked for Cade. I didn't know why but never mind. Then, based on what Pick told him, Cade was going to decide what to do with Pick and then us. I concluded he would decide there was no reason to keep us alive and therefore have us killed. We were probably just minutes away from that happening.

Anywhere else other than Montana (OK, maybe Texas), I think people in our situation would have waited, hoping not to be killed, and then got killed. Here, we did things differently. The relaxed posture of the Russians showed me they didn't understand that. I glanced at Ray who still had his hand on Amelia's back. He shifted his eyes and I understood why his hand was where it was. It was time to move. I didn't run. I walked, crossing the open ground between me and where Tanya lay.

"Where are you going, Mike?" Cade asked.

"To see if Tanya is alive," I said, which made the Russian who'd murdered her laugh.

I went down on my knees beside her. Jeanette called out, "Mike, she's gone. You can't do anything."

What happened next took just seconds but I will describe it in slow motion. I cradled Tanya into my arms, turning her so I had the back of her bloody head leaning against my chest. The Russian who'd shot her came at me, his pistol raised. I lifted Tanya up, keeping her between me and him while my hand went into her front pocket where she'd put the .22 pistol I'd given her. I released its safety, pulled it out, and fired it. The bullet struck the Russian in his right eye with a satisfying spurt of blood. To my disappointment, it apparently didn't have enough energy to penetrate his brain, probably lodging in a sinus cavity. It was, however, a definite distraction. He screamed and staggered around. "Run to the dig!" I yelled.

Jeanette, Brian, Philip, and Laura didn't hesitate. They ran, scrambling up Blackie Butte. The Russians fortunately concentrated on me, their bullets striking Tanya's corpse. I ignored them and shot at Cade with my little pistol, hitting him in the leg. Amelia knocked Edith down with a hard right to the jaw and took away her pistols. Ray withdrew Amelia's pistol, hidden in the small of her back, and fired at the Russians, who all scattered. Ray then handed her pistol back to Amelia and took back his .44 before they ran together over to Blackie Butte. The Russian I'd shot in the eye was still staggering around, but Ray put him out of his misery by providing a little .44-caliber medicine. Ranch kids. You got to love them.

I scurried over to Edith, who was sitting up but dazed. I grabbed her by the back of her shirt and dragged her with me. The path up to the dig led slightly behind a fold in the hill, giving us cover. At the dig, I threw Edith down and did a quick count. We were all there—me, Jeanette, Ray, Amelia, Laura, Brian, and Philip—with sandstone boulders providing us with some cover. Pick was there, too, the little sandy-haired, pony-tailed rat.

I ducked as bullets ricocheted off the boulders. I had Tanya's .22, Ray had his .44, and Amelia her .38 and Edith's, too. "Jeanette, do you have your pistol on you?"

"No, Mike. I'm sorry."

So that was it, four pistols and just the ammo that was in them. Amelia silently handed Edith's pistol to Jeanette. The shooting stopped and Ray peeked around a slab of sandstone. "They're just standing there, looking up at us."

"Do you see Cade?"

"Yeah. He's on his back, pushed up on his elbows, looking around. There's blood on his jeans. No, wait, he's getting up and limping over to one of our chairs."

"Flesh wound," I said. "I hoped I'd hit bone."

Laura said, "Pick, what's all this, anyway?"

Pick was huddled against a boulder. "I'm sorry," he gulped. "I messed up."

"No shit!" Laura snapped.

Pick hung his head. "Where do I start?"

"The beginning is always good," I said.

Everyone was looking at him. He looked back, then shook his head. "When I was in Argentina, Cade sent me an e-mail with just the photographs Ray put in his paper. Cade said they were bones he'd found on his property and he wanted to sell them. He wanted to hire me to come find the rest of the skeleton. I kept telling him that it was the science that was important, but if a baby T. rex skeleton was found, I could raise the money to see that he was paid. He agreed to that so I came. When I got here, he gave me a complete copy of Ray's paper and started telling me about the complications, that the bones weren't on his property but maybe on the BLM and I had to get permission to cross the Square C and all that."

Laura asked, "Why didn't you leave?"

Pick looked around. "Did anybody bring any water?"

"I've got two liters in my backpack," Laura said.

"Don't give him any until he tells us the rest of his story," I said. I also calculated how long eight people could survive on two liters of water in the blazing sun. Nine, counting Edith. The answer was not long.

Pick took a weary breath and said, "I swear I had no idea that Cade would bring men like this after us."

"How about the mayor?" I asked. "What's her part in this?"

"I think she was the one who first got hold of Ray's paper and showed it to Cade."

That made sense. As mayor, Edith probably checked the high school Internet site occasionally and there would have been the English teacher's posting of the paper.

Pick went on. "Edith was at Cade's ranch when I met with him. She gave me the BLM permit and said her husband would let me remove the bones with no problems."

"And Toby?"

"He was there, too. He was very knowledgeable of paleontology and understood what it meant to find a baby Tyrannosaur. He said he had friends with lots of money who would finance future expeditions. I agreed to go see what I could find and then we'd talk more. That's all I agreed to. But then something happened. Could I have some water now?"

I nodded to Laura and she handed him a bottle. "Just a swallow," she warned.

Pick got his swallow and went on. "I spent the night at Cade's ranch and then drove to the Square C the next day. After I talked to you and Jeanette, I was surprised to find Mayor Brescoe and Cade were waiting for me just inside the BLM fence. They made it clear that, despite what was said the day before, I was working for them. That's when they killed that black cow. They said that could be me."

"My bull!" Jeanette gasped.

"Cade had a rifle and shot it. When it didn't die right away, the mayor went over to their truck, got a shovel and a big knife, came back and hit the cow in the head with the shovel that broke. The cow was still alive so she cut its throat. It was awful. She also cut the fence, saying no one would suspect a local would do such a thing."

Jeanette stared at Edith who was lying where I'd dropped her. I noticed her head was a bit bloody, seeing as how it had bounced off a sandstone rock. I hadn't meant to do that. She was occasionally groaning. Otherwise, she seemed to be out cold.

"How could she do that to a poor, dumb animal?" Jeanette demanded.

"I'd never seen anything like it," Pick said. "I mean she acted crazy. She was laughing the whole time. Cade finally told her to settle down."

"So you agreed to play ball," I said.

"It was either that or run away. I really wanted to look for that little T. rex. I figured if I found it, something could be worked out. When we started finding more than I ever imagined and not on the BLM, it got a lot more complicated. I just kept putting Cade off about it."

"Your head in deep time as usual," Laura accused. "Look, I want everybody to know Tanya and I had nothing to do with this."

"That's true," Pick said. "I called you both to come help and I didn't tell you about the complications."

"What you did got Tanya killed," Laura hissed at him. "And it might get us all dead before this is over. Pick, you're a complete idiot."

I thought that was a bit of an understatement as bullets began to *ping* on our little rock castle and whistle overhead. Brian said,

"Maybe we could head for the lake and get some walleye fishermen to pick us up."

It wasn't a bad idea except for the news Ray gave us next. He was keeping his eye on things below. "They've got automatic weapons. Looks like AK-47s. And one of those guys has moved around behind us on the lake side."

"What are we going to do, Mike?" Jeanette asked.

I appreciated her asking, which effectively put me in charge. I gave it some thought. I checked Edith to see if she had her satellite phone with her. She didn't, so I asked, "Anybody got a radio?"

"I do," Laura said.

"Start calling. See if anyone answers. We're safe for now, I think. I don't see those guys charging up here, at least during the day."

Laura moved off to the other side of the dig and started talking into her radio. A few minutes later, she said, "Nothing. I've tried a number of frequencies, including the emergency channel. I'll keep trying."

This was a disappointment but not a surprise. The radios didn't have much range and there were hills higher than Blackie Butte all around us. That's why Laura hadn't been able to raise Pick the night we all came into the ranch.

"OK," I said. "When it gets dark, I'm thinking Brian's right. We head toward the lake. If they only have one guy guarding that route, we should be able to get past him."

"Why not go for the ranch?" Jeanette asked.

"Lots of fences to cross. Anyway, they'll be expecting us to go that way. It's wide open to the lake."

"There's a full moon," Ray pointed out.

"That will make it harder," I acknowledged. "When we go, I'll start shooting to keep their heads down. Ray, you take everybody else and head out. If that guy between us and the lake starts shooting, find him and kill him."

"I'll take care of him," Ray swore.

"Mike, you can't stay behind," Jeanette said.

"Somebody has to. I won't wait long before heading out, too."

"They're doing something," Ray said. "They have a big net they're spreading out."

I crawled over to have a look. It did look like a big net but for what purpose I couldn't imagine. Then one of the Russians went over and started rolling one of the jacketed bones toward it."

Pick was watching. "They're going to destroy the bones!" He stood up. "Cade, tell them to leave the bones alone! They'll break the jackets!"

This was answered by a round flying past Pick's head. Ray reached up and pulled him down. "Don't do that again, Dr. Pickford," Ray said.

Down below, Cade pushed himself out of his chair and limped closer to our hill. "Pick, if you don't want these bones destroyed, come down here, and show us what to do. We've got a helicopter coming for them."

That was news. It was going to have to be a damn big helicopter to lift the plastered bones of two T. rexes. "They can't let us live," Jeanette said. "If they take the bones and we're alive to alert the state police, a helicopter is going to be easy to trace."

This wasn't news. From the moment Cade and the Russians had shown up, I knew they meant to kill us. Their mistake was not to do it right away. "Pick, where do you think they'll take the bones?" I asked.

Pick mulled my question over, then said, "Toby mentioned Mexico when we were still talking about only the baby skeleton. He said there would be less questions that way. Mike, we can't let them get away with those bones. We must bring this knowledge to the world."

"Hey, Pick!" Cade called. "Dammit. The boys just dropped a bone. It's all busted up."

"Stop it!" Pick screamed.

"Remain calm, Pick," I said. "Give it some thought. They want those bones to sell. They're not going to damage them."

Pick nodded although I could tell he was unconvinced. I thought about the helicopter. Likely, rather than trying to fly with a huge load a long distance, it would transfer the bones to trucks somewhere. Then it occurred to me there was one among us who would know exactly the plan.

I prodded her with my boot. "Edith, get up. We need to talk."

It took a few more prods but she finally sat up. She was holding her head. "Mike, you hurt me."

"I should have killed you."

She began to weep. "I didn't mean any of this to happen."

"Yes, you did. Now, Edith, the only way you're going to get out of this is to tell me the truth when I ask you some questions. Will you do that?"

Sniffing, she nodded and I asked, "Tell me about the helicopter. What's the plan?"

"It belongs to the buyer," she said. "I don't know his name. Cade and Toby set it up. Some rich Mexican."

"OK. Who are the bully boys below?"

"You know who they are."

"Well, tell me, anyway."

"Russian mob. Cade owes them a lot of money from when he made movies. Toby came to collect. He had worked with Cade on the movies and liked him. Rather than beat him up or kill him, he tried to help. Toby was very interested in everything and said he was an avid amateur paleontologist. When I showed him a copy of Ray's paper that I got off the school Web site, he thought it would be a great idea to sell dinosaur bones to offset Cade's debts. So they started looking around the Net and found out about Pick. He was not only a respected paleontologist, but they found evidence that he sold fossils from time to time. So Cade sent him an e-mail. It didn't take long for him to respond."

"What was Ted's part in this?"

She looked away for a moment, then said, "He wasn't part of it. I asked him to give Pick a permit and he agreed. Then he got all bent out of shape about his precious BLM. He just couldn't leave it alone."

"Did Ted kill Toby?"

She smirked. "I told you my husband doesn't kill men."

"Where's Ted now?"

Her expression was distant. "Swimming with the walleyes."

I felt a cold chill down my back. My questions seemed to be bringing out another Edith, one I had never known. "Did you kill Toby?"

Her eyes bored into me. "I found him on his knees in front of my husband. Call me a jealous wife. Anyway, I just wanted to do it. I got a hammer, used it on the back of Toby's skull." She smiled. "Ted took off running. I wasn't going to kill him, the fool. I still needed him or at least I thought I did. Anyway, I got a hacksaw blade and sawed open Toby's throat, then put that note on him just to throw you off track. Yeah, I figured you'd start investigating. You're no cowboy, Mike, just a cop in cowboy clothes."

"How did you get Toby into the lake?"

"I told Cade what I'd done. We waited until the dance was over and dragged him to the lake. We thought he'd sink but he didn't."

"Did you kill Ted, too?"

She shrugged. "Well, after he started threatening to tell the police I'd killed Toby, Cade shot him. Then I cut his throat."

I still couldn't believe this was the same Edith I'd cared about. "How did you get mixed up in all this?"

I guess she figured she didn't have anything to lose by telling me more. She said, "Cade said if we got enough money, we'd leave here and go to Mexico. There is a very big man there, the one buying the bones, who would take care of us, set us up." She looked at Jeanette. "I would do anything to get out of this county and away from these ranchers. You're a bitch, Jeanette. You always have been. But you ended up marrying Bill Coulter and climbed on top of the pyramid. Me? I was just mayor of a shithole married to a prick."

"You killed my bull," Jeanette said. "And cut my fence."

At this, Edith started to laugh. It was a harsh, mean laugh and I knew now that she was insane. Completely and utterly. "You see, Mike?" she said. "She cares more about that damn bull and her fences than people. Cade, Toby, and I decided to throw everybody off track by killing more cows and cutting more fences, leaving behind that stupid Green Monkey note. Ranchers are all paranoids. I knew exactly how to sucker them."

"It's time to be quiet now, Edith," I said.

Edith made a sudden grab for Amelia's pistol. Amelia pulled back in time, but Edith vaulted over the sandstone and ran down the hill, screaming for Cade. I don't know how many bullets struck her. She fell, then rolled until she hit the sand at the bottom.

32

"They're leaving Mayor Brescoe where she fell," Ray said, peeking around a sandstone boulder.

"How about Cade?"

"He's just sitting over by the tents. He's got a bandana wrapped around his leg. The men have moved about a dozen of the bones into the net, but now they've stopped."

When I heard the *whop-whop* of blades, I knew why. The noise grew louder and then a helicopter appeared. It flew over us once, then turned around and came in to land behind the camp, its rotor wash tossing tents around. It was a Bell UH-1, the famous utility helicopter of Vietnam, painted a dark blue with no other insignia. Its turbines whined down and two men, the pilot and co-pilot I presumed, emerged and walked over to inspect the bones on the cargo net. They also conferred with one of the Russians and then Cade limped over. There was a lot of waving of arms and pointing at the bodies of Tanya and Edith. Then one of the pilots started walking back to the helicopter. He apparently meant to leave as this earned him a bullet in his back. The other pilot suddenly got a lot more cooperative. All the talking and gesticulating stopped and he started lifting the edge of the cargo net. Two of the mobsters helped him and they pulled it together over the bones and cinched it at its center.

There was some pointing in our direction and then the pilot and one of the Russians carrying an AK walked over to the helicopter and got in. As the rotors started to turn, I realized what that was all about. "We're going to get strafed," I said, thinking fast. "The cave by the mama T. We've got to get there."

"No!" Pick yelped. "If they attack us there, they'll hit her!"

"Shut up, Dr. Pickford," Ray said. Then, to me, "Guess we'd better get going. I'll lead."

"OK. Ray then Amelia, Jeanette, Laura, Brian, and Philip. Pick, you and I will go last."

The helicopter rose and dipped its nose to gather speed and gain altitude before turning back toward us. "Go!" I barked and Ray took off, Amelia on his heels. Jeanette was right behind her. Laura and the brothers tore after them, too. I pushed Pick ahead of me and we scrambled—falling, rolling, getting up, and running again. The helicopter came roaring overhead but if there were shots, I couldn't hear them because of its rotor and engine noise.

We reached the cave and fell inside. Pick collapsed and started whining. "They'll destroy the nest."

I didn't care about Pick and at that moment, not much about the dinosaurs. "Ray, get over here, help me set up a defense." We stacked up some rocks and I motioned everybody to lie down.

When Pick kept complaining, Amelia said, "Dr. Pickford, didn't you say that the mother T would watch over her nest forever? You said you could feel her. Won't she still do that?"

Pick shook his head. I guess he didn't have confidence in his own mystic philosophy when things got rough. Funny how that works.

The helicopter made a pass but the AK fire out of it was ineffective. Then, two Russians on foot appeared below us and sprayed bullets into our cave. Fortunately, the bullets didn't ricochet but were absorbed into the ancient mud of the Hell Creek Formation. I traded pistols with Amelia—the .22 just didn't cut it for distance or impact—and Ray and I fired back, carefully squeezing off only a single round apiece, trying to make them count. Happily, I hit one of the Russians in his arm. He twirled around, then fell, before getting up and running away. The other Russian went with him. That was good but we were in a cave, not able to see much of anything, and that was bad. I said, "Ray, you and I need to get to the top of this hill."

"No," Jeanette said. "I'll go with you. Ray, you hold the line down here. You're the better shot."

Ray hesitated and I said, "She's right, Ray. We need you here." I looked up, trying to recall the terrain above. We would need to go all the way to the top where there was a layer of sandstone slabs for protection. I told Jeanette what we were going to do.

"Now or never, Mike," Jeanette said, catching a water bottle Laura tossed to her.

"Let's go," I said and we bounded out of that cave like Butch Cassidy and the Sundance Kid. I guess I was Butch. We scrambled up, sending little landslides behind us, and were up that hill in a few seconds, falling down on top of it. No one shot at us. We crawled over to some boulders. I looked toward the camp and could see the helicopter had landed but just about everything else was blocked by the truncated top of Blackie Butte. To the north was a series of hills that we'd need to cross if we tried to break out toward the lake. There was no sign of the Russian sent to guard in that direction. No matter. We were stuck until nightfall.

Then I saw something interesting on the western horizon. "Look," I said, nudging Jeanette. "Something coming our way."

"Whoa," she said, "a big'un."

It was a "big'un" all right. The layer of slate-black clouds blanked out the entire westward sky. Well, like old Bill Coulter said. A quiet day in Fillmore County is a temptation to God. We were going to be hit by a terrible blow.

The UH-1's rotors started up, then it lifted off and moved to hover where the bones had been stacked in the net. When it rose, the net with its load was dangling beneath. The chopper flew over us to the east, the *whop-whop* of the blades diminishing to nothing in a few minutes. "There go our dinosaurs," Jeanette said, sorrowfully, "at least part of them. How do you think they'll move them, Mike?"

"The way I'd do it," I said, "would be to have some big trucks waiting out there somewhere, maybe over by the Ogallala Indian Reservation where there's hardly any traffic. I'd load up the trucks and drive south on the Interstate. Crossing the border into Mexico shouldn't be much trouble with the right payoffs."

"I've been such a fool," Jeanette said. "You tried to warn me."

"Well, maybe I should have listened to myself," I said. "I've had a hunch for days we should get the hell away from here."

She leaned back and allowed a sigh. "I'm sorry about Tanya."

I hadn't been able to think much about Tanya, not while dodging bullets and such. I didn't want to think about her now, either. Time for that later if I was still alive, a doubtful proposition. "She was a fine woman," was all I had to say.

The hours ticked by. I saw Cade once or twice limping around and then a couple of the Russians. They were moving more jacketed bones into another cargo net. Then I heard a small rock slide below. It was Pick climbing up to us. He fell over the top and crawled over. "What do you want?" Jeanette asked him in something less than a happy tone.

"I want one of your pistols," he said. "I don't intend to let them destroy the mother T and the nest. If necessary, I'll go down fighting."

"I told you," I said, "that they're not going to destroy anything. They plan on selling it."

"They can't remove the bones at this site. None of them are jacketed. All they can do is tear them up trying to get at us. Let me have some dignity, Mike. If the greatest discovery in paleontological history has to be destroyed, I'd just soon die with it."

"No," I said. "It's not happening. We're going to break out tonight."

"Until then, can I stay up here?"

"The helicopter might try to strafe us again when it comes back."

"I'll take my chances. I don't like that cave."

I looked at Jeanette and she rolled her eyes. "All right," I said. "Just don't cause any trouble."

"No, no. Of course not."

Pick was a bit too agreeable to suit me but I had other things on my mind. The mobsters plus Cade were probably trying to figure out how to get at us. Two of them were wounded, one of the Russians in his arm, Cade in his leg, but no big thing to determined men. Most likely, anyway, they'd send the still healthy Russians to flush us out, then pick us off. But how? When I stopped to think about it, Pick was right. The best approach to the cave was over the mother T and her nest and I didn't want that beautiful site destroyed, either.

Darkness started to settle in on us while the big storm edged ever closer. We could see flashes of lightning within its core and occasionally a flickering blue-white streak between the clouds and the ground. Thunder rumbled menacingly. If I'd been in my trailer, I might have decided it would be a good night to spend in the barn. It took me back to the night before Pick arrived. Beneath that storm, we had brought new life into the world. On this night, there was no chance of that. We were all potential killers.

Then we saw headlights from a vehicle coming across the Square C. It was a sport utility vehicle and out of it came four more men dressed similarly to the Russians. What was with the Hawaiian shirts? Blackie Butte wasn't exactly the beach of Waikiki. Anyway, there they were, four more Wolves to come and get us. Where they'd come from, I didn't know. Maybe an auxiliary group within a day's drive or maybe they had been coming all along. Maybe they got lost. It wouldn't be the first time city boys got lost in the vast state of Montana and Fillmore County. It didn't matter. They were here and we were in even more trouble.

"We don't have a chance, do we?" Jeanette said, more as a statement than a question.

"Well, to paraphrase Wellington after the Battle of Waterloo, it's going to be a close-run thing."

"I want to at least get Ray and Amelia out," she said. "You and I need to create some sort of distraction."

There was only one distraction I could think of. Jeanette and I could charge the camp, pistols blazing. Maybe then the others could get away. There was more than one problem with that, of course, but a major one was that the cave was on the southeast side of the hill and Ray, Amelia, and everybody else needed to go north. They'd either have to detour by going around the hill or climb up and over. Both routes would expose them to the gunmen. But it was at least a chance. I told Jeanette what I was thinking.

"We'll go when you say," she said.

"When you go, I'll head down to the mother T," Pick said.

"I still don't see what good that would do," Jeanette replied. "What are you going to do when they come? Yell at them?"

Pick rolled over on his back and looked up at the sky. "I don't know. I just know that I've got to stop them somehow."

I was keeping my eye on the Wolves. Two of the four new ones,

AK's on their shoulders, disappeared as they walked toward the butte, then reappeared, dragging the bodies of Tanya and Edith behind them. They pulled them inside the cook tent, left the bodies there, then came outside. I was surprised when one of them fell down. The other one looked at him, then another Russian walked over. It was hot, even with the approaching storm stirring up a breeze, and I suspected heat prostration. But then the others turned and looked north, then retreated into the camp.

What had *that* been all about? The downed Wolf just laid there, not moving. It would have been a good time to have binoculars. Another Wolf walked to the supply tent. He inspected his buddy on the ground and then he also fell down and didn't move. Jeanette had been watching, too. "What's happening?" she asked.

"Beats me," I said and it did.

We saw no more movement in the camp for the next hour or two. The storm came upon us at dusk. It started with a brisk wind, then all hell broke loose. Darkness fell across us and the rain came in a deluge. Lightning cracked and thunder shook the ground.

"We should go now," Jeanette said.

I thought she was right but we'd forgotten something. It was nearly impossible to walk on the wet gumbo, much less run on it to get to the camp. This was demonstrated by Pick standing up and his feet flying out from under him. Covered with mud, he crawled to the lip of the hill and said, "I'm going down to the dig. I can slide there on my belly."

I said, "All right, Pick. But I still don't know what you're going to do."

"I want to be with her. I can't explain it."

Jeanette put her hand on his shoulder. "Pick . . ."

"I know," he said. What he knew, I didn't have a clue, but I guessed it had something to do with their roll in the hay. Pardon me if I don't put a romantic spin on their moment.

"Stop at the cave and tell them to sit tight," I told him.

Pick nodded, then slid over the lip and down the hill. He made it to the cave, stopped there, then wallowed on to the nest, which had turned into a gumbo hole. Pick huddled there, waiting. They would kill him when they found him, of course, but there was nothing I could do about that.

Mainly, I was trying to figure out what to do. Even if the storm was short-lived, the gumbo was going to be too slick to walk on until the sun came out to dry it. We could crawl but that was about it. Of course, that meant the Wolves weren't going to be able to climb up to get us, either. We were in a stalemate.

"Mike, I don't understand what happened to those two who fell down by the supply tent," Jeanette said. "They've still not moved."

"There's probably a lot of fat in their diet. Maybe they had heart attacks."

"Mike."

"I don't know, Jeanette."

We hunkered down. And then, when the thunderous displays of lightning paused, I heard that strange mechanical sound again. What the hell was that?

It got darker and the rain began to diminish. I guess the helicopter had been waiting for a break in the weather as I heard the whopping of its blades toward the east. That was when the Wolves attacked. They had been sneaking around to the south and assaulted the hill, guns and AKs blazing. Of course, as soon as they started up, they slipped and fell down. They started up again, only to meet the same fate. I guess they don't have gumbo in Russia. Jeanette and I squeezed off a couple of rounds, missing our targets in the low light.

I didn't detect any shooting from the cave, probably because they were pinned down by all the fire coming their way.

Then the helicopter roared overhead. It was in one big hurry, rolling over in a tight turn and settling in on the camp. It didn't land but hovered above the jacketed bones. I guess somebody on the ground attached the net because when the chopper rose, the net was dangling beneath it. It made a circle toward the east, then began to gain altitude. That was when a bright light stabbed out of the darkness from near the hills toward the lake and lit up the helicopter. The chopper turned away but the spot of the light stayed with it. Then a red streak leapt from the source of the light, tore through the rain, and plowed into the UH-1. It jerked at the impact, then rolled over on its side and went down with a massive fireball rising from its twisted remains. The light switched off and everything was quiet but the thunder and the grumble of a burning helicopter. All I can say is I was more than a bit confused over what had happened to the chopper, but grateful.

Below, the Wolves were coming at us again, just raising hell with their automatic weapons. I doubted that they knew their helicopter had been blasted out of the sky since all the action had occurred on the other side of our hill.

Standing before the bas relief of the mama T, Pick was screaming at the Russians to stop. It was none other than Cade Morgan who managed to scramble up to the dig. He proceeded to point a pistol at Pick, then stopped to look with awe at the great headless beast squatting there.

"Yes," Pick said, "it is another T. rex. A mother T and she is on her nest, protecting it. It is the wonder of wonders. Nothing in paleontology has ever been seen like it before."

The rain was picking up again, heavy drops striking the dig. To Pick's horrified eyes, the leg bones of the T began to come apart, sliding into the muck. "Help me, Cade," Pick said. "We need to lay a tarp over it."

Cade was over his initial shock. "I've got two sets of bones. I don't need another. No, I guess I need to kill you."

Pick backed up against the side of the hill. The mud was flowing around him in a small river, coating his head, his shoulders, and his back. It was as if he was melting into the wall of mud. Above him, something was forming out of the mud. Cade saw it and laughed. Pick looked up and saw the muzzle of the mama T coming out of the mud. "Damn," Cade said, "that's an ugly thing."

Then there was a roar behind Cade and he turned to see what had made it. Pick took the opportunity to reach up, grasp a foot-long steak knife of a tooth, and pull it free before launching himself to plunge the tooth into Cade's back. Cade screamed and threw his head back as a huge light switched on, flooding the entire side of the hill with a blue-white fluorescence.

Jeanette and I slid down the hill, reaching the cave. "We're OK," Ray said and I kept going to the lip of the dig. Pick was standing there over Cade who wasn't moving, mainly because there was a big brown tooth in his back. Then I noticed the snout, the teeth, and the bony brows of a giant skull protruding from the muck. "Hello, Mama," I said. "You took care of your child, didn't you?" She didn't reply but I thought she looked happy for a sixty-five-million-year-old Tyrannosaurus rex.

I shaded my eyes from the glaring light, which suddenly switched off. I turned away, trying to get my night vision back, and then I heard the shriek of metal on metal and a thumping noise. It sounded like a steel hatch being thrown open. A huge reddish-purple dot was hanging in my eyes but as it faded, I slipped and slid my way around the dig and down the hill. On the way, I fell across a body. By its Hawaiian shirt, I saw it was one of the Russians lying on his back.

There was an additional color to his shirt, a florid, bloody spot at the chest where there was also a big hole. Whatever kind of bullet had struck him was armor piercing.

I heard a voice I recognized but did not belong to the scene. "Mike, you OK?"

A big hand reached down and grasped mine and drew me up. It was Sam Haxby. I looked past him to what I now recognized was an armored car. Its engine noise was very familiar. I had been hearing it at night for weeks. The face painted on its front had reptilian eyes and a great, grinning mouth of teeth. Then I noticed Sam was carrying a huge rifle with what looked like a night scope and a big silencer on its barrel. He kicked the dead Wolf. "I think this is the last of them. Sorry it took so long for us to plug 'em. We wanted to make sure of our shots."

"Sam," I said. "What are you doing here?"

He looked at me as if I was daft. "Why, on regular patrol, Mike. Since them Green Monkey Wrench ecoterrorists hit us, we've been keeping an eye on our ranch and the BLM, don't you know? We've been watching your tent city for more than a while. You looked like you weren't doing nothing but digging in the dirt so we left you alone. But then Cade Morgan and these fellows arrived and we couldn't figure it out. Heard your radio calls, too, but we thought we'd just sit tight to see what was what. But when that damn black helicopter arrived, we knew it was time to stand up to these bastards. What are they, FBI, CIA, or some government agency we don't know about?"

"Russian mob," I said. "And I think the helicopter was navy blue, not black."

Sam took this disappointing news gracefully. "Well, I suppose that's almost as good."

I was still in a mild state of shock. "You . . . you shot down the helicopter?"

"Naw. Jack did. Got her good, didn't he? Tell you what. Them old Soviet shoulder-mounted SA-14's work pretty good."

"What else you got in those bunkers, Sam? Nuclear weapons?"

He laughed. "They're too much trouble. Did you know a nuke degrades in ten years?"

I honestly didn't know that and said so while Sam kept laughing.

Jeanette slid down beside me and I helped her to her feet. She said, "Thank you, Sam. You saved us."

Sam took off his hat as Carl and Jack climbed out of the armored car. They took off their hats, too. "Happy to help a neighbor, Jeanette," Sam said.

Ray, Amelia, Laura, Brian, and Philip slid down the muddy slope, too. Amelia got up and hugged Sam and his boys. Hell, I felt like hugging those survivalist bastards, too.

Jeanette put her hand on my shoulder and leaned against me. "Thanks, cowboy," she said. "What do we do now?"

I was reminded of something old Bill Coulter used to say. When you get to where you're going, it's probably time to stop.

"Let's go home," I said, and after Ray and I gently wrapped Tanya in a sleeping bag and placed her in our truck, that's what we did.

ONE YEAR LATER...

I AM WRITING ON my patio beneath the awning attached to my trailer. Beside me on a small round table is a g&t. Before me is the land of the Square C and above me is the big sky of Montana. In short, I am in a perfect spot. Right where I want to be. It is time to be thankful and a time to move past mourning to what lies ahead. It is also a time to recall what happened after the events on Blackie Butte.

I am still cowboying and Jeanette is still my boss. Work never ends on the Square C and, after a few days of dealing with the authorities after the events out there on the Hell Creek Formation, Jeanette, Ray, and I had to bring in our wheat and hay. This we did and continued the life of the rancher through the seasons, the same things every year, only with different problems.

Jeanette is as unchanging as the land. She is still the most competent and courageous woman I've ever known. Yes, I still love her. She knows that, of course. She also knows that Tanya will forever have a place in my heart. Whether she cares about that, or whether she ever intends to express any feelings for me, I don't know. We haven't talked about it. For some reason, I feel content with that.

Ray and Amelia are now preparing to go off to college. Both chose Montana State University in Bozeman. Ray will major in ag business and Amelia in paleontology. They are going to do well. Whether they will end up together, I can't say. They're eager to start their studies and they seem very happy together. I guess, with teenagers, that's the best anyone can ask. Jeanette is going to really miss Ray and so am I. We had a family, whether we knew it or not. I guess we still do only we're getting to be an empty nest, not counting the cows, of course.

Speaking of family, Superdog survived. Cade Morgan winged him in the hip but, though he bled a great deal, he hung onto life until we returned. We opened up the surgery immediately and Jeanette removed the bullet. Ray and I assisted. Soupy is fine now, though I think his hip hurts when there's bad weather on the way. I love that dog. Lucky for old Delbert, he was out on the Mulhaden pasture when Cade and the Russians swept through on the way to Blackie Butte. When Cade said he'd shot Soupy, I didn't think to ask whether he'd also shot Delbert. I guess my excuse is I was a little distracted at the time.

As might be imagined, there was a lot to explain concerning all that happened on Blackie Butte. The Haxbys suggested that we bury all the bodies and bulldoze the helicopter into a coulee, then go about our business. Tempting as that prospect was, Jeanette decided to call in the authorities. This did not prove all that easy. She phoned the state police in Billings and they took it as a crank call. We finally had to get Frank Torgerson to call, explaining that his mortuary had a number of corpses he didn't know what to do with.

The state sent Trooper Philpot, the same youngster who had come up to investigate Toby's murder. He stopped in at the mortuary where Frank showed him the bodies and went over the various wounds. Trooper Philpot instantly decided all this might be above his pay grade, turned around and drove back to Billings and convinced his superiors that the FBI should be called.

The Feds were unimpressed by the call from the Montana State Police but finally deigned to send an agent from Salt Lake City to check all this nonsense out. His name was Agent Tim Conway who reminded me a bit of the comedian of the same name. I met ol' Tim at the mortuary, then drove him out to Blackie Butte. Laura and Pick were still there, guarding the bones of the mama T and patching up the jacketed bones that were damaged in the helicopter crash. Of course, Pick wanted to remove all the dino bones at the first opportunity, but Jeanette insisted that they remain where they were until we got everything settled. I went out and helped Pick and Laura construct a cover for the mama T, which we otherwise left as we found it. Even the skull protruding from the mud was left until it could be carefully moved and jacketed.

With the slow-motion act of the state and the feds, the bones carried away by the helicopter on the first pass had disappeared. We presumed they were put on a truck, which headed for Mexico and crossed the border. Pick says they are almost assuredly lost forever, disappeared into the black market for dinosaur bones or into a private collection.

Agent Conway was impressed by the evidence littering the Blackie Butte site. There were lots of bullet casings, bullet holes, bloody rags, a tent full of various pistols and automatic weapons, and one rather bent UH-1 helicopter. Agent Conway was so impressed he started yelling at everybody and telling us we were all going to prison for a long time if not forever. We stood there and took it for a while, then Jeanette told him to get serious and bring in somebody who knew what they were doing. When Agent Conway continued to yell, she told me to shoot him because the feds had sent us a turkey. I didn't shoot the agent, but I did convince him to shut up and call for reinforcements.

Agent Conway called and a platoon of federal agents from the

FBI, ATF, and other acronyms related to the Department of Homeland Security arrived. They marveled over the dead Russian mobsters, and then declared everything was a secret and that no one, and they meant NO ONE, was to find out about this by which they meant the press. We managed that quite well because we didn't want to get in the newspapers or on television and lived in a county where no one wanted it, either. Oh, a few things got out, mainly that Jericho needed a new mayor because the other one had died due to mysterious circumstances. No national news organization picked it up. They don't care, you see, and that's fine with us.

The helicopter's registration proved to be Mexican. Its pilot and co-pilot, presumably working for a shadowy bone collector south of the border, were completely and utterly deceased and therefore unable to testify against their boss. The navy blue paint job on their chopper was, according to my FBI informant, probably for night operations. Unluckily for them, the Haxbys thought it looked black. Black helicopters over eastern Montana. Not a good idea.

The Haxbys are fine even though the feds got a court order to inspect their ranch. Other than their surface-to-air missiles, they owned nothing illegal and opened their bunkers up for inspection. Their remaining missiles, of course, were buried so the Homeland Security folks didn't find them. Still, the feds threatened the Haxbys, told them that there was evidence of a SAM strike on the helicopter, and if they didn't confess, they would be locked up forever or at least until they were executed. The Haxbys said nothing and kept saying it. Nice thing, the Constitution of the United States, which the Haxbys had actually read.

Eventually, the Homeland Security folks claimed the Russian bodies and left. Our attorneys in Billings assured us the investigation was over and we could all go about our business. The state of Montana, however, took note of the bones and sent the state paleontologist to have a look. This he did and recommended a careful removal of them for preparation and protection at the Museum of the Rockies. Jeanette and Pick agreed with this plan and a team from the museum soon arrived. The bones are still in Bozeman, being studied. Pick and Laura went with the bones. Laura called just a week ago and said she had taken a position as a research assistant at the Museum of the Rockies. Pick signed a contract with the museum to help catalog the bones and write a description of them. I think he's found a home but we'll see. The boy does like to travel.

Brian and Philip Marsh, the two Green Planet brothers, were questioned closely by Homeland Security but, for the most part, kept their traps shut. Both swore they had no idea how the helicopter came to blow up. The downed chopper, by the way, seemed to upset the feds more than having dead mobsters littering the BLM, or the greatest paleontological find of all times discovered and nearly destroyed. Since Brian and Phillip haven't written, I've kind of lost track of them. Maybe they joined the Peace Corps and are using their new expertise with shovels and picks to dig wells for remote villages.

The one aspect of all this that surprised Jeanette (but not me, cynic that I am) was that when the survey was done by the BLM, lo and behold, it was found that Blackie Butte was, just as old Ted suspected, on BLM land and therefore the bones all belonged to the federal government. That's now tied up in the courts but I don't expect a good outcome for the Square C. Looks like we're still going to have to work for a living and not live off the sale of old bones. I don't much think Jeanette minds losing the bones or even the money but she wants Blackie Butte back. To get it back, she's got the ear of some state politicians. She's also supporting a couple of new faces for the U.S. Congress. If that doesn't work, she might get some dynamite and just blow the hell out of the damn thing so nobody can have it. Don't ever count Jeanette out when it comes to her land. The powerful environmentalist organizations, their lawyers, and the federal government might consider that as they work to combine the BLM, CMR, Missouri Breaks Monument lands, and private property into a giant swath of buffalo prairie off limits to everybody but themselves. The ranchers aren't going to just step aside into history. They mean to fight. As Bill Coulter used to say, there's things a whole helluva lot worse than being dead and one of 'em is not being free.

Ted Brescoe was found floating in Fort Peck Lake by fishermen. After Edith had killed him, and perhaps recalling how Toby had floated, Cade had dumped Ted with twelve feet of logging chains wrapped around him, but failed to take into account the internal gas bodies tend to produce. The resulting buoyancy bobbed Ted to the surface in just a few days.

Ted and Edith were buried side by side in the Jericho cemetery. The locals thought that was punishment enough for both of them. The BLM had a new man in Ted's position in just a couple of weeks. He's another Brescoe, this one a graduate in land management from the University of Montana. Seems like a nice guy. I heard he bought a round of beer for everybody the other night in the Hell Creek Bar. It's a start.

Cade Morgan's body with the mama T's tooth removed, went with the Russians and is probably in a federal freezer somewhere. His property went up for sale. Joe the bartender told me the buyer was someone from Alabama, but he hasn't shown up yet. Anyway, we expect him to be a good neighbor, whoever he is. After we educate him in our ways, of course.

It is illegal to bury someone on a Montana ranch even with all of our thousands of square miles of prairie. So after I did due diligence in searching out Tanya's family, and finding none, I had her cremated and buried beside the little baby pioneer Nanette Mulhaden. I planted wildflowers around their graves and visit them often. I think Nanette and Tanya will have much to talk about across deep time. Eventually, if I have my way, I'll join them there.

But, for now, here I am on the Square C, the top and only hired hand of the queen of the prairie. I'll finish my g&t and then crawl into my bunk. Or maybe I'll just stay where I am and breathe in the summer aroma of the Square C, which is manure, wildflowers, dust, and fresh-cut hay. When I look up, a ribbon of stars endlessly unwinds, the edge of our galaxy lying on the ebony blanket of the universe. If I watch for only a little while, I'll see a satellite speed across the sky or perhaps a meteor will break into the atmosphere, throwing yellow sparks behind.

A silence envelops the land except for the occasional low moo of one of our cows talking to her calf, or the yip of a passing coyote, and the following snort of Nick catching its scent. The coyote will keep going. It knows Superdog is probably already coming after it.

Now, here come Rage and Fury, finished with their day of mousing and wanting to get some strokes for their labors. I'll happily give them and then surprise them later with some crunchy snacks from a bag of store-bought cat food I've got hidden away. It is always good to keep your cats happy.

I smile, stretch, have another drink of g&t. Life is the way I like it right now. Sure, storms will come. They always do but I'll handle them. That's what we do out here. That's what we expect. That's where we live.

Montana.

ACKNOWLEDGMENTS

My introduction to dinosaur hunting came through Joe Johnston, the director of the film *October Sky*, which was based on my memoir *Rocket Boys*. Joe also later directed a little movie titled *Jurassic Park III*. While visiting his home, Joe told me he was heading to Montana to work in the field with Dr. John (Jack) Horner, the famous paleontologist who is the technical consultant for all of the *Jurassic Park* movies. This sounded like an adventure so it took me less than a second to ask, "Can I go, too?" After giving it some thought, Joe finally allowed as how he guessed maybe it would be OK. Big mistake. I tend to get carried away by adventures and, sure enough, that's what happened.

Jack Horner hangs his hat at the Museum of the Rockies in Bozeman so that was our first stop. As it happens, Bozeman is also where my good buddy Frank Stewart lives. Frank, an avid sportsman, was also interested in going out to the dino hunting grounds and so he joined me on my first journey to Garfield County in eastern Montana, otherwise known as dinosaur country. Under Jack's tutelage, it didn't take long before Frank and I were hooked on poking through the famous Hell Creek Formation, home of the iconic Tyrannosaur rex, Triceratops, Hadrosaur, Ankylosaur, and other creatures of the

Cretaceous. For the next decade, every summer would find Frank and me along with numerous other interested amateur paleontologists and friends journeying to Garfield County. We did this, of course, under the direction of Dr. Horner with all the required permits. Fossil hunting on public land without permit is illegal and proper training is a must. Everything we found was carefully documented, then turned over to Jack who is also Montana's state paleontologist.

It turned out we were pretty successful dinosaur hunters. Before long, Frank discovered a T. rex, which Jack dubbed the F-Rex and sent a team to collect the bones. A couple of years later, I found the bones of an ancient animal Jack called the H-Rex and again a team was dispatched to dig out the remnants of what turned out to be a rare juvenile Tyrannosaur Frank and I were having a great time and learning a lot, not only about dinosaurs, but about the country in which we were hunting and the people who lived there, too. In fact, it didn't take me too long before I was more interested in the people of Garfield County than the ancient animals which once lived there. That's just the way I am. People interest me, especially interesting people.

The people of Garfield County are, for the most part, ranchers, farmers, cowgirls, and cowboys. They still live very close to the land, the seasons meaningful to them in ways city dwellers of today cannot imagine. Over the years, I was gradually allowed to be a part of their special community and getting to know them has been a privilege. They are a strong, hardy, well-educated people who add a special dimension to life and discourse in the United States. We are lucky to have them among us. Getting to know them prompted this novel, so as to bring them to life through the fictional characters of the mythical Fillmore County.

I extend my thanks to Dr. Horner for his patient teaching, and to Frank Stewart, faithful dino buddy, and fellow dino hunters Al Cunningham, Bill Hendricks, Art Johnson, Claus Kroeger, Lee Hall, Bob Harmon, Carl Campbell, Laura Wilson, Nels Peterson, Kim Wendell, Mark Goodwin, David Varracchio, and many other fine professional and amateur paleontologists, all of whom have been helpful to me every step up and down those glorious badlands.

Thanks also to Shelley McKamey, Pat Lieggi, and all the staff of the Museum of the Rockies, which honored me by allowing me to be on the museum advisory board. Thanks are also tendered to the Fellman and Phipps families in Jordan, Montana. They have been especially helpful in my quest to catch the wily dinosaurs. Of course, little could have been accomplished without the Hell Creek Bar to repair to for cool, liquid libations (not to mention fried chicken and onion rings) after a hot, sweaty day chasing dinosaurs. A tip of the expedition hat to barkeep Joe Herbold and the present owners of this grand watering hole.

This novel would not have been possible without the assistance of my reviewers and fact checkers, which included Mary Pluhar, Laura Wilson, Frank Stewart, and, always my first reader (and wife), Linda Hickam. Their expertise was required to breathe truth into Mike Wire's tale. Thanks are also due to David McCumber who generously allowed me to use his brilliant memoir, *The Cowboy Way*, as a resource for the novel. Similarly, my heartfelt thanks are extended to Walter W. Stein for the practical knowledge I learned from his excellent book, *So You Want to Dig Dinosaurs? A Field Manual on the Practices, Principles, and Politics of Vertebrate Paleontology, Second Edition*. Of course, any errors in this novel are entirely my own.

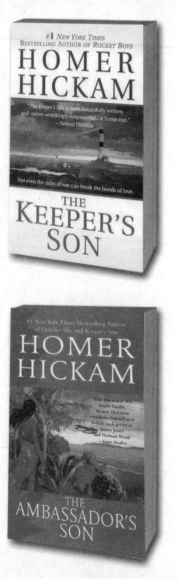